"Wh___ ___ ___ about?" Kat asked.

"Never mind," Stefan said evasively. "I discern that politics bore you." Suddenly, he grinned again. "You are much more curious about men and women, is that not so, little Kat?"

"Fie, sir," retorted Kat, backing off a step. "What is there to know of men and women except that they marry, mate and beget? Is that not what makes the world go 'round?"

The glib response that Stefan was about to utter died on his lips as he looked deep into those wide, questioning, green eyes. "You are the one who says so," he murmured. Then, in a voice that Kat did not hear, he added to himself, "I'm not sure."

Dear Reader,

Our titles for September include a new novel from June Lund Shiplett, *Boston Renegade*. When spinster Hanna Winters inherits a ranch from her long-lost brother, her quiet world is suddenly turned upside down.

In *Bodie Bride,* by Isabel Whitfield, Margaret Warren is furious when her father brings home a live-in guest, especially one who's so good-natured about disrupting her well-ordered life.

Knight Dreams is a wonderful story from first-time author Suzanne Barclay. Lord Ruarke Sommerville was drunk when he rescued French noblewoman Gabrielle de Lauren and impulsively wed her. Now he must learn to live with the consequences.

Mary Daheim's *Gypsy Baron* is the author's third book for Harlequin Historicals. Set in England and Bohemia during the early years of the seventeenth century, it is the story of an English noblewoman and a mysterious half Gypsy who draws her into a web of political intrigue.

Look for all four novels from Harlequin Historicals each and every month at your favorite bookstore.

Sincerely,

Tracy Farrell
Senior Editor

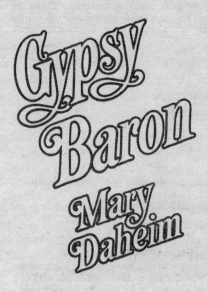

Gypsy Baron

Mary Daheim

Harlequin Books

TORONTO • NEW YORK • LONDON
AMSTERDAM • PARIS • SYDNEY • HAMBURG
STOCKHOLM • ATHENS • TOKYO • MILAN
MADRID • WARSAW • BUDAPEST • AUCKLAND

Harlequin Historicals first edition September 1992

ISBN 0-373-28742-9

GYPSY BARON

Books by Mary Daheim

Harlequin Historicals

King's Ransom #54
Improbable Eden #87
Gypsy Baron #142

MARY DAHEIM

Mary Daheim started writing at the age of eight and finished her first novel, a mystery, when she was eleven. She put that career on a back burner, however, while she made her mark in public relations. She had risen to be under consideration as the first woman vice-president in her company when she "took a look at the existing vp's and decided that, compared with marriage and a family, corporate life made exhausting demands and was...uh, er, DULL." So she decided to marry David Daheim instead. At the age of forty, and pregnant with her third daughter, she finally hauled eight hundred fifty pages of historical romance off the top of her refrigerator for a rewrite. That book was published in 1983, and Mary has been writing successful historical romances ever since.

For my family—*Devlesa avilan*

Chapter One

London, 1612

Lady Katherine de Vere had made up her mind: she would wear mourning and never love again. Henry, Prince of Wales, was dead, and Lady Kat could belong to no other man. She had insisted that her parents accompany her to London to attend her beloved's funeral. Kat had loved Henry above all else, and eighteen was too young to die, especially for a strong, handsome prince.

They had known each other for almost five years, yet it had been only in the past six months that Kat had realized her infatuation with Henry was not one-sided. She had outgrown the awkwardness of adolescence, with her slim figure budding into womanhood. Her oval face was a medley of shimmering green eyes, a wide mouth, a fine small nose and that determined little chin. The dominant features had the impact of bold beauty; nature's softer touches suggested an attempt to rein in Kat's more reckless side. Prince Henry had been captivated. They had embraced; they had kissed. They had even dared speak of the future, though Henry's fate was in the hands of his father. While the king would look askance at a union between his heir and the daughter of a mere baron, such a dream was

not impossible, and Katherine de Vere had never been one
to avoid a challenge. Indeed, she could not imagine being
married to anyone else.

But that had been in sweet Maytime, and now, under
December's bitter reign, Kat's future looked as bleak as the
heavy gray skies that hung over London. Henry had not
died on a storm-tossed sea or in the fever of battle, but over
a period of agony-racked weeks that had sapped his ener-
gies and eroded his strength. Ever brave, he had tried to
conceal his illness, even from the king and queen. From
Kat, too, to whom he had written a brief but apologetic
letter in early October, begging her forgiveness for his pro-
longed absence from Windrush. She had not believed the
news of his death when it reached her the first week of November.

Now, a month later, a chill wind blew up from the
Thames. Attired in an outdated black gown and cloak her
mother had worn almost a decade earlier for Queen Elizabeth's passing, Kat felt herself jostled by the crowd lining
the way to Westminster Abbey on that gloomy December
seventh. Lord and Lady de Vere had been separated from
her by a half-dozen somberly clad merchants and their
equally decorous wives. Kat felt no kinship with the other
mourners. As the Prince of Wales, Henry was claimed by
his subjects, but as a man, he belonged only to Kat. She felt
cut off from the rest, almost as if she somehow soared
above them to a special place where she could see Henry's
handsome, serious face returning her adoring gaze.

"You're standing on my foot," said a deep, faintly accented voice directly behind Kat. "Please move."

Kat turned awkwardly, hampered by the thick veil that
hung from stiff wire loops. Tentatively, she shifted her
stance. The boot on which she had inadvertently trodden
belonged to a dark-visaged young man with striking features and intense black eyes. Kat mumbled an apology, then

turned away to see if the royal guards were still ushering in the select few who would be admitted inside the Abbey. Over three hundred years after Henry III had rebuilt Edward the Confessor's masterpiece, the west front of the church wore an unfinished air. Yet Kat found the Abbey and its surroundings impressive, especially the Dean's Yard with its stately elms, the Great Sanctuary and its bell tower, and the Abbot's Lodgings, which were situated close by the old Benedictine order's farmlands.

Despite her grief, she was anxious to see the interior of the great church, having heard wondrous accounts of its rich treasures as well as its soaring architecture. Her father, whose kinsman was the Earl of Oxford, would be entitled to a place at least midway up the nave. But even on tiptoes, Kat could not see the guards or her parents. A wave of apprehension crept over her; she could not imagine anything worse than not being part of the service that would bid farewell to Henry.

Battling not only the press of people, but her unwieldy mourning garb, Kat tried to push forward. The onlookers stood wedged together like an insurmountable barricade. Helplessly, Kat twisted around, searching for an ally.

The dark eyes of the man directly behind her locked with her uncertain gaze. Swiftly, she took in the rugged features, the sharp angles of chin and nose, the straight black hair and the bronzed skin. "Sir," she began, almost losing her balance when a portly gentleman edged sideways at her elbow, "can you signal to one of the guards for me? I'm too short."

The dark face turned quizzical. "Signal?"

"Yes, yes," she answered with a trace of impatience. The man must be a foreigner; perhaps he didn't understand English very well. "I have a place in the Abbey. With my parents. I must join them," she said with as much dignity as her sixteen years and cumbersome costume permitted.

A tinkling laugh erupted close by. Kat's veils caught in the wind, obscuring her vision. Vexed, she yanked at the silken hangings and noted that the man was flanked by two young women, a lavender-eyed blonde in brilliant yellow and a tall, voluptuous redhead in bright green.

"Tut!" exclaimed the blonde to Kat. "King James despises gloomy colors. You should have worn red."

Before Kat could respond, the shrill voice of a guardsman called out, "The Countess of Essex." The redheaded young woman moved forward as the crowd parted. The swaying movement of her rounded body gave the lie to her demure manner. Kat politely stepped aside as well, trying not to stare at the young Countess of Essex who, like so many of the Howard women, always seemed to be at the center of various scandals.

The guardsman called out again, this time for Lady Susan Howard. The blonde stopped smirking and tugged at her escort's arm. "Come, Stefan, we must go inside. The procession draws nigh."

Kat again stood on tiptoe, teetering precariously as she scanned the roadway with its arching gates. Again she could see nothing, but the muffled sound of drums rolled in the distance. At her back, the man called Stefan shrugged off the invitation. "I'll stay outside. I'm a foreigner, after all."

"Then why did you come with us?" Lady Susan demanded in a querulous voice.

Kat saw an enigmatic look cross the man's face. "I knew your prince well. I liked him. But I care not for funerals. I'll bid my farewell in the open air, under God's free sky." He jerked his head heavenward, and Lady Susan, with a disdainful expression, sailed off toward the Abbey in a swish of yellow taffeta.

Yet more names were called out—Villiers, Tyrrell, the Earl of Arundel. Anxiety crept over Kat like an ague. The procession was now in sight, with young Prince Charles at its head. Verging on panic, Kat turned back to the foreigner who was watching the proceedings with a bemused countenance.

"Sir," she said, speaking more slowly this time, lest he have trouble comprehending her words, "will you aid me? I must get into the Abbey."

The stranger gave Kat another quizzical look. "You should have gone with them," he said rather absently, gesturing in the direction the Howard women had gone. "Or with your... parents, was it?"

"We were separated in the crowd," Kat said, forced to shout above the shuffling throng. "They probably thought I'd meet them inside."

The man shrugged his shoulders. "Then do so," he suggested. Though he could have passed for a Highland Scot, his voice held no echo of the North. Kat was reminded instead of dangerous, secret places, of steep, jagged mountains, of dense, sunless forests, of swift rushing streams. Most of all, she was disconcerted by those penetrating black eyes. Her usual forthright manner was sufficiently dampened; she did not feel like trying to explain English protocol to a foreigner.

"All right, I will," said Kat, taking up the challenge. Wherever he came from, this ungallant brute knew nothing of chivalry. Setting her jaw, Kat lowered her head and prepared to push her way through the crowd. Instead, she stumbled and would have fallen had the foreigner not caught her by the waist.

"Forgive me," he said in that deep, disturbing voice. "This time I have trod on you." The dark eyes glanced down at the cobbles where his black leather boot stood on Kat's hem.

"Oh!" Aghast, Kat tried to jerk free. The fabric, which had grown brittle with age, ripped at the waist, just under the wide verdingale. Kat cried out again, this time in horror. The black skirts sagged, revealing her petticoats. Frantically, she pulled her cloak around her and was about to berate the foreigner when a great murmur went up from the gathering.

Prince Charles, at the head of the procession, was riding up to the Abbey's entrance. At twelve, the heir to England's throne was small, spindly and unimpressive, despite a mass of golden curls and bright sapphire eyes. Kat's heavy sigh echoed the crowd's. Compared to Prince Henry's robust figure, Charles seemed so vulnerable. Yet he was alive and his older brother was dead. Kat felt tears sting her eyes. It was too late. She would not be allowed to join the other mourners inside the great church.

Blindly, Kat tried to fight her way out of the crowd and away from the Abbey. Her trembling hands clutched at her ruined gown, and she was well aware that a number of the onlookers were staring as much at her as at the catafalque with its waxy effigy of Prince Henry. Finally free of the crush, she stopped to catch her breath outside the Abbey gatehouse. She was not pleased to discover that the man called Stefan was coming toward her, his long stride easy, yet purposeful.

"You will, I suppose," he remarked in a calm, self-possessed tone, "blame me for missing such a state spectacle. But there will be others. The queen is unwell, and your king practices unwholesome habits."

Kat's green eyes flashed in anger. "I'm not a ghoul! And you have no right to say such things! You are neither English nor Scot, I'll wager."

"True." The dark-eyed young man seemed unaffected by her accusation. He bowed briefly. "I am Stefan Dvorak, of Prague and Oxford University. Magdalen College, to be precise."

Oxford lay only a few miles to the south of Kat's home at Windrush. The university's fanciful spires had always intrigued her, so much so that she had begged to attend one of its famous colleges. But a girl, even an only child who was an heiress, did not require academic knowledge. It rankled that this foreigner from Prague should benefit from English book learning, while she, a proud de Vere, was barred.

But such logic would be lost upon this stranger, Kat reasoned. "I knew Prince Henry," she said with a proud lift of her head. "He and the Princess Elizabeth have been dear friends to me."

Stefan Dvorak tipped his head to one side. The wind had picked up again, sending dried leaves swirling over the patch of grass on which they stood. "I, too, know their highnesses. I met Prince Henry at Oxford." Again he spoke casually. Kat had the feeling he was not an easy man to impress. "I deplore these rumors about Henry's untimely demise," he went on in a musing tone. "Who would poison so fine a prince?"

Kat, who had been discreetly trying to hitch her torn skirts up under her verdingale, stared at Dvorak. Secluded almost a hundred miles from court at Windrush, she had heard no such ugly tales. "Poisoned? Rot! It was a fever, virulent and swift."

Dvorak shrugged. "No doubt." Despite the company he kept with princes and the Howards, he was dressed more like a yeoman, in plain dark hose, leather jerkin, muslin shirt and a short brown cape. At his hip hung an unusual sword, long and lethal. The sense of danger Kat had heard in his voice assailed her once more. Anxiously, she glanced back toward the Abbey. Most of the crowd still lingered, though the procession had wound its way into the church and the doors had been shut. Kat put a hand to her head, feeling suddenly desolate.

"I can't stay here...I must be with.... Oh, this isn't fair!" she wailed. "I've come all the way from Windrush!"

"Your prince isn't inside those cold ancient walls," Dvorak pointed out. "He's somewhere that we can't see or reach. He's..." The dark-eyed gaze suddenly veered away from Kat, scanning the leaden skies. Dvorak's lips grew thin, his jawline taut. "He's free. God help him, he's finally free."

Momentarily diverted from her pain, Kat threw Dvorak a curious look. "Free? Of course. He was always free. He was a prince." The man spoke nonsense; perhaps that was how foreigners thought. Kat marveled at how different other people were from the English. It was, she thought, a pity.

But Dvorak was slowly shaking his head. "You don't understand, do you, Mistress...? Who are you who mourns your princeling with such hot green eyes?"

Kat drew herself up to her full, not particularly impressive height. The old-fashioned mourning costume made her look older than her sixteen years and not unlike a somber butterfly. "I am Lady Katherine de Vere, daughter of Edgar, Baron Cheltenham, and Lady Beatrice de Vere of Windrush, Gloucestershire."

Kat's bloodlines did not seem to impress him, either. Indeed, Stefan Dvorak looked bemused. "Such a lot of names," he remarked lightly. "You should have been ushered to the dean's chair for the service."

His apparent flippancy ignited Kat's temper. The tears dried as her anger heated. "How dare you? What can you know of English ways? Prince Henry loved me! We would have wed, had King James been coaxed into giving permission! Why, I might have been queen of England!"

It seemed that Stefan Dvorak was having difficulty keeping a straight face. He started to respond, then went silent. His right hand reached out to touch Kat's ear. "Like this?" he said. With a deft movement, he palmed a playing card with a picture of her royal majesty, Queen Anne.

Kat's jaw dropped. "What? Where did you get that?" She saw the black eyes spark with amusement. His jest was at her expense, and she was further infuriated. "What are you? A cheap conjurer? A Gypsy charlatan? I'm disgusted!"

Dvorak slipped the card inside his jerkin. "Some, such as this very queen, are vastly entertained. No, I'm not a conjurer. But yes, I am a Gypsy. At least in part."

Kat was appalled. Gypsies were the lowest sort of creatures, pagan vagabonds, given to the most depraved practices. Still grappling with her skirts, she started to stomp away, heading back towards the Abbey. "I should have guessed you were no gentleman, foreign or not," she declared. "No wonder you carry rumors of poison. Such foul deeds are common Gypsy fare!"

Dvorak stepped aside to let her pass. "It's not Gypsies who are accused of murdering your poor prince," he said, and though his voice was low and matter-of-fact, it carried on the wind. "It was supposedly a woman whose love was rejected. No names, of course. You English are too discreet."

Kat whirled, her fists clenched in anger. "Of course we are! And what you say is nonsense! Englishwomen do not resort to poison, no matter what the cause!"

Dvorak gave that aggravating shrug. "Perhaps not. I only repeat what I hear. Farewell, Lady Katherine. My condolences."

"Rot!" snapped Kat, all but running to escape the vexing presence of Stefan Dvorak.

She had almost reached the roadway when her skirts fell off.

* * *

Kat's parents were not happy with their daughter. Though they doted on their only child, both had felt that the trip to London was unnecessary. Indeed, any journey to court was to be avoided as far as Edgar, Baron Cheltenham, was concerned. As Sir Walter Raleigh's comrade-in-arms, he had been with the great adventurer at the brilliant raid on Cadiz in 1596. But later, when Raleigh had been charged with treason, Sir Edgar's outspokenness over Raleigh's imprisonment had earned the ire of King James. Kat's father had been banished from court, but his exile at Windrush had proved so pleasant that when James finally relented, the royal invitations were politely declined. The occasion of Prince Henry's funeral was the first time Sir Edgar had deigned to visit London in ten years.

"I cannot think how you could have gotten lost right in front of Westminster Abbey," Sir Edgar scolded his daughter when at last they were reunited in their temporary lodgings at Whitehall after the services.

"And your dress!" exclaimed Lady Beatrice, her fine features puckered with dismay. "*My* dress. It's ruined! It cost a small fortune!"

Kat let her parents vent their wrath. As a spirited child, full of lively curiosity, she had frequently earned their displeasure, mainly by causing them considerable worry. Though mother and father could rebuke at length, both were rarely incited to further punishment. Kat would let their anger run its course; in this instance, explanations were useless. Kat's self-reproach far outweighed her parents' recriminations.

With a hand to his graying temples, her father shook his head sadly. "We'll return to Windrush tomorrow. London is no place for us. Nothing but trouble comes from living too close to kings and queens."

Kat didn't argue, though she thought she noted a glimmer of defiance in her mother's hazel eyes. It was well and good for Sir Edgar to rusticate amid the comfort and pleasures of Windrush. But Kat knew her mother occasionally yearned for the sociability and excitement of court. While Kat cherished her home as a bird loves its nest, she, too, felt the lure of London. Even without Henry's presence, the city stirred her blood. And there was still Elizabeth, that vivacious princess with a zest for life that equaled Kat's own.

In the waning hours of the de Veres' visit, Kat sought out Elizabeth Stuart in her suite of apartments known as Whitehall's Cockpit. The princess, surrounded by long-faced maids of honor, welcomed her childhood friend with a wan smile. Her honey-blond hair was uncharacteristically limp and there were dark circles under her blue eyes.

"I didn't think you'd come for the funeral," she said, keeping her voice low as the other young women withdrew to hover over an unfinished tapestry in the corner of the chamber. "I didn't see you in the Abbey."

Kat's face tightened. "That's a tiresome story." She was still unwilling to admit to her failure at gaining entrance to the church, and worse yet, of her humiliation at having been left in her petticoats outside the Abbey Gatehouse. At least Stefan Dvorak had not been so ungallant as to laugh, but had merely glanced back once and then walked on into the crowd still lining the cobbled street.

"Bess," Kat began, resorting to the familiar childhood nickname, "I heard something alarming today. Pray put my mind at ease."

Elizabeth's usually open, animated face was drawn. She and Henry had been extremely close. A wrinkled handkerchief clutched in her fingers indicated that she had not yet shed all her tears. "What, Kat? How could anything be more alarming than Hal's death?"

Kat was looking grim as she cast a covert glance at the maids of honor, who appeared not to be listening. "The manner of it," she replied shortly. "I heard there was talk of poison."

Elizabeth's pink-and-white complexion turned pale. "God's eyes! Who says so?"

Kat lowered her lashes. "A man I met by chance. A foreigner." Swiftly, she put a hand on Elizabeth's arm. "Never mind, I should not have mentioned it. Such tales don't bear repeating."

"Such tales are too common," retorted Elizabeth bitingly. "Any personage of rank who dies unexpectedly is said to have been poisoned." She smiled at Kat, a bit more brightly this time. "Don't fret on it. Think only of the pleasant times we all had together. There were many, praise God."

Elizabeth was right. Six years ago, Kat had been in her bedroom, looking out over the long tree-lined drive when Henry had first paused at Windrush en route to visit his sister at Combe Abbey.

Even at twelve, the prince had shown promise of growing into a handsome young man. Kat had been smitten, moved in a childlike way not only by Henry's grave good looks, but by his innate compassion and kindness. As for the prince, he had been intrigued by Sir Edgar's early career at sea and his allegiance to Henry's hero, Sir Walter Raleigh. From that time on, whenever the prince rode north to visit his sister, he made Windrush his natural resting place.

In a house where other children seldom came to play, Prince Henry's visits were eagerly awaited by Kat. When the Princess Elizabeth, who was also two years younger than Henry, arrived at Windrush for the first time, Kat felt as if she'd finally found the sister she'd always wanted. The two young girls had formed an immediate bond, giggling into the night, applying Lady Beatrice's purloined cosmetics, combing and recombing their hair into the most outrageous concoctions. Henry indulged them both, the adored sister and the chestnut-haired hoyden who could make them both laugh in a most immoderate manner.

Reflecting upon those carefree times, Kat offered her friend a tremulous smile. "I will miss him so. As will you," she added quickly.

Elizabeth sighed. "Oh, yes. Were it not for Freddy..." She stopped, closing her eyes as if to keep back fresh tears. "At least I will soon be married and have a family of my own, God willing," the princess continued, referring to her courtship by the young Elector Palatine.

In the far corner, there was a rustling of the maids as someone rapped upon the door. Lady Susan Howard, whom Kat had not noticed upon her arrival, glided across the Persian carpet. To Kat's surprise, a moment later Stefan Dvorak was admitted.

"Stefan!" cried Elizabeth, causing Kat to marvel at the warm greeting as much as at the foreigner's arrival. "Where have you been? My lady mother is distraught!"

Dvorak, with Susan at his side, moved easily to kneel before Elizabeth. "As ever, I'm at the royal disposal. What will it be, your highness? Tales of our darkling Bohemian forests? Ancient mystic Gypsy lore? A pigeon up my sleeve?" Despite the heavy black hangings and the oppressive air of grief, Stefan's eyes twinkled.

Elizabeth sighed. "Just comfort," she said. "His royal majesty is worthless in such situations. He pretends that death doesn't happen, especially when it strikes so close. My lady mother is bereft. If only you would offer her some words of consolation." Elizabeth bestowed a fond smile on the foreigner, who had now risen to his feet. "She thinks highly of you, Baron Ostrov."

Kat gave Dvorak a sharp glance. Not only had the insidious foreigner inveigled his way into the royal bosom, but it seemed he bore a title as well. Of course it must be Bohemian, and as such, of little value, especially if the man went around pulling cards and pigeons out of his sleeve. Kat gave a little sniff.

The dark eyes slid in Kat's direction, but he gave no sign of recognition. Perhaps he didn't remember her, since she was now attired in her own garments. "Her majesty is still at Whitehall, I presume?" Dvorak inquired of the princess.

"Oh, yes," replied Elizabeth with faint irony. King James's predilection for male companions was well-known—and well-mocked—in his domain. Though he and his consort had once led a comparatively happy domestic life, in later years they had gone their separate ways, with Queen Anne residing at Denmark House. Only a state occasion, such as the death of their eldest son, could bring them together under the same roof.

"Poor lady, she is all undone, I hear," remarked Dvorak, who struck Kat as unlikely to be undone by almost anything. She wondered where he fit into the scheme of the court. Foreign Oxford students, even of noble rank, were not generally called upon to offer succor to the royal family. Stefan Dvorak's position struck Kat as very strange.

"So are we all," sighed Elizabeth. A bit sheepishly, she turned to her friend. "Dear Kat, would you mind? It would not be appropriate for Baron Ostrov to call on her majesty unattended."

Kat suppressed a sigh. She did not wish to share Stefan Dvorak's company, even for a short time. Nor was she anxious to call upon the queen, who, though a kindly soul, was reputedly given to lengthy discourses on her most recent ill health, the lack of kindness on the part of her husband, the difficulties of being a daughter of Denmark in the kingdom of England, and now, understandably, the anguish of losing a son.

But Kat had no choice. Briskly, she marched to the door and led Stefan Dvorak down the shadowy corridor, where occasional flickering sconces lit the way. It was only after they had gone about twenty feet that Kat realized she had no idea where she was going.

She said as much. Dvorak grinned, revealing white teeth in his bronzed face and somehow making Kat feel uneasy. "It's the other way," he said. "You haven't spent much time at court, I gather?"

Kat's expression was pugnacious. "I prefer Windrush," she said, not with complete candor. "There's too much intrigue at court. You, obviously, know your way about, especially for a foreigner."

"True," Dvorak acknowledged. "Prince Henry and I had become good friends these past months, especially since it appears that the Princess Elizabeth will wed Frederick of the Palatinate. His country is near my own, you see."

Kat blinked. "It is?" She recovered quickly. "Yes, of course it is, to the south."

"The west," put in Dvorak. "The fate of the Palatinate is intertwined with the future of Bohemia. My people seek to be independent, just as the German principalities desire autonomy. The Holy Roman Emperor threatens us all."

Kat ignored the political diatribe. "Bess and Freddy love each other. That's all that matters." She started off in the opposite direction.

As ever, Dvorak seemed unimpressed by Kat's pronouncements. When they reached the door to the queen's apartments, Kat paused just short of the two halberdiers who stood on duty. "I must return to my parents. I will see you as far as her majesty's antechamber."

"Well enough," agreed Dvorak.

Kat hesitated. "Tell me," she inquired, "why does our queen rely on your talents to amuse her?"

Hearing the resentment in Kat's voice, Stefan lifted one black eyebrow. "Her majesty is not the sort to amuse herself," he said carefully, unwilling to call the consort shallow and stupid. "Even before the Prince of Wales died, she was highly agitated. King James's fondness for Robin Carr has upset her more than such attachments usually do."

Even in the relative isolation of Windrush, Kat had heard about the king's latest favorite, Robert Carr, newly created Viscount Rochester. A tall, lanky, fair-haired Scot, Carr had been pushed into James's fawning embrace by his mentor, Thomas Overbury, who happened to be a neighbor of the de Veres. The young Scot had been no friend to Prince Henry, who despised his fatuousness and considered him a self-seeking adventurer. Hal had sheepishly recounted to Kat that at one point, during a heated tennis match, he'd actually taken a swing with his racquet at the latest royal pet. Kat had been mightily amused.

"Carr is said to be stupid and shallow," said Kat, not nearly so tactful as Dvorak. "Hal disliked him, as well he might."

Dvorak was beginning to show signs of impatience. "Indeed." He gave a little shake of his head. "A simple triangle. The prince and Robin Carr both vied for Fanny Howard's attentions. Henry won. For a time, she was his mistress."

Kat froze in place. Dvorak's statement was impossible. Henry had had no mistress. He had loved only Kat. There was no room in his life for dalliance. Stefan Dvorak must be wrong. Or a liar. Kat had to fight down the urge to scream her rebuttal.

"That's absurd," she said at last, trying to keep her voice low enough so that the halberdiers could not overhear. Yet such a triangle might explain Hal's antipathy toward Carr.

But Kat refused to believe the tale. "Surely, sir, you've been misinformed."

Stefan only shook his head again. "No, it's true. She's a most fetching creature. As are all the Howard women." He spoke matter-of-factly, meanwhile moving backward toward the royal chamber. The stormy expression on Kat's oval face told him he had said the wrong thing. Stefan made a sharp gesture with his hand. "You are a fetching wench as well," he said to make amends. Then his eyes sparked with amusement. "Especially when you are properly dressed. Did you ever recover the rest of your skirts?"

Kat's temper was on the verge of exploding, but she didn't dare give vent to her wrath in front of the guardsmen. "You need no help from me," she snapped. "Seek the queen on your own. Or," she added, whirling on her heel, "conjure up a proper maid from your shirtsleeve!"

Kat stomped off down the corridor. Stefan cocked his head to one side, watched her disappear around the corner and smiled. He wasn't sure exactly why.

Chapter Two

The manor house of Windrush, with its creamy brick facade, had begun its history in a stormier era. Swiftly, Kat descended the stone steps of the square tower that had been built for defense some one hundred and fifty years earlier but was now used primarily for storage. Changed, too, was the moat, reduced to a duck pond that ran the length of Windrush's front lawn. Now, in more placid times, all was given over to comfort and function. Kat loved Windrush as if it were another member of the family, but on this drear February day she spared not a glance for its warm exterior or fanciful chimneys or playful gargoyles. She was headed for the stables, where her favorite mare, Leda, anticipated her mistress's whim. The house stood staunchly at Kat's back, haven, shelter, protector, patiently waiting to welcome its wayward daughter upon her return.

A canter to Leigh Wood should lift her flagging spirits. The hint of snow that had tinged the morning air now seemed to have drifted off to the west, toward the Welsh Marches. Kat felt the brisk breeze on her cheeks and spurred Leda into a gallop. Almost recklessly she cleared the rambling brooks and the low-lying stone hedgerows. Kat could not thrust Henry's memory aside, but at least she could regain some sense of peace in the pastoral setting of her country home.

Or so Kat hoped. Close to the village of Temple Guiting, where outcroppings of white rock jutted from the ground and the beech trees stood shorn of leaves, Kat encountered a strangely garbed woman near the ancient packhorse bridge. Curious, Kat slowed Leda to a trot and studied the woman, who wore a motley dress of orange, gold, purple and green. She also sported a peculiar hat, with a crown like a church steeple. Somewhat to Kat's surprise, the woman called out a greeting.

"Do you want my help?" Kat inquired, guiding Leda to the ford.

The woman looked up from the footpath where she'd been gathering dried elderberry curds and putting them in a wicker basket. "Not I, my lady," she responded in a high, yet musical voice. "But you want mine."

Kat blinked. "For what? Explain yourself, good dame."

Under the tall hat, the woman's face was unlined, yet her eyes looked ancient. Dark but flecked with gold, they seemed to mirror time itself, turning inward on the past and outward into Kat's very soul. The woman smiled sagely. "You are from Windrush, are you not?"

"Why, yes," Kat answered, shifting uncomfortably in the saddle. "How did you know?"

The smile remained in place. "I know many things. You are sad. You have lost your lover." She slipped the basket over one arm and held out her hands. "Here, give me your palm. I'll tell you not only what has been, but what is yet to come."

Instinctively, Kat pulled back. "No! I don't believe in such superstitious blather! I know what is to come—I've planned my life."

"Tch!" clucked the woman, still smiling. "Only God can do that." She gave a shrug of her motley-clad shoulders. "Very well. But should you change your mind, I'll find you."

Under Kat's hands, Leda seemed to shudder. Kat suddenly felt cold, despite her fur-lined cloak. She leaned down to speak soothingly to her mare. "Good day," Kat mumbled, setting spurs to Leda's flanks. But when she looked up, the woman was gone.

Not five minutes later, Kat saw a Gypsy caravan halted along the roadside. Such visitations were not unusual, but for the first time, Kat's interest was more than cursory. She reined Leda in atop a small knoll and watched the Gypsy children tumble about in the tall grasses, their rainbow-colored clothing brightening the winter landscape like early spring flowers. Their presence might explain the woman on the footpath. But except for her unusual clothing, she hadn't looked like a Gypsy. Her features were clearly English and she was well-spoken. Kat dismissed the idea.

No doubt the adults in the caravan were eking out a living as tinkers or jewelry menders. Perhaps they performed feats of magic. Kat frowned as the image of Stefan Dvorak, palming a card, leaped into her mind's eye. It was not the only time she had envisioned that bemused, self-possessed foreigner since leaving London two months earlier. To Kat's dismay, Dvorak's rugged features had materialized on several occasions...whenever there was a mention of mountains, the sound of rushing water or a reference to Oxford.

Kat was about to guide her mare south of the village and on to Leigh Wood when a half-dozen farm lads came down the road with a cartload of firewood. Sighting the Gypsy caravan, they stopped. Words were exchanged, and though Kat could not make out exactly what was said, the meaning was clear: the farmers were harassing the Gypsies. The children fled back to their elders who, Kat now realized, had been attempting to affix a lost wheel. One of the farmers swung a stout tree branch at an aged Gypsy man, who had had the temerity to offer an argument. The blow missed by a scant inch, but the flash of a knife came in answer, the blade sailing past the farmer's head. It appeared that the battle was joined. Kat hesitated, then urged Leda into a trot. A moment later, she was calling out to both farmers and Gypsies.

"Cease! Do any of you want death on your souls?"

Men, women and children all looked up at the young woman who, despite her youth and fragile appearance, sat astride her mare with an air of authority. The farmers backed off; the Gypsies actually seemed to cringe.

"A bit o' sport, that's all," said one of the lads, a towhead with pointed ears who was probably not much older than Kat. "Gypsies are fair game, after all."

Kat knew he voiced the opinion of most Englishmen. Indeed, Gypsies were hunted like wild game in some parts of the Continent. Yet she suddenly found her countrymen's attitude repugnant. "If you must brawl, do so with each other," she admonished. "There's a tavern in the village High Street. You can get drunk as dogs, and beat yourselves black-and-blue."

Some of the Gypsies were clambering back inside their red-and-green-painted wagon. But the farmers weren't so easily put off. The one who had spoken first shot Kat an insolent look. "Why should we harm our own kind, mistress? Is it not better to rid this road of vile vermin? They're child stealers, dirty, even cannibals!"

Fleetingly, Kat asked herself why she was so insistent on defending this feckless Gypsy band. But logic was not always her strong suit. Kat preferred to act rather than reason. "Because I said so," she declared, brandishing her riding crop. "Would you care to have me report your villainous behavior to the sheriff?"

At least two of the farmers uttered a lame laugh. "Sheriff indeed," snorted the eldest of the group. "What would he care about some thieving Roms? Why, we hear the guilds in London have outlawed Gypsy craftsmen.''

Kat neither knew nor cared about the city guilds. She saw instead the upturned faces of five small children, their dark eyes big and beautiful. Inexplicably, Kat was moved. She dismissed the guilds with a flick of her riding crop.

Briefly, the farmers shifted about in the roadway, then the oldest—and burliest—of the bunch waved a pitchfork. ''This be the devil's own tool,'' he announced in a thick voice. ''Would yon Roms recognize it as their own?'' His face split into an evil grin.

At the sight of the pitchfork, the children clambered onto the wagon. One of the Gypsy men leaned against the vehicle, squinting at the farmers from under the brim of a battered hat. Kat's heart fluttered in her breast. Should these yokels again turn violent, she had no way to stop them. Unless the Gypsies were armed with more than the knife that had been thrown. But as far as Kat could tell, they were outnumbered—she had seen only the one younger man among the women, children and what appeared to be a grandfather.

Kat forced herself to utter a hoot of derision. ''How brave to frighten babes! Will you use your pitchfork on me first?''

For one breath-snatching, terrifying moment, Kat read the menace in the farmers' eyes and realized that she, too, might be fair game in their present mood of mischief. Her only hope was to make her escape on Leda and seek help in the village. Yet she could not abandon the Gypsies. Even while she debated with herself, the farmers turned as the sound of approaching hoofbeats reached their ears. Anxiously, Kat scanned the horizon. From under the stone bridge, a lone horseman came into view. Kat saw the strange sword before she recognized the rider. Stefan Dvo-

rak reined in his big black gelding and surveyed the roadside scene.

"Lady Kat!" He grinned at her, then directed his attention to the farm lads. "You're here to help these Gypsy
folk, I take it? No right-minded soul would hinder them,
I'm sure." His smile remained, but his eyes were hard, like
flint.

The towhead took in the long sword and gulped. "We're
sowing," he blurted, pointing over the hedgerow to a newly
tilled field. "Early wheat."

Stefan inclined his head. "Your grain will not thrive on
this rough road," he remarked mildly.

"That's so." The towhead choked on a laugh. "We'd a
mind to have a drink."

"Then have it," returned Stefan, resting both arms in
front of him. "But not here."

"And why not?" It was the burly farmer, still clutching
his pitchfork. He stared up at Stefan. "You look like one
of them, for all your fine speech. Go back where you came
from, and take these poxy pests with you!" He lowered his
head and lunged at Dvorak's gelding with the sharp imple-
ment.

Both horse and rider were amazingly agile; Stefan managed to wheel his mount out of harm's way just in time.
The farmer fell flat on his face in the roadway. His humiliation only served to incite his companions. The towhead
and a somewhat older man rushed Dvorak, pulling on his
bridle.

"Come down and fight like a man!" the towhead yelled,
his small eyes burning with rage.

Incensed by the unfair advantage of numbers, Kat swung
her riding crop at two of the farm lads who were holding
back. She missed one, but caught the other's cap, knocking it off. "Don't be fools! You'll end up in the stocks for
this!" Anxiously, she saw Stefan, with an air of resigna-

tion, leap down from his horse. The Gypsies, perhaps as
many as a dozen, were now all leaning out from various
openings in the wagon. But they did not come forward. Kat
cursed them along with the farmers.

Somewhat to Kat's surprise, Dvorak did not reach for his
sword. Instead, he put one booted foot on the neck of the
burly man who was still sprawled on the ground, grabbed
the towhead by the neck and threw him back against his
companion. Both men gasped but didn't go down. The two
lads who Kat had warned off were clearly vacillating; upon
closer inspection, Kat realized they were mere boys, no
more than twelve.

But the sixth farmer, who until now had hung back,
made an attempt to plunge into the fray just as his two
stunned comrades collected themselves and again made for
Stefan. Kat pulled on Leda's reins, urging her to rear up.
The flying hooves sent the newcomer reeling off to the side
of the road. Kat whirled about, just in time to see Dvorak's fist connect with the towhead's jaw. The other farmer
hesitated, then apparently decided that his manhood was at
stake and went for Dvorak's throat. Kat was on the verge
of dismounting when Dvorak pulled free and landed a hard
blow to the farmer's midsection. The man crumpled like
old clothes.

Momentarily free of his assailants, Stefan finally reached
for his sword. "Don't make me use this," he said in a calm,
controlled voice. "This is all too absurd to cause blood-
shed."

The burly man was struggling to his feet; so was the
towhead, who was also rubbing his jaw. Stefan gestured at
the Gypsies with his free hand. "Go! Seek safety elsewhere!" He spoke again, but this time in a language Kat
did not understand. Heads were drawn in, the various
openings in the wagon were closed and the mules were
urged to move as swiftly as they could. The wheels wob-

bled, evidence of incomplete repair work, but moments later, with the incongruous sound of bells a-jingle, the Gypsy caravan had disappeared over the old stone bridge.

Warily, Kat eyed the farmers, who were still scrambling around in the road, tending to their various injuries. Dvorak stepped to one side, the dangerous sword still raised. He waited until his former antagonists were huddling together by their cart, then reached inside his jerkin and extracted a handful of coins.

"Have your drinks at my expense," he called, tossing the coins at the abject group of farmers. "But if you do, swear to toast, not curse, the Roms."

All but the two boys dared to give Stefan malevolent looks. The towhead's small eyes, lusterless under the wintry sky, darted toward the coins. "To the devil with ye," he muttered, and spat on the ground. With a show of bravado, he joined the others in clambering back onto the haycart.

Stefan did not sheathe his sword until the cart had disappeared over the horizon. Only then did Kat breathe a sigh of relief. "They might have killed you," she said in a small, strange voice, and vaguely wondered why the prospect alarmed her so. "Why didn't those feckless Gypsies help you?"

With a casual air, Dvorak strolled over to the scattered coins, retrieved them and got back on his horse. "I suspect they would have if things had gotten out of hand," he said with a little shrug. "But contrary to your *Gajo* lore, Roms don't ask to borrow trouble. Who would believe them in a court of law?"

Briefly, Kat considered. "Mayhap. But six to one is still an unfair fight."

The dark eyes sparked with amusement. "Not quite. I had you."

Kat flushed. "I hate seeing people take advantage. After all," she went on more briskly, "they might have attacked me. You came just in time. I was stalling. For all I know, those Gypsies have been stealing from villager and farmer alike. Perhaps they deserved to be mishandled." Feeling suddenly perverse, she gave Dvorak a defiant glare.

His black eyes stared her down. "Do you believe that?"

"Well...no." She eyed him questioningly. "Whatever brought you here in the first place?"

"I'm returning to Oxford," he said, gesturing beyond Leigh Wood toward the site of the university. "I'd paused by the brook to let my mount drink." His black eyes danced. "This seems to be a place of strange encounters for you."

Momentarily puzzled, Kat suddenly realized that Stefan must have seen her talking to the strangely garbed woman. "You've been spying on me!" she charged.

But Dvorak shook his head. "Not I, Lady Kat. I came upon the scene just as you departed it. You did not look amenable to further conversation."

"I was put off by that odd creature," Kat said, now on the defensive. "She claimed to know my mind. Nonsense, of course. I've never seen her before in my life."

"A witch-woman, perhaps," mused Dvorak, seemingly as unimpressed by the notion as he was by most other occurrences. He gazed off over the rolling fields to a distant farmhouse, where a spiral of gray smoke drifted into the sky. "Before I return to Oxford, I must first call on your sire. I bear a message from the king."

Surprised, Kat peered at Dvorak. Leda was growing restive. Overhead, the dark gray clouds were again coming down from the north. The air had grown very chill and Kat's fingers felt stiff on the reins. "What sort of message do you bring?" Her tone was suspicious.

"It's for your father," said Dvorak.

Kat sniffed. "He'll ignore it. He always does."

"I think not."

"Rot. You don't know my father." She peered at the road, which crested over the ancient stone bridge. "What do you study at Oxford?" she asked, trying to keep the envy out of her voice.

Dvorak allowed his mount to crop at some short, tough grasses next to the hedgerow. "History, mostly. I'm interested in events that have shaped the world."

"People shape the world," countered Kat, "not events."

He shrugged. "It's the same thing."

"No, it's not. That's a very different point of view. People aren't events, they're . . . people." She had grown dogmatic, imagining a lecture hall jammed with eager students, all male, and judging from Stefan Dvorak, not necessarily English. The thought galled her. She did not wait for Dvorak's response. Putting spurs to her horse, Kat led the way to Windrush.

For almost an hour, Kat's parents listened to Stefan discuss what was taking place in the restless city of Prague. Edgar de Vere was fascinated by the young man's reports of the latest Bohemian turmoil. Lady Beatrice was intrigued by their visitor's faintly exotic appearance and virtually flawless English.

Kat was bored. The conflict between Protestants and Catholics in faraway lands with unpronounceable names held no interest for her. The political quarrels struck her as petty, mere family disputes between one king named Rudolf and another called Matthias. Where the Holy Roman Emperor fit into this scheme of things eluded Kat. She nibbled on a cold pheasant leg and watched the rain fall outside of the mullioned gallery window.

But Stefan Dvorak had not come to Windrush to offer a discourse on Bohemian nationalism. At last Kat and Lady

Beatrice withdrew, to let Dvorak speak privately with Sir Edgar.

"His majesty is at Windsor bestowing the Order of the Garter on the Elector Frederick," explained Lady Beatrice when they reached the hallway. "This charming Bohemian was dispatched with a message of importance." She gave her daughter a swift glance. "Think you what it could be?"

Kat was unperturbed. "An invitation to Bess's wedding, no doubt. It's finally been set for St. Valentine's Day, next week." Picking up one of the latest litter of terriers, Kat allowed the little animal to lick her cheek. "I should go, I suppose. I may not see Bess for a very long time now that she will be moving with the elector to Heidelberg."

Lady Beatrice's high, smooth brow puckered faintly. Her complexion, like her carriage, was still the envy of other women. Kat admired her mother's élan, while also resenting her for it. "You think it's of Elizabeth's marriage that this Dvorak was sent by the king?" A curious light gleamed in Lady Beatrice's hazel eyes.

Kat frowned at her mother. "Of course. What else? Surely his majesty doesn't expect my sire to make another voyage this late in his life? Our family seeks no advancement at court. We ask nothing of the king. He need ask nothing of us." She spoke firmly, but her expression was questioning.

Lady Beatrice did not respond. She was off to the kitchen to confer with the cooks, should Stefan Dvorak stay on for supper. Kat lingered in the corridor outside of the gallery, playing with the pup and vainly trying to make its floppy ears stand on end.

When her father emerged a quarter of an hour later, Kat feigned indifference to his summons. Before he could introduce the topic at hand, however, the de Vere steward, Anthony Robbins, begged permission to enter, apologized for intruding and announced that Lord Edgar's mare was about to foal, courtesy of Sir Nicholas Overbury's prize stallion. Kat's father begged his guest to forgive him for taking a brief leave, and requested that Kat entertain Dvorak in his absence. Under ordinary circumstances Kat would have been eager to join Lord Edgar and Anthony Robbins in the stable, but she felt compelled to remain in the gallery. Her father was grateful. "Such a coincidence," he remarked on his way out, "with all this talk of mating between our families."

Puzzled, Kat sat down in the chair her father had vacated. Stefan Dvorak was opposite her, his attire casual, his manner at ease. He was drinking a cup of Scottish usquebaugh and sampling smoked oysters from a silver tray.

"What is my sire talking about?" Kat asked abruptly.

Stefan regarded her with detachment. "It's not for me to say," he answered easily. "Wait until he returns."

But Kat was not put off so readily. "My parents don't shelter me from the world," she asserted. "You may speak as freely in front of me as in front of them. Is this about the Princess Elizabeth and the Elector Palatine or not?"

Briefly, Stefan considered. "Inasmuch as I must leave for Oxford within the hour, I suppose you're right. The business of foaling can take much time." He inclined his head, and in the momentary silence, Kat heard the rain patter against the windows and the terrier bark outside the door. "King James has arranged a match for you." He paused just long enough for Kat to open her eyes wide and let her jaw drop. "With Thomas Overbury, the son of the family whose stallion has sired your new foal."

Although the de Veres and the Overburys lived within an hour's ride of each other, Kat scarcely recalled their son. Once or twice, when she was very small, a most superior adolescent had spurned her company when his parents had come to call, she remembered. Then, she supposed, young

Thomas had gone away, abroad or to court. His mother and father remained friendly, but Kat had seen little of them and thought less of it. Her reaction to Dvorak's announcement was one of disbelief.

"There must be some mistake. Surely Master Overbury is already married. Why, he must be at least thirty!"

Dvorak gave one of his annoying shrugs. "Such disparities are common. As for Overbury's marital status, I assure you," he said in a dry tone, "the man is . . . eligible."

Now unsettled, Kat gripped at the arms of the chair, which were carved into cat's paws. "You know this Overbury? Isn't he a poet or some such literary personage?"

"Indeed he is," Dvorak agreed, taking another oyster from the tray. "Talented, I'm told. But better known at court for his connection with your king's current favorite, Robin Carr. The two are thick as pudding pie." The black eyes danced with amusement, the source of which was lost on Kat. It occurred to her that not only was Stefan Dvorak's mastery of the English language beyond reproach, but that he also understood the nuances amazingly well.

Kat was on her feet, pacing in agitation. "Poet or potter, I won't have him," she declared. "I've vowed not to marry, and that's that." She darted a glance at Dvorak. He was sipping his usquebaugh and, as usual, looked unruffled. "Well? Do you find me unreasonable?" demanded Kat.

"Definitely," Stefan replied with a wry expression. "But it's probably a folly of youth. How old are you? Fourteen?"

"Fourteen!" Kat stamped her foot. "I'm going on seventeen, sir! Have you an eye disease?"

His attempt at humility was a failure. "Forgive me. I was judging from your actions, not your appearance. Going-on-seventeen is rather old to be unwed, is it not? I'm told that the usual age for a girl's betrothal in this country is twelve.''

Whirling away, Kat strode to the window, where the rain was beginning to desist while the clouds blew south in gray, scudding masses. "Age is of no matter in my case," she said in a severe voice. "I told you, I will not wed. I've lost my only love, and shall spend my days a spinster."

Regarding her very seriously, Dvorak also got up. "So. It seems a waste. Your beauty will be stunted." Though the words were well spoken, Kat heard only indifference.

"I've no idea what you're talking about," she insisted. "What I look like is of no matter. The only thing that's important now is that when the time comes, I can manage Windrush on my own."

"Windrush?" Stefan glanced at his surroundings, the well-appointed room with its portraits of various de Veres and its collection of Italian artifacts. "This house, you mean."

Kat lifted her chin. "Of course."

He looked vaguely puzzled. "It matters that much to you?"

"Certainly," replied Kat. "It means the world to me."

Dvorak uttered a short little laugh. "What good is a house when all is said and done? A roof to keep away the rain and snow. The heavy limbs of a sturdy tree would do as well. Why do you English make so much over your homes?"

Kat was aghast. "An Englishman's home is his castle! We take great pride in our properties! Our ancestors worked and fought for every square inch of soil! This house is my heritage. It's who and what I am!"

Dvorak did not look convinced. "I'm glad I don't think that way. I should hate to believe I am what I came from. Particularly," he added on a bitter note, "since it no longer exists. I prefer to dwell not on the past, but the future, illusory as it may be." He picked up his short green cloak and tossed it over his broad shoulders. "I must head for Oxford. I fear your good sire may be up all night awaiting the birth of his foal. My compliments to him and your lady mother." He touched his forehead in salute. "And to you, Lady Katherine, on your imminent betrothal."

Infuriated at his calm acceptance of her fate, Kat waved her fists at Dvorak. "How dare you! I will not be betrothed! I will be a spinster! I've sworn it!"

Stefan eyed Kat with that black, sardonic gaze. Despite her unreasonable nature and ill humor, the little wench amused him. She reminded him of a cat he'd had at Falkenau, as green-eyed as she and just as feisty. He'd never tamed the animal, but he'd eventually won her affection. Stefan frowned suddenly, wondering why such long-ago images had flashed into his mind. He preferred not to think of Falkenau at all.

"You will wed, Lady Kat," said Stefan in a quiet, assured voice. He moved a step closer, ignoring the waving fists. "You will love again, too. You are, I'll wager, made for love."

Kat's hands fell to her sides; the green eyes widened with astonishment at his temerity. Dvorak held up a big hand, and for a brief moment, Kat thought he was going to touch her. She recoiled. To her further surprise, he broke into a grin, made a mockery of a bow and wheeled out of the gallery, with the short green cloak billowing behind him.

A dozen stinging retorts leaped into Kat's mind, but it was too late to give voice to any of them. Next time, she promised herself, she'd unleash them all. It did not occur to her why she expected there would be a next time with Stefan Dvorak.

As a loyal English subject, Kat was forced to respect James Stuart as her sovereign. But she held him in contempt as a man. He was crude of manner—probably a result of his upbringing in Scotland—and his preference for male companionship offended Kat. But most of all, he had not been receptive to Prince Henry's attachment for the de Vere heiress. Had Henry lived, Kat was convinced she and her beloved would have eventually prevailed. After all, they had Elizabeth on their side. But Henry's death had slammed the door on Kat's future. Stefan Dvorak was right—she felt blighted, and could not help but put some of the blame on the king.

Naturally, James was oblivious to Kat's feelings. When he arrived unannounced at Windrush two days after Dvorak's visit, he expressed a desire to partake of the gracious hospitality the de Veres had shown to his daughter and much-lamented son. Yet, as Kat feared, sociability wasn't uppermost in his mind.

"We gather you think we're being unreasonable," James said dryly, shoveling sweetmeats into his mouth and ignoring the debris he was leaving on the Persian carpet. "Why is your daughter not more enthused about the Overbury match?"

Sir Edgar had already explained Kat's position at least twice. Surely the king couldn't be so obtuse as to not understand why the death of his elder son had affected Sir Edgar's only daughter. Kat's parents had not been pleased by her obstinacy, but they were loath to force her into marriage.

James glanced at Sir Edgar, then spat out a piece of candied fruit that displeased him and absently stroked the hand of his gentleman-in-waiting, the handsome, fair-haired Robert Carr. "Your wife's dower house, is it not?" James was saying as Kat brought the wine. "A pity she's ill."

Sir Edgar's expression was guarded, but it was Kat who spoke. "These spells come upon her without warning. They leave just as swiftly." Nothing in Kat's visage indicated that the present "spell" would go away precisely when King James departed Windrush. Like her daughter, Lady Beatrice did not approve of her sovereign's unnatural predilections, and she despised his estrangement from Queen Anne.

"Our children brought back wondrous reports of Windrush's charms," the king said, drinking freely while he ran his other hand over the shimmering green brocade that covered the arm of his chair. "They did not exaggerate."

Sir Edgar inclined his head. "Your majesty is most generous. To us, it is our home, a haven from the heckling world."

"It needs children," James said abruptly, suddenly sitting up straight and turning to Kat. "How old are you?"

"Sixteen, Sire, seventeen come June." She kept her hands clasped at her waist, a slim, unyielding figure in her gown of black silk with its delicate wire ruff.

"That old!" exclaimed James, not without humor. "And pretty, too. Our Henry found you so, at least," he added with a fond glance at Robert Carr. "You must wed so that this magnificent house won't fall into disuse."

Kat actually took a backward step. "Alas, Sire, I have vowed not to wed. Spinsterhood suits me well since the death of your beloved son."

Under his graying beard, James's mouth drooped. "We need no reminders of our loss," he said without rancor. "Yet life goes on. Your youth and beauty should not be wasted. We have selected a neighbor of yours, Sir Thomas Overbury. A fine fellow, is he not, Robin?" The king plucked at his favorite's pleated sleeve.

Robin gave his master a languorous look. He was handsome enough, Kat had to admit, and under that practiced fey charm he possessed a certain virility.

"Tom is most amusing," Robin said in a thick Scots accent. "Yet he can be overbearing." A giggle escaped from his lips. "Overburying, should I say, m'lord?"

"Zounds, Robin!" the king exclaimed with a hoot of laughter, wielding his goblet like a jester's baton and sloshing wine on the carpet, "your wit delights us! If Tom is overbearing—" the king paused, apparently trying not to guffaw again "—then it's clear he needs a wife to bear Overburys, eh?"

Monarch and favorite all but fell about with mirth while Kat and her father exchanged baleful glances. Robin squeezed the king's narrow, ermine-clad shoulder and slapped his well-molded thigh. Kat longed to turn her back, but remained in place, seething inwardly. Surely her parents wouldn't allow James to force her into wedlock with Overbury? She looked again at her father, this time in mute appeal, but he seemed uncharacteristically ill at ease. Kat set her jaw and made up her mind: she would not—could not—argue with His Majesty. But neither could she marry Thomas Overbury. The fact was, even if she had been of a mind to wed, there was something about the way people spoke of Overbury that disturbed her. Her recollection of him was sketchy. Yet her parents would know the truth; certainly they would not permit an unsuitable match. Caught up in her thoughts, Kat barely heard her father's attempt to ease the strained atmosphere. "Perhaps your grace would enjoy a stroll in the gardens. It's grown quite fine for February. False spring, my lady wife always calls it."

James was amenable to the suggestion. Indeed, the weather had changed dramatically, with a hint of soft warmth in the air and green shoots in the orchard. Coyly, the king leaned on Robin Carr, like a lapdog courting attention.

Sir Edgar fell in step just behind them. Kat's black mood hovered over her like a veil. She longed to saddle up Leda, gallop heedlessly across the countryside and let the fresh breezes clear her mind. Instead, she woodenly walked at her father's side.

James had stopped, his eyes raking over the carefully tended gardens with the Dutch bulbs peeking out of the rich, damp earth, the precious, sheltered orange trees from Spain and the Italian fountain where Neptune reigned supreme. "Charming," murmured the king. His slack mouth evolved into a little smirk as he gazed at Kat and Sir Edgar. "What a pity to lose such a property by default. Tell me, my sweet Robin," he inquired of the young man at his side, "do you find Windrush agreeable?"

"Indeed I do," Robin smiled back. "But you've already been too generous with your gift of Sir Walter Raleigh's fine home."

Next to Kat, her father winced. Sir Edgar had been outraged when the king had confiscated Raleigh's manor house, Sherborne. The implication was not lost on either Sir Edgar or his daughter. Kat bridled, and was about to speak up when James yawned unrestrainedly, revealing several rotting teeth in the process. "We must be off, since our daughter's wedding is four days hence. You will attend, we trust?" Despite the question in his voice, there was no doubt that the king had given a command.

Sir Edgar bowed, a rigid gesture that conveyed only the merest suggestion of obeisance. "If my lady is recovered, we will come," he said quietly. "However," he went on, meeting the king's gaze squarely, "if she worsens, I would not dream of leaving her. In my opinion, a man is measured by his devotion to his wife."

For once, the king's slack mouth snapped shut as he glared at Sir Edgar. But when he spoke, his words were mild enough. "Well put," he said, letting go of Robin Carr's

arm. "In your place, we will hope to see Lady Katherine."
He offered Kat a crooked smile, rotting teeth and all.
"Accompanied, of course, by her betrothed, Sir Thomas
Overbury." Idly, James took one last inventory of Windrush, with its mellow stones and graceful chimneys and
charming gardens. "Tom will enjoy this place," remarked
the king, again clinging to Carr. "Think you he'll like it as
much as you do, Robin?"

The favorite sniggered and threw Kat an insinuating
look.

Chapter Three

The Princess Elizabeth had broken with tradition and insisted on wearing white for her wedding. Kat thought the satin gown, richly embroidered with silver, was beautiful. But she had no wish to follow her friend's steps on the road to matrimony.

"Your sire all but threatened us," Kat confided to Elizabeth after the final fitting on the day before the ceremony. "His majesty is most insistent that I marry this Overbury. My parents are heartsick, but fear they can't prevent the match."

Elizabeth wore a sympathetic expression, though her mind was clearly on other, more personal, matters. "It will all work out for the best," she soothed, taking one last look at herself in the long beveled mirror in her apartments at St. James. She had moved there only the previous week from the Cockpit at Whitehall, while Frederick spent a few days hunting with King James and Prince Charles at Hampton Court. "Oh, Kat," sighed Elizabeth, "do you think Freddy will find me fetching?"

"He already does," replied Kat dryly. To Kat's mind, Elizabeth did not need the embellishments of her trousseau, including the twenty-six gowns, hundreds of buttons, yards of ribbon and rows of lace. Indeed, Kat thought the extravagant fashions of the day, particularly the jutting farthingales, were all but ridiculous. Her mother concurred, which was well enough in the relative isolation of Windrush, but at court, Kat found herself being coaxed into Florentine cloth of silver with reams of decoration, including four dozen sugar-loaf buttons.

"You must attend me with the others," Elizabeth insisted. "Don't fret, there's plenty of material for an extra gown. I had five hundred and twenty yards of the stuff sent just for the occasion. You are," she added with her warm smile, "my dearest friend. I wish you were coming with me to Heidelberg."

Fond though she was of Elizabeth, Kat considered Heidelberg almost as far away and as exotic as Araby. "You have other good friends going with you," Kat demurred. "And you will make more. People take to you, Bess. Your new subjects will be enthralled."

Elizabeth gave a toss of her head. "We'll see. I intend to do my best to win them over." She gave Kat a rueful look. "We have grown up, dear friend. Has the loss of Hal also made us lose our sense of fun?"

Kat was momentarily taken aback by the question. Laughter didn't bubble up the way it used to; there were no more comic pranks played on unsuspecting residents at Windrush. The sense of adventure had seemed to slip away, virtually unnoticed. "Life becomes more serious as we get older, I suppose," ventured Kat, with a pang of regret.

"It does at that," admitted Elizabeth. "And I must take my responsibilities in the Palatinate most seriously. At least," she added with a wry expression, "I don't have to bring along any of those loathsome Howard women. Which reminds me—could you fetch Susan? I purchased seventeen pairs of stockings and I can't find any of them. She's tucked them away someplace and forgotten to tell Lady Harington where they are."

Kat obliged willingly. Lady Harington was Elizabeth's governess, a kindly woman with handsome if faintly pinched features and a maternal disposition that was lacking in Queen Anne. Kat had become acquainted with the governess on the three occasions that she'd visited Elizabeth at the Haringtons' manor house of Combe Abbey.

But if Kat was well-acquainted with Lady Harington, she was much less conversant with the Palace of St. James. Kat had never been inside the royal residence until her arrival the previous day. To make matters worse, the palace was a-bustle with the wedding preparations, and no one seemed inclined to stop long enough to give directions. Kat finally found a vague-looking maid carrying a pile of linen who thought Lady Susan's temporary quarters were close at hand, overlooking the park.

The antechamber the maid had indicated was empty. Three doors led off of it, presumably to the bedrooms assigned to the princess's ladies-in-waiting. Kat tried them all and got no response. She decided to leave a note for Lady Susan, but could find neither parchment nor pen. Tentatively, she pushed at the door on her left; it swung open reluctantly, revealing a small darkened room where a naked man and woman were standing in a close embrace. Kat let out a startled cry, her stunned gaze locked with the lavender eyes of the woman who was facing her some six feet away. She appeared more vexed than surprised, her golden hair cascading over her paramour's broad shoulders. Even in the dim light, Kat recognized Susan Howard. She was positive she knew that bronzed masculine form even before he turned his head. It was Stefan Dvorak.

Mesmerized by the sharp profile, Kat suppressed an urge to scream. Dvorak's body may have held the other woman captive, but his eyes seemed to devour Kat. She felt as if she were as naked as Lady Susan.

"Sweet Jesus," she murmured, one hand at her breast, the other gripping the doorframe. Falling over her hem, she turned and stumbled out of the room.

Banging the heavy door behind her, Kat leaned against its stout oak and gasped for breath. Her mind was no longer functioning properly. Forcing composure upon herself, she tried to obliterate those black eyes, the chiseled features, the rumpled hair that rivaled the raven. Despite her efforts, she felt faintly dizzy, with a pounding in her ears. She was disturbed, even angry. Intruding on an amorous couple was embarrassing enough, but to find Lady Susan, a sprig of that infamous Howard family, entwined with Stefan Dvorak somehow struck Kat as shocking. She was trembling from head to foot, and didn't know why.

Awkwardly, Kat crossed the antechamber and headed into the passageway. She had trudged along for almost five minutes before she realized she was hopelessly lost. In her path, a door flew open and a slim, brown-haired man almost fell over her.

To Kat's surprise, he turned not to her in apology, but back toward the chamber he had so precipitously left. "Will you never leave the company of that base woman?" he cried to an unseen audience. Then he slammed the door and glared at Kat. "Why do you eavesdrop, mistress? Have you no business of your own?"

In truth, Kat was beginning to feel like a voyeur. She flushed guiltily, and for once had no sharp response. "I'm on my way back to her royal highness's apartments," she said, trying to regain her aplomb. "I think I'm lost."

Smoothing the ruffled hair back from his temples, the man let out an impatient breath. "You need to reverse your step, then go to your right. In fact," he continued, his own heightened color beginning to recede, "I'm about to call on the princess myself. I'll show you the way."

"Thank you," said Kat, falling into step with the
stranger. He was of medium stature, with a short, spade-
shaped beard, a long straight nose and intelligent, if aloof,
gray eyes. His attire was impeccable, the slashed doublet
and falling ruff in the latest French mode. He certainly
looked more like a courtier than the casually garbed Stefan Dvorak in his plain linen shirts, leather jerkins and well-
worn boots.

But instead of Dvorak's clothed form, Kat's mental image showed her only his bare shoulders, broad and bronzed.
She made a face and walked faster. Neither she nor her
companion spoke as they made their way through the corridors of St. James's.

"Here," said the man at Kat's side, gesturing at the entrance to Elizabeth's quarters. "Are you a servant to her
highness?" His keen gaze took in Kat's plain black gown,
still devoid of decoration in deference to Prince Henry's
passing.

Kat's green eyes snapped. "I am a friend of the Princess
Elizabeth," she said with as much dignity as she could
summon. "Are you in her train of attendants heading for
Heidelberg?"

"Zounds, no," responded the man, looking down his
long nose at Kat. "I've been abroad, to France. Foreign
parts annoy me." He grimaced as a halberdier bade them
enter Elizabeth's chambers. "I've come to collect my bride-
to-be, though I've no stomach for it. Still," he added with
a shrug, letting Kat precede him, "it's my duty, I suppose.
I shall have to make the best of it, no matter how homely
or stupid the chit may be."

Elizabeth was in the middle of the room, attended by
Lady Harington and her daughter, Lucy. "Look," announced the princess, swinging a handful of silken stockings, "what was lost has been found! Oh!" she exclaimed,

seeing that Kat was not alone, "Sir Thomas Overbury! What a surprise!"

Kat whirled about, staring at the man who had accompanied her to the princess's rooms. Elizabeth was speaking again, this time in a confused rush. "You've already met? You've not? But how could...?" She let the question dangle as Kat and Overbury stared at one another.

"I'm not stupid," averred Kat. "I was merely lost."

"Well." Overbury was clearly abashed. "You have me at a disadvantage, my lady. I am not usually as ill-tempered as you found me just now."

At least, Kat thought to herself, *you were dressed.* But she had to stop letting that disturbing image of Stefan Dvorak and Susan Howard intrude. "Fie, sir, it's of no matter. I'm sure you had good cause for berating whoever it was on the other side of the door. But I gather you are as unenthusiastic about this forced match as I."

Overbury looked at her askance. If Kat had hoped for an ally in her putative fiancé, she was about to be disappointed. "Our enthusiasm is not required," Overbury asserted in his haughty manner. "Only our acquiescence is necessary. We must, of course, do as the king commands."

"But my lord," Kat protested, "you don't wish to marry me any more than I wish to marry you."

Elizabeth and her ladies were watching with a mixture of bemusement and embarrassment. Taking her royal responsibilities seriously, the princess intervened. "Dear Kat," she said, clasping her friend by the hand, "I know how distressed you are over my brother's death. But the world must keep on spinning. Tom here is a neighbor of yours, a brilliant poet, a man of culture and accomplishment. Given the fact that you have forsworn love, where could you find a better mate?" Before Kat could react, Elizabeth turned to Overbury. "And you, Tom—I give you

my sincere assurances that Lady Kat is the most delightful
and intelligent of companions. My life would have been
much the poorer but for her friendship.'' Handing the
stockings to Lady Harington, she also took Overbury's
hand and joined it with Kat's. "Don't spoil my happiest of
days by denigrating the married state. Promise yourselves
that you, too, can find happiness as I have done with
Freddy.''

Given the circumstances, as well as the burden of royal
decree, Kat and Thomas Overbury could do little but submit, at least for the moment. Overbury gave Kat's hand the
faintest of squeezes; Kat offered an uncertain smile. Elizabeth beamed on them both.

"Come," she exclaimed, relinquishing her hold, "it's
time to watch the pageant! We shall have a marvelous view
from the privy stairs at Whitehall." She fairly danced across
the chamber. "Best of all," she said in an excited voice,
"Freddy will be there! I haven't seen him for almost a
week!''

Kat tried to widen her smile for Elizabeth's sake. She
even attempted to conjure up an image of the elector's
dark-haired, strong-featured, pleasant face.

But all she saw was Stefan Dvorak.

Amidst lavish scenery set up across the Thames, the
Christian Navy defeated the forces of the Infidel. Some
thirty-eight righteous vessels pummeled the Turkish fleet
for more than four hours. Kat admired the performance for
the first sixty minutes, but eventually grew bored. Her gaze
wandered to the far side of the river, where Lambeth Palace was all but obscured by Turkish minarets and rocky
cliffs. Directly below, a barge had been tied up at the palace landing, and a privileged crowd of Londoners watched
the doings with more enthusiasm than their betters on the
privy stairs. During yet another lull, a bright blaze of color

on the barge caught Kat's eye: a concoction of orange, gold, purple and green stood out among the more soberly clad burghers. Kat saw the tall hat, too, and was momentarily mesmerized. Could this be the same woman she had met by the ford at Temple Guiting? Surely not, Kat told herself, and looked again. But the motley figure had been swallowed up by the crowd. Kat returned to her state of torpor.

Her boredom was apparently shared by the king and queen, who withdrew in mid-display. Even Prince Charles became restive and retired before the denouement. But Elizabeth and Frederick, holding hands and watching each other as much as the exhibition, stayed on to the very end.

Thomas Overbury had also retired early, much to Kat's relief. He had made only the most perfunctory attempt at conversation, which was just as well, as far as Kat was concerned. His vaunted urbane wit did not seem to be in evidence when it came to courting his alleged betrothed.

Kat noticed Susan and Frances Howard among the onlookers, but saw nothing of Stefan Dvorak until dusk. He came sauntering up the privy stairs, his green cloak rippling in the breeze. The good weather had held, a boon for the bride and groom. Kat eased her stiffened limbs and watched Dvorak pause to speak with the elector. Yet another fusillade erupted, this time signaling the sinking of the Turkish admiral's flagship in the middle of the Thames. Kat squirmed in her place on the hard stone steps. At least the fireworks of the previous night had been mercifully brief, mainly because of a mishap with St. George and the Dragon, which had injured several bystanders. Kat was not only tired, but irritable. Dvorak, who had bowed to the elector and kissed Elizabeth's hand, was now heading up the stairs in her direction. Somewhat hastily, she stood and started to turn back into the palace.

But she was too late. Stefan had seen her. "Mistress!" he called, sounding unusually good-natured. "Hold!"

Kat regarded him with a cool expression. "Excuse me," she said, "I didn't recognize you at first with your clothes on."

To her dismay, Dvorak grinned. "We seem to keep encountering each other in a semigarbed state," he remarked, unexpectedly taking her by the arm and guiding her inside. "I hear your betrothal is official. Congratulations."

Once out of public view, Kat jerked her arm free. "It's not official! We're merely humoring Elizabeth on her wedding eve. Overbury is no more anxious to have me than I am to wed him. How dare you taunt me?"

The grin faded. "I don't taunt you. Indeed, I sought to apologize."

Kat stiffened. "For what? It was I who intruded." To her annoyance, she felt her cheeks grow hot. "I was looking for a . . . pen."

Dvorak's forehead furrowed. "What? A pen? I referred to my abrupt departure Sunday last from your family home."

"Oh!" Kat pressed her fingers against her pink cheeks. "I thought you meant . . . that is, today I . . ."

"Oh, that." Dvorak shrugged. "Careless of us. We should have locked the door. But Lady Susan is as impetuous as she is ardent. Do you know her well?"

Kat was nonplussed. "Not nearly as well as you do," she retorted.

Dvorak ignored the barb. "The fact is, I came upon that Gypsy *vurdon* the next day in the Vale of Evesham. The Roms told me how you defended them from the farmers before I arrived. They asked me to give you these as a token of their gratitude. I forgot I had them until I saw you just now." From inside his jerkin, he produced a pair of tortoiseshell combs, exquisitely decorated with jet. Kat had half expected rabbits.

"How lovely," said Kat faintly, recalling the appeal in the dark eyes of the Gypsy children. She was rattled by her conversation with Dvorak, disconcerted by his nonchalant attitude toward the amorous encounter with Susan Howard. Shifting about uncomfortably, Kat tried to think up an excuse to take her leave. From outside on the privy stairs, she could hear applause as the Christian admiral claimed total victory. It was virtually dark, and close to the supper hour.

"I wanted to write a note," she blurted.

Puzzlement still clouded Dvorak's brow. "A note? To me? Why?"

"No, no, no." Kat waved her hands. "To Susan. About the stockings." She swallowed hard, her wideset green eyes seeking comprehension.

The cat of Dvorak's youth at Falkenau slipped through his mind. Despite those other ugly, dreadful memories, he smiled. This little English wench with her plain black garb and forthright, if baffling, manner beguiled him. She was very different from the women he had known at the Bohemian court in Prague or here in London. Perhaps it was because she was a country lass. Whatever the reason, he was intrigued. But then Stefan Dvorak was frequently intrigued by women, no matter what their station. To his everlasting gratitude, they usually returned the favor. He wouldn't have it any other way.

"Let me understand this," he said carefully, pointing a finger in the direction of Kat's upturned nose. "You wanted a pen so that you could write a note to Susan Howard. That's despite the fact that Lady Susan was present at the time. Correct?"

"But she didn't answer my knock," Kat said doggedly. "I thought she was elsewhere." The discussion was ab-

surd; Kat had an illogical desire to laugh out loud. But that
wouldn't do. Instead, she pressed a hand to her head. Her
reaction to Dvorak couldn't possibly come from amusement. There was another emotion she didn't recognize, an
elusive sensation, almost a longing. Kat had no idea what
it meant. She refused to dwell upon it further. "What difference does my explanation make?" she demanded, now
testy. "It's suppertime. The festivities are concluded. I must
attend her royal highness."

Dvorak inclined his head. "And I must do the same with
the elector. What do you think of your friend's bridegroom, little Kat?"

Kat started to balk at the familiarity, but thought better
of it. Perhaps that was how people in Bohemia addressed
their peers. Kat knew little of foreign ways, except that they
were inferior. "I have not seen much of him," she replied
cautiously, "but he clearly dotes on Bess. Does anything
else matter?"

Stefan considered. "For them, no," he said at last.
Abruptly, he shook himself. "Yes, it does. It matters a
great deal. But neither the princess nor the elector will see
it. Yet," he added on an ominous note.

Perplexed, Kat gazed up at him with a questioning expression. "Do you mean as husband and wife or
as...something other?"

"I have accomplished my task," he murmured, more to
himself than to Kat. "They make a happy couple. Why
should I sense failure?" He stared out through the arched
doorway to the river, where darkness was swiftly falling
over the Turkish ruin.

Kat grimaced. "Whatever are you talking about?"

"Never mind," Stefan said evasively. "I discern that
politics bore you." Suddenly, he grinned again. "You are
much more curious about men and women, is that not so,
little Kat?"

"Fie, sir," retorted Kat, backing off a step as the sound of the departing audience resounded on the stone stairs just below, "what is there to know of men and women except that they mate, marry and beget? Is that not what supposedly makes the world go round?"

The glib response that Stefan was about to utter died on his lips as he looked deep into those wide, questioning green eyes. "You are the one who says so," he murmured as the royal party emerged from the privy stairs. Then, in a soft voice that Kat did not hear, he added to himself, "I'm not sure."

The wedding ceremony had been splendid. Frederick was suitably grave and just a trifle nervous, while Elizabeth was radiant and completely unselfconscious. Kat, who was serving as one of fifteen official train bearers, marveled at her friend's aplomb. The service was conducted in the chapel at Whitehall, and except for being overlong, Kat thought it was a flawless occasion.

The wedding festivities did not end with the Archbishop of Canterbury's pronouncement that Elizabeth and Frederick were now man and wife. Indeed, the week that followed swept by on a tide of entertainments and feasts that left much of the court breathless. By the next Saturday, Kat was surfeited and told the princess it was time she went home.

Elizabeth's face fell. "But you can't! Freddy and I won't leave for Germany until April! You must stay on! Who knows when we'll see each other again?"

Kat was surprised at the princess's vehemence. Since Elizabeth had been so wrapped up in her bridegroom, Kat had felt her departure would not be missed. "But Bess," protested Kat as they enjoyed a rare quiet moment between performances of a play, *The Dutch Courtesan,* and a masque, *Depicting the Marriage between Thames and*

Rhine, "until this very afternoon, we have had no opportunity for even the briefest of chats. You will be feted by yet more worthies and you must prepare for your journey. Then there are all the arrangements for your train of attendants. For my part, I find much of this mummery tedious. As for the food, I've had an upset stomach these past two days."

Elizabeth shooed away one of her Irish hounds, which was threatening to chew up a down-filled bolster of Milan fustian. "The worst is over, dear Kat. My royal father leaves Monday for Theobalds and Newmarket. Except for the baptism of the Cecil baby on Tuesday, Freddy and I will have most of our daytimes free. We can ride and hunt and gossip, just as before." She gave Kat a pleading look. "Please?"

Kat sighed. "I'm not cut out for court," she insisted. "Even this," she declared, making a sweeping gesture over her borrowed dark blue silk grosgrain skirts with their mauve petticoats, pink stomacher and heavy, padded sleeves, "is not for me. Where do I put my hands when I stand up?" She jabbed at the huge farthingale that jutted out more than a foot in circumference.

Elizabeth regarded Kat with sympathy. "I know, that's always been a problem. In fact, farthingales are about to be outlawed." She dimpled at Kat. "Several of the ladies at the wedding ceremony wore some that were so wide there wasn't room for everyone who was invited to watch the ceremony. Isn't that amusing?"

Kat made a droll face. "Not for the people who had to stand outside. I thought at the time there were some outlandish costumes present. But then we don't adhere strictly to fashion at Windrush." Her expression suddenly grew serious again. "If you really wish it, I'll stay on for another week. But Bess," Kat continued earnestly, "you must help me with Overbury. He insists on going ahead with this idiotic betrothal. I simply can't do it.''

Yet another dog, an island breed that Elizabeth had received as a wedding present, leaped onto the elaborately decorated nuptial bed. Deftly, Elizabeth snatched away the pillow it had pounced on and set the dog in her lap. ''You're making too great a fuss over this match, Kat. Tom Overbury is brilliant. He's handsome and reasonably well off. The only criticism I would have of him is…'' Her voice faltered and she frowned. ''Well, he's very proud, and he's not terribly gallant. That is, unlike so many men at court, he isn't one to pursue the ladies. But that would no doubt make him a faithful husband.''

The conversation was curtailed by the return of Elizabeth's ladies-in-waiting. Kat tried to ignore Susan Howard, who was looking exceptionally beautiful. To Kat's further dismay, Fanny Howard was with her cousin. The pair fell upon their knees in front of Elizabeth, whose honey blond hair was being curled with a crimping iron for the evening's masque.

''Your highness,'' Susan began, the lavender eyes downcast, ''my cousin, the Countess of Essex, is being persecuted in the most vile manner. We beg your generous intervention.''

At Susan's side, Frances Howard knelt wide-eyed, for all intents and purposes the very portrait of aggrieved innocence. It occurred to Kat that the Howards were taking advantage of Elizabeth's newlywed euphoria.

Elizabeth, constrained by Lucy Harington's efforts with the curling iron, did her best to look down at the two women. A flicker of distaste passed across her visage as she saw Fanny. Kat sympathized with her friend's feelings, but was still not convinced that the Howard chit had been Prince Henry's paramour. Kat had yet to meet Frances, although she had been on the fringes of most of the wedding festivities. But, Kat told herself, a rumor was only a rumor, and this one recounted by a foreigner, at that. She would try not to let tittle-tattle influence her. Yet the opulent beauty of the young countess might be well-nigh irresistible for even the most high-minded prince. Kat wished all the Howard women could be set adrift in the North Sea.

"Present your predicament," Elizabeth commanded with a faint sigh.

"It's quite simple," Susan began, but was cut short by the electress.

"Can't your cousin speak for herself?" demanded Elizabeth, wincing as Lady Lucy wound a curl too tight. "I've never yet met a Howard who was mute."

In a suitably demure manner, Fanny launched her recital: how at twelve, she had been forced into a loveless match with Robert Devereux, the Earl of Essex. Either because of incapacity or indifference, he had never consummated the marriage. Fanny wanted an annulment. She had fallen in love with Robin Carr, and as she was a virtuous maid, she would not dream of fulfilling their ardor until they were lawfully wed.

Though startled by Fanny's declaration, Kat was not without sympathy. While arranged marriages were common, the Howard girl's plight was remarkably like her own. The only difference was that Kat had no intention of falling in love with anyone.

Elizabeth, too, seemed caught up in the story. "I know that my royal sire is not opposed to a wedding between you and Robin," she said, voicing James's oddly magnanimous attitude toward his favorites' matrimonial ventures. "So if you can get your annulment, where's the rub?"

Fanny passed a graceful hand over her smooth forehead. "The rub, your highness, is Thomas Overbury. He is the sole obstacle to our everlasting happiness." Fanny wrung her hands, the fingers of which were covered with expensive gems. "Mayhap Overbury fears that once we are wed, his influence with Robin will diminish, and thus Thomas's hold on the king will loosen. Otherwise, it makes no sense. Indeed, Overbury encouraged us in the beginning. But now he stands between us and holy wedlock!" She offered Elizabeth a tremulous smile.

The electress paused while Lucy gave a final twist to the crimping iron. "It seems to me that you must first procure your annulment. I don't see how Sir Thomas—despite his great influence at court—could prevent your marriage to Robin Carr. Perhaps you're overwrought."

Fanny's wideset eyes snapped, momentarily flawing the demure portrait she had so carefully created. "He calls me a strumpet! And base! Imagine the effrontery!"

Kat blinked. It dawned on her that Fanny must be the "base woman" Overbury had mentioned when Kat had overheard him the day before Elizabeth's wedding. Obviously, he had been berating Robin Carr. Thomas Overbury's meddling in Carr's marital designs struck Kat as odd—and unfair.

Elizabeth motioned for the Howard women to rise, but before she could offer any more advice, the door burst open and a nondescript young man stormed into the room. He remembered his manners quickly enough to bow before Elizabeth and apologize for the intrusion, but his words were for Fanny Howard.

"We have caught the thief, madam wife," he announced. "She was making off with a purseful of coins."

Fanny jumped. "'She'?" The blue eyes narrowed at the man who was obviously her husband, the Earl of Essex. "A servant, then?"

Essex shook his head. Kat had seen the young earl at the royal wedding but had not realized who he was. Certainly he bore little resemblance to his famous if unfortunate father, whose reputation for looks and daring had cost him his head. This Robert Devereux was of medium height, with a wide, stolid face, an unprepossessing physique and bland blue eyes. She could see why Fanny preferred Robin Carr, but the idea of this inconsequential-looking young man resisting his wife's opulent charms struck Kat as funny. She had to turn away briefly to compose herself.

Elizabeth appeared exasperated. "Will you settle your domestic problems elsewhere? I am about to leave for a masque."

But Essex had dug in his heels, looking not unlike a worrisome terrier. "Highness, this took place inside these palace walls...."

Elizabeth waved an impatient hand. "I don't care if it took place under my bed! I'm celebrating my marriage! Make out a report and send it to the king. We're off to be amused."

Kat, however, could hardly bear any more theatricals. Having regained her control, she bobbed a curtsy at Elizabeth. "Allow me, your highness, to handle this matter. I am willing to sacrifice the evening's entertainment to be of service."

Elizabeth shot Kat a grateful glance. "So be it."

Swiftly, Kat ushered the Earl and Countess of Essex out of the royal chambers. In the passageway, two halberdiers guarded the culprit. To Kat's astonishment, the accused thief was the woman in motley. Kat gaped.

"She has already stolen a diamond ring and a pearl necklace," said Essex in his unremarkable but dogged voice.

The woman, who had apparently lost her steeple-crowned hat in the course of the incident, regarded Kat with an unperturbed countenance, but no apparent sign of recognition. "I'm not a thief," she announced calmly. "I was merely claiming my just wages for services rendered."

"What services?" asked Kat, recovering herself.

The sanguine smile Kat remembered from the footpath crossed the woman's face. "That," she said, with her fathomless eyes resting on Fanny Howard, "is between her ladyship and me."

"Nonsense!" snapped Fanny. "The bawd's a thief! Take her away!"

The halberdiers hesitated, but Essex nodded. Before anyone could move, the Elector Frederick and a half-dozen companions emerged into the passageway to escort Elizabeth to the masque. Among the company was Stefan Dvorak, for once dressed in formal, if subdued, courtier's attire. The others, including the elector, marched past without more than a glance, but Stefan caught Kat's eye and stopped.

"What is all this?" he inquired in that deep, casual voice.

Essex gave the explanation, terse and trenchant. Stefan nodded, then studied the motley-garbed woman. "Who are you, mistress?"

She returned Stefan's dark gaze without flinching. "I'm Mary Woods, of Stratton Strawless, near Norwich. I'm employed by the Countess of Essex. She can tell you why."

But even as Dvorak turned a questioning look on the countess, she put both hands to her ginger-colored hair and uttered a little shriek. "Lies! All lies! Let the bawd go! My nerves are all undone!" With a crackle of silk and taffeta, Fanny fled the scene.

"God's eyes," grumbled Essex, "my lady wife is unpredictable!" He turned to Stefan. "Frankie," he said, using the nickname that his wife supposedly despised, "may not want to prosecute, but I do. The ring and necklace were gifts from me. This woman must be punished."

Mary Woods retained her poise, the strange, deep eyes flickering over Kat. "That one knows me. She lives at Windrush. Her star is obscured by clouds for now, but will rise again."

Kat gaped at the woman, but before she could speak, Mary Woods turned to Stefan Dvorak. "And you, a stranger in our midst, dwell with uncertainty. Forget your homeland. All is lost."

Stefan's eyes narrowed, but he kept silent. His visage tightened as he appeared to consider the woman's warning. Kat again started to protest, but Essex cut in. "This sounds like witchcraft as well as thievery! Guards, have her removed to await my formal charges."

Stefan gazed from Essex to Mary Woods and back again. He fingered his impressive chin and shook his head. "I think not. There may be wisdom in what she says. Let her go."

The halberdiers exchanged stymied looks. An English earl outranked a foreign baron any day, but they knew authority when they heard it. Essex, however, had his hand on his sword.

"You meddle, sir! This is a matter of honor. No one can rob the Earl of Essex blind!"

"If robbery was done, it was of the Countess of Essex, and she's quit the field," Stefan said dryly. "Let your wife and this woman settle things between themselves. And pray take your hand off your sword. It would not serve you well against my *schiavona*." Idly, he flicked his fingers toward the long, dangerous-looking weapon that hung at his side.

Essex glared at Dvorak. "I mislike your impertinence, Baron Ostrov. It's no wonder that you've been sent into exile. You're a rebel, I'm told."

As ever, Stefan was unruffled. "Your king is not unsympathetic to my rebellion," he remarked calmly. "Indeed, your country has been hospitable to Bohemians ever since your King Richard II married our Anne. She was much loved by the English."

Essex was not assuaged by Stefan's conciliatory manner. He muttered something Kat could not hear and stomped off. Stefan grinned at Kat. "Contrary to what you've just seen, Essex is a brave man in battle. But where women are concerned, he, too, prefers to quit the field."

Kat was annoyed as well as mystified by the whole episode. "This all seems like a bollix to me. Perhaps Mistress Woods can enlighten us."

But of course, when she turned around, Mary Woods was gone.

"You are certain you never saw this woman until you met her by the bridge near Leigh Wood?" Stefan Dvorak asked Kat as they strolled through the torchlit gardens at St. James's.

"Of course I am," said Kat, who had been grateful to Dvorak's suggestion that they go outside and clear their heads. "But I saw her since, last Saturday night, at the pageant on the Thames." She paused, suddenly aware that it was still February and quite chilly without a cloak. "Why did she tell you to stay in England? Why did Essex call you a rebel?"

Stefan was frowning. "I have been outspoken in advocating freedom for Bohemia. Emperor Matthias, who is also king of Bohemia, wants to keep us under the Hapsburg yoke," he said with a weary air. Clearly, the subject was not a happy one for Stefan. "My views are not popular with the self-styled rulers of my homeland. But this Norwich woman doesn't know me any more than she knows you." He gave Kat a puzzled, sidelong glance. "If she's indeed a practitioner of the black arts, I'd be curious to know why the countess has employed her. There's something odd about all this, don't you think?"

"Yes," agreed Kat. "But I'm even more curious to find out what possible interest she could have in either of us. I don't believe in such things as soothsayers. Do you?"

"I believe in very little," Dvorak said, faintly grim. "But many people, including your king, set great store by astrologers and necromancers and such. They don't trust themselves, so put their faith in whimsy."

For once Kat was finding herself in agreement with Stefan Dvorak. It was an odd sensation to realize she had something in common with this foreigner. "I'm inclined to believe Mary Woods, not Fanny Howard. But then I don't trust the Howards in general. They're too ruthless." The words tumbled out heedlessly, and Kat gave Stefan a guilty look. "Forgive me, I didn't think of your...friendship with Lady Susan."

"Friendship?" Dvorak seemed genuinely puzzled. A crescent moon hung over the gardens, distant and cold. Kat shivered. "I wouldn't call it that," he said at last. "An accommodation, perhaps. Susan can be very provocative company. She is well versed in the arts of love."

So matter-of-fact was his tone, so casual was his attitude that Kat had to fight down the urge to berate him for his lack of moral fiber. "It's not seemly in this country to speak so freely of illicit liaisons," she declared in her primmest manner. "Englishmen do not behave as if bedding women meant no more than chasing rabbits."

Stefan's dark eyes were quite serious. "Perhaps your English gentlemen aren't as candid in the presence of women. But don't mistake my meaning. Making love is much more important than catching rabbits. Besides," he added, and now his black gaze held a glimmer of amusement, "the rabbits don't want to be caught. Most women do."

"Rot!" exclaimed Kat, her temper flaring. "The women I know best guard their virtue zealously. Nor would any honorable Englishman even think of tampering with a maid unless he intended to make her his wife!"

Stefan raised his eyes to the darkened heavens. "Oh, my! Where have you been for sixteen years, little Kat? Up on yonder moon?"

Kat planted both feet firmly on the ground and set her fists on her hips. "You would teach me about my own people? How dare you! I am well acquainted with the world. I've been loved by a prince! It's only women like those Howard sluts who are so easily seduced! Or Gypsy whores!"

Kat gasped as Dvorak grabbed her by the shoulders, snapping her head back. "Don't ever speak so of the Roms! My mother was a Gypsy, as good and virtuous as the fine English lady who bore you!" One hand swung up, then his mouth clamped shut and he dropped his arm at his side. "You're a fool, Katherine de Vere," he said, his face wooden but his eyes flashing. "Like most of the English, you're a smug, ignorant boor."

Kat's temper was boiling, but her mind was a blank. He was a brute, a savage, a half-breed foreigner with nothing to his credit but an Oxford education. "If you think so little of English ways, why ever did you come here?" she demanded.

An odd, pained expression crossed Dvorak's face. "You heard Milord Essex. I am not welcome in my own country. I had nowhere else to go," he said, and his voice sounded hollow. Strange, he thought, that Kat's opinion should matter. She was of no importance to him, merely a silly wench he'd met at a state funeral. He grabbed her wrist with his other hand, pulling her so close that her breasts brushed his doublet. It would do no good to try to shake sense into the chit. She was too obtuse, too self-righteous, too *English*. "I told you," he said curtly, "you don't understand." The black eyes glittered with anger, and for a brief moment Kat thought he might actually strike her. Instead, his lips came down on hers in a crushing kiss. Kat

reeled with the sensation of that hard mouth on her lips.
This was not at all like Henry's gentle embrace, soft and
sweet as morning rain. She tried to escape, but his arm was
at her back, holding her captive. In the pit of her stomach,
an alien sensation welled up, muddling her brain and stirring her senses. Kat was afraid, and at the same time exhil-
arated. She wasn't entirely aware that her lips were
responding to Stefan's as if they had a will of their own.

Abruptly, with the anger still in his veins, he let her go.
Kat momentarily lost her balance, falling backward against
a stone wall. Stunned, she searched his face, hazily noting
that while his annoyance hadn't faded, the dark eyes had
softened. With a sigh of vexation, Stefan shook his head.

"Excuse me. That was a foolish action. A good shaking
would have served as well." He was aware of the rough edge
in his voice and inwardly cursed himself. Impulse was not
his way with women; passionate interludes were carefully
calculated, based on mutual consent. Stefan felt like an
unruly schoolboy.

Kat swallowed hard and tried to regain her composure.
"I'm not a trifle," she declared, sounding quite lame. "My
upbringing has not accustomed me to such . . . dalliance."

For a brief moment Dvorak looked as if he might smile,
but he did not. "No," he said flatly. "That's clear." With
a little bow, he strode away from her, up the path toward
the palace.

Kat stayed in the garden, not wanting to follow for fear
of further confrontation. Stefan Dvorak had no right to
kiss her, especially in anger. Indeed, no honorable man
should kiss any virtuous woman except as part of courtship. His behavior was as inexplicable as it was unsettling.
Along the torchlit path, Kat felt the first soft drops of rain.
She must go in, as soon as Dvorak was out of sight. Tentatively, she touched her mouth. It felt bruised. It felt

wonderful. Kat didn't understand the conflicting emotions. Slowly, she walked up the path, shivering with cold. Yet inside she felt quite warm.

Chapter Four

The following day, which was the Sabbath, Kat forced herself to concentrate on the enigma that surrounded Mary Woods. She came to no solution, however, other than the obvious, which was that Mistress Woods was precisely what she had said she was—a Norwich soothsayer who had probably been employed by the Countess of Essex to cast her horoscope or make some other predictions about Fanny's tumultuous love life. The semihysterical reaction to Mary Woods's alleged theft was no doubt triggered by Fanny's wish to keep the seer's revelations from the Earl of Essex. Or so Kat reasoned, worrying over the matter for an inordinate amount of time. But at least it was better than letting herself dwell on Stefan Dvorak's stolen kiss. Kat absolutely refused to allow the foreigner's impudent behavior to disrupt her life. Clearly, it had been the action of a man who had no other resources with which to silence a disputatious woman. If she'd been a man, he'd probably have resorted to his strange-looking sword. Kat sniffed with disdain as she headed for the stables. Now that Sunday services were concluded, she was free for at least two hours. A gallop in nearby St. James's Park would refresh her spirits.

Kat was walking past the old tiltyard when she heard her name called. Frowning, she turned to see Sir Thomas Overbury coming stiffly but purposefully toward her. Kat suppressed a sigh of vexation. Her would-be swain was the last person she wanted to see. Except, perhaps, for Stefan Dvorak.

"Lady Katherine," said Overbury, dressed once more in the very height of elegance, "I was told you'd gone this way to the stables. Pray spare me a few moments of your time so that we may converse." He sounded as if he were delivering a speech.

"About what?" blurted Kat.

Overbury's thin mouth turned down in his spade-shaped beard. "About our future. We should sign the prenuptial contract within the week, probably at Windrush. My own parents are content. I visited them a fortnight ago, and they would like to be present when we are formally contracted." He glanced up at the sky, which had brightened considerably after a heavy rain during the night. "I should like to see your family home again. It's been years since I was there, and as I recall, it's a fine property. But I prefer the city. Once your parents are gone from this world, perhaps we will sell it."

"What?" shrieked Kat, aghast. "Sell Windrush? Are you mad? I wouldn't sell Windrush if I were starving in the gutter! As for my parents, they're still young and healthy as—"

"Tut." Overbury cut into Kat's diatribe. "Life is unpredictable. No one knows the hour or the day, as it's said in Scripture." He paused, somehow dismayed by his own words. Kat eyed him curiously, though she was still angry. "The point is," Overbury went on quickly, "my memory of Windrush is dim, and I would like to refresh it before we wed."

"Hold, Sir," put in Kat. "You're forgetting yourself. I haven't yet consented to marry you."

Overbury sighed heavily. "Don't be a fool. The king has arranged this match, and so it shall be. Do you imagine that I'm enthused?" He looked at Kat as if she were debris.

A pair of stable boys passed by, carrying bridles and riding crops. Kat waited until the lads were out of hearing before she spoke again. The respite gave her time to collect her thoughts, none of which she found very appealing. "You seriously believe we can't avoid this marriage?" she inquired, trying to keep her temper in check.

Inspecting his fingernails, Overbury didn't so much as glance at Kat. "Of course we can't. As for my own part, it's time to wed. I'm thirty-one, and must consider posterity. We shall do well enough, as long as you remember your place." Ignoring Kat's startled expression, he tipped his head to one side and began to recite,

"Birth, less than beauty, shall my reason bind,
Her birth goes to my children, not to me."

He finally looked at Kat. "You know my works?"

"Not a syllable," retorted Kat. "Most of the authors I read have been dead for years. I trust their sons-in-law sold off their properties." She had to bite her lip to keep from laughing.

But Kat's arch response was lost on Overbury, who had resumed reciting his lugubrious stanzas, this time alluding to total meekness in a wife. Kat tapped her foot and kept her mouth shut. Overbury droned on, while Kat's mind wandered. To her surprise, she conjured up not the image of Prince Henry as she usually did when daydreaming, but of Stefan Dvorak. His dark face was bent over hers, his arms tightened around her body, his black eyes searched her face. . . .

"She frames her nature unto his howsoever:
The hyacinth follows not the sun more willingly."

Overbury finally ran out of breath and folded his arms across his slashed velvet-and-satin doublet. "Inspiring, don't you think?"

From the vicinity of the stables, Kat could hear the neighing of horses. In the kennel, several hounds barked. And overhead, on a recessed window ledge, a pair of pigeons cooed at each other. Kat preferred any of their noises to Overbury's verse. But she supposed she shouldn't say so.

"Most edifying," she murmured, then gave a brisk swish of her riding habit. "I must be off, milord. The day is waning. If you insist, we shall ride to Windrush on Saturday next. I've promised the electress that I'd stay in London until then."

"Very well." Overbury bowed stiffly. "I don't intend to visit for more than a day. My court duties consume me. You realize, of course, that the running of this country falls more and more on me." He feigned an air of reluctance and assumed a burdened expression.

"So I'm told," said Kat dryly. "How does it go? 'Carr rules the king and Overbury rules Carr.' So, in fact, you rule England. How bothersome for you."

"Indeed," sighed Overbury. "But necessary, I fear."

Kat considered offering him her hand, thought better of it, and instead gave Overbury the faintest of smiles. "You go ride herd on the country then, Sir Thomas. I'll settle for riding a horse." *Which I prefer,* she thought despite her docile expression, *to you, you horse's behind.*

"Until next Saturday," he replied stiltedly.

"Mmm, yes," she agreed, again struck by the urge to laugh, and wondered why the seriousness she had so carefully cultivated seemed to have deserted her of late. Eliza-

beth had been wrong; though Kat mourned Hal's loss, she
had not forgotten how to laugh.

As for Overbury, thought Kat, as she watched him strut
away, he had no more wish to see her in the intervening
week than she had to see him. Kat's spirits plummeted.
Bleakly, she looked down the long road of her life and tried
to imagine how it would be with Thomas Overbury at her
side.

The prospect was definitely gloomy.

In the palace still-room, Kat and the other ladies-in-
waiting were busily preparing the cosmetic stores for the
electress to take with her to Heidelberg. The newest meth-
ods, developed by the Marquis Frangipani, were used to
steep dried fruits, herbs, flowers and spices in alcohol. Lady
Harington supervised the task, which involved carefully
preserved quantities of eglantine rose hips, goat's milk, ce-
darwood oil, sunflower seeds and almonds. The varied
smells in the room ranged from sickly sweet to sharply ac-
rid. Kat held up a cucumber and frowned.

Bess Apsley's dimples showed in a merry smile. "They're
for the complexion. Lettuce, too, and carrots. Mother Nature provides so many ingredients to give us what God forgot," Bess rattled on in her loquacious manner. "What do
you use, Kat? Your skin is very fresh."

"Buttermilk," replied Kat. "When I remember." Guiltily, she recalled her mother's constant reminders about using buttermilk soap and applying honey water for special
occasions. Lady Beatrice was most assiduous in her beauty
regimen; Kat, never so conscientious, had become haphazard since Henry's death. Perhaps it was time to adopt
better habits. Though, Kat told herself, there was really no
reason. Her appearance certainly didn't matter to Thomas
Overbury. She addressed herself to a vial of birch oil and
tried to ignore an arch glance from Susan Howard.

"You're a bit pale," Susan said, deftly sifting lavender into a small jar. "You need more practice in the cosmetic arts. I would suggest a heavier powder and a good deal of rouge. A beauty patch or two might help as well."

Annoyed, Kat gave Susan's own carefully made-up face a sidelong perusal. Before she could retort that if she had a patch, she'd like a large one to put over Susan's mouth, Fanny Howard swished into the still-room and drew her cousin aside.

Out of the corner of her eye, Kat noticed that the cousins were apparently conspiring in a frenzied manner. That morning, the last Wednesday of February, 1613, a rumor had circulated that the Earl of Essex was being asked to submit to an examination of his manhood. How, it was asked, could he not have consummated his marriage to the luscious Fanny unless there was some impediment? The court was agog over this latest sensation.

Lucy Harington was at Kat's side, examining a bottle of Hungary water. "The Howards are up to mischief, I'll wager. Fanny's request for an annulment doesn't sit well with Essex, but her family has cozened the king."

Kat leaned back against a glass-fronted cupboard and fingered a slice of orange peel. "If I were Essex, I'd be glad to get rid of her. She—and Susan—strike me as troublesome."

Even as Kat spoke, the Howard women were heading toward her, obsequious smiles plastered on their pretty faces. "Dear Kat," said Susan, her attitude much changed, "we hear you're off to Windrush this weekend to formalize your betrothal. How pleased you must be!"

"As much as if I had pox," retorted Kat. "Happily, there's no date fixed for the wedding."

Susan's lavender eyes grew round. "Oh? I heard it was to be in May. Ascension Thursday, to be exact."

Kat gave Susan a sharp look. "Then you hear more than I do," she said a trifle tartly.

Making a soothing gesture with her graceful hands, Susan drew Fanny closer, somehow managing to excise Lucy Harington from the little circle. "We beg your help, dear Kat. Now that you are about to become Sir Thomas's bride, you must have some influence with the obstinate man. Do exert your charms and try to make him see reason. He must not oppose my good cousin's marriage with Robin Carr. Surely Tom is behaving in a most contrary manner!"

Fanny nodded vehemently. "He's an arrogant swine. He fears he'll lose his hold on Robin. If so, he'll lose his power. But I care not a fig for politics, only for love. Tom Overbury can run the world, as far as I'm concerned." Her color rose, and she fanned herself with her hand. "Sweet Mother of God, I want to be Robin's wife, not his overseer!"

It struck Kat as odd that while Thomas Overbury seemingly could prevent a marriage that had been given the blessing of the king, he was powerless to stop his own. Kat took in Fanny's beautiful, determined face, and wondered if she in turn could intercede with Overbury.

"Tom and Robin are close, are they not?" Kat asked.

Fanny's expression tightened. "They were. Now they are on the outs. Why do you inquire thusly?"

"If," Kat said carefully, "I try to help you, I would expect you to return the favor by helping me. I don't want to marry Overbury any more than you wish to stay married to Essex."

Fanny and Susan exchanged quick glances. "Of course," said Fanny blandly. "I'll do whatever I can. But you must convince Tom that we will wed whether he wishes it or not."

"Then why do you care what he thinks?" Kat asked, genuinely mystified.

Fanny's flush deepened. "Because we do," she snapped. "It's imperative that he stop meddling."

Again, Susan made a calming gesture, this time directed at her cousin. "Now, Fanny dearest, you know the reason." She gave Fanny a hard stare. "He used to be Robin's friend. You want his good will for the future. You can't bear to think of people being estranged from each other. Love must have its way." She turned to Kat and smiled. "You will help us, of course. It's so romantic."

"I'll do what I can," Kat said vaguely. "But I make no promises."

Fanny's mouth curved into a smile. "That's as well. Promises are often made to be broken." In a rustle of scarlet silk, she turned away.

Kat didn't hold out much hope of convincing Thomas Overbury that he should withdraw his opposition to the Howard-Carr match. Nor did Kat understand how Fanny could be so sure she would get her annulment in the first place. While the countess claimed to be a virgin, it was bruited about the court that she had been conducting an adulterous affair with Carr for months. If proof was needed of Essex's impotence, then it would also be required for Fanny to give evidence of her maiden state. It was a provocative situation; Kat wanted no part of it. She went to Elizabeth to say so.

But the electress, on this rainy February afternoon, was abed with her elector. Kat rubbed at her forehead and wondered if she should talk to Lady Harington. There was no one else at court in whom she could confide. But Elizabeth's governess had remained in the still-room, and Kat didn't wish to go back, lest she again encounter the Howard cousins. Frustrated, Kat braved the rain and went outdoors, where she saw Eustace Norton, Prince Charles's falconer, testing a fledgling's wings.

In the shelter of the doorway, she watched unobserved for some minutes until another figure approached from the direction of the river. It was Stefan Dvorak, and Kat wished to avoid him.

But like the falcon, his eye was too quick. He caught sight of Kat just as she was opening the heavy door and called to her. "Little Kat," he said, with a deft bow, "do you hunt?"

"Certainly," replied Kat with a touch of frost in her voice. "Hunting is excellent at Windrush."

"Have you ever caught one of these?" asked Dvorak, reaching under his cloak and producing a pigeon.

Kat cried out as the bird squawked, fluttered and flew off. Stefan laughed. "I should have brought an eagle. But they're much harder to hide." With a wave for Eustace Norton, Dvorak opened the door with what appeared to be a flick of his fingers. "Why so glum?" he inquired when they were inside. "Is there bad news? I've been at Oxford these past three days."

Kat's initial reaction was to turn mulish and insist that all was well in her world. But his trick with the pigeon had already lightened her mood. She gazed up into the black eyes and found a flicker of sympathy. Or at least she took it for such, since no one else seemed inclined to lend an interested ear. "It's the Howards and Overbury," she said, and then the story tumbled out in a rush, intertwining her imminent betrothal with Fanny Howard's plight. Stefan's understandable confusion ebbed as she slowed down and became more precise.

"So I don't know why Fanny and Susan asked me to intervene with a man who sees me only as a necessary nuisance. All I want to do is go home to Windrush and ride my mare." She turned a pugnacious face up to his. "I don't suppose you could pull Leda out from under your cloak, could you?"

Dvorak looked puzzled. "Leda?"

"The name of my mare." The hint of a smile touched Kat's mouth. "You aren't a mind reader, at least."

"Not usually," Dvorak admitted, looking bemused.

"There's more to my plight," Kat moaned, leaning back in the window embrasure where they'd sat down, near the entrance to the magnificent banqueting house Inigo Jones was designing for King James. "Thomas Overbury says he may sell Windrush after my parents die."

Stefan Dvorak raised an eyebrow. "And when has his exalted efficiency scheduled their demise?"

Kat laughed. "Well, he hasn't. At least I hope not. But the mere idea makes me cringe."

Dvorak rested his dark head against his half of the embrasure. "Ah, yes—Windrush, your personal paradise. How you treasure those four walls and fertile ground!" He caught Kat's swift change of mood, and touched her hand. "Nay, I meant no insult. You glower like a winter storm." His eyes roamed over the chestnut curls that clustered at Kat's temples. "You're wearing the combs the Gypsies gave you, I see." His tone held approval.

Kat's anger faded as she looked down at the long dark fingers covering her small white hand. "They're very pretty," she conceded, "and Elizabeth insists that I wear my hair in this artificial fashion. It takes too long to crimp and I scorched myself twice this morning." Kat heard the grumble in her voice, but her mind was elsewhere. "You should not have kissed me," she murmured.

"Why not?" He realized she was making no attempt to pull away.

"I told you," she countered, "such dalliance is not seemly."

Stefan looked out the window where the rain fell steadily on the plane trees. "Oh, I don't know. I found it very seemly. As," he went on, catching and holding her gaze, "did you."

"Rot!" cried Kat, pulling her hand back. "Now you pretend you can read my mind! I found it . . . disturbing."

"Ah!" Stefan grinned, and Kat could have sworn the devil danced in his eyes. "That's even better."

Kat's small chin jutted. "Better than what?"

His answer was to lean forward and capture her face in his hand. "Better the second time," he said in a calm, low voice.

Kat tried to move away from him, but her back was already up against the embrasure. He was so near that she could see her reflection in his eyes. The effect was hypnotic; a strangled gasp escaped Kat's lips.

But there was no kiss. A voice called out, angry and imperative, "Katherine de Vere! You sully my name!"

Kat and Dvorak both turned, almost bumping heads. Thomas Overbury stood in the entrance that would lead to the new banqueting house, his long face suffused with indignation.

Dvorak stood up without haste, then gave his hand to Kat. Slowly, he looked at Overbury. "Lady Kat does not yet bear your name, sir. Thus, she cannot sully it. I believe she has two more days before you can claim her as your intended. Surely you will allow her the freedom to pass that short time as she pleases?"

Dvorak's effrontery caused Overbury's face to flush darkly. "Zounds! You have learned very little at Oxford! In England we do not behave like feckless Gypsies! Begone, and never come near Lady Katherine again!"

To Kat, Stefan seemed more exasperated than insulted. He gave an incredulous shake of his head, then took three steps toward the other man. "No one," he said very quietly, "ever tells me what to do or where to go." He paused just an instant to make sure the words had sunk in, then he grabbed Sir Thomas by the doublet and yanked him up on his tiptoes. "No one. Is that clear?" Just to make sure, he gave Overbury a sharp shake.

Overbury had turned from red to white. "You cur!" he snarled. "How dare you?"

With an indifferent shrug, Dvorak cast Overbury aside just as King James appeared with a small entourage, apparently bent on inspecting Inigo Jones's plans for the proposed banqueting house.

"Hold!" cried the king, looking uncertain. "Do we have dissension here?" His wavering gaze flicked from Dvorak to Overbury to Kat and back again.

"We have insolence," responded a breathless Overbury with a stiff bow. He jabbed a finger at Stefan. "This foreigner has assaulted me!"

James looked much put upon as he studied both men. "God's eyes, we want no quarreling in our midst! Make peace, both of you." He hesitated, apparently waiting for the two antagonists to fall into each other's arms. Kat would have intervened, but James was waving a long arm in an awkward fashion. "Few things are worth fighting over," he declared rather testily. "Not women, not honor, not even money, though at least that's a tangible quantity. When one has it," he added a bit wistfully. "Now sort out your differences and reconcile."

Kat noted that Stefan was already composed, but Overbury's hackles were still raised. "You don't understand, your majesty," Overbury insisted, giving the king an imperious stare. "Not only did this knave lay hands on me, but he dared to dally with my fiancée!"

Kat flushed and Stefan rolled his eyes. However, James, who normally might have found such a situation amusing, glared at Overbury. "You forget yourself, Thomas. You address your sovereign lord, not some illiterate lackey. We suggest you mend your manners, lest we decide you would feel more at home in a foreign post." To underscore his threat, James smirked at the members of his retinue, who had been observing the little drama with suitably expressionless faces.

For an instant, it appeared to Kat that Thomas Overbury was about to contradict his monarch. But after what appeared to be a tremendous effort at self-control, he bowed his head in assent. "You know, your majesty, my greatest wish is to serve you. In England."

"Mmm." James's head lolled to one side. "We shall try to remember as much," he replied in a bored voice. Then, with an ineffectual snap of his fingers, the king commanded his courtiers to follow him down the passageway. "You, too, Thomas," he added as an afterthought. "We must receive the Venetian ambassador."

With a set look on his face, Overbury obeyed. Kat was left with Stefan Dvorak, who was wearing an unusually thoughtful expression. "Now," she moaned, "you've ruined my reputation!"

Dvorak looked more annoyed than surprised. "For that you should be grateful. Perhaps Overbury will not want to marry you after all. Where, little Kat, is gratitude?" Over his shoulder, he gave her a glance of reproof as he started striding off in the opposite direction.

"Gratitude?" Kat was almost screeching. Yet Dvorak was right; as far as she could foresee, the worst thing that could come of the encounter with Overbury would be his refusal to make her his wife.

Kat would not know for some time what a tragic mistake she had made.

Chapter Five

Sir Edgar and Lady Beatrice were not happy. Yet as much as they disliked coercing their daughter into marriage with a man she didn't love, they considered the prospect of losing Windrush, paled at the possibility and surrendered.

Kat understood. If there was one thing she could accept, it was her parents' desire to hold on to their beloved home. They had been shocked by her revelation that Thomas Overbury might one day sell Windrush, but had put the notion aside.

"He'll have to outlive us," Lady Beatrice had averred with uncustomary cynicism. "In truth, he's not that much younger than I am."

She was right, of course, having turned forty only the previous autumn. But it was the king, not Overbury, who had put fear into the de Veres. James was ruthless, especially when it came to pleasing his favorites, and the confiscation of Walter Raleigh's property served as a frightening example.

So, on a damp Sabbath on the last day of February, 1613, Lady Katherine de Vere and Sir Thomas Overbury affixed their signatures to a prenuptial contract, while both sets of parents watched with varying degrees of anxiety. Indeed, the jocular presence of Sir Nicholas Overbury and his plump wife was a special source of comfort for Sir Edgar and Lady Beatrice. Surely the union between the children of old friends had to turn out well. The two families tied a red ribbon around the contract, exchanged embraces, and settled down to drinking malmsey.

The exception was the groom-to-be, who excused himself, put spurs to his horse and headed back to London. The court—and possibly the world, Kat reflected wryly—could not move forward without him. Kat preferred to stay on at Windrush, probably until after the nuptials, which had been set for the first week of May at the village church in Naunton. She intended to enjoy the comforts of her family and her home for as long as possible. Once wed, she would be mewed up at court, tied forever to the fortunes of Thomas Overbury. Kat could not bear to dwell upon the future.

Instead, she sought diversion in the wooded water meadows and beside the rippling river. In years past the Windrush had been known to flood, but as spring promenaded its greenery, the threat faded for another year. Kat listened to the quavering song of the tree-creeper, saw the warblers choosing their nests and smiled at the wagtails as they flaunted their yellow breasts in flight. She seemed to be committing each ash, hazel and willow tree to memory, mentally sketching the old stone cottages in the villages, and willing the cowslips to bud before their time.

Occasionally, unbidden tears would well up in her eyes, but Kat would grit her teeth and set her jaw and urge Leda into a trot. Perhaps there was still some way out of this nightmarish marriage, Kat would think. If only Thomas Overbury would refuse to wed her. If only the king weren't so covetous. If only Prince Henry had lived. If only some bold knight errant would ride up to Windrush and rescue her....

Kat was jarred by the recurring image of Stefan Dvorak. "He's bold, in truth," she'd mutter to herself, "and I'm fanciful." She would set the thought aside, and concentrate instead on her surroundings, serene and charming, rustic and familiar.

Only weeks away, the noisome, teeming, reeking city of London awaited her. So did marriage and Thomas Overbury. Kat cringed. But she would not weep. She would think only of the day when she could come home to Windrush. As her mother had said, Thomas Overbury would have to outlive them. Including, Kat reflected grimly, herself.

On the second Monday of April, Stefan Dvorak had ridden out from Magdalen College, beneath the stately tower and over the bridge that spanned the placid Cherwell. That morning, fine and fresh, with purple-and-white pasqueflowers lining the pathways, Stefan had received a message. He was to meet old friends in a quiet dell in the Windrush Valley. The prospect both intrigued and troubled him.

At the village of Kineton near Leigh Wood, he dismounted at the top of the hill and led his gelding down a winding footpath into a sun-dappled clearing. The wind sang softly in the willow trees; the air smelled new, almost primeval. Stefan waited.

Within a quarter of an hour, two figures materialized as if from nowhere. Stefan registered no surprise; Gypsies often seemed to sprout up from the ground. The pair moved leisurely toward him. The younger man was square of jaw and shoulder; the older Rom was faintly stooped and bearded. They doffed their caps.

"Devlesa avilan," the younger man said in greeting. "We thank God for bringing you here."

Dvorak grinned. "No supernatural power brought me—my horse did. You met up with the Englander Roms, I hear, Kore."

Kore nodded. "They told us you had passed this way a month or more ago. We only came to this country eight days past. We will not stay." He glanced at the older man for confirmation. "Eh, Grandfather Yojo?"

"Islands are not good places," declared Yojo through broken teeth. "They hem you in."

Dvorak regarded the men with affectionate humor. "So why come at all?"

Kore, ever alert, darted his eyes in the direction of a thrush, taking food to its babies in a nearby ash tree. "To see this land. To escape Bohemia. To give you news."

Though Kore spoke without emphasis, Stefan knew the importance of the last reason. But he kept his tone as casual as Kore's. "What news?"

Kore answered with another question. "When did you last see Albrecht Wallenstein?"

For once, Dvorak didn't try to conceal his surprise. "Brecht? Ten years ago." His face hardened. "But it's been fifteen since I spoke to him."

"He doesn't hate you," Grandfather Yojo interjected. "He grieves almost as much as you do, especially for your mother."

The slashing gesture Dvorak made with his right hand was explosive, shattering the bucolic calm of the little dell. "Traitor! He has no right to grieve. He was enough older than I that he might have stopped those murdering bastards. He could have summoned help, but he hid. The craven coward hid from those fiends who killed my parents!"

Kore and Yojo both looked away from Dvorak, anxious to avoid the pain and rage they could see in his glittering black eyes. "He is a soldier now," Kore said at last in a quiet voice. "He could help Bohemia. He could help us. He could even help you."

There was a silence, filling the dell and calming Dvorak's shattered temper. He shifted his weight from one foot to the other and shook his head. "I don't want his help. I don't need it," he asserted, again under control. "Don't be fooled. He won't help Bohemia. Brecht is a Catholic. He was Jesuit reared. If it comes to a fight, he'll serve the emperor."

Both of the Gypsies looked cowed, but neither appeared convinced. "He was like a brother to you, Stefan," said Kore. "You might persuade him otherwise."

"No." The word was curt, final. Then, seeing the disappointment in his friends' faces, Dvorak put a hand on each man's shoulder. "See here," he said, his features softening, "I will be finished with my studies soon. Then I will return to Prague, at least for a time. Until then, I'll think on this matter. If I conclude there is even a chance of claiming Brecht's loyalties for Bohemia, I'll see him." He paused, grimacing. "I would do that for my homeland, not for myself. I would rather stick a knife in Brecht's heart than go begging to him."

Grandfather Yojo narrowed his faded old eyes. "You did not always feel that way, Stefan."

"No," Stefan agreed with a little shrug. "I did not. Brecht and I were raised like brothers. And as such, I loved him. But much has changed. People change, too." He saw his own sorrow reflected in the faces of the Roms. "And change again," Stefan added on a more hopeful note that surprised him as much as his Gypsy friends. "Where will you go next?"

Kore looked up at the sky, as if the birds could lead the way. "To Spain? Or Italy. And someday, back to Bohemia." He gave Dvorak a crooked grin. "As it's said, the Gypsy may wander the world, but he always comes home."

Dvorak grinned back. "So they say. May we all meet again in Prague and share a bottle of pinard wine."

Kore put out a callused hand. *"Bater,"* he said. "May it be so."

The two men disappeared into the trees, leaving Stefan alone in the peaceful dell. Slowly, he untethered his mount and rode off in the opposite direction from which he'd come. There was no reason to hurry back to the university. This isolated, gentle part of England soothed his soul. He needed its peace just now, for the Gypsies had resurrected terrible memories: of pillage, murder, and unbearable loss. In one heartbreaking afternoon, Stefan Dvorak's whole world had been devastated. His parents had died, his home had been destroyed, his faith in other human beings had been shattered.

But regrets were futile. Grief was wasted. Stefan Dvorak allowed the gelding to amble aimlessly. The horse made a circle, out of the dell, across the river, beyond the village and back to Leigh Wood. Without knowing it, Dvorak was at the packhorse bridge where he had watched Katherine de Vere talk to the strange woman known as Mary Woods. Almost two months had passed since that day, and winter's barrenness was camouflaged by spring's lush greenery. Stefan wondered if Kat were nearby; he'd heard she was at Windrush. Perhaps he should ride that way and inquire after her marriage plans.

Stefan frowned at the notion. Kat and Overbury had no doubt signed their nuptial contract and were caught up in making their wedding arrangements. By now, Kat was probably adjusted to her fate and flinging herself into the future with enthusiasm. She would not, Stefan reflected, be overjoyed at his intrusion.

Or, he thought, recalling the naive ardor of her embrace, would she? But again he shrugged off his caprice. More to the point, why should he care?

Why indeed? an unfamiliar voice asked him, but Stefan Dvorak tugged on his horse's reins and headed not for Windrush, but back to Oxford.

* * *

"If you fail to come, I will leave England wreathed in even more tears than is my due," wrote the Electress Palatine in a frenzied script. "If your dear face is absent from the well-wishers, I shall not feel well wished at all, but rather consigned to strangers in a strange land."

The importunate request was overblown, but it impressed Kat nonetheless. Elizabeth was scheduled to leave Whitehall on April 10. For Kat, it would mean arriving in London almost a month sooner than she had planned. But she could leave as soon as the electress's entourage sailed down the Thames to Greenwich. With some reluctance, Kat prepared for her journey. Since her parents did not wish to go along, she was accompanied by the family steward, Anthony Robbins, and his wife, Dorothy. Neither had ever been to London and were excited by the prospect. Kat was not.

Arriving at Whitehall on the day before Elizabeth's departure, Kat was chagrined to find the electress caught up in last-minute arrangements. The two young women had no chance to talk until late that night. Elizabeth insisted that Kat accompany her to Margate, where the royal party would set sail for the Continent. Having come this far, Kat gave in. She had never been to Canterbury, which would be one of the stopping places en route to the coast, and she felt duty-bound to visit its famous cathedral. Anthony and Dorothy Robbins were dismissed from their responsibilities, heading back to Windrush full of London's sights and smells and sounds.

"So," Elizabeth said to Kat as they awaited word of a favorable wind six days later, "your wedding plans move apace."

Kat sipped from a goblet of red wine and gave her friend a wry look. They were staying in the deanery at Canterbury. The king and queen had taken leave of their daugh-

ter at Rochester, exchanging tears and tokens. Prince
Charles remained with his sister, being charged with the
official duty of seeing her off to a new life. "You sound almost gleeful when you speak of my nuptials," Kat chided.
"How can you be so enthused when I am not?"

Elizabeth dimpled, a merry, secretive flame dancing in
her eyes. "Now that we're alone and my father is gone, I
can tell you something most intriguing." She flipped aside
the damask hangings, as if she half expected to find an
eavesdropper hiding somewhere in the canopied bed.
"Your bridegroom is being posted to the Low Countries.
He will leave within a week after your wedding. You and I
will be virtual neighbors, a few days' traveling time apart.
Just think, we won't have to wait years and years to see each
other after all!"

Elizabeth's excitement was not contagious. Kat's face
fell. "He's . . . I'm—we're going abroad?" She made the
word sound indelicate.

It was the electress's turn to look dashed. "I thought
you'd be pleased! I am! Why, you know that if you weren't
about to be married, I would have insisted that you be appointed as one of my attendants."

Kat assumed a penitent air. "Yes, yes, I realize that." She
gave Elizabeth a shrewd glance. "But you should also know
I might have refused. I've never had a yen to live in a foreign land."

"Nor I," asserted the electress with spirit. "But I have no
choice. Now," she added with a touch of spite, "neither do
you."

Kat's temper started to erupt, then she took in the tears
welling up in her friend's eyes, and uttered a heavy sigh.
Clearly, Elizabeth wanted company in her misery. No matter how much she loved Frederick, the sacrifice she was
making as his wife had elicited a burdensome price.

"Forgive me, Bess," begged Kat, shooing away one of the dozen dogs the electress was bringing along to Germany, "but I'm stunned by your news. And upset. I hadn't ever considered living anywhere but England."

"I've always had to consider it," Elizabeth replied with some bitterness. "I've carried around a map of Europe in my head like a millstone. France, Spain, Germany, Savoy—I never knew until a year ago. But we have to make the best of it, both of us, don't you see?" She stared earnestly at Kat, the tears still glistening, yet unshed.

Kat scooted back on the bed, drawing her feet up under her and wrapping her arms around her knees. Elizabeth was right; neither of them had any choice. The miracle that Kat had hoped for was proving elusive. Slowly, she turned to the electress and shook her head. "When your dear brother died, I vowed not to wed. I thought I could determine the course of my own life. I should have known better."

Outside, the bells of the great cathedral chimed for vespers. Elizabeth gave Kat a sad little smile. "Yes," she said softly. "So you should. But you can still determine whether or not you will be happy. That much you have in your power."

Kat emitted a sound that was half laugh, half snort. "Can I? I wonder. My fate seems entirely out of my hands."

To some extent, Kat was right. Some eighty miles away, in London, her immediate fate had already been decided.

The *Prince Royal* had been christened in honor of Kat's beloved Henry. Despite the ship having gone aground on her maiden voyage from Chatham, Elizabeth had no superstitious fear of any vessel that bore her late brother's name. However, she and Kat both became speechless, lost among their memories, when they caught their first sight of the stately craft resting at anchor in Margate Harbor. The

Royal Standard and the Union Jack fluttered in the wind. A favorable wind at that, and the electress and the elector were ready to sail.

The previous day, Prince Charles had bid adieu to his sister. Now, of the large company that had ridden out from Whitehall almost a fortnight earlier, only Kat and a handful of others remained with the travelers. Charles Howard, Lord Nottingham, father of Lady Susan and uncle to the Countess of Essex, had announced that the voyage to Holland would be his last official act in his capacity as lord high admiral. Despite the doughty old seaman's valor in helping fend off the Spanish Armada more than twenty years earlier, the Howards' enemies were glad to see him go.

But Kat was not glad to see Elizabeth leave England. Now that the actual moment to part had arrived, Kat was having second thoughts about moving to the Low Countries. Not only was Elizabeth her childhood friend, but she was the only real link Kat had to Prince Henry. There was, she had to admit, some morsel of comfort in the fact that the electress would be relatively close by.

So it was with only a hint of tears that Kat and Elizabeth embraced under a patchy sky. The admiral's barge was crammed with gentlemen attired in black suits, tall hats and white ruffs. A trio of men-of-war rested on the outgoing tide, grim reminders that not everyone wished Elizabeth and Frederick well.

"You will visit this summer," Elizabeth insisted, with one wary eye on the heavily bound trunks that were being loaded into a longboat. "Promise me. I want you to help me plan an English garden."

"I will," Kat assured the electress, giving her a final hug. "I'll bring bulbs from Holland."

At Elizabeth's side, Frederick looked very young and very solemn. "We will give your princess whatever she likes. My people will try to please her. As," he added, taking his wife's hand, "will I. I have sworn to King James that she will be the most important personage in the Palatinate." Though Frederick spoke earnestly, Kat thought he winced a bit. James, as ever, had extracted the highest possible price from his son-in-law.

Moments later, Elizabeth was being conveyed into the admiral's barge. Kat waited on the dock until the slow-moving vessel had reached the flagship. Then she lifted her arm in one last wave, and turned away from both her friend and the ship that bore the name of the only man she had ever loved.

The black gelding was lathered, the rider begrimed. Stefan Dvorak dismounted and flung the reins at a startled pot-boy in the courtyard of the inn outside Canterbury. "Water my mount," he ordered, then stopped in mid-stride to toss some coins at the lad. Framed in the doorway of the inn stood Kat de Vere, looking as surprised to see Dvorak as he was to find her here in this out-of-the-way resting place.

"Were you at Margate?" he asked without preamble.

"Yes. We're on our way back to London...." she began, gesturing vaguely at a small group of courtiers struggling with their baggage in the rain.

"Have they sailed?" interrupted Stefan, ducking under the low archway.

Kat regarded him quizzically. "I don't know. Just after we left Margate, this storm blew in."

He nodded once. "Then they have not. I shall still have time to reach the elector."

"Why for?" asked Kat, not giving way to Stefan, who was obviously trying to move inside the inn.

But he merely shrugged. "Frederick sent for me. I didn't get the message until three days ago. I rode like a demon from Oxford. My poor horse is half-dead. I'll borrow one here and go on to the coast." He put a hand on Kat's arm to edge her out of the way, then suddenly stopped, his grip tightening. For the first time, he seemed to take in her presence.

"Lady Kat," he said, almost in surprise. "Have you heard?"

Kat stared up at him. The expression on his face frightened her. Despite herself, she shivered inside her traveling cloak. "Heard what?" Her voice was breathless.

Dvorak regarded her curiously. "Thomas Overbury. He refused the embassy to the Low Countries." His hand went to her waist. "He has been arrested and sent to the Tower."

Chapter Six

In the depths of Kat's soul, some basic swell of compassion overcame her urge to cheer. Afterward, she was grateful for the charitable reaction. But in the shock of the moment, she actually swayed against Stefan and was left quite speechless.

His arm still steadied her as he waited for the news to sink in. "It's probably a mere whim of James's," he said, trying to contain his impatience to move on. "No doubt the king wishes to chastise Overbury and make him come to heel."

"No!" Kat had found her voice and used it with emphasis. A glance at Dvorak's probing expression caused her to turn away, ashamed of her sudden change in attitude. "That is ... I hope so. I mean, I pray that James will be merciful. But Thomas should not have behaved so arrogantly. He's too proud." She jerked her head up and down in affirmation. "Yes, that's it—his pride has brought his downfall. You're right, he'll have to give in." Kat nodded some more, her words uneven, one hand resting on Dvorak's chest.

Somewhat confused by her reaction, Dvorak finally pulled her inside the common room. A trio of Kat's fellow travelers, including Thomas Howard, Earl of Suffolk and the lord high admiral's elder brother, was seated in an

inglenook, eating from a joint of lamb and drinking cider.
They glanced up, displaying only mild interest in the newcomers.

Her thoughts still jumbled, Kat allowed Dvorak to sit her
down at a small table, discreetly placed behind a stout
wooden beam. He called for beef and ale, then sat opposite Kat and tried to decipher her reaction.

"You're relieved," he said at last, in a low voice.
"You've probably been praying for a miracle. Now perhaps you've got it."

Eyes wide, Kat started to protest, then sank back against
the rickety chair rails. "You of all people know I didn't
want to marry Overbury. Or anyone else, if it comes to
that," she added, lest Dvorak make any mistake about her
avowals. "I certainly don't wish Thomas ill, but obviously
his majesty can't insist that I marry a man who is in
prison." She turned silent as their host brought two tankards of ale, a platter of rare beef and a loaf of brown bread.
"James may find some other candidate for me," she mused
as Stefan began to slice off slabs of meat, "but he may also
forget about my marriage. He may even forget about
Windrush. He's like that, I think."

"He can be whimsical, that's true," Dvorak allowed,
proffering a piece of beef. "Here, you ought to keep up
your strength. You've had a shock."

Kat ignored the twinkle in Dvorak's black eyes. "I've lost
my appetite. How could I eat anything when my betrothed
is in the Tower?" Furtively, she peeked around the oak
beam. None of the other guests seemed to be looking her
way. "Well . . . a few bites. And some bread, please," she
added, taking a big sip from her tankard. "Is there any
butter?"

Dvorak suppressed a grin and handed her half the loaf.
Kat did not demur.

* * *

Within the hour Kat was on the road again, along with
the other courtiers. She said nothing to them about the latest sensation from London. Indeed, she scarcely knew any
of her traveling companions and was just as glad, since she
was thus free of the need to make conversation.

Stefan had devoured his meal in about a quarter of an
hour and left for Margate. Kat had been unexpectedly distressed to see him go. But, she told herself, that was only
natural; she had suffered a shock, and he was the one person with whom she could discuss the matter. At least at the
moment.

Three days later, when she arrived in London, Kat had
to confront her dilemma. Should she try to see Overbury in
the Tower? Should she request an audience with King
James and make some attempt to discern his attitude toward the prisoner? Or should she simply continue on to
Windrush and let the comfortable old house wrap its arms
around her?

In the end, it was Kat's inherent decency that won the
day. She could not be so callous as to leave London without so much as an inquiry after Thomas Overbury. But beyond that decision, she was stymied. The king had gone
hunting at Windsor; the queen was in progress to Bath. Kat
barely knew Prince Charles, and he was still only a child.
There was no one in all of the teeming, bustling city of
London in whom she could confide.

Until Stefan Dvorak returned the next day. She saw him
ride into Whitehall in the late afternoon under a bright
spring sun. The weather had held for the past two days, and
no doubt Elizabeth and Frederick had set sail for the Continent. Kat hesitated in seeking Stefan out, but encountered him by chance in the Cockpit. He had, she guessed
with annoyance, been calling on Susan Howard.

"You saw the elector?" she asked, not wanting to bring up her own problems first.

Stefan nodded, but avoided her gaze. "Fortunately for me, they were held up another two days. By now they should be in Holland." He looked unusually somber.

"Well." Sensing his mood, Kat didn't press him for details. Instead, she launched into her own predicament. "So," she concluded, "I can't find any recourse. What little I've gleaned indicates that his majesty is very much put out with Thomas."

Stefan's dark eyes flickered over Kat's upturned face. "Is that all you've gleaned?"

Since Kat had no intimates at court, she had been lucky to gather that much. "What else could there be?" she demanded, irked by the hint of reproach in Stefan's tone.

Dvorak peered down the long corridor. At one end, two middle-aged men were deep in conversation outside an open door. At the other, a trio of servants was heading toward them. Taking Kat's arm, Stefan led her into a cramped room cluttered with feminine possessions. Kat recognized a lavender satin overskirt as belonging to Susan Howard. Despite herself, she sniffed with disdain.

Appearing not to notice, Dvorak picked up a flurry of gold tissue petticoats from a chair and tossed them onto a trunk. The gesture was at once both proprietary and indifferent. Kat frowned. The man's attitude toward his paramour puzzled her.

"It's true that Overbury refused the foreign embassy," he began, resting one arm on the fireplace mantel. "It's also true that James considers such defiance as treasonable. But," he continued, lowering his voice even though there was no one to overhear him, "it is rumored that the king knew in advance that Overbury would never consider going abroad. Your fiancé was manipulated into this position. Someone who knew him well arranged that he would be arrested.''

Kat's forehead creased as she sat down on the chair that Dvorak had cleared off. ''But how dreadful! And why? Who? Except . . . oh, dear!'' Her hands flew to her cheeks. ''Stefan,'' she began, unaware that for the first time she had addressed him by his Christian name, ''I can think of no one but me who wished him . . . out of the way.''

Stefan leisurely crossed the six feet that separated them and pulled up a large packing crate. Gingerly, he also sat down, his knees almost brushing Kat's skirts. ''That's not so. Queen Anne despises Overbury. The king has come to resent his arrogance and self-aggrandizement. Fanny Howard wants him out of the way. Maybe Robin Carr does, too. There are others, as well. He has waxed too self-important. Your betrothed is not a popular figure at court.''

Kat sighed. ''Oh, dear! What a bollix! I almost feel sorry for him.''

Taking her hands in his, Stefan smiled at Kat's admission. ''You are like that, I think—sympathetic to the underdog.''

''Well...'' Attempting introspection, Kat tipped her head to one side. But her thought process was a bit muddled. Stefan's fingers felt warm and strong. The rugged, bronzed face was fixed on hers with a kindness that she had hitherto not suspected of him. She recalled his kiss, bit her lip and tried to concentrate on Overbury's plight. ''What should I do?''

''Nothing.'' He gave one of his little shrugs, and she felt the tug on her fingers. ''It's up to his majesty. You might as well go home and wait.''

''For what?'' Kat wondered if she should try to free her hands; but Stefan was being so sympathetic—he might consider her rude. Or ungrateful.

"For events to follow their natural course," replied Stefan, never letting her wide-eyed gaze escape.

"For. . . who?" Kat couldn't remember her question.

The smile broke into a grin. "For Overbury." He leaned closer, his nose touching hers. "Little Kat, your mind is wandering. How can I read it when it's somewhere else?"

"But it's not!" Her response was almost fierce. "That is..." she started to explain, but was stopped by his mouth on hers. His kiss lingered, clung, probed. Kat slid forward on the chair, balancing precariously. Stefan let go of her hands and put his arms around her waist. Carefully, he drew her onto his knees, still keeping her lips captive. Kat struggled for breath, made small pushing gestures with her hands, and then, with her brain reeling from the sweet sensation of his embrace, wrapped her arms around his neck.

His hands roamed to her waist, where a tiny mirror dangled from a gold chain, to the curve of her hip under the gimped brown silk, to the rounded buttocks beneath the overskirt and petticoats. Kat made an ineffectual protest, but the little sound was swallowed up in a flurry of more kisses, while his fingers worked expertly at the laces that held her bodice intact.

Neither of them heard the door open. Susan Howard froze on the threshold, her lavender eyes flashing like the amethysts at her ears. "Knave! Slut! How dare you sully my chamber! Go to the stews, where you belong!"

Startled, but seemingly unperturbed, Dvorak released Kat and assisted her to her feet. "Susan," he said mildly, also standing up. "I thought you'd left for Audley End."

Lady Susan marched across the room, her grass green taffeta skirts crackling. She shot a furious look at both Kat and Dvorak, then snatched up her petticoats. "I'm leaving, all right," she snarled. "I forgot these." Whirling on Kat, who was still supported by Stefan's arm, Susan lashed out with the voice of a virago, "Is this how you console

your imprisoned betrothed? What will the world think of
a wanton who betrays her intended husband while he lan-
guishes in the Tower?''

"What will the world think of a traitor who defies his
king?'' Kat snapped.

Susan's angry expression changed, though Kat felt the
sudden, sly smile was no improvement. "So! You agree that
he's guilty?'' The voice had dropped to a purr.

Kat lifted her little chin. "He's been accused. That's all
I know. His guilt is yet to be determined.''

"That's not what you just said,'' Susan countered, the
smile evaporating. She turned to Stefan, who had been
watching both women with bemused tolerance. "As for
you, Baron Ostrov, the minute I walk out the door it seems
you seek your pleasures elsewhere!''

Stefan offered no argument. "Yes,'' he replied amiably,
and stared Susan down.

"How could you!'' she gasped, aware that she was losing command of the situation.

"How?'' echoed Dvorak. "Well, it's quite simple. I come
upon another pretty wench and succumb to her charms. It
happens all the time.'' He spoke good-naturedly, and Kat
didn't know whether to laugh or cry.

Susan, however, reacted by brandishing the petticoats
and all but shrieking, "Ooh! You're a faithless viper! You'll
pay for this! I won't be mocked!'' She started to storm out
of the room, but stopped in the doorway and glared at Kat.
"You'll pay, too! No one tramples the Howard name and
gets away with it!''

The door slammed so hard that two small ornaments fell
off the mantelpiece and smashed on the hearth. Kat blinked
several times, then shook her head. "Susan's very vexed,''
she said in a small voice.

At last Stefan removed his hand from Kat's waist and went to the hearth to scoop up the scattered shards. "Susan is often vexed. She'll get over it."

Kat watched Dvorak dump the bits and pieces into the unlit grate. "But is she right?"

He looked up. "About what?"

"You." Kat's green eyes were speculative. "Is it true you can't be trusted with women?"

Dvorak looked genuinely perplexed. "Did Susan say that? I think not." He strolled from one end of the room to the other. "I told you, I find women enchanting. When they are also willing, the enchantment is shared between us. Like this." With a grin, he produced a white silk kerchief. Under it, in his palm, was a small ivory heart.

In spite of herself, Kat was amused. Yet she hoped Stefan would retract what he'd said to Susan and confess that he'd merely been trying to annoy her. Instead, it appeared he had spoken the truth.

Kat assumed her primmest, most dignified air. "I told you before, I'm not the sort who dallies with men. I must leave now. I shall go home to Windrush."

Stefan was tucking both kerchief and heart inside his jerkin. "I must ride back to Oxford. Shall I accompany you?"

"No!" Kat was aghast at his temerity. "I'd rather ride with the devil!" She began to back out of the room.

"You'll have to ride with *someone,*" Dvorak pointed out calmly. "Not ten minutes ago, I could have sworn you enjoyed my company."

Kat flushed. "I was upset. I let my emotions carry me away."

"And a good thing," he remarked, moving to her side. "You are too much inclined to let your head rule your heart. It's not always wise."

"Don't lecture me!" Kat wagged a finger at him. "I'll hire an escort. I'll pay for a carriage. I'll send for a servant from Windrush."

"I'm leaving in the morning." Dvorak again spoke matter-of-factly, though he was vaguely puzzled by this obstinate, perverse little wench. Any other woman reacting in such a contradictory manner would lead him to believe she was playing a game. He did not think it was so with Kat, however. She seemed to believe what she was saying. Clearly, she was too young and inexperienced to know she was lying to him—and to herself.

Even as Dvorak spoke, Kat was taking stock of the options she'd already given herself. A hired escort might not be trustworthy. A carriage would take three days. Sending to Windrush for a servant would take even longer. Kat chewed on her lower lip and made up her mind.

"Very well," she agreed. "You may ride with me. But you must not take any more liberties. Your own words show that you are not a man of honor where women are concerned."

Stefan considered arguing the point, saw the stubborn expression on Kat's face and thought better of it. He believed himself to be the most honorable of men, especially where women were concerned, but Kat would never understand. At least not now. On the other hand, he wasn't making any promises he couldn't keep. That would not be honorable, either.

"I will not force you against your will." He spoke solemnly, and Kat was so intent upon the words that she missed the twinkle in his eye.

"Well and good," she declared, waiting for him to open the door for her.

But Dvorak made no move toward the latch. Instead, he gazed at her bosom. "I suggest you lace up your bodice before we enter the corridor. As charming as I find the view, it might shock some of the king's staid divines."

Looking down, Kat gasped as she realized that the deep cleft between her breasts was showing through the parted laces. With fumbling fingers, Kat tried to fasten her clothing. But neither holes nor laces would cooperate, and Kat stared cross-eyed at her clumsy attempt.

"Here," said Dvorak at last, with a good-natured sigh. "Let me."

"No!" Kat jumped away from him, hitting her backside against the door. "I can do it!"

"No, you can't," Stefan said reasonably. Firmly, he pulled Kat's hands out of the way, then set about to lace up the bodice. Even as she tensed, he finished quickly, then stepped back to admire his handiwork. "There. Though I regret covering up such beauty, you're a proper noble maid again."

Kat was still flushed, but her mouth had curved into a faint smile. While Dvorak's hands had been businesslike, the touch of them against her breasts had tantalized her. So, she had to admit, had his kisses. She wished she knew why his embrace was so different from Prince Henry's. Maybe it was because Dvorak was a foreigner. Kat found that idea convincing. "Thank you," she said primly.

"You're welcome," said Dvorak, and allowed her to precede him from Susan Howard's chamber. Kat could not see the broad grin on his face.

Kat's concern about letting Stefan Dvorak accompany her to Windrush turned out to be groundless; two Oxford dons, one from Magdalen College and the other from All Souls, rode with them. The journey, which was made in fine May weather, turned into a seminar on ancient history, with Kat surprising the others with her book learning.

Stefan said as much to Sir Edgar when they arrived at Windrush. "Your daughter's knowledge is commendable. Minoans, Mycenaeans, Hittites—Lady Kat is well-versed in antiquity."

Kat's father looked pleased. "Her lady mother and I both felt that as an only child, our Kat had the right to an education, even though she may never need it as a woman."

In the background, under the shadow of the yew hedge, the two Oxford dons nodded sagely. But to Kat's surprise, Dvorak demurred. "The better educated a woman is, the better wife and mother she will make. That is one of the things I admire about your country, Sir Edgar. A hundred years ago, your women were encouraged to study. Queen Elizabeth was a shining example of feminine intellect. But in recent generations such accomplishments have been frowned upon. I think it's a pity. But I hail your personal commitment to Lady Kat's education." He made a little bow, first to Sir Edgar, then to Kat.

Sir Edgar beamed. "I thank you, milord. Now that Kat will be staying at home indefinitely, she will have more leisure to study history and literature, as well as science and the arts."

"It will be time well spent," said Dvorak, making ready to take his leave. And so it would, he thought, though there was one art in which Kat was unschooled. *The art of love,* he said to himself, and sensed that Kat might prove an apt pupil. It was a shame that he could not stay in England long enough to teach her. But Stefan Dvorak already knew that before the green leaves turned to bronze, he would be gone.

For once, the open road lacked its usual luster.

Sir Nicholas Overbury was much distressed by his son's imprisonment. He visited twice at Windrush, bemoaning the injustice of the charge and the king's capriciousness. Sir Edgar and Lady Beatrice were sympathetic, but they were also relieved. Kat was safe at home, and their secluded little world was again revolving on its comfortable axis.

Kat should have been elated at having been freed—at least temporarily—from the prospect of marriage. Sir Nicholas had agreed that nothing more should be done about the betrothal until his son was set at liberty. That, he realized, could take years, and meanwhile, he reluctantly acknowledged that should another suitor seek Kat's hand, the prenuptial contract would have to be nullified.

Kat, of course, was hoping that no such potential bridegroom would appear. And as spring blossomed into summer and the long hours of sunlight washed over the gentle countryside, there was no further word from the king. Kat rode and read and stitched and hunted. She savored her parents' company, visited with the tenants and gossiped on the village green. Yet it was not the same. A year ago, under a younger August sun, she had been carefree—and in love with Prince Henry. Now, despite her reprieve, she felt restless, even anxious. Kat did not understand her unsettled emotions. Unless they sprang from grief.

At last, in the waning days of summer, she wrote to Thomas Overbury. She had intended to do so sooner, but after a half-dozen false starts, she could not approach the subject of his incarceration without awkwardness. On this last try, she kept her words brief and to the point.

"It is a source of sorrow to me that you remain in the Tower." That much was true; Kat's compassion was genuine. "Your punishment might be ameliorated by contrition, perhaps even earning you his majesty's gracious pardon and your freedom." So it *might,* Kat reflected, though James could be unpredictable. But it didn't hurt to make the suggestion; Kat had to say something. "If there is any way in which my family or I could be of service, please ask of us what you will." The de Veres and the Overburys were old friends, after all. It was the least she could do to make the offer. Kat pondered the closing for a full ten minutes. "I remain your devoted admirer," she finally penned, and signed her name without her usual flourish. Admirer was a bit strong, Kat felt, but she could think of no better word. The letter was dispatched to London with a touring company of actors traveling from Ludlow to London. Kat then sat down to write to Elizabeth. She had already heard from the electress three times, her missives filled with glowing reports of Heidelberg and the Palatinate. The only sour note was her complaint regarding Kat's postponed marriage.

"Your Thomas has proved not so true by my sire's reckoning," she wrote rather waspishly, "and thus has deprived me of my boon companion. Who now will help me plan my English garden?"

Kat did not know, but Elizabeth's lament pricked at her conscience. Two days later, her niggling sense of guilt was replaced by alarm when a message bearing the royal seal arrived at Windrush. It was not, as she feared, another match proposed by James, but rather a summons for her father. The king was considering the release of Sir Walter Raleigh to undertake an expedition up the Orinoco in the New World. His majesty wished to confer with Sir Edgar about the matter, since he was not only an experienced seaman, but a former comrade of Raleigh's.

Sir Edgar hemmed and hawed, but in the end, he submitted. Lady Beatrice was ready, even eager, for another visit to the capital. Somewhat reluctantly, Kat agreed to join her parents. They arrived in London on the last day of August, taking up temporary lodgings in Whitehall.

Kat was surprised when Fanny Howard called on her and Lady Beatrice while her father was in conference with King James. The countess was at her most demure, all fluttering eyelashes and nervous gestures. Beatrice de Vere was gracious; Kat was wary.

"I came to offer my condolences about your fiancé," Fanny began, fidgeting with the delicate ruff at her throat. "Thomas Overbury has been such a staunch friend of Robin's. We are both much distressed."

"Naturally," said Lady Beatrice in an exaggeratedly soothing voice. Then, more seriously, "Our families' ties go back some twenty years. It's a sad situation."

Fanny inclined her head, the mellow late summer sun catching in the ginger curls. "Life can be so sad. It's a shame that Thomas has taken ill. I hope he recovers soon."

Kat lifted her eyebrows. "Ill? I didn't know."

The countess fanned herself with her hand. It was very warm, and the small chamber at Whitehall was quite close. "Yes, he's been ailing for some weeks now. Perhaps it's the weather. I, too, have felt unwell." Her eyes grew very round and innocent as she regarded Kat. "But you haven't heard from your betrothed? Is it true that he's allowed no letters?"

Kat and Lady Beatrice exchanged glances. Fanny Howard looked as healthy and sleek as a frisky colt. "Perhaps," suggested Lady Beatrice coyly, "you're with child."

"Oh, no!" Fanny looked genuinely shocked. "That's just the problem! I will never bear a babe as long as I stay married to Essex. He won't come near me. And that," she added in a weak voice, "is what I must prove to secure my annulment. Yet how can I, when I feel so...frail?"

"Frail," huffed Lady Beatrice. "My dear countess, you look about as frail as one of my spaniels." She took note of Fanny's offended expression and waved a hand. "No, no, they're handsome animals, intelligent, too." She paused, darting yet another glance at her daughter. "Clever, at any rate. I suspect you merely have the vapors."

Fanny sank back against the brocaded armchair. "True. Yet this dreadful weakness overcomes me so unexpectedly.

And often. That's why I can't go through with the examination."

"What examination?" asked Kat, who was getting anxious for their guest to leave so that she could go outside into the fresh air.

Tugging nervously at a pearl eardrop, Fanny surveyed the ceiling. "The examination to prove my virginal state. Of course," she went on earnestly, "I'm still a maid, Essex refusing to consummate our marriage. But I know I could never endure such a humiliating experience. I'm far too delicate." She sighed heavily, then suddenly gazed at Kat with big, startled eyes. "Oh, Lady Kat—would you consider taking my place? I'd be so grateful! So," she added meaningfully, "would all of my family!"

Kat gasped at Fanny. "Of course not! The mere idea is appalling!" She turned to her mother, who was also looking stunned. "Surely you'd refuse permission?"

"Surely," asserted Lady Beatrice, getting to her feet. "The idea is indecent. I must insist that you make your coarse offer elsewhere, madam. We de Veres have as much pride—and more dignity—than any Howard."

Stiffly, Fanny got to her feet. Despite Kat's indignation, she could not help but admire the other young woman's beauty. The ginger hair so perfectly coiffed, the flawless skin, the perfect features were sufficient to turn any man's head—except, it seemed, her husband's. Perhaps, Kat thought with a pang, Prince Henry had not been immune. What if, as Dvorak had put it so facilely, when one woman was not around, Henry had found another? Was Kat's royal prince any different from the Gypsy baron? But Henry Stuart was not Stefan Dvorak. Yet Fanny was unwilling to undergo an examination of her virginity. Was Henry the reason? Or was it Robin Carr? So caught up in her musings was Kat that she barely heard Fanny's tart farewell.

"You will regret your lack of generosity in coming to my aid," she warned. "We Howards forget neither a kindness nor an insult."

"Brazen baggage," muttered Lady Beatrice, when Fanny had swept out of the room.

"She pretends to be so demure," remarked Kat, "but you're right, my lady mother, she is most brazen." And Kat, now having been threatened by two of the Howard women, hoped that Fanny wasn't vindictive as well.

Chapter Seven

"The king's a fool," Sir Edgar railed as they rode past the royal mews at Charing Cross. "He's asking me to join Raleigh on this ill-conceived voyage to the New World. If Wat wants to trade his imprisonment for the opportunity to risk his neck, that's up to him. But I refuse to be a part of such folly."

"Why is it such a foolish venture?" Kat asked of her father. The de Veres were heading for the Tower, where Sir Edgar planned to visit Raleigh and dissuade him from accepting the royal commission.

Sir Edgar was still looking vexed. "James is insistent that any English exploration of the Orinoco will not provoke conflict with the Spanish while I think it will. He hopes that Prince Charles will wed the Infanta. A papist match!" her father grumbled. "The next thing we know, we'll be under the thumb of the pope and the Holy Roman Emperor! Pah!" He spat upon the ground, eliciting a series of barks from a mongrel dog that had been following their mounts. "I'll be glad to leave this place tomorrow. London has never suited me, not even in my youth."

Lady Beatrice shot her husband a wry look as they passed by Lord and Lady Harington's palatial town house in Convent Garden. "Need I remind you, dear spouse, this

Orinoco enterprise was originally Wat's idea. He's been pressing the king about it for years."

"Yes, yes," replied Sir Edgar testily. "The poor fellow's been imprisoned for most of the past twenty years! And for what? Merely annoying his sovereigns! How can you shut a brilliant man like that away for life only because he's a bit of a nuisance?"

The question, of course, was rhetorical, and both wife and daughter knew it. It occurred to Kat that the same query could be made concerning Thomas Overbury. A monarch's displeasure, whether it be that of Queen Elizabeth or King James, could result in unjust punishment. But Raleigh, unlike Overbury, was much admired and well liked. His prison was said to be as lavish as any palace suite, his wife and two young sons lived nearby on Tower Hill, and he even had a laboratory where he conducted his scientific research. "Only my father," Prince Henry had once remarked dourly to Kat, "would keep such a bird in a cage."

Following the sluggish Strand past the Temple and St. Paul's, the de Veres rode eastward along the busy Thames toward London Bridge, and eventually, the Tower. Their progress was slow, for London's narrow streets were jammed with carts, carriages, coaches and wagons. New buildings seemed to be going up everywhere, with half-timbered fronts already jutting out over the crowded lanes. Hawkers shouted their wares at every corner, knots of city dwellers congregated to exchange the latest gossip, servants, apprentices, merchants and goodwives scurried about under the pall of smoke and reek of sewage. Kat wrinkled her nose and wondered if any of the Londoners noticed. Like her father, she could not wait to get back to the sweet, fresh haven of the country.

But it occurred to her that, as long as she and her parents were going to the Tower, it might be courteous to inquire after Thomas Overbury's health. Fanny Howard had mentioned that he was ill. Prisoner or not, officially he was still her fiancé. She made the suggestion to her parents; after a brief exchange, they agreed that their daughter was showing Christian consideration.

The lord lieutenant of the Tower, Sir Gervase Elwes, did not see things in the same light. Overbury was closely watched; he was allowed no visitors or letters. Kat wondered if Thomas had received the missive she'd sent him some weeks earlier.

Elwes, who, despite his refusal, struck Kat as a bland if affable sort, apologetically informed the de Veres that Raleigh could see visitors only one at a time. Some restrictions had also been placed on him in recent months. While Lady Beatrice hadn't seen Sir Walter in years and Kat barely remembered the great adventurer at all, the two women had come along only for the outing. Vaguely disappointed, they agreed to wait for Sir Edgar in the lord lieutenant's cozy parlor.

In a quarter of an hour, Sir Gervase returned from showing the visitor to Raleigh's prison in the Brick Tower, commenting that he saw no need to oversee what appeared to be a discussion of sea routes and savage natives.

"It's all charts and compasses and maps with your lord and Sir Walter," said Elwes with a shrug as he poured sack for himself and his guests. "It's gold they seek, I suppose." He sat down in a comfortable chair and shifted his paunch. "Ah, yes...gold. It's a commodity that both kings and commoners find themselves short of these days." He gazed at Lady Beatrice expectantly.

Mother and daughter exchanged swift glances. "Now, Sir Gervase," began Lady Beatrice with an amused twinkle in her hazel eyes, "don't tell me his majesty is stingy with your wages!"

Sir Gervase made a face. "His majesty is stingy, period. Everyone knows that. It takes nothing away from his sovereign glory, mind you," he added hastily, "but this royal assignment is like any other—one must pay to get it in the first place, and then the compensation is far from ample." He wiped his forehead with a kerchief, for the day was warm. "It's the privilege of serving the king, not the remuneration. Yet privilege doesn't buy much in the marketplaces of the world."

"Well." Lady Beatrice palmed the little suede purse that dangled on a chain at her wrist. "What could we buy in the marketplace at the Tower?"

Sir Gervase inclined his head and lowered his voice. "Ah, let me think . . . it's difficult, of course." He watched Lady Beatrice dump several gold coins into her lap. "And quite against orders," he added. Kat's mother shook out three more sovereigns and gazed unblinkingly at the lord lieutenant. "But exceptions can sometimes be made." Elwes cleared his throat and stood up. He bowed not to Lady Beatrice, but to Kat. "Come along, my dear, your beloved is in the Bloody Tower. I'll show you the way." Nimbly, he held out his hand, awaiting Lady Beatrice's bounty.

"But," Kat started to protest, "I thought we were going to see Sir Walter . . ."

"It's fitting that you call upon Sir Thomas," her mother broke in, handing over the bribe. "After all, you suggested it yourself." She gave Kat a helpless look.

Her mother, of course, was right. The misunderstanding with Sir Gervase was probably all for the best. Sir Edgar and Raleigh would no doubt prefer not being interrupted, and Kat was duty bound to see Sir Thomas now that she had the chance. Docilely, she followed Elwes to the Bloody Tower, though the very name made her shiver.

While Fanny had remarked upon Overbury's state of ill health, Kat was not prepared for what she found in the small, dank prison cell. The dapper, arrogant Thomas Overbury Kat remembered was hardly recognizable in the withered shell that huddled in a corner under a much-patched blanket. Overbury had lost not only a great deal of weight, but most of his hair and, Kat noted upon closer inspection, his fingernails. Halfway across the boxy room she paused, realizing that Overbury was naked under the thin covering. Embarrassed for him as well as for herself, she glanced at Sir Gervase before speaking to the prisoner. The lord lieutenant nodded encouragement; Kat should speak to Overbury.

"My lord," she began in an uncertain voice, "I'm very sorry to find you unwell. Is it an ague from which you suffer?"

Hollow eyes stared out at Kat. "Fever," croaked Overbury. "And vomiting."

"The weather, I'd guess," said Kat in an effort to minimize Overbury's sufferings. "It's been unseasonably warm. But autumn is coming—mayhap you'll feel your old self soon."

Overbury's mouth twisted in his unkempt beard. "Nay," he asserted in that weak, rough voice. "I am done for. Done to death."

"Oh, no!" Kat protested, taking a step nearer. Not only did a rank odor permeate the cell, but a pair of rats with hostile eyes rooted about in a moldy bowl of uneaten food. A single narrow window, some ten feet up on the stone wall, seemed to distill the sunlight and cast long, ominous shadows across the room. Kat turned to Elwes for moral support, but the lord lieutenant was gone. Nervously, Kat's fingers twitched at the thin gold chain that hung from her waist. "How long have you been feeling poorly?" she inquired of Overbury.

He shook his head, and the gesture triggered a violent trembling of his entire body. Overbury seemed to be all arms and legs, bones barely covered by flesh stretched taut. "Water," he gasped, one hand flailing in the direction of a pitcher set not far from where the rats were feasting.

Terrified, Kat edged toward the vessel. The rats darted one last venomous look at her before skittering off through a hole in the wall. With fingers almost as unsteady as Overbury's, Kat sloshed water into a chipped cup. An insect floated on top; she tried to remove it with her finger, failed, and thrust the water at Overbury.

"Drink, sir. Your thirst must be powerful."

Greedily, Overbury consumed the contents of the cup. Some foreign emotion stirred behind those burning eyes. Gratitude, Kat thought, and tried to smile.

A moment later, Overbury was convulsed on the floor. The blanket slipped away as he began to retch. Kat could stand no more. She raced to the door and called out to the guard who stood on duty a few yards from the passage. With a lugubrious air, he sauntered in her direction.

"Sick again, eh?" he drawled, glancing in at the prisoner but making no move to help. "'Twill pass."

Kat grabbed the man by the sleeve of his homespun shirt. "Go to his aid! Bring fresh water! Fetch a physician! Have you no Christian charity under your loutish hide?"

Startled, the guard shook himself free and entered the cell. "Waste o' time," he muttered. "This one's almost gone." But as Kat moved away on shaky legs, she saw the guard bending over her betrothed. The last she saw of Thomas Overbury was his thin, pale bare legs writhing in agony on the cold stones of the Bloody Tower.

The next day he was dead. Kat heard of his death just as she and her parents were about to leave Whitehall. Stunned, Kat stared at the bearer of the news, Eustace Norton, the royal falconer, who happened to be in the stables when the de Veres arrived to claim their horses.

"Fever," breathed Lady Beatrice, patting her daughter's shoulder. "Our Katherine saw him only yesterday. He was pitifully weak."

Kat nodded dumbly. As little as she'd cared for Thomas Overbury, and as loath as she had been to marry him, his death still came as a blow.

Norton, a rangy young man with fine gray eyes as sharp as the birds he trained, gave Kat a sympathetic look. "He was ill for some time, I'm told. If it was fever that took him, it must have been a different type than that which finished off Prince Henry. His highness went much quicker, rest his soul." Somewhat to the de Veres' surprise, he crossed himself in the papist manner.

Shuddering at the reference to Henry's demise, Kat turned as a tall, handsome woman entered the royal stable and came toward them. Norton broke into a smile. "Nan!" He turned to the de Veres. "'Tis my sister, Anne Turner. She's a widow, with several young children to raise."

Kat and her parents allowed themselves to be introduced. Mistress Turner had the same sharp gray eyes as her brother, but unlike his open countenance, there was something sly in her manner. Kat felt uneasy, even as she accepted Anne Turner's glib condolences.

"Fret not," said Mistress Turner. "Another husband will be found for you soon enough. That's one thing about men—when one is lost, there's usually another just around the corner."

The advice seemed jarring from a widow, but Kat dismissed Anne's words. Prospective husbands weren't important to Kat; what grief she felt was for the waste of a life, not the loss of a mate. Kat followed her parents to the stall where their horses were kept and allowed a pair of stable boys to fetch the gear. A quarter of an hour later, the open road lay before them, and all three de Veres thankfully bid farewell to London.

A fortnight later, autumn touched upon the city, bringing a fresh breeze and a softer light. From Whitehall Palace, Stefan Dvorak could see the mist settling in over Lambeth Marsh across the river. But he was more interested in the contents of the chamber in which he stood than its fine view. Robin Carr's quarters were cluttered, not only with the usual accoutrements of daily life, but with an accumulation of riches that the favorite had been purchasing for the home he hoped to make with his future wife. Saddles of Spanish leather, paintings by Italian masters, Belgian lace and French tapestries were crammed into every spare nook and cranny.

Yet Stefan paid these treasures little heed. He was searching not for valuables, but for evidence. For several months now a rumor had circulated around the court that some of those closest to the king were in the pay of Spain. If James were to be coaxed into a match between Prince Charles and the Infanta, England's support for Protestants all over Europe would be weakened. One of the reasons Stefan had come to Oxford was because of the old ties between Bohemia and the English people. But a Catholic queen, especially one from Spain, would doom any alliance of Protestant sympathizers in both countries.

Certainly, Dvorak reflected as he rummaged through drawers and listened for any warning sounds in the passageway, Robin Carr was a likely target for Spanish gold. So, he had come to learn, were the Howards. Susan had hinted as much, lying replete in his arms one warm night and murmuring about her uncle, Northampton, and his secret source of income from what she'd quaintly called "the orange trees."

But after a quarter of an hour searching Carr's belongings, Stefan uncovered no sign of bribes offered or received. Carr might be stupid, but perhaps he had enough sense to be careful. Gazing around the chamber, Stefan could see no other hiding places. He'd tried secret panels, recesses in the floor, even the bricks in the fireplace. As an occasional conjurer, he knew that the best place to hide anything was in plain sight. His eyes fell on a Bible, the newly translated version authorized by King James. Dvorak picked up the heavy volume and noted that it was in virtually pristine condition. Apparently, he thought with a wry smile, Carr was not devout. That fact came as no surprise.

The half-dozen sheets of paper tucked in between the New and Old Testaments did give him a start, however. They were not from the Spanish ambassador, Gondomar, but had been written by Carr himself. To Thomas Overbury in the Tower. Stefan frowned. It struck him as strange that Carr would bother not only to retrieve his correspondence to his former mentor, but to conceal it.

Masculine voices filtered in from the passageway. On impulse, Stefan folded the letters and put them inside his jerkin. The sound of a latch being lifted sent him to the window. With easy grace for so big a man, he launched himself over the sill and steeled his body for the ten-foot drop to the ground.

Across the Thames, the mist enveloped Lambeth, shrouding even the archbishop's palace. Evening was settling in, cool and damp. Stefan walked purposefully toward the river and hailed a bargeman. In the morning he would be gone from England, perhaps forever. The thought made him melancholy, and he wondered why. As the barge was untied from the wharf, a cat crouched on its rough deck, then leaped onto the shore, with a jump as neat and quick as Stefan's descent from the palace. He stood for some moments, staring into the mist where the cat had disappeared. Instead of the turrets and chimneys of Whitehall, he saw an oval face with green eyes and a turned-up nose. Forever suddenly sounded like an impossible word. Stefan Dvorak made up his mind that some day, against all odds, he would return to England.

A few weeks later, news trickled in to Windrush. The Electress Palatine was expecting her first child early in the New Year. Was it possible that her dearest friend could join the midwife who would be coming from England to Heidelberg to attend the birth? With a slight pang, Kat thought not.

In a more sensational vein, the de Veres learned of the latest developments in the Howard scandal. Fanny, swathed in heavy veils, had been examined by a group of matrons and pronounced *virgo intacta*. Her marriage to Essex would be annulled forthwith. Yet Robin Carr's hold on King James was said to be slipping. Without his mentor, Thomas Overbury, the favorite's counsel was less wise, more frivolous, not nearly as astute as in times past. But Robin retained James's affections, if not his confidence. As for Overbury, his remains had been hastily buried within the Tower precincts. His father, Sir Nicholas, had been dismayed by the preemptory interment, and had ridden posthaste to Windrush to seek the consolation of the de Veres.

"Poor old Nicholas," sighed Sir Edgar on a bright, crisp October afternoon in the small orchard that lay between Windrush's formal gardens and the river. "He is distraught, as you might imagine. But his ramblings about poison are nonsense. I fear he is falling back on that trite explanation for the death of anyone who is taken relatively young." Her father gave Kat a sad little smile. "You remember how it was with Prince Hal, my dear?"

"Oh, yes," Kat replied in a thin voice. "I remember. Too well." Stefan Dvorak had carried that rumor to her, some ten months earlier, at their first meeting on the day of Henry's funeral. As a south wind stirred the dry leaves, Kat wondered if Dvorak was still at Oxford. The great university lay only a few miles to the southeast, yet to Kat, barred from its lecture halls, it always seemed a world away.

"Life is not fair," she announced, causing her father to lift both eyebrows in the act of inspecting the last of the windfall apples that lay beneath the trees.

"What?" He frowned at Kat, took a bite out of an apple, then cast it away in the direction of the river. "Not fair, you say? Of course not!" Fondly, he took her arm as they began to walk along the riverbank, downstream toward the weir. "You speak of Prince Hal, dying so young?" Sir Edgar inquired gently.

To Kat's surprise, it was not of Henry that she had spoken. For the first time since his death, she realized that her railing against the Fates was directed not at her beloved's untimely passing, but at something else. "No," she answered a bit uncertainly. "I spoke of...Oxford. I think."

Sir Edgar chuckled and patted her hand. "You are still being educated. Your studies have not been neglected these past months. Do you wish us to hire a new tutor?"

But Kat shook her head. Over the years, she had been instructed by a series of tutors, the last of them having moved on to Paris the previous year. Her parents had sought a replacement, but before they could find someone suitable, Henry had died. Kat apparently had lost interest in formal studies, preferring instead to read on her own and then engage her father in discussion.

"I'm seventeen, I can follow my own paths to knowledge now," she said. "I've crammed enough ancient history into my head and I've little gift for mathematics. It's time to learn more about the present world. The farther reaches of Europe, perhaps, or even the Ottoman Empire.''

Sir Edgar eyed his daughter curiously. Across the river, a grouse flew up out of a clump of blackthorn bushes. ''A pity you didn't consider starting that area of study sooner. We might have engaged that foreign fellow—what is his name?—to instruct you.''

''Who?'' Kat kept her voice even.

Sir Edgar waved a hand. ''Oh, you know who I mean. He called upon us with the message from the king and was your escort from London along with the Oxford dons. A Bohemian name; it eludes me now....''

''Stefan Dvorak,'' Kat said a little too promptly.

''Yes, yes,'' replied her father. ''That was it. He seemed a bright sort, especially for a foreigner. Excellent command of the language. You might have benefitted from his instruction. But now he's gone.''

''Gone?'' Kat stopped in midstep, almost tripping her father. ''Where? When?''

Both father and daughter were surprised by the unexpected desperation in Kat's tone. Sir Edgar registered consternation. ''A month ago, mayhap more. I heard of his departure when I last called on Cousin Oxford,'' her father explained, referring to the de Vere who had inherited an earldom but very little else. ''This Dvorak had returned to his homeland. Trouble is brewing, I gather. But then it usually is. Those foreign countries are like that.''

For some unknown reason, Kat's heart felt like a stone. She had not seen Stefan Dvorak for months, but she had thought about him. More, perhaps, than she cared to admit. Unbidden, he would creep into her thoughts, occasionally her dreams. And somehow the knowledge that he was close by had given her comfort. But now he was gone. Kat turned a stricken face to her father.

''Is he coming back?''

"I don't know," Sir Edgar admitted. "I didn't ask." His eyes, so like Kat's, studied her carefully. "Why, my dear, are you upset? I didn't realize you...it...he mattered!"

Kat tried to compose her features, gripped her father's arm tightly and began walking again. "No," she said, her voice low. "Neither did I. Maybe I don't. At least," she added with a quick intake of breath, "I shouldn't. And I won't."

The vow was not taken lightly. But even as she spoke, Kat knew her intention was in vain.

A half moon hung over Prague as Stefan Dvorak entered the Old Town from the Charles Bridge. The night watch on the other side was known to Stefan, and had let him pass without more than an exchange of banter. Stefan was headed for a small but pleasant house behind St. Salvator's Church. The owner was an elderly banker with Bohemian leanings and a winsome young wife. The arrangement worked out very nicely for all concerned.

On the edge of Knights of the Cross Square, he paused, aware of a figure in the shadows by St. Salvator's Church. It was Jesuit built, part of the Clementinum that housed the order's college. Stefan was immediately on guard. The figure in the black serge cloak and hood might have been a priest, but as Stefan warily approached, he recognized Albrecht Wallenstein, despite the decade that had passed since the two men had last met.

"Stefan." Wallenstein peered about the empty square to make sure no one was lurking. "I heard you were back in Prague."

He studied the long thin face under the hood. Stefan had come to despise that face, to hate the heart that beat inside the man who had abandoned the Dvorak family in their hour of greatest need. Yet now, confronting Wallenstein for the first time in so many years, Stefan was curiously devoid of emotion. "I heard the same about you. Odd, isn't it, that we should return to Prague within a few days of each other."

"Maybe," replied Wallenstein, looking strangely furtive and ill at ease. He was close to thirty, lean but fit, with sad brown eyes, a long face and a well-kept beard. "Maybe not."

Stefan shrugged. "It appears that you've sought me out. Have you had me followed?"

"Of course. How else to find you?" Wallenstein's tone was dry. "I'm also told you've been with Count Thurn. Have you cast your lot with that empty-headed rebel?"

Stefan's dark gaze was steady. "Shall I argue that Thurn is Bohemia's only hope?" He saw the light flare in Wallenstein's eyes and laughed sardonically. "Oh, Brecht, what would you have me do? Ask Count Thurn to kiss the Pope's arse and shear him of his nationalist aspirations?"

Wallenstein started to look away, then met Dvorak's intense stare head-on. "Scarcely. Thurn is impossible." His narrow face grew very grave. "Uncle Heinrich and my cousin Vilem have great influence with Emperor Matthias. Let's be blunt. The emperor is not well, and he's childless. Matthias will name Ferdinand as his heir, but the wind blows in favor of a Protestant successor. It's very likely that when Matthias dies, the Bohemians will name their own king."

Stefan inclined his head. "They should. They are in the majority, after all."

With a sniff of disdain for majority rule, Wallenstein leaned toward the younger man. "We know where Spain and France stand, we have no questions about the Netherlands or Scandinavia. You've been in England. Where do King James's sympathies lie?"

Fingering his long upper lip, Stefan regarded Wallenstein dubiously. "James is changeable. He despises war. He will not commit himself unless he is forced to do so."

"But," argued Wallenstein, "his daughter has married the head of the Protestant union."

"So?" Stefan lifted his eyebrows. "His son is rumored for a Catholic match with Spain or France." He gave Wallenstein an ironic look. "That should please you, Brecht."

Wallenstein drew back inside the folds of his heavy cloak. "Do you think dissension pleases me? Do you take me for a warmonger?"

"You're a soldier. You make your living off war," Stefan responded reasonably. "You've been fighting the emperor's petty battles in Italy. Why should I think you won't be willing to fight for him and the pope in Bohemia?"

"I don't want civil war." Wallenstein's gaze was unwavering. "You could help me prevent it, Stefan. Convince Thurn and the other rebels that only tragedy will come of persisting in their Protestant beliefs. This independent national church is nothing but heresy, a path to perdition. Surely you don't support Father Comenius and his like? They are rabble-rousers, out for their own selfish ends."

For a long moment, Stefan did not reply, but kept his dark eyes fixed on Wallenstein's face. "Rot!" he exploded, banging his fist into his palm. "Comenius is a holy man! I give not a fig for formal religion under any guise, but at least the Bohemian church allows men and women freedom of conscience! It's you and your Jesuits who care not for the people! It is the Catholics who are Hapsburgs and Holy Roman Emperors! I'd rather hang than be your dupe!"

Wallenstein's sallow face hardened, revealing the core that was capable of rallying ten thousand men against overwhelming odds. "How noble, Stefan. How stupid. What will Count Thurn and his ilk do with your Roms?

Would you sacrifice your Gypsy friends for the sake of sentiment?''

Stefan raised his chin. "I am a Gypsy. Half, anyway. Or don't you remember my mother?" The words were pointed, like small stilettos.

Wallenstein shook his head sadly. "Don't taunt me. Keja cast my horoscope, she taught me how to bind up wounds, she brewed me herbal draughts for—" He stopped abruptly, his eyes clouding over. "Believe me, Stefan, I would have saved her if I could! But I was forced to flee when she was condemned to the stake!"

"I was there." Stefan turned toward the hill above the city, feeling the breeze from the river. Above the placid Moldau, the cluster of ancient buildings that formed the Hradcany brooded over Prague. "It was there that she was condemned as a witch, and out in the square that she was burned." He spoke quietly, yet there was a throb beneath the words. "I was only ten, but I watched. I heard her screams, I saw the flames, I smelled the flesh...." His voice had risen and he whirled on Wallenstein. "I was there, Brecht! I was there, too, when my father was murdered by imperial soldiers for defending the Protestant church at Laun. I tried to save him, but I was barely thirteen, and no match for fifty men. I marvel they didn't kill me, too!" The hot black eyes bore into Wallenstein. "Now," he continued, dropping his voice, "do you expect me to serve the emperor and his minions?"

Wallenstein gave a little shake of his head. "You've every right not to trust the emperor," he conceded, edging sideways as if to gain breathing space. "But who sent you to Oxford? Didn't my Catholic uncle see to it that we both got an education? Didn't he arrange for you to receive the scholarship set up by the canon of St. Vitus's Cathedral? Why won't you trust me?"

Silence filled the vast square, broken only by the call of an owl in the bell tower of St. Salvator's Church. Stefan put his hands on his hips and closed his eyes. Wallenstein's words had hit their mark: Brecht's childless uncle had taken both young men under his wing, a pair of orphaned boys whose schooling he had sponsored. The generous old man had been dead for many years, but Stefan remembered him fondly. He was looking again at Wallenstein, the black eyes riddled with rebellion. "I'd rather you fought with me than against me, Brecht. By God, I would."

Wallenstein gathered the heavy serge cloak against his body. "It can't be that way," he said softly. "Not your way."

Stefan nodded once, then turned a wry face to Wallenstein. "Nor yours."

The young colonel stared past Stefan to the Old Town Bridge tower outlined in the moonlight. "Because of the past, we should be friends." He took a deep breath. "And because of Keja, of course. She was a mother to me, too."

"Yes." Stefan watched as Wallenstein scanned the square. "Why did you flee?"

Wallenstein paused, a hand at the neck of his cloak. "The soldiers threatened to kill me." Carefully, he pulled away both collar and shirt to reveal his right shoulder. In the moon's pale glow, Stefan could make out a three-inch scar, dark red and puckered. "Indeed, they tried. But I got away." He swallowed hard as he replaced his garments. "I'm sometimes sorry that I did." On impulse, he reached out for Dvorak. "I've forgotten—what is the Rom word for 'brother'?"

Stefan hesitated, then gripped the proffered hand. "The words don't matter. It's the deeds that count. *Nais tuke,* brother."

"God keep you," murmured Wallenstein, backing away across the square. "May He preserve the cause that is right."

Stefan's mouth twisted in an ironic smile as the half moon slipped behind a cloud. "I wonder," he mused, "if God cares?"

Chapter Eight

Kat knew her parents fretted over her future. At twenty-one, she was well past the marketable age for a bride, yet her dowry of Windrush would commend itself to any man. In the past few months, both Sir Edgar and Lady Beatrice had frequently hinted as much, but Kat was obdurate about remaining a spinster.

"I vowed I'd wed no one but Prince Henry, and I meant it," she told her parents, and that was that. Still, in the soft summer twilight or on brisk autumn mornings, Kat would succumb to pangs of longing that did not seem quite suited to the comfortable unmarried state she'd promised for herself. Her books, her horses, the land and the house itself all gave her a sense of satisfaction, but from time to time, especially upon waking in the still small hours of the night, she had to admit that something was missing from her life. One day seemed very like another. Certainly she didn't laugh as much. Elizabeth had been right after all; there was nothing particularly funny about growing up—or growing old. Especially alone.

Often she would have these dark feelings after receiving one of Elizabeth's effusive letters overflowing with news of her domestic bliss in the Palatinate. Two sons, Frederick Henry and Charles Louis, had been born to the elector and the electress in less than three years. Elizabeth seemed anxious to provide another babe for the royal nursery. The experience of childbirth had not tempered her zest for life.

> "The doctors would fill me with the most noxious of medications that, upon their leave-taking, I pour into a basin. Instead, I have my own cure for easing pain, which is to rumble it away with riding to the hunt."

Kat had smiled fondly at Elizabeth's bravado. Briefly, she considered a visit to Heidelberg. But Germany was so far away, and despite Elizabeth's assertions that her new country was both fruitful and beautiful, Kat could not imagine any foreign land living up to such an enthusiastic description.

Indeed, the rest of the world seemed so far removed from Windrush that when a trio of king's men rode up on a golden October afternoon, Kat could not imagine that their arrival had anything to do with her.

"Don't tell me," she whispered to Lady Beatrice as Sir Edgar greeted the contingent, "that the king is still badgering my father about Sir Walter Raleigh's failure in the New World!"

"I hope not," replied Lady Beatrice, with some alarm. "Now that poor Raleigh has lost his head over that disaster, I should think we've heard the last of it."

Indeed, the de Vere family had been most distraught over the recent news of Raleigh's execution after his failure to find gold along the Orinoco. The Spanish ambassador, offended by the English incursion into what his monarch claimed as Spanish territory, had hounded King James into sentencing Raleigh to death. Despite their grief over the man's fate, Kat and her parents had been relieved at Sir Edgar's steadfastness in refusing to join his old companion on the voyage. Yet now Kat's father, moving away from the door, was turning an ashen face to his wife and daughter. "Kat...my dear..." he began, then hurried forward to take her hand. "This is most dreadful! His majesty is insisting that you go to London to answer some questions."

Kat's brow creased in puzzlement. "Questions? About what?" She gazed from her father to the king's men, stolid and sturdy. All she could think of was another match proposed by James. But what questions there could be eluded her. "Now? Why so urgent?"

Sir Edgar was trying to compose himself. "It's something to do with Thomas Overbury." He gave both Kat and Lady Beatrice an apologetic look, as if he were to blame for this terrible intrusion. "It seems poor old Nicholas may have been right. Despite great obstacles, his dogged persistence all these years has been rewarded. Thomas Overbury was in fact poisoned. The king's justices want to ask if you had any reason to commit murder."

Kat's reaction was to burst out laughing. Under the circumstances, it was not a wise thing to do.

In death, Thomas Overbury cast a longer shadow over Kat than he had in life. The miracle she had hoped for at the time of her betrothal now turned into a nightmare. Her parents were discouraged from accompanying her to London, and Kat tried to make light of the situation by insisting that she would be back home within a few days. With anxious eyes and heavy hearts, Sir Edgar and Lady Beatrice watched their only child ride off under the close guard of armed men.

With Windrush behind her, Kat's spirits fell. She was barely conscious of the sights along the road to London. If the city had changed in four years, Kat did not notice. She was too distressed—and puzzled—over the long-delayed verdict in Thomas Overbury's death. More to the point, she was afraid. The mere suggestion that she might have been

involved in her late fiancé's death was sufficient to undo
any young woman, even one as sensible as Kat de Vere.

The king's men who had brought Kat to London apparently were under orders to reveal nothing about the matter
at hand. After a few attempts at asking what was going on,
Kat gave up when the men politely refused to enlighten her.
Perhaps, she considered, they didn't know. But somehow
she had the feeling that the least of King James's servants
knew more than she did.

At Whitehall, the magnificent banqueting hall had just
been completed. Its handsome windows and graceful lines
made the rest of the hodgepodge of royal buildings look
even more decrepit and ugly. As Kat was ushered into the
Cockpit to meet with Sir Edward Coke, she felt a pall of
melancholy descend upon her.

Finally left alone by the guards who had brought her
from Windrush, Kat studied her surroundings. The room,
which she judged to be close by the suite Princess Elizabeth had occupied in this same part of the palace, was lavishly appointed, considering that it was the headquarters of
the king's chief justice. Most of the furnishings were from
an earlier era, and though worn, were decorated with opulent brocade, damask and silk. The hangings were heavy
dark red velvet, the wall sconces shaped like stout, gilded
arms.

Kat wondered if she should sit. But before she could
make up her mind, a door opened across the room. To her
surprise, it was not Sir Edward Coke who entered the room
but Stefan Dvorak. Kat was so nonplussed that she could
not speak.

"Little Kat," said Dvorak in apparent wonderment. "I
couldn't believe my ears when I heard you were coming
here."

"Neither," gulped Kat, unceremoniously flopping down
onto a green damask-covered footstool, "could I." She

blinked several times, watching Dvorak make his leisurely way across the room. He had changed, she thought, grown leaner, darker, with a few added lines in his chiseled face. The years fell away, and, unbidden, she remembered his kiss, his touch, the strength of his arms. Such a reaction, Kat sternly reminded herself, was most inappropriate. "What are *you* doing here?"

Dvorak sat down in an armchair a few feet away, one leg thrown casually over the side. "I've been in England for some months. The elector and electress hoped to visit London in the spring, but Elizabeth's latest pregnancy changed their plans. Since Queen Anne is so ill, the electress begged me call on her mother. Her majesty is fond of my little tricks, as you may recall. Elizabeth thought I might cheer her, and thus ease her disappointment over the canceled visit." He gave one of those little offhand shrugs that Kat remembered so well.

"You've been here all this time?" Kat asked in a faintly incredulous voice. *And not so much as paid a visit to Windrush,* came the unasked-for thought that made her flush guiltily—and without reason, since Stefan couldn't read her mind. Or so Kat hoped.

"I've spent most of my time trying to convince King James he should help my fellow Bohemians," explained Stefan. He made a face. "I've not yet been successful. James is still playing a double, nay, a triple hand, with Spain, with France, with the emperor. Your king will not commit himself to any cause, it seems."

But Kat was not interested in politics. Her primary concern was for herself and the reason for her presence at Whitehall. "I mean, why are you *here*—in this room, where Sir Edward Coke ought to be? You've heard about Thomas Overbury?"

Brushing at the sleeve of his plain cambric shirt, Stefan nodded. "That's why I'm here. Because you are," he lifted his dark eyebrows a notch. "You're in trouble, it seems."

"Am I?" Kat shivered, despite the unseasonably warm October weather. "But why? I don't understand any of this."

"Nor do I," Stefan admitted. "All I know is that Overbury's father—your family friend—was never satisfied that his son died of natural causes. In recent months, rumors began to spread. It was more than the usual talk of poison. There were names, high up, and a long list of people who might have wanted Thomas dead. Yours," he added, leaning forward in the chair, "was among them."

Kat shrank back on the stool. "Oh! But why? Why me?"

Dvorak was looking quite somber. "According to Lady Susan, you didn't want to marry Overbury. If he died, you were free." Stefan spread his hands; the argument sounded simple. And convincing.

"Lady Susan!" Kat spat out the name. She hadn't thought of Susan Howard in years. "What a venomous thing to say!"

"Perhaps." Dvorak spoke in that familiar, easy manner. "There are others, of course. Some have even dared whisper the names of the king and queen."

Kat was aghast. "That's absurd!"

But Stefan kept to his reasonable style. "The king resented Overbury's interference, his arrogance, his presumptions. As for Queen Anne, Overbury had been insolent to her on at least two occasions. In her grief at hearing of Prince Henry's death, she cried out that Robin Carr and Thomas Overbury must have poisoned him." He saw Kat wince, but continued, placing a hand lightly on her knee. "I wouldn't take those accusations too seriously. The queen probably never truly believed the prince was murdered. Nor is she a vindictive sort. And James had other, more legal means at his disposal."

Kat felt his touch and quivered. How long it had been since she'd rested in his arms! How little she had yearned for the embrace of any man—except this one. Kat could admit that to herself now, that long-suppressed secret she had not dared confront because it seemed so hopeless. She stared into the intense black eyes and wondered if he'd thought of her over the years. There had been no messages, no sign, not even a letter to tell her he was back in England. Yet here he was, speaking with her as if they'd never been apart, and apparently concerned because she was, as he'd put it, "in trouble."

"Stefan..." she said on a breathy note, then drew back and gave herself a little shake. "I'm upset. Forgive me. My mind's a-jumble." Frowning, Kat gnawed at her lower lip. "See here," she said more briskly, "do you think I poisoned Thomas Overbury?"

He let out a short laugh. "Of course not."

Somewhat reassured, Kat passed her hand over his but did not touch it. "I couldn't have," she said, more to herself than to him. "I was at Windrush."

"You could have had agents work for you," Stefan pointed out. "Whoever did kill him no doubt had the poison administered that way."

Kat stared again. "What? Oh...well, yes. I suppose that's true." This time she did put her fingers on the back of his hand. She knew she was in terrible trouble. But her spirits felt brighter than they had in years. Was it because of Stefan? Surely not. Yet Kat felt a change come over her as if conjured up by one of his magic tricks. "Stefan, who do you think killed poor Thomas?"

Stefan turned slightly, staring off in the direction of a tall bookcase crammed with weighty tomes bound in tooled leather. "I think I know. But I can't prove it. Yet."

"Oh!" Kat drew in her breath. "But who? And how do you know?"

He removed his hand from Kat's knee and squeezed her fingers. "Will you come away with me to Heidelberg? Now?"

With a gasp, Kat shook her head. "I couldn't! It would be improper! And it's so far away!"

Dvorak gave an impatient shake of his head. "It also might be necessary. England may not be a safe place for you right now."

"But that's ridiculous," argued Kat, as the sound of voices trickled in from the passageway. "England is my home. I can't go traipsing off to a strange land just because of some silly rumor. What would my parents think?"

"There isn't time for anyone to think, including you," declared Stefan, abruptly releasing her hand and getting to his feet. "Coke is on his way. And I must be, too—through the other door." In a half-dozen swift strides, Dvorak left the way he had come. The latch had just clicked behind him when Sir Edward Coke, like a ghost from the era of Elizabeth, materialized behind Kat.

"Well," he boomed, "Lady Katherine! Don't get up, stay as you are, this shan't take long." With a heavy sigh, he dropped into the chair Stefan had so recently vacated. Coke was still a handsome, imposing figure of a man even in his sixties. Bearded and florid of face, he had a swaggering air. "How was your journey? No jarring incidents, I trust?"

"None." Kat tried to focus on the king's chief justice. "Are we here to talk of travel or of Thomas Overbury?"

Coke erupted with hearty laughter. "Both, if it pleases us. But since you mention poor Sir Thomas, let us get straight to the point." The heartiness fled, replaced by cold blue eyes and a chin that seemed to jut through the graying beard. "Do you know a Mistress Mary Woods?"

At first, the name meant nothing to Kat. She started to say as much, and then, floating through the mists of time, a motley-clad figure rose up in her mind's eye. "She was accused of theft...." Kat began somewhat vaguely. "She was from Suffolk—or was it Norfolk? Yes, I met her once or twice, years ago."

"Ahh." Edward Coke folded his hands over his deep blue velvet doublet. "Excellent. Mistress Woods offered you her services, did she not?"

Kat gave Edward Coke a puzzled look. "Services? To what end? I don't recall. Was she a servant? A cook?"

Coke's shake of his head was decisive. "No. Think, my lady. Did you not hire her?"

"Oh, no," Kat responded quickly. "My mother does all the hiring at Windrush. Mistress Woods worked for someone else." She hesitated, wanting to be accurate. "Frances Howard, when she was the Countess of Essex. Now I remember." She leaned forward, eager to recount the incident between Mary Woods and the Essexes. "The earl accused Mistress Woods of stealing jewels, or money, or perhaps both. But Fanny—the countess—refused to press charges. So the guards had to let her go. I never saw Mistress Woods after that."

Coke nodded rather absently. "But you'd met her before, near Windrush."

"Yes," Kat agreed. "It was a chance meeting."

"I see." Again the chief justice spoke indifferently. "And Mistress Anne Turner?"

Kat's expression was blank. "Who?"

"Anne Turner," repeated Coke. "Her brother, Eustace Norton, is the royal falconer."

"Really?" It was Kat's turn to sound disinterested.

"Really." Now Sir Edward spoke dryly. "You know Mistress Turner?"

"I don't think so," replied Kat. "I may have met her at court, but I really don't remember..."

Sir Edward's voice began to rise, echoing in the confines of the sumptuous chamber. "And both Mistress Woods and Mistress Turner were purveyors of potions that could induce love—and death." The cold blue eyes bore into Kat.

"Oh!" Kat's hands flew to her face. "They were? But I never...why, I scarcely spoke with Mistress Woods, and as for Mistress Turner, I hardly recall..."

Edward Coke jumped to his feet with the alacrity of a much lighter and younger man. "Save your denials!" he roared, jamming a blunt thumb in the direction of Kat's anxious face. "You were seen speaking with Mary Woods near Windrush, you met with Mistress Turner and her brother here in London, you have often been seen in the company of a Bohemian Gypsy who dabbles in magic and sleight of hand! You visited Thomas Overbury the day before he died, having your lady mother bribe the lord lieutenant of the Tower into letting you see the poor prisoner to ensure that he would pass away before another day was out! Deny any of this, and I shall produce a dozen witnesses who will testify to the contrary!" Coke paused to take a breath. His impressive velvet-clad figure loomed over Kat. "Well?" he rumbled. "What say you now?"

Kat's hands slid from her pale cheeks to her breast. She felt like a doe caught in a snare. Visions from the past floated through her mind: of the brightly dressed figure in the pointed hat by the packhorse bridge, of Eustace Norton introducing his widowed sister, of Sir Gervase Elwes complaining about his wages, of Thomas Overbury, rail-thin and naked, writhing on the floor of the Bloody Tower....

"This is stupid," said Kat, jerkily getting to her feet and confronting Sir Edward. "I refuse to be browbeaten. Why would I poison Sir Thomas? His imprisonment virtually nullified our betrothal. Even his father agreed to that. Look elsewhere for your murderer, sir. I had nothing to do with this heinous crime."

Sir Edward snorted. "Nor with the untimely demise of our beloved Prince Henry?"

Kat's jaw dropped. She could scarcely frame her protest. "Henry! How dare you!" She gasped and took a backward step, almost stumbling over the footstool.

Edward Coke smirked. "You were jealous. Of Fanny Howard, or so I'm told. He preferred her charms to yours. So you poisoned him. And then," he went on, that booming voice building, "you wanted to make sure you could avoid Thomas Overbury's bed because he preferred having a man in it! So you killed him, too!"

Kat reeled. The accusations against her were sufficient to cause a lesser female to swoon. But the allegation concerning Overbury struck her dumb. She gaped at Coke, a trembling hand searching for the support of the footstool behind her. "He...*what?*"

"Come, come," coaxed Sir Edward, dropping his voice a few notches. "Surely you knew that Sir Thomas shared Robin Carr's favors with the king? What's the harm? Some men, including our sovereign lord, are like that."

Dimly, Kat recalled Elizabeth's comment that Overbury was not one to pursue the ladies of the court. With a vague sense of anger, Kat wondered if Elizabeth had known the truth. Not that it mattered now. Kat ran her hands through her hair, displacing the slashed felt riding hat she had worn on her journey. It floated to the floor, the jaunty plumes drooping on the Moorish carpet.

"Good God Almighty," she murmured. "Who hates me so?"

Sir Edward guffawed. "No one, my lady. We only seek the truth from those who know the facts. Just be thankful that we have no real evidence in the matter of Prince Henry.

Of course," he added lightly, "we have no need, with such testimony regarding Thomas Overbury well accredited."

Kat was despondent, but not yet defeated. "This is farcical," she declared. "What," she asked, with a defiant toss of her head, "do you intend to do now?"

Implacable, self-satisfied, Sir Edward again folded his arms across his velvet doublet. "You will be formally charged and escorted to the Tower. Then you will be tried, no doubt convicted, and executed." He shook his carefully cultivated beard. "English justice is fair—and swift."

Within her breast, Kat's heart sank. English justice was those things and more. It was also often mistaken. Sir Walter Raleigh was a sad case in point. "May I go to the chapel and pray first?" she asked, appealing to Coke with her wideset green eyes.

He waved a magnanimous hand. "Of course, of course. We are ever merciful. Fifteen minutes, that is all. I, of course, shall accompany you."

"Of course," agreed Kat. She gave Coke a swift, sidelong glance. He might be quick to get out of a chair, but he probably couldn't run more than ten feet without turning purple. Assuming a docile manner, she allowed him to lead her from the chamber and toward the chapel royal. In the open space outside the Cockpit, Kat took her chance. She stopped abruptly, bent down as if to inspect her footgear, and then swerved, racing back toward the palace proper. Coke swore, then started after her. But Kat had judged rightly; the king's chief justice was no longer fleet of foot. Kat was inside the palace and down the passageway before Coke could get through the door.

She had no idea how to find Stefan Dvorak. Fleetingly, she wished she had prayed first, asking for divine guidance. Instead, she raced along the corridors until she reached the tiltyard. There she found two young boys playing shuttlecock in the twilight. Hoping against hope, she tried to keep her voice casual as she inquired after the foreign gentleman from Bohemia. The lads returned blank faces. Kat's heart plummeted. She started back inside the palace, frantic and frightened. She almost fainted when she ran straight into Stefan Dvorak's arms.

Chapter Nine

"**Y**ou should have known," he said a few minutes later as they hurried toward the river, "that I wouldn't have abandoned you to that brute's clutches. But I couldn't watch too closely. He might have had his minions waiting for me."

"Oh, Stefan," gasped Kat, clinging to his arm, "what are we going to do? He even accused you of being an accomplice!"

"That comes as no surprise," remarked Dvorak, signaling to a bargeman and glancing over his shoulder to make sure they weren't yet being followed. "You English never trust a foreigner. No doubt Coke and his ilk think Overbury was poisoned by Gypsy lore."

"No," breathed Kat, watching the bargeman's torch flicker in the oncoming darkness. "He spoke of Mary Woods and Anne Turner and . . . I forget."

Behind them, urgent shouts floated down to the river. Stefan pulled Kat onto the bobbing craft, then urged the bargeman to make haste. With agonizing slowness, the barge drifted out onto the Thames, heading downriver.

Kat looked up toward Whitehall, where the flames of a half-dozen torches could be seen heading for the quay. "They can't be sure we went this way," Stefan said to Kat, a hand on her shoulder. "We'll head for Tilbury, then take horses to the coast."

Kat, who was still nervously watching the scramble of lights at the river's edge, barely heard him. "Can't the guards commandeer a swifter craft?" she asked with apprehension.

"That would take time," he replied as they bobbed along past Lambeth Marsh. "If they're sure we escaped by barge, they'd be better off to go by land and try to stop us when we disembark. That's why we're going all the way to Tilbury. They would probably guess we'd leave the river at Southwark and cross back over London Bridge."

The hint of a smile touched Kat's lips as she craned her head to look up at Stefan. "Mayhap you *can* read people's minds. At least I hope so."

Dvorak grinned, but his eyes were without their usual humor. "So do I," he said.

To Kat's relief, the torches had faded from view. The barge slipped around the bend in the river, with the lights above the Strand reflected in the pale, black waters. For the first time since the king's men had come for her, Kat relaxed, just a little.

In the dawn, with fog rolling in off the North Sea and the tang of salt in the air, Kat was amazed to find a ship ready to set sail for Ostend. She was even more astounded when Stefan produced papers for their passage.

Once aboard, she found herself staring incredulously at her savior. "However did you manage all this?" she inquired, even as the fog began to evaporate and the crew prepared to lift anchor.

He gave a slight shrug. "It was simple enough, actually. I was already planning to leave today. You remember Lady Harington, the electress's governess?"

"Of course," replied Kat as the breeze stirred her tangled hair. "She is a most kind lady who has suffered tragic losses of late. Both her husband and her son died within weeks of each other."

"Exactly," Dvorak nodded. "She had returned to England from Heidelberg for the christening of her grandchild. But tragedy struck. Lady Harington has not yet recovered from the double blow. I suggested to her that Elizabeth might be well pleased to have you take her place. Thus, you will be chaperoned, since there are other courtiers bound for the Palatine court."

Above them the sails billowed and filled as the ship edged out to sea. Kat was still gaping at Dvorak. "But... how could you know I'd go?"

"Rumor told me you would need to," he answered, shifting his weight on the slanting deck. "I took precautions. I misliked Coke's intentions. It seemed to me that someone had been whispering in his ear."

"Who?" demanded Kat.

But Dvorak shook his head. "Again, I can't be absolutely sure. The real murderer, probably. I doubt that it was Sir Nicholas Overbury. Had you been brought to trial, I suspect he would have testified in your defense."

Leaning on the rail, Kat sighed deeply. "Just a few hours ago, I was on the brink of going to the Tower. Now I'm headed for Heidelberg. Oh, dear!" she exclaimed, turning to Stefan in alarm, "what of my parents? How can I reassure them of my whereabouts?"

As ever, Dvorak was unruffled. "Lady Harington will inform them. She planned to return to Combe Abbey, so will pass by Windrush shortly. As for Edward Coke, I doubt that he'll exert further effort to arrest you. He will not want to admit he was hoodwinked by a slip of a girl."

"But," protested Kat as England began to recede on the horizon, "he thinks I poisoned Overbury!"

"For all his years, Coke is still an impulsive man," explained Dvorak. "He acted precipitately. Cooler heads, such as Francis Bacon's, will prevail."

Kat hoped so. Yet on the face of it, Sir Edward's evidence had been damning. Whoever had brought him so many bits and pieces that tied her to the crime had certainly laid the groundwork well. Kat wondered who the viper could be. But Stefan wouldn't tell her, and now, headed for a foreign land, she might never know. Tears of regret—for leaving her parents, Windrush, England, everything familiar and dear—sprang into her eyes. Yet, as she caught Dvorak's outline from the corner of her eye, she felt strangely comforted. A foreigner he might be, but a stranger he was not. If Kat must be cast adrift, she found unexpected consolation in the fact that Stefan Dvorak was at her side.

More than a dozen courtiers made up the party headed for the Continent. With favorable winds, the crossing would take no more than a day. Kat was to share a tiny cabin with Elizabeth Apsley, the electress's maid of honor, who had spent the summer back in England with her family. And, she confided to Kat once they were settled in, to find a husband.

"German men are intolerable," sniffed Bess. "They expect wives to wait on them like Nubian slaves." Her plump little body quivered with indignation. "Anne Dudley has married Colonel Schomberg, who thinks he runs the Palatinate. Let's see how he runs that shrew of an Anne! Schomberg has even dared to lecture our princess about economy! Imagine the temerity of foreigners! I was very glad to spend some time at home, I'll tell you that!"

Briefly, Bess's wagging tongue ran down. Kat remembered her vaguely from the weeks she'd spent at court upon the occasion of the royal wedding. She was a buoyant girl, but not overly bright, as Kat recalled, and poles apart from Anne Dudley's calm, intellectual demeanor. It was no wonder that the two young women apparently didn't get along.

"...so I said to Anne, 'Just because you're now a countess, you think you can speak to me in such a high-handed way. Well, think again, Lady Fancy-Boots. I won't put up with...'" Bess rattled on, giving Kat a headache.

Somehow Kat managed to extricate herself from the diatribe. Even though she was extremely tired, she knew there would be no chance to sleep until Bess Apsley had worn herself out. Claiming a need to catch the fresh sea breezes, Kat made her way up onto the deck, which was almost deserted except for the watch and a lone figure standing at the rail.

"Stefan," Kat called softly, walking as fast as the rolling deck would permit. "My fellow passenger babbles like a brook. If I had a ball of cotton wool, I'd stuff it in her mouth."

He turned, giving Kat a crooked grin. "The Apsley? I believe she was sent home so that the electress could rest her ears. A good-hearted wench, though. A pity no match could be made for her while she stayed in England."

Kat clung to the rail, watching the black, heaving sea pitch the ship from side to side. "Oh, I don't know. Too much fuss is made over marriage. Not every woman needs a man."

At her side, Dvorak shifted an inch or so nearer to Kat. "Really? I've yet to meet a lass who didn't pine for a husband and children." He had turned serious, though Kat thought she caught a flicker of humor in his black eyes. "Except, of course, for you."

Kat lifted her chin. "I took a vow. And," she asserted, meeting his gaze head-on, "I've kept it."

"So you have." His expression did not change. Silently, he studied the oval-shaped face with its wide mouth, pert nose and brilliant green eyes. The bud of beauty he had first seen over five years ago had not yet blossomed. The promise was still there, smoldering innocently behind those long-lashed eyes and deep within the curving bosom. Strange, he thought, how he'd almost—but not quite—forgotten how appealing she was in her prim, self-imposed virginity. Deliberately, he put his arm around her neck and drew her closer. "But why?"

Kat stiffened at his nearness. "Why what?" Her voice was breathless.

His face was a scant two inches from hers. "Why keep such a reckless vow? Whom do you punish? Yourself? Or all the men who would want you?"

"What men?" Kat demanded, sounding surprisingly cross. "I've noticed no path beaten to Windrush's door."

"You barred the way." Casually, he brushed his lips across hers. "Who would dare assault such a citadel?"

"I'm not a citadel," Kat protested, trying to lean away from him. "I'm a virtuous maid, content with my studies and my horses and my..." She faltered, her mind going suddenly blank.

"Rabbits?" suggested Dvorak, putting his other arm around her waist. The wind rippled through their garments; the waves whispered secrets from the sea.

"Rabbits!" gasped Kat. "You compared women to rabbits! I'd almost forgotten!"

He nudged his noise against hers. "But you didn't. So you must have remembered me as well, eh, little Kat? Did you remember...this?" He brought his mouth down on hers with tantalizing slowness, savoring her lips, touching her tongue. Kat's resistance was feeble. She remembered all too well, but memory had played her false. Dvorak's embrace was more than stirring, deeper than passing pleasure. Kat's pent-up emotions flooded her senses, overtaking her will and inciting a response that startled him as much as it did her. With clutching hands and eager lips, she returned his ardor, clinging to his kisses, feeling the muscles of his back and shoulders, relishing the sensation of his body pressed against hers.

Both surprised and elated by her passion, Stefan let his hands outline her hips, her buttocks, her waist, and at last her breasts, full and taut beneath the serge of her traveling gown. Shuddering with delight, Kat felt a flame kindle deep inside, as if her very soul had been ignited. She let her head fall back, accepting Stefan's kisses along the curve of her throat, even as his fingers teased the tips of her breasts. As thrilling as this moment was, and as far beyond what memory had anticipated, Kat knew intuitively that there was more. She dug her fingernails into the fabric of Dvorak's leather jerkin, urging him to lead her to that mysterious, elusive goal.

The odd sound that Kat dimly heard over the beating of her heart and the song of the wind was the creaking of the ship or the snapping of the sails. Or so she thought at first, until abruptly, Dvorak loosened his grip and spoke over Kat's head in a faintly disconcerted voice. "Sir Henry! I didn't see you approach." For once Dvorak did not sound quite so sure of himself.

"So I gathered," replied the other man dryly. "One does hate to intrude, but the matter is somewhat urgent." He looked apologetically at Kat, who had twisted around in Stefan's arms to observe the newcomer.

Sir Henry Wotton was an ordinary-looking man with extraordinary slate gray eyes and a reputation for keen wit. He had been the ambassador to Venice for a number of years, but still kept in close touch with events in England. Wotton was one of the few courtiers that Sir Edgar liked and respected.

"There may be little opportunity to speak privately during our sojourn," Sir Henry began as Kat and Stefan reluctantly broke apart. "While in London, I heard disturbing news about you, Lady Katherine. For the sake of my old friendship with your father, I felt the need to make inquiries." Though his voice was as bland as his expression, the gray eyes were animated.

Kat swallowed hard. "About Thomas Overbury?"

Wotton inclined his head. "A sad affair. Not," he insisted, spreading his hands, "that I think you had anything to do with his unfortunate demise. Ned Coke can be a bullheaded fool. But there may be a method to his madness. If," he added with a lift of his thick graying eyebrows, "you understand my meaning."

Stefan intervened, and slipped his arm protectively around Kat's shoulders. "He questioned Lady Kat. Most harshly."

Wotton nodded. "I heard he intended to do so. That's why I was surprised to see Lady Kat on board this ship. I feared she might have been bound for an uglier destination." He gave Kat and Dvorak his bland, yet sympathetic smile. "But Coke did not act on his own. You know that, I'm sure."

"I guessed as much," said Kat, with a swift glance up at Stefan. "Who urged him on?"

Wotton's expression remained innocuous. "Who urges us all? And who finds Windrush a most enchanting property? His majesty, of course."

Kat stared at Sir Henry. "King James? Oh!" She edged closer to Stefan. "Is this a plot to gain my family home?"

Wotton shrugged his ermine-trimmed shoulders. "That's merely part of it. But if you were guilty of poisoning Overbury, then King James could rightfully confiscate Windrush."

Kat's jaw hardened. "For himself? Or Robin Carr?"

Wotton laughed. "My dear, you have been away from court too long! Robin is no longer the king's fair-haired darling. Now it's that Villiers pup, young George. He's even more acquisitive than Carr. I trust your parents are on their guard."

Helplessly, Kat turned to Dvorak. "How could they know? What will happen in my absence? Oh, Stefan, I should never have left England!"

Stefan looked grim. "You had no choice. Your father and mother will have to fend for themselves."

Kat let out a deep sigh. "It's all my fault...I did nothing wrong, yet I'm to blame. Heaven help me, I can't let the king steal Windrush!"

Sir Henry stroked his short, full beard and eyed Kat with compassion. "You have two formidable allies," he remarked.

Wotton again inclined his head, his eyes on the scatter of stars above the restless sea. "The electress. And the truth. You know the one well. The other you must still search out."

Kat, with Dvorak's arm still around her, stood very straight. "And I will, Sir Henry. I promise you that. I will not lose Windrush for lack of resolution."

The keen gray eyes probed Kat's face. "No," agreed Sir Henry. "I didn't think you would."

Heidelberg Castle was as handsome as Elizabeth had boasted. Its cluster of rose-colored sandstone buildings clung to a hill overlooking the town. Like Windrush, it had originally been constructed as a fortress rather than a home. But subsequent centuries had tamed the structure, with sprawling additions including the new ballroom that Frederick was building for his wife's pleasure. Kat was impressed, not only by the rosy-hued castle, but by the charming town that nestled along the cheerful Neckar

River. The marketplace, the university, the Church of the Holy Ghost and the old bridge with its quaint towers brought murmurs of appreciation from most of the English party. Indeed, the fruitfulness of the Rhine, the lush vineyards of the Palatinate, the earnest hospitality of Frederick's subjects had made the journey most pleasant. In spite of herself, Kat was impressed.

Climbing the steep road that led up to the castle, they passed over a covered drawbridge. The gateway before them was adorned with heroic statues of prancing lions and armored knights. Inside the walls, Kat recognized a collection of buildings, erected in different styles and eras. She was about to comment to Stefan about the eclectic yet harmonious architecture when a hunting party appeared below them on the road, dressed in bright colors and emanating high spirits.

"It's the elector and the electress," Stefan said, gazing down to where the gold and red leaves of the linden trees shaded the jaunty group as they made their way up the hill.

Recognizing Elizabeth in the lead, Kat smiled. "She is with child again, yet see how she rides. Bess defies nature, it seems."

"But not her father," murmured Stefan. "Yet."

Kat gave him a curious glance, but he said no more. In the week since they had docked at Flushing, she had seen little of him. Without so much as a word of discussion, it had been assumed that Kat would keep to the company of the other ladies in the party, rather than with the foreigner who had brought her aboard ship. Reluctantly, Kat had accepted the decision. But she had been disappointed, her senses brought alive by the renewed promise of Stefan's embrace.

And now they were at journey's end. Kat watched eagerly as she heard rather than saw the approach of the horses over the covered drawbridge.

"Bess!" she gasped, and beamed at the pert figure who was the first to emerge into the autumn sunshine. The electress was garbed in jonquil and rose, with a high-crowned hat set at a rakish angle, her handsome features radiating good health. So caught up in the excitement of the chase was she that her horse almost ran over Kat, who had dismounted and was waving her arms.

"Sweet Jesus!" cried Elizabeth, reining up while the rest of the hunting party struggled to avoid colliding behind her. "Kat de Vere! Whatever are you doing in Heidelberg?"

Kat remembered to bob a curtsy, but before she could reply, Stefan Dvorak stepped between her and the electress. "Lady Katherine is here to serve your highness. It was thought you would appreciate an old friend as a replacement for Lady Harington."

The Princess Palatine's smile was brilliant. "Baron Ostrov, you've wrought a miracle! No wonder Freddy thinks you're a wizard!"

Edging up beside Elizabeth, Frederick of the Palatinate made a formal bow. He had matured in the intervening years, a boy evolved into a man. His brown hair and swarthy complexion enhanced his virile, if not quite handsome, image. "We are pleased to welcome you, Lady Katherine," he said in accented English. "My wife has never stopped wishing for your company." He turned in the saddle to thirstily quaff wine from a hunting cup held out by a crimson-clad servant. Elizabeth, suddenly remembering her royal duties, raised her gloved hands in greeting to the others. Kat drew back, studying her old friend's regal manner. Elizabeth Stuart had changed, too, from frisky princess to gracious consort. With a burst of introspection, Kat wondered if she, too, had been altered by time. But no, a small voice said, she had merely grown older.

Within a quarter of an hour, Kat was soaking in a tub of hot water while the Princess Palatine lounged on a velvet-covered chaise and devoured a plate of chicken wings. Even as a child, Elizabeth had possessed a prodigious appetite, yet her tall figure remained surprisingly slim, except for the budding life beneath her peignoir.

"Your third baby!" Kat exclaimed, feeling an odd pang of envy. "Shouldn't you abstain from hunting with a child on the way?" There was a trace of reprimand in her voice, a reminder of their former days as playmates.

Elizabeth laughed, shooing one of her numerous hounds off to a satin-covered bed in the far corner of the room. "My bairns learn to hunt even before they're born. I'm stronger than my horses, the doctors say. Besides," she added with the mischievous gleam Kat remembered so well from their adventures at Windrush, "they can't stop me."

Reunited with the colleague of her youth, Kat was undergoing an unaccustomed bout of sentimentality. It hadn't been until she and Elizabeth were left alone in the royal apartments that Kat realized how much she had missed having a friend and confidante.

Elizabeth, however, was off on a different track, her nimble if undisciplined mind grappling with Kat's dilemma. "I am utterly flummoxed at Sir Edward Coke's accusations. He must be getting senile. Indeed, I can scarcely believe that Overbury was poisoned in the first place. It seems like so long ago. Why, he was arrested right about the time Freddy and I left England!" The electress made a face and shook her head. "I'm writing to my father this very day to tell him that you are completely innocent and to keep his avaricious hands off Windrush. Even he wouldn't be silly enough to act otherwise."

Kat emerged from the wooden tub, a thick towel wrapped around her body. "He thought the worst of Raleigh," Kat pointed out. "What I don't understand—and never did— was why Thomas was imprisoned in the first place. Refusing an embassy hardly strikes me as treason."

Elizabeth disposed of the last chicken wing and daintily wiped her fingers on a lace-edged napkin. "You're not my father. Refusing any of his commands is treasonable. He thinks he speaks for God. Or *is* God, if it comes to that. Really, he may be the wisest fool in Christendom, but he's also the most annoying. Sometimes," she added hastily, reminding Kat that even as far away as Heidelberg, King James had ears close to the ground.

Kat hugged the towel closer, then sat down on a lavishly embroidered footstool next to the chaise and the silver platter littered with chicken bones. "My parents must be terribly upset. I shall write to them tonight."

"I suppose," Elizabeth mused, sliding open a small compartment in the little mahogany table next to the chaise, "I should be grateful. At least this misfortune has brought you to Heidelberg. Here, have some sweets. It's marchpane, a great favorite of mine. It always cheers me."

"It tastes like paste," remarked Kat, but accepted a handful of the confectionery, which had been made in the form of various flowers. Elizabeth's indomitable spirit buoyed her. It was, she thought fleetingly, a bit like having Henry back. Yet, she realized, how little she had thought of her prince over these last few years! Time was said to heal all wounds. Surely that was not true for her. Kat suddenly felt guilty.

Elizabeth swallowed a rose, a tulip and a daffodil in one gulp. "Let's talk no more of troublesome matters. My lady mother is a-dying, my father plays the fool, I haven't seen my little brother in five years. I've been agonizingly impatient to ask you about Baron Ostrov," she said with her mouth full and her blue eyes wide. "How did he come to rescue you?"

"By chance." Kat sampled a marchpane daisy and looked unwontedly prim. "He was returning to the Continent and arranged for my passage. He's actually very kind.

And civilized," she added, and wondered why she felt the necessity to say so.

"Hal knew him at Oxford and Freddy regards him highly, but he looks a proper devil to me," said the electress, sorting through the remaining candies. "My lady mother found him a great source of amusement."

"He's clever," said Kat in a bit of a mumble. Even to Elizabeth, Kat was not yet ready to reveal the emotions Dvorak had stirred within her. She needed time to reflect, to think, to discover why Stefan Dvorak seemed able to alter her disciplined outlook on life, even to restore her sense of laughter. "I believe he's had an unfortunate life," Kat added in what she hoped was an indifferent tone. Suddenly anxious to change the subject, she became practical. "Do you really think I can replace Lady Harington, at least for a time?"

Like Kat, Elizabeth was seldom less than forthright. The electress stuffed two more pieces of marchpane into her mouth and regarded Kat levelly. "No one can replace her. But you will be yourself and that's all I ask." Unexpectedly, her eyes glittered with tears. "In fact, there are two vacancies in my train. Anne Dudley, who married dear Count Schomberg, died a fortnight after giving birth. I've already asked my royal sire to appoint someone else." The electress sighed. "I miss Dudley terribly, but at least there will be less discord. She and Bess Apsley were always at sixes and sevens. I trust my father will send an amiable soul to take Dudley's place." In a sudden, typical shift of moods, Elizabeth dabbed at her eyes and all but bounced up and down on the chaise longue. "Oh, Kat, we shall have such wonderful times together! The new baby is coming, my two boys are a delight, the grape harvest has been wonderful, there will be festivals and visits to the Upper Palatinate, and the hunting is always excellent! The most beautiful books in the world are at Hornberg Castle, and

Dilsberg has a knightly ghost! We can explore all these things, Kat, and laugh away the night, just as we did at Windrush!" She stood up and stretched, the fruitful curve of her belly jutting beneath the sheer silk robe de chambre. "Come, let us find you clothing and get you fed." She paused in front of a gilt-edged mirror, inspecting the tiniest of blemishes on her otherwise perfect complexion. "What about your Stefan? Did he try to make love to you?"

Kat stiffened. Elizabeth's unfettered tongue suddenly irked her. "He's been very helpful," she declared, grateful that her friend was absorbed in the mirror. "For a foreigner, he's remarkably well-bred, as I said. Why, he's no different from you or me."

Elizabeth wrinkled her nose at the dreaded blemish. "Oh, yes, he is." Her blue eyes danced. "In case you haven't noticed, he's a man."

Kat knew that all too well.

Chapter Ten

The Elector Frederick was training a new gyrfalcon, and having little success. The young German prince slipped the hood from the bird's eyes, but could not get it to leave his arm. Frederick swore, then reached with his free hand for a silver goblet all but overflowing with a fine white wine from the vineyards of Castle Schaubeck.

"Here, highness," offered Stefan Dvorak, adjusting the band on the bird's left talon. He spoke to the gyrfalcon softly in Rom, then stepped back. Flapping its wings, the bird took flight, soaring above the castle walls.

"What magic words were those?" Frederick demanded, his swarthy features faintly suspicious. "I know of no such language."

"The language is unimportant," replied Dvorak easily. "It's the tone that matters. Talk to the gyrfalcon as you would talk to your ladylove. The results will be equally rewarding."

Frederick drank deeply of the wine and gave Dvorak a surprisingly engaging smile. "Ah, of love I understand! But then I've been blessed with my beautiful Elizabeth."

"You have indeed," Stefan agreed as the gyrfalcon circled above them, a bright spring morning with sparse clouds blowing off to the north and the sun warm enough to remind its admirers that winter was still being held at bay.

The paddock was a busy place, the hub of the castle's equestrian passions. "Thus far, you have led a charmed life."

"You are most gracious," Frederick murmured, signaling for a lackey to refill his goblet. "We are pleased to have you join us as our ambassador from Bohemia."

Dvorak shot a puzzled glance at the young elector. Perhaps Frederick's mistake was due in part to the absence of Colonel Schomberg, who was away on business in Heilbronn. Dvorak had served as the elector's eyes and ears for several years, in England and on the continent. His capacity was unofficial, but indispensable. It was also a secret, known only to Frederick and Colonel Schomberg. Even Christian of Anhalt-Bernburg, Frederick's uncle and chancellor, was unaware of Dvorak's role. At the moment, Prince Anhalt was near the kennel, absorbed in conversation with Dr. Abraham Schultz, the royal chaplain.

"I'm only passing through, your highness," said Stefan. "I have never held an official capacity. You've merely asked me to keep you informed. Remember, we first met when I was a student at Oxford and you were wooing the electress in England."

Frederick looked up from his goblet just as the gyrfalcon swooped down onto his hand. "Ah! England! My lady wife and I were supposed to visit there this past summer. But she is enceinte again. So home we stay. And glad I am. Her royal sire makes me nervous." His brown eyes had grown troubled, if faintly unfocused.

Stefan grimaced. The elector's mind seemed as cloudy as his eyes. "You also wish news of Bohemia," Stefan said carefully. "I am going there almost at once."

"Prague? Some call it the crossroads of Europe. Would I like it there, I wonder? Would Elizabeth?" The elector's attitude was more whimsical than practical. He was adjusting the gyrfalcon's hood, spilling some of his wine in the process. He giggled, then handed the bird over to a groom. "We'll test this one in the field tomorrow," he announced, shaking wine drops from his sleeve before turning back to Dvorak. "What's happening in Prague? Is Count Thurn truly in control?"

Dvorak refrained from gnashing his teeth in the face of Frederick's naiveté. "I haven't been in Prague for over six months." He nodded toward Christian of Anhalt, whose handsome blond head was still bent close to the black flat cap worn by the royal chaplain. "Your chancellor must have the latest reports."

"He should," Frederick replied carelessly. "It's his responsibility, after all. The Elector of Saxony and I have been asked to intervene with the troubles there. I can't think why. Do you suppose old Matthias is dying?"

"He's been ill for some time," Stefan pointed out, trying to mask his astonishment at the elector's lack of knowledge about the tenuous political situation across his frontier. "Of course his cousin, Ferdinand of Styria, has already been appointed his successor as King of Bohemia."

"Ferdinand!" Frederick scoffed. He took another drink and spat on the ground. "He's—how do the English put it?—poor as the churchmouse, also blind in one eye and can't see out of the other. So says my Elizabeth. Pah!" He spat again.

Stefan recognized the futility of trying to clarify the political upheaval in Bohemia with Frederick. "Matthias is concerned primarily with religious suitability," he said somewhat tersely. "Ferdinand is a Catholic."

Frederick was requesting yet another refill of his goblet. Dvorak glanced at Anhalt to see if he was monitoring his master's consumption, but the chancellor and Dr. Schultz had wandered off toward the dovecotes.

"Ferdinand is a fool," the elector was saying in a voice that had grown fuzzy. "He's likely to be made Holy Roman Emperor, as well as King of Bohemia, damn his homely hide." Frederick teetered a bit on his heels. "Not right for one man to make another king in his own lifetime. Stupid idea. Stupid Matthias. Stupid world." The swarthy face grew very dark, all previous signs of good cheer replaced by gloom. The elector lurched, then threw the half-empty goblet across the paddock, startling a pair of nuzzling yearlings.

At that moment, Kat and Elizabeth rode in through the outer gate. Taking in the scene, the Princess Palatine didn't wait for assistance, but jumped from her mare and rushed to meet her husband.

"Milord!" she exclaimed, her dazzling smile in place, "we've been to Mosbach! The townspeople gave us two bushels of tasty apples! Kat picked a whole bushel by herself!"

Slowly, Frederick's eyes came into focus. "Apples? Oh, marvelous! I'm fond of apples." Although the elector was a well-built young man, he was of average height, not more than a half inch taller than his willowy wife. His knees buckled briefly, and he leaned against Elizabeth like a weary child. "Let's go inside, sweet Bess. I've an ague."

"Of course, my love. They do beset you at such inconvenient times." Still smiling, she wrapped an arm around his waist, leading him toward the castle. "We'll dine on apples and dream of the babe to come. Who could ask for more?"

Kat, who had also dismounted, was watching the royal couple with a curious, concerned expression. She wanted to ask Dvorak what was wrong, but all she could think of were his kisses. In the four days since their arrival at Heidelberg, she had seen him only at table with the other courtiers. Vexed at his failure to seek her out, Kat pretended she hadn't noticed him, and started to head back toward the castle.

"Little Kat." Stefan's voice was low but commanding.

Reluctantly, Kat turned, and to her horror, realized she was blushing. "I must go change," she blurted. "I'm covered with dust." As a distraction, she started to tug off her kid gloves, saw the scratches from the apple tree branches on her hands and quickly yanked them back on.

"I'm about to ride out," Stefan replied, not quite as at ease as was his custom. He took Kat by the arm, steering her out of hearing range of the milling servants. "The elector is drunk, in case you were about to ask." He no longer tried to conceal his disgust.

"Ride out where?" Kat barely noted what Stefan had said concerning the elector's condition.

"For Prague." Dvorak didn't look at Kat, but seemed to be studying a pair of doves roosting under a chimney.

Kat felt her pink cheeks turn pale. "I thought you planned to stay in Heidelberg," she said, hating the petulant tone in her voice.

"I never said that." With a frown, he finally gazed at Kat. "My homeland is headed for civil war. I can't sit here in the Palatinate and pull cards out of my sleeve. Besides," he went on, suddenly sounding unusually formal, "Frederick desires firsthand news."

"Frederick desires another drink, from the looks of it," Kat asserted angrily, though deep down she knew her temper had not been ignited by the elector, but by Dvorak. "So you're heading out, just . . . like that?"

"That's the way I live," Stefan replied, wishing the grooms and stablehands and other retainers would evaporate. The wind had changed, and overhead, gray clouds began to drift in from the east. It occurred to Stefan that the weather wasn't the only thing that was changing. For all of his adult life, he had been accountable to no man—or woman. At least not on a personal level. Yet here was this little English chit, about to upbraid him for not discussing his departure. It was ridiculous. It was annoying. It was also making him feel uncharacteristically guilty.

"See here," he said, keeping his voice low and jabbing at Kat with a forefinger, "I come, I go. It's my nature. In this case, it's my duty as well. The Protestant majority in Bohemia is being ground under by the Catholic minority. But if Matthias dies, the will of the people may be able to challenge the new emperor. Even though Ferdinand has already been named king of our country, and will probably be elected Holy Roman Emperor, defiance runs rampant in Bohemia. Our people could choose our own king and thus—"

"Oh, fie on the emperor and the king!" snapped Kat, waving her riding crop. "Why don't you have hereditary kings and queens like sensible countries do?"

A flicker of amusement flashed in Dvorak's eyes. "Like England, you mean?"

Kat planted her feet apart, stopped wielding the crop and put her fists on her hips. "Well, of course like England!"

A clap of thunder sounded in the distance. The doves took flight and, in the kennel, several dogs began to bark. Stefan planted his forefinger on Kat's nose. "Then why did your sensible country hold its breath for years, waiting for Queen Elizabeth to name her successor? Which, I might add, she never actually did."

Kat, backing away from Stefan's touch, was momentarily flustered. "Everyone knew James would become our king. He was in the direct line of succession, after all."

Dvorak's expression was wry. "Had James been a Catholic, I suspect someone else would have been crowned. The day may come, little Kat, when your orderly English government will find itself as confused as any other. Life's like that. You can't command it to run a certain course."

"*I* can," insisted Kat. "And so can England. We're a very disciplined people."

Lightning flashed, just above the hill where the castle nestled so comfortably. Kat sucked in her breath, waiting for the thunder, which swiftly rolled nearby. Drops of rain began to fall, sending most of the retainers running for cover. Both Kat and Stefan held their ground.

"The fact is," he was now saying in his reasonable manner, "what happens in Bohemia is closely tied to this very place." He gestured expansively, taking in the cluster of buildings that made up the castle, the tree-covered hill, the town below. "Some think Frederick should be named King of Bohemia."

"Frederick!" Kat was temporarily diverted from her pique. "But...do you agree?"

Stefan said nothing. His doubts about the future of Bohemia were not put to rest by the elector's behavior. Reports had indicated that Frederick was not only young, but was inattentive to duty, unusually moody—and, as Dvorak had just seen for himself, overfond of wine.

"The Princess Palatine thinks the world of her husband," Kat was saying in the vacuum left by Stefan's reticence. "They dote on each other."

"She knows how to manage him," Dvorak remarked absently, his thoughts clearly elsewhere.

The rain was now pouring down. Kat felt it pelting her face and her light woolen riding habit. Stefan put his hand on her elbow and steered her toward the castle. Surreptitiously, she glanced up at the chiseled profile. He was going away; it was possible that she'd never see him again. Kat felt a surge of panic.

"Will you be gone long?" She posed the question in a tremulous voice.

His dark eyes were unreadable. "It depends." He let go of her arm, hooking his thumbs in his belt. The distress in

Kat's green gaze and the flush of her smooth cheeks weakened his usual ramrod will. "I'll be back early in the new year." He could scarcely believe his own words; he had not made promises to anyone for almost twenty years. Stefan Dvorak wished he could take the words back, but Kat gave the impression that she was holding them close, like treasured gifts.

They were in an alcove, the door to their backs, the rain pouring down just inches away. Another crackle of lightning, another shudder of thunder made them both pause, gazes locked. "I must go," Stefan murmured, bending down with his hands resting on the stone wall in back of Kat.

"In this deluge?" asked Kat breathlessly.

He shrugged. "It will pass." The black eyes searched her face. "You will be here when I return?"

Kat nodded. He was so near, yet he would soon be gone. She leaned forward, face tipped up. His lips touched hers, tenderly, then with a touch of fire. Kat wrapped her arms around him, willing him to stay. But with the hunger still in his eyes, he broke away and walked purposefully out through the driving rain.

Kat had never felt so alone in her life.

The hunting at Zwingenberg was even better in the fall than in the summer, Elizabeth had told Kat as they cantered along the Neckar River. Boar abounded in the woods that surrounded the thirteenth-century castle. Now, in November, the royal party would seek stags and perhaps a few hare.

The weather was crisp, with the river sparkling in the autumn sun and bright red toadstools sprouting in the grasses. The quaint tollhouses with their curving towers and turrets, the rich vineyards sloping down to the river, the great stone castles perched on high cliffs like huge aeries heightened Kat's appreciation of Elizabeth's adopted homeland. Yet Kat had to make an effort to shake off her cares in order to match Elizabeth's ebullient mood. In the weeks that had passed since Stefan Dvorak's departure for Prague, Kat had discovered loneliness. The separation from her parents was difficult enough, but to her dismay, she found that she missed Stefan even more than Sir Edgar and Lady Beatrice. It was a situation Kat could not have imagined even a month ago.

She had written to her parents twice, but so far had received no reply. Nor had Kat received any word from Stefan Dvorak. She hadn't expected to, and yet she found herself taking heed of every post rider who galloped into Heidelberg Castle. Elizabeth had teased Kat about her keen interest in the dispatches that arrived almost daily. Kat put the electress off by telling her that she was anxious to hear from her mother and father. Elizabeth's own sire had written within the past month, but had not mentioned Kat or Windrush. Instead, he had rambled on about his impecunious circumstances, his new Villiers favorite, whose pet name was Steenie, and that plans moved apace for the match between Prince Charles and the Spanish Infanta. As an afterthought, he mentioned that Queen Anne's health was worsening.

Yet England and its troubles seemed very far away on this crystalline November morning. Within the shadow of Zwingenberg's massive red sandstone walls, the hunting horn sounded, the hounds set off amid raucous barking and the beaters fanned out into the forest to flush their prey. Kat's arrows managed to find their mark on a couple of large rabbits, but it was Elizabeth who brought down a six-point stag in the middle of a clearing about a half mile from the river. The elector led the applause for his wife, who brandished her crossbow and laughed with exultation.

"A veritable Diana," declared Christian of Anhalt-Bernburg, bringing his gelding up beside Kat's mare. Prince Anhalt was a tall, handsome man of middle age, with impeccable manners and wary eyes. "Do all your fellow countrywomen hunt so well?" he inquired in his precise, guttural English.

"We are a sporting people," said Kat, rearranging her wide-brimmed beaver hat with its high crown and rakish ostrich plumes. With a portion of the wages that the electress had finagled out of Colonel Schomberg, Kat had been able to supplement her wardrobe. "Tennis, bowling, draughts—and golf, since King James came to the throne."

"Enchanting!" exuded Anhalt, with a glance at the huntsmen who were tying the big stag to a pair of saplings. "Our ladies think that sport is unseemly. Of course, despite their personal feelings, they must try to emulate the electress." He dropped his voice as Bess Apsley, Baron Christopher Dohna and Dr. Schultz rode by. "You are fond of the electress, I gather? And she, of you?"

Anhalt's probing gaze put Kat off. She looked straight ahead, as if admiring Elizabeth's fallen quarry. The electress was still elated over her triumph, sharing a stirrup cup with Frederick. "We have been friends since girlhood," Kat responded.

"Just so. You have influence with her, eh?" Anhalt, as ever, sounded jovial.

"I don't know about that." Kat forced a girlish laugh and soothed her restive mare. The hounds had begun to bark as the party prepared to return to Heidelberg.

"How well do you know Baron Ostrov?" inquired Anhalt in his suave manner.

Kat was momentarily blank. "Oh—Stefan Dvorak!" She felt a faint flush on her cheeks. "I met him years ago, when he was a student at Oxford. I never think of him by his title, only his given name."

"Just so," agreed Anhalt as they joined the rear of the hunting party on the sun-dappled road. "He disdains its usage. No wonder, since his properties were confiscated by the emperor years ago. But his family has been prominent over the centuries. It was his father's Hussite religious views that ruined the Dvorak name. And the fact that he married a Gypsy."

Kat pondered Anhalt's revelation. "I gathered as much," she remarked casually. "Certainly he is no mere . . . *Zigeuner*." Where, she asked herself, had she heard that word? Perhaps from Stefan himself? Kat saw his image before her, dark and forceful. She shook herself.

"Stefan Dvorak is an ardent champion of Bohemia," Kat declared.

"So? What does that mean?" Anhalt guided his gelding closer to Kat. "Is it true he supports Frederick as the future king of Bohemia? Is it true that Elizabeth is reluctant to let her husband accept the crown if offered? Come, my dear Lady Katherine, you know these two quite well. A clever woman can learn more than a band of Spanish Inquisitors could." He gave Kat a winning smile.

Puzzled, Kat shot Anhalt a sidelong look. "What do you ask of me, highness? To pry—or spy? You are the elector's uncle, you are this country's chancellor. Surely you know the answers better than I."

Anhalt retained his polished demeanor. "Baron Ostrov keeps his own counsel," he agreed as they wound along the shimmering river. "As for the electress, the man she loves stands on a precipice. Believe me, milady, Frederick needs her whole-hearted support. And in the process, that of her father. Will you help me help them?"

Kat considered her old friend. "Goody Palsgrave," Queen Anne had called her daughter in disdain, convinced that the young elector was an inferior match for the King of England's daughter. But Elizabeth would have no other man as her mate. It occurred to Kat that the electress would make any sacrifice required of her to promote her husband's career and make him happy.

"I can't promise anything," said Kat. "I'm not well versed in court intrigue, if that's what you expect of me."

"Intrigue!" Anhalt's smile was disparaging. "I ask only for encouragement, to make Elizabeth see that her future—and Frederick's—is not limited to the Palatinate. And Baron Ostrov must recognize Freddy's suitability. Oh," he continued, reining in his impatient mount, "my nephew is still young, of course. He has his lapses. But he's a fine fellow, intelligent, hardworking, and, as you can see, prolific. What more could Bohemia want?"

Perplexed, Kat stared down at the green-and-red embroidery on her riding gloves. What more, indeed? It made no difference to Kat if Bohemia chose Frederick of the Palatinate or the Tsar of Russia to run their paltry little country. It sounded to her that whoever was unlucky enough to get the crown would be inheriting a box of bees.

But Kat said nothing more. She would wait and see how Elizabeth felt about becoming a queen. At present, the electress was wrapped up in her family and the baby that was due in less than two months. Elizabeth, like Kat, wasn't particularly interested in politics.

As for Stefan Dvorak, Kat could only wait until he returned to Heidelberg. *If*, she thought, suddenly chilled despite the mellow autumn sun, he returned.

Two weeks later, on November 27, 1618, Elizabeth gave birth to a daughter. Dark like her brothers and her father, she was named for her mother. Kat held the tiny babe and felt an unfamiliar warmth engulf her being. She had never seen, let alone touched, such a small person before. Her cousin Oxford's children hadn't visited Windrush until they were toddlers. Kat never paid much attention to the de Vere tenants' offspring until they were old enough to play in the fields. An infant was a new experience for Kat, and she discovered a heretofore unsuspected emotion when she cradled little Bess against her breast.

On the first day of December, with snow clouds hovering over Konigstuhl, the hill above the castle, Kat heard from her parents. Sir Edgar wrote in veiled terms that all seemed well at Windrush, despite ". . . certain ill humors which blew in from London." Kat assumed that gossip about her near-arrest had traveled to her family home and that her innocence was not yet an accepted fact. "We hear, too, from Sir Nicholas," her father continued, "that the matter regarding his late son has not yet been put to rest. Speculation is rampant, with fingers pointing in divers directions. For his part, Sir Nicholas has his own mind made up, but can prove nothing."

The rest of Sir Edgar's letter recounted the recent harvest, heavy rains and the threat of flooding in the Windrush Valley. Lady Beatrice, more effusive, had added several pages, devoted almost solely to her fervent wish for Kat's safety and early return. Fondly, Kat read and reread the missives, then immediately set pen to paper to reply.

But there was still no word from Stefan Dvorak.

Through the snows, the Yuletide season and into the new year, Kat waited. News trickled across the frontier, mainly to the effect that Bohemia was on the brink of civil war. When fresh reports that Emperor Matthias was near death reached Heidelberg in mid-January, Kat took the opportunity to broach the subject with Elizabeth.

The electress was trying to juggle the new baby in one arm and fend off her pet monkey, Jock-o, with the other. "There are all sorts of candidates besides Ferdinand for the crown of Bohemia. I give not a fig whether Matthias has named him as his heir. Freddy is the ideal choice. Uncle Kit will do his best to secure the crown for him."

The statement was the first that Elizabeth had made to that effect since Stefan Dvorak's departure for Prague. Kat looked up from the mug of hot chocolate she was sipping. "Does Uncle Kit—Prince Anhalt, I should say—know how you feel?"

Jock-o took a swipe at wee Bess, the electress slapped the monkey's backside and both babe and pet began to howl. Elizabeth called for Bess Apsley to remove the two offenders.

"I'm already chief governor to all the monkeys and dogs," complained Bess, though not without humor. "Am I now in charge of the royal nursery as well? By heaven, highness, this castle is a menagerie, a zoo!"

"Yes, yes," agreed Elizabeth, keeping her patience with the loquacious Apsley. "And all its members are dear to me. You, too, Apsley. Now, shoo!"

Bess Apsley, leading Jock-o by his silver-studded collar and clutching the small baby against her shoulder, exited among much clucking and coaxing. Kat waited until the door was closed before she posed her next question. "Bess—you're so happy here in Heidelberg. So is the elector. Do you really want to be queen of Bohemia?"

Elizabeth lifted one shoulder, then nibbled on a slice of candied orange. "Why not? Freddy is head of the Protestant Union of German Princes. Who would serve better? Not Charles Emmanuel of Savoy, not that lazy pig John George of Saxony, not those Catholic candidates, especially not the heir-designate, Ferdinand! He's a vicious anti-Protestant who has already violated the agreement to let the Reformers alone. Even my father will support Freddy. He's said as much in his letters."

Kat stiffened at the mention of King James. Despite Sir Edgar's reassurance, she didn't trust the king an inch. "Has your sire given his word?" Kat asked dubiously.

Elizabeth turned evasive. "He is praying on it," she said, not looking at Kat.

"If I may say so," asserted Kat with her little chin thrust out, "God might be slow to hear him."

Elizabeth's gaze was unusually frosty. "Nonsense. God chose him. He will provide."

Kat stifled a snort of derision. She didn't appreciate Elizabeth's change of attitude. Perhaps, Kat hoped, like the winter snows, it would pass.

At Herr von Imhoff's secluded castle not far from the German border, a servant carved a haunch of venison while Stefan Dvorak and Albrecht Wallenstein drank beer from tall tankards and eyed each other with mutual wariness.

It was very quiet. They could hear the lowing of the cows, brought down from the Alpine pastures for the winter. Their host had retired to join his wife in a game of backgammon. Herr von Imhoff did not know the names of his guests, only that the Bishop of Innsbruck had provided them with safe conduct. Imhoff never inquired after his visitors' identities. He was a lawyer who knew when to ask the right questions, and when to ask none at all.

"In three years," said Wallenstein, slicing a piece of *roggenbrot* from the fresh-baked loaf, "you have been all over Europe."

Stefan slit open a roasted potato. One of their host's hunting hounds, smelling the meat, struggled up on uncertain legs and loped over to the table. "You have not been idle, either, Brecht," Stefan remarked.

Wallenstein's sallow face darkened. "I might as well have been. The Protestants are threatening to confiscate my property. Perhaps we'll both end up impoverished, Stefan."

"It's possible." The glint of satisfaction in Stefan's eyes was tempered by a sympathetic shake of his head. "We could both be sent packing, like a pair of wandering Roms." He tossed a bone to the hound, who gave a feeble bark of gratitude. "You still have your commission in the imperial army, I gather?"

"Certainly," Wallenstein replied a trace testily. "Matthias is near death."

Stefan chewed thoughtfully on a piece of venison. "And Ferdinand waits in the wings."

"But the majority despises him." Wallenstein cut a turnip in half. His brown-eyed gaze was irritable, like a man who has exchanged gold for dross. "They will try to set one of their own kind in his place. Will England send troops to fight for the Protestant cause?"

The hound had finished with the bone, depositing it under Stefan's chair. Surfeited, the animal ambled back to the hearth and resumed its place in front of the fire. Stefan watched the flames dance in the grate, sending sparks up the massive stone chimney. "King James will not spend a ha'penny on a Calvinist cause," he said at last. "He will promise the moon and deliver only moonbeams. The man genuinely deplores war, but more to the point, his purse is lean, and what he has he'll squander on his pleasures."

"The Dutch are worth ten times the English," declared Wallenstein with unusual fervor. "Is the emperor assured of England's neutrality?"

Stefan gave Wallenstein a wry smile. "Not if Prince Charles marries the Infanta. Spain would give its backing to Frederick of the Palatinate. It would be all in the family, you see."

In an uncharacteristic gesture, Wallenstein flung his knife across the room, startling the old hounds out of their deathlike sleep. "Spain be damned! Philip is a Hapsburg, too! He wouldn't betray his cousins!"

Dvorak shrugged. "It could happen. But it won't."

Wallenstein had quickly regained control. He rested his hands on the table, regarding Stefan with judicious eyes. "Are you sure?"

"Reasonably." The gazes of the two men locked and held. It was an unconscious yet familiar exchange to both of them.

Wallenstein took a drink from his tankard and gave his cousin a thin smile. "Who do you support as king of Bohemia, Stefan?"

Dvorak's mouth set in a tight line. "The best man. Whoever he may be."

"You mean the Elector Frederick?"

"Did I say that?" His heavy eyebrows lifted slightly, then he drained his own tankard and pushed away from the table. "I'm going now, Brecht. I've come a great distance out of my way to meet you here. For naught, it seems. I thought you might have changed your mind."

"You haven't changed yours." Wallenstein got to his feet. "It's late, Stefan; it's snowing. Why are you in such a hurry?" His voice held a note of supplication. "We could talk the night away, philosophize, theorize, the way we used to do at Falkenau. Even then we rarely agreed, eh?" Wallenstein uttered a little laugh, one hand making a mock jab at Dvorak's midsection.

"Those days are gone forever, Brecht." Stefan sounded suddenly weary. He picked up the *schiavona* and sheathed it at his hip. "I think it will be best if we don't meet again."

"Stefan!" For all that he was the elder, a hardened soldier and a leader of men, Wallenstein's voice broke. "Soon, maybe in a few months, this will all be settled! We can sit on the banks of the Moldau and laugh about our adventures! All our differences won't mean a thing!"

Stefan put a hard hand on Wallenstein's shoulder. The black gaze was steady, though tinged with sadness. "That's the trouble with you, Brecht. It *won't* mean anything—to you. Nothing does. You fight because you have a knack for it. But you have no cause, only a master. I would give anything to see you embrace your Bohemian brothers and lead us into battle. With you as our general, we would win."

Wallenstein looked away, into the long shadows of the dining hall with its fine tapestries and rich paneled walls. "I can't." Slowly, almost painfully, his brown eyes returned to Stefan's face. "You know I can't. I despise rebellion under any name. And I'm a Catholic."

Stefan dropped his hand. "That much is between you and God. But you're a Bohemian as well. So am I. We are much alike." He fingered the cat's-head pommel on his sword. "But not enough."

He left Wallenstein in the flickering firelight, with the hounds still sleeping and the snow piling up against the windows of the schloss. Above the village of Alpbach, the great mountains rose to touch the sky. Dvorak knew he should head back to Prague, where trouble flowed as freely as the Moldau. But he had a promise to keep. He saddled his horse and rode through the night toward the German frontier.

Chapter Eleven

Sir Henry Wotton had finally left the comforts of Heidelberg and gone on to his post in Italy. He had left behind his nephew, Albert Morton, as the electress's new secretary. Kat found Albert a clever, amusing young man who was anxious to please not only his new mistress, but her attendants as well. He was also unmarried, and Elizabeth had been weaving a fantasy in which Kat and Albert made a happy match.

"He's good-natured, well-spoken, gentle and kind," the electress said as they prepared for the ball that would belatedly celebrate the new baby's birth and Elizabeth and Frederick's sixth wedding anniversary. "What more could you want in a husband?"

The question took Kat aback. Briefly, she caught herself actually trying to answer it. But it was a useless point of inquiry. "I've told you, I don't want a husband at all." She concentrated on placing a topaz set in silver in the electress's upswept coiffure. Albert Morton's image danced before her eyes, with his engaging smile, button blue eyes, slight stature, jug ears and all. Kat had to suppress a giggle. She liked Albert, as did all the ladies at court, but he was not the type to inspire romantic notions. He was not at all like—*for example only,* Kat told herself—Stefan Dvorak.

But it was already March, with the scent of spring in the air, and Kat had still not heard from Stefan. At Windrush, her parents watched and waited. King James had passed through on progress, making much over the property and singing its praises to George Villiers, who had recently been made Earl of Buckingham. The visit had made Sir Edgar and Lady Beatrice very nervous.

And when Kat learned of it, her own apprehension increased. She felt helpless and frustrated being so far away in Heidelberg. Yet her mind was not on Windrush as she accompanied the electress to the ballroom Frederick had just completed for his wife in the huge round tower known originally as the *Dicker Turm*. Under a hundred wrought-iron chandeliers, the polished mahogany floor reflected the shimmering fabrics and scintillating jewels of German aristocracy. Hanging snout by jowl with portraits of the elector's ancestors were mounted heads of boar, stag, bear and even a lynx, their dead glass eyes staring down at the glittering assembly. A juggler, a pair of acrobats and a fool with a red, bulbous nose had taken a brief leave from the Frankfurt Fair to perform at the castle. The atmosphere was merry, the guests exuberant. Elizabeth was radiant in purple and silver, Frederick looked regal in crimson and white, Prince Anhalt preened in green and gold. Even Frederick's mother, the Dowager Electress Louisa Juliana, had put on her best brocade. Kat, in a gown of deep blue velvet with a flaring white ruff and matching cuffs, wore a silver pendant at her breast and an aigrette feather in her hair.

"You're lovely tonight," remarked Prince Anhalt as he guided Kat through a series of intricate steps. "Is it true that you and Albert Morton are betrothed?"

Kat practically fell over her own feet. Elizabeth's fantasy was getting out of hand. "By heaven, no!" She gave

Anhalt a sharp look as he carefully restored her balance. "The electress enjoys playing matchmaker, that's all."

Anhalt's shrewd eyes strayed to the dais, where Elizabeth was tapping her toes and plying Frederick with roasted quail. "She wants everyone to be as happily wed as she is. The electress is a dutiful, fruitful wife," he commented as the musicians on the balcony above them finished off the final notes with flair. "Elizabeth is fit to be the mother of kings and queens. I pray she agrees."

Kat gave Anhalt a piercing glance as they made their formal bows to conclude the dance. "Surely you know the answer to that by now."

Anhalt's expression was deceptively blank. "Do I? Her highness tells me she awaits the advice of her father. As for Frederick," he went on, with a nod in the direction of the dowager electress, "his mother begs him to refuse any crown that might be offered. I fear she suffers from unnecessary misgivings."

Kat's eyes strayed to Elizabeth's formidable mother-in-law. In the past, the two women had not seen eye-to-eye on a number of occasions. Indeed, the dowager electress spent most of her time away from court, at her various dower houses. But this was a special celebration, and all seemed well between Elizabeth and Louisa Juliana on this festive night.

"I know only that the electress gladly supports the elector in whatever path he chooses to take," Kat said primly.

A spirited Giovanetta had been struck up by the musicians, but Anhalt made no move to ask Kat to join him with the other dancers. His eyes studied her thoughtfully as the sea of merrymakers swirled around them. "I'm pleased to hear that," he said, his smile fixed in place. "This very day I have learned of the Emperor Matthias's death."

"Oh!" Involuntarily, Kat took a backward step, almost colliding with Christopher Dohna and his dumpy wife,

Trina von Solms. She gave not a fig for the emperor, dead or alive, but was still surprised at the news. "I had not heard," she said, puzzled. Raising her voice above the din of musical instruments and flying feet, Kat posed a question, "Do Elizabeth and Frederick know...?"

Anhalt did not wait for her to finish. "No." He began to artfully guide Kat away from the dancers. "Why spoil the celebration? Not that they will mourn Matthias. Far from it. But his passing would distract the court from this important occasion."

A clang of cymbals and a blare of horns ended the lively dance. Next to the long, lavish buffet, Kat fingered a dainty sugar cake. "How did you hear of his death?" she inquired, wishing Anhalt would take his leave of her company. His suave, self-assured, faintly patronizing manner made her edgy.

The chancellor was accepting a goblet of wine from a liveried servant. "From an unimpeachable source," he replied, taking a sip and looking pleased with the vintage. He gazed past Kat and inclined his head. "That one."

Kat turned. In the entrance to the big round tower room stood Stefan Dvorak. He was not alone. Susan Howard, attired in three shades of green, with golden stars sprinkled in her blond curls, was clinging to his arm.

"Dvorak," murmured Anhalt. "And I believe that's the electress's new maid of honor, just arrived from England. Lovely creature, isn't she? I don't recall the name..." He turned back to Kat.

But she had fled the ballroom.

Kat clenched her fists and gritted her teeth. The knock on the door grew more insistent. She pressed her knees together with both feet flat on the floor and refused to get off the bed. Stefan Dvorak could rap away until his knuckles fell off as far as Kat was concerned. She had no desire to exchange even the most minimal of greetings with the wretched man.

"I know you're in there," Stefan shouted for the third time. "Don't be a brainless fool!"

Kat didn't move. Outside, the rain was pouring down, as befitted the last day of winter. But he had not sought her out the previous night. Instead, Bess Apsley reported that he had presented his compliments to the elector and electress, spoken briefly with Prince Anhalt, and disappeared with Elizabeth's newly appointed maid of honor, Susan Howard. Kat had been infuriated. She'd spent a sleepless night, imagining all sorts of things she knew nothing about going on in one of the bedchambers that formed part of the castle's new wing.

Now it was almost noon, a gray, wet day with the early blooming flowers drooping on their stalks in the castle gardens and the electress absorbed in mending the results of the elector's overindulgences of the night before. Kat dug in her heels as Dvorak knocked again.

"You must open this door." His voice was even, almost cold. "I've come about Windrush."

Kat sat up on the bed. Stefan Dvorak had uttered the one word that could bend her obstinate will. Uncertainly, she slipped off the bed and crossed the little room. The latch rattled under her hand as Dvorak pounded once more on the door. With fumbling fingers, Kat slipped the bolt.

Stefan Dvorak was still dressed for travel in his leather jerkin, white shirt and black breeks, with the high, cuffed boots of Russian leather. If possible, he was even more bronzed than when she had last seen him, a season past. The dark eyes flashed; the rugged chin was set. Kat's heart leaped in her breast. It was absurd; despite everything, she was elated at the sight of him. But she would not let it show.

"Well?" Her own voice was chilly, though anxiety betrayed itself in a slight tremor. "What of Windrush?"

"Here," he said, thrusting a travel-stained scroll of paper into her hand. "You can read, I take it?"

"You know I can!" Kat snatched at the paper, then stared dumbly at the seal, which bore her family coat of arms. "Where did you get this?" she demanded sharply.

"Susan Howard carried it from England." He flung out his hand, gesturing at the room's interior. "Shall I come inside, or do we discourse on the threshold for all to hear?"

A bit clumsily, Kat gave way, letting Stefan in. He closed the door behind him with a bit more emphasis than was necessary, and went to the tall mullioned window with its tiny rain-spattered panes. He stood with his hands behind his back, looking out into the dreary day, while Kat read the words penned by her father.

The letter was not at all reassuring. Sir Nicholas Overbury might believe in Kat's innocence, but there were some at court—unnamed, of course—who did not. Until Thomas Overbury's murderer was brought to justice, the de Veres were in disgrace, and Windrush stood in peril.

"Since the royal visit of some weeks ago," Sir Edgar wrote in his precise, if unusually cramped style, "our tenants are in distress, requiring warrants of protection and continued custody. Your lady mother ails, being so beset with worry not only about our home, but about our dearest daughter as well. If the remedy is in your hands, pray let us share in it so that this cloud may pass overhead and leave us once again in peace."

Her shoulders slumped as Kat rolled the letter back up and felt a sense of helplessness overwhelm her. The desperate tone was so unlike her father. Nor was it characteristic of Lady Beatrice to succumb to adversity. Surely the guilty party would be found. Unless, Kat thought miserably, the king did not want to see justice done....

"Elizabeth failed me," Kat said dully. "Or did her father fail her?"

Stefan turned away from the window, hands still behind his back. "What do you mean?"

Angrily, she pitched the letter across the room, just missing the tiled fireplace. "Bess wrote to James, beseeching him to keep his greedy paws off Windrush. The man's a swine! He gives not a fig for his daughter, only for his fatuous favorites!"

Dvorak's attitude was dispassionate. "True. The man not only thinks he's omnipotent, he is obsessed with his creatures." Casually, he moved to the hearth, retrieved the letter and carefully placed it on the mantel. With an indolence that seemed slightly feigned, Stefan examined an exquisite Dresden figurine on the mantel. "Nor will he help his daughter and her husband when their time comes, alas."

Kat dismissed his last remark with an angry wave of her hand. Her own problems were most urgent; Dvorak seemed to be referring to some hypothetical situation that could not matter a jot in comparison with Windrush.

"You once said you knew who killed Thomas Overbury," said Kat. "Were you boasting?"

Stefan looked at her over his shoulder. "Boasting? No. I never boast."

Impatiently, she approached him, fists clenched together. "Then who? This is no game! It's my life in question!"

He gazed down at the oval of her anxious face, then brushed at his dark hair. "It's not that simple. I haven't been in England since you and I ran away. I've no proof, nothing except ideas. There were some letters I found once, but they don't seem to mean anything specific."

"What letters?" demanded Kat.

But Stefan shook his head. "It's pointless to discuss it. Dangerous, maybe. I would have to go back to England, ask questions, find witnesses, piece together the—"

"Then do it!" Kat stamped her foot, her face hot with anger. "I'll go with you!"

Dvorak waved a big hand. "I can't. Not now. Good God, Matthias has just died. Bohemia is in turmoil. My people may be at war in a matter of weeks, even days! I must head for Prague, not London! Be reasonable, wench! There is more here at stake than a house in the country!"

His own voice had risen, his self-control noticeably ruffled. Kat's eyes widened, almost as fascinated by his loss of aplomb as she was infuriated by his attitude. "What about my reputation?" she demanded, trying to refrain from pummeling his chest with her fists. "Am I to live out my life in exile, with suspicion trailing me like a stray dog?"

"Exile!" Stefan spat out the word, his chiseled face twisted with contempt. "I've been in exile for years! It's my life, you little fool!" He grabbed Kat by the shoulders and shook her. "Don't you see that? I have nothing; I am nothing! And you whine about Windrush!"

For a fleeting moment, Kat plumbed the depths of his intense dark eyes and forgot her own predicament. But fear was a dreaded disease, the symptoms sometimes put at bay yet always a threat. Kat glared up at Stefan but it was too late. He had caught the sudden softening of her features. His kiss overtook her before she could reply.

For months she had waited for this moment, remembered, cherished, envisioned it. But anger did not flee. Rather, it fueled her emotions, kindling fire against fire, urging her hands to grasp at Stefan's shoulder and back, forcing her body to mold itself into his. Kat felt his tongue thrust inside her open mouth, allowed herself to be crushed by his hard-muscled embrace. Her heart pounded in her ears, playing a strange, dangerous song. Outside, the rain still pelted down, in rhythm to her throbbing pulses. When Stefan lifted her in his arms and carried her to the bed, Kat did not resist.

The beige lingerie collar parted, the satin stomacher was undone, the tiny rosette that had rested on her bosom was gone. Kat's eyes grew enormous as Stefan tugged at her silk chemise, baring her breasts.

"Stefan," she protested, albeit feebly. "I'm not a rabbit like Susan Howard!"

Half lying on top of her with his chin leaning on her stomach, he grinned wickedly. "Not like Susan, no. But you are all soft and cuddlesome. I've even seen you hop."

Despite herself, she giggled. Whatever had happened between Dvorak and Susan did not matter. Not now. Kat, not Susan, held Stefan in her arms, and all the Howards could rot in Hades. Kat wriggled provocatively, if innocently. "Stefan, you're mad! You must stop. Now." The lack of urgency in her voice surprised her. But not Stefan.

"No." He sounded unconcerned, cupping her naked breasts in both hands and uttering a deep groan of pleasure. "I judged rightly," he said, moving up so that his mouth was against her left side. "You are beautiful." He was grinning at her even as he fondled her body in the most unimaginable, tantalizing ways. The grin softened as his touch grew more aggressive. "You are as fair as any forest creature. You are like the scent of spring among the mountains that stirs a man's soul and makes his heart feel alive. Little Kat, you could lure the chamois from his lair!"

The words were like a poem in Kat's ear; by comparison, any other man's flattery would hold a hollow sound. Even Prince Henry's long-ago praises seemed to fade in the mists of time. Kat put her fingers in Stefan's dark hair and pressed his face against her bare throat.

"I missed you so!" she confessed, a little wail in her voice. "I thought you'd never come back!"

"We Roms always come back," he said, kissing the underside of one breast as his fingers plied her nipple. Kat writhed at his touch, that deep longing catching fire and sending a shudder throughout her entire body. Whatever she had imagined between Stefan and Lady Susan came to vivid, importunate life. Kat knew she was as wanton as any Howard, as any Gypsy wench, as any woman who ever desired her man. But in that rush of sensual discovery, she didn't care.

Stefan was slipping the big velvet sleeves off her shoulders, easing the gown from her hips. Staring into his dark eyes, Kat was awed by the naked desire she saw, and even more amazed by the unexpected vulnerability. Stefan Dvorak's hard edges seemed to have been melted away by passion, the perpetual irony dispelled by the mingling of their flesh. Kat yanked at his cambric shirt, exposing his chest to her eager hands.

The knock at the door went unheard at first. When Kat finally noticed, she stiffened and swore softly. Dvorak lifted his head, turning slightly. "The electress may be summoning me," she whispered.

"Ignore it," he said, burying his face anew in the cleft between Kat's breasts.

But the pounding was almost as insistent as Stefan's own assault on Kat's door had been a few minutes earlier. *Damn all the world,* Kat thought hazily, until a muffled masculine voice called Stefan's name.

It was Dvorak who now cursed, more vehemently than Kat had done, and with a glimmer of anger in his eyes. "Who is it?" he called in annoyance, sitting up with Kat cradled in the crook of one arm while reaching for the *schiavona* with the other.

For a long moment, there was no answer. Then the muffled voice came through the oak, firm if barely audible. "A poor priest. From Moravia."

Stefan looked down at Kat and heaved a deep sigh. "I must speak with this priest." He pulled his shirt on and smoothed his dark hair. "Will you wait for me?"

Kat suddenly felt empty inside. With limp fingers, she tried to put her clothing back in order, but fumbled with the laces and struggled with the sleeves. Stefan was at the door, carefully undoing the latch. "When?" she breathed.

Stefan turned, taking in the disheveled chestnut hair, the flushed poignant face, the wide, anxious green eyes. "Always," he wanted to say. But such words were foreign to him. Instead, he gave a ghost of his usual grin, a parody of his customary shrug, and slipped into the corridor.

Heidelberg Castle had one of the finest wine cellars in Europe. It held the great tun, a container so large that it loomed like a small mountain. Standing among the collection of casks, with their gilded emblems and vintners' crests, Kat reflected that it was no wonder Frederick enjoyed his drink so much. In the Palatinate, fine wines were as plentiful as they were tempting. However, to Kat's uneducated English palate, one vintage tasted much the same as any other.

She didn't hear Stefan Dvorak's approach. For a big man, his tread could be surprisingly light. But she saw his shadow, cast against the far wall by the torches that flared on stanchions set in the cellar's dirt floor.

"Isn't this rather ridiculous?" Kat whispered, indicating the secrecy of their meeting place. "Why not one of the secluded student prison cells at the university or a raft in the middle of the Neckar?"

He wasn't nettled by her sarcasm. "The cells aren't secluded—they're usually filled with young rowdies. As for the Neckar, it's running too high this time of year." Stefan drew Kat along a row of smaller casks to the far end of the cellar. "Father Comenius has come incognito to Heidelberg to observe Frederick. He is uneasy in his mind."

"So?" Kat had never heard of Father Comenius. "Is he here to help Dr. Schultz?"

Stefan gave an impatient shake of his head. All signs of
the previous day's ardent lover were gone. He was self-
contained, businesslike, aloof. And as usual, he seemed put
off by Kat's political naiveté. "Father John wants me to
return to Bohemia with him." He ignored Kat's look of
dismay. "The people—the peasants, the poor, the common folk—are not rallying to Count Thurn as expected.
Without them, the movement for independence is doomed.
This priest thinks I may have some influence. He's wrong,
of course, but I must try."

"What on earth for?" exclaimed Kat, wishing he'd take
her in his arms instead of standing there like an icon with
his thumbs hooked in his belt. "Who is this priest? Who is
Count Thurn?"

Dvorak kept his patience, though not without effort. Kat
could be as exasperating as she was enticing. But for now,
he must put aside the desire that she kindled in him even at
her most vexing. "John Comenius is a young priest from
Moravia who studied here in Heidelberg. He has preached
widely in Bohemia, gaining much public support for his
views on religious freedom. Naturally, the conservative
Catholics despise and fear him. As for Heinrich Matthias
Thurn, he is the nominal military leader of the Protestant
majority in Prague. I admire Father John, but Count
Thurn is a hotheaded fool. However, he's all we've got. For
now. The Catholics have Wallenstein and Tilly. Both are
brilliant. Protestant Bohemia must defend itself or die."

"Oh, good heavens!" Kat rolled her eyes at Dvorak's
solemn pronouncement. "Why can't they just be sensible
and get themselves a proper king? We got James from the
Scots."

"An arguable accomplishment," murmured Dvorak.
Then he held up a hand to stop Kat's retort. "I've no time
for word games today," he said abruptly. His dark eyes
glanced around the cellar to make sure they were still alone.

"Father Comenius is anxious to get to Prague. In my absence, I must ask a favor."

Kat brightened. Perhaps he was going to exact a promise of her fidelity, or exchange tokens of affection, or even declare himself. She looked up at him with expectant green eyes, her lips parted, her pulses quickening.

"You must speak with the Princess Palatine about her ambitions for Frederick," he was saying in low, brisk tones. "She trusts you—you're a childhood friend. Convince her that the elector should refuse the crown of Bohemia, if indeed it is offered to him. Make her see that he must withdraw his name at once."

Kat clamped her lips shut and narrowed her eyes. She could hardly believe that the cool, detached man who stood before her with his litany of political requests was the same Stefan Dvorak who had all but devoured her half-naked body less than twenty-four hours earlier. She had been wrong about him. But he had been wrong, too. Making love to women meant no more than chasing rabbits, after all. Kat's temper flared.

"I'm no intriguer! You're as misguided as Prince Anhalt! It's none of my affair what Elizabeth and Frederick do! Go off with your Moravian meddler and recruit the dregs of the earth! I've got troubles of my own!"

Stefan's eyes snapped, but he stood very still. "It's the way of the world." Idly, he reached up to the top of the nearest wine cask. A flip of his hand revealed a playing card. "The queen of spades. She bodes ill for all of us." There was no merriment in Dvorak's eyes.

Nor was Kat amused. "It would be better if you could conjure up the proof I need to defend my honor," she asserted, still with anger in her voice.

Stefan inclined his head. "Or a military genius to lead Bohemia. When I've finished there, I'll be back." Scowling, he wheeled about, no longer bothering to keep his footsteps silent.

Clutching a solid oak tun for support, Kat watched his shadow lengthen, then disappear. He had no right to ask her to interfere in her friend's dynastic plans. She was furious as well as frustrated. For a landless half Gypsy, the man behaved like an omnipotent despot. Next to the oak tun lay the card Dvorak had palmed. Kat stared at it, wondering why its placid, lifeless features should convey such menace. She squared her shoulders and thrust out her chin, trying to ignore the small voice that told her she would have gladly done Stefan's bidding if only he'd kissed her goodbye.

Chapter Twelve

The electress was unhappy. She did not like having her will thwarted, and throughout her pampered life, Elizabeth had rarely been forced to cope with adversity. Except for the death of her beloved brother, she had been spared many of life's ordinary disasters. But now she was faced with two disheartening, though very different, sets of circumstances.

Her mother, Queen Anne, had died of dropsy. Her death was not unexpected, nor had Elizabeth and Anne been particularly close. But the queen had been her mother nonetheless, and her passing seemed to show the electress how far removed she was from her homeland and what remained of her family.

The second occurrence struck at Elizabeth's inner circle, and threatened to break yet another bond with England. Feeling uncharacteristically depressed, the electress summoned Kat and sent the other attendants away.

Attired in a plum-colored robe de chambre, with Jock-o chattering at her feet, Elizabeth handed Kat a sheaf of papers. "Read this," she commanded without preamble.

Puzzled by her friend's gloomy countenance, Kat assumed the missive pertained to the late queen. But as her eyes skimmed down the first page, Kat realized with a growing sense of alarm that the letter concerned herself.

Dictated by King James, it declared that Lady Katherine de Vere was still suspected of a most heinous crime, namely the poisoning of Sir Thomas Overbury, and that the electress should cease and desist giving shelter to such a person. The king went on at length in his pedantic manner, going so far as to suggest that showing favor and friendship to Kat could harm Frederick's chances for the crown of Bohemia. Kat was appalled.

"This is an outrage!" she exclaimed, slapping at the sheaf of papers. "Who has planted such inane notions in your sire's mind?"

Dolefully shaking her head, Elizabeth allowed Jock-o to climb into her lap. "I've no idea. Lady Susan brought the letter when she arrived last week. I've been mulling it over for days, but Freddy says my father is right—we cannot afford any scandal at this juncture. Oh, Kat, I know it's unfair! I know it's untrue! But it's very likely that Freddy will be offered the Bohemian throne. The Protestant majority is ready to set Ferdinand aside at any moment. Think of it—I could be Queen of Bohemia!" Her blue eyes were shimmering, the melancholy gone.

Kat withdrew her hand. Her face was set, the green gaze cold. "And I will become a wanderer, like Stefan Dvorak and the rest of the Roms?"

Elizabeth turned vaguely sheepish. "Of course not. You could..." She frowned, seemingly unaware that Jock-o was cheeping at her hem. "If you don't think it's safe to return to England, perhaps we could find a place for you with the Dowager Electress. Or at the court of Freddy's brother, the Duke of Simmern. He's a very pleasant fellow. I suppose," she mused, finally giving in to Jock-o's pleas to resume his place on her lap, "we'll have to forget about the match with Albert."

"Albert!" Kat shrieked. "Bess, don't be a ninny! I have no wish to marry Albert Morton!" Angrily, she began to

pace the room. "Nor will I take charity from your in-laws.
The best thing I can do is go home. In England, perhaps I
can find the truth and be done with all this calumny. I refuse to act like a furtive criminal, hiding out all over Europe. Especially," she added pointedly, "if you don't want
me."

"Kat!" Elizabeth's cry was full of genuine anguish.
"You know that's not the case! I had to choose, between
you and Freddy! He's my husband—what could I do?
What would *you* do?"

Kat stared blankly at Elizabeth. Until now, the question
would have held no meaning for Kat. But in that moment,
with the electress's bright blue eyes demanding a response,
Kat understood the predicament. She had no husband, had
forsworn the married state; but if she were forced to make
a choice between Elizabeth and Stefan Dvorak, Kat knew
what the outcome would be. And with the knowledge came
the realization that Kat loved the penniless, homeless,
footloose, aggravating Gypsy baron.

"Don't fret over me," said Kat in a toneless voice. "I'll
be gone before sunset."

"Kat..." Elizabeth again stretched out a hand.
"Please...wait until the weather clears."

But Kat was already gone.

The south side of the palace that Frederick had built for
Elizabeth overlooked the English garden, the moat and the
forest that covered the Konigstuhl. Kat was heading for her
own chamber to pack up her few belongings. No matter
what the danger, she would return to England. In truth, she
had nowhere else to go.

Just outside her room, she encountered Susan Howard.
The two attendants had not exchanged more than a passing nod since Susan's arrival the previous week. Elizabeth
had not been pleased by her father's appointment, but had

behaved graciously toward the newcomer. The electress, after all, had more important things on her mind than her maids of honor.

"Lady Katherine," purred Susan, a vision in mauve satin with a graceful ruff at her throat. "You look out of sorts. Is aught wrong?"

Kat could barely look at the other woman. Was it possible that Susan had lain in Dvorak's arms since their arrival at Heidelberg? Of course it was, Kat told herself savagely. With a man like Stefan Dvorak, anything was possible.

"I'm leaving," Kat muttered, trying to make her way past Susan, who seemed determined to block her passage. "Pray excuse me."

"Leaving?" Susan blinked at Kat, the long, dusty lashes thick as cobwebs. "La, mistress! I thought you and the electress were boon companions!"

Kat darted an annoyed look at the other young woman. "We are. But I must go home. My mother is ill."

"Oh, dear." Susan sighed with exaggerated sympathy. "A pity. But I wouldn't return to England if I were you." In a swish of satin, she sidled closer to Kat. "There's been *such* talk in your absence. It may be nonsense, of course, but why take chances? And all for the sake of a silly old house! Steenie tells me it's quite quaint, but I prefer Audley End."

"Steemie?"

Susan wrinkled her nose. "*Steenie*. The king's new darling, George Villiers. I can see you're out of touch with the English court." She made a clucking noise with her tongue. "No wonder you're considering such a reckless course. Perhaps you'd be better off living in The Hague, or Amsterdam."

"I'm not that fond of cheese," snapped Kat, wishing that Susan would budge.

"But you seem to like rats," remarked Susan, her face hardening a jot. Unexpectedly, she uttered her tinkling laugh. "Kat and rats! How amusing! How appropriate!"

"How stupid," retorted Kat. "You babble, mistress. I haven't the remotest idea what you're talking about."

Susan stiffened, then put a hand on Kat's arm. Emeralds and diamonds glittered at Susan's wrist. "You and the baron from Bohemia. There's talk, you know. Here and in London. You're said to be lovers and to dabble in necromancy." The lavender eyes narrowed. "Who would believe it, to look at you? La, to think I was almost fooled! At least I got rid of that Gypsy half-breed before he broke *my* heart!"

Kat's free hand shot out so fast that Susan had no warning of the sharp slap. Stunned, she gaped at Kat, then unleashed a volley of venom better suited to a stewsmonger than the daughter of a noble house. Kat tried to push her way past Susan, but the other woman grabbed her by the hair. They wrestled, more with their cumbersome gowns than with each other, until Kat broke free. Susan was on her heels, but as Kat turned a corner, she stopped abruptly and put out a foot. Susan tripped, cursed and fell, sprawling onto the passageway floor. Kat ran as fast as she could, down the corridor and out through the first door she could find.

She fled blindly, and at last found herself in the castle herb garden. The early spring plantings looked forlorn after the heavy rain. The air was cool, with more dark clouds moving in over Konigstuhl. Kat shivered and turned to go back inside the castle through a different entrance.

The outer door to the chapel was locked. Kat went through Elizabeth's privy garden, with its heroic statue of Frederick. Through the windows on the terrace, she could see Christian of Anhalt engaged in conversation with Colonel Schomberg. In her disheveled state, Kat couldn't

bear to face either the debonair chancellor or the courtly
soldier.

The rain began to fall again. Growing more chilled by the
moment, Kat slipped through a gate at the other end of the
garden. She had never gone this way before, and found
herself in the tiltyard. The tennis courts were to her right;
she was sure of that. Through a slit in the wall, she could
see the town below, and the Neckar River.

As if her feet had a will of their own, Kat exited the tiltyard through a big wooden door. She was outside the castle walls, on a little slope covered with drooping shrubbery
and budding fruit trees. Across the valley the neat, fertile
fields had been put to the plow. But Kat was in no mood to
appreciate the prosperity of the Rhineland. Down the hill
she went, her shoes getting wet, her rumpled clothing
damp, her chestnut hair streaming over her shoulders. A
narrow street led between half-timbered houses and a small
church with a single spire. The city wall was nearby, but
came to an abrupt end at a tollhouse by the river's edge.
Kat kept walking.

Upriver, she could see the covered bridge that spanned
the deep, dark waters. Directly across the river was the
Heiligenberg, a high hill crowned with the ruins of an ancient basilica. Twin turrets framed the city gates; a square
tower stood at the other end. There was virtually no traffic
on such a chill and gloomy afternoon. A lone horseman
rode into Heidelberg, while downriver, two small boys
stood on a little dock, skipping stones across the ripples.

Sinking to her knees on the marshy bank, Kat let out a
desolate sigh. Except for the rumbling of the river, it was
very quiet. The past walked over her with heavy boots. Kat
shuddered, huddling on the strand like an abandoned kitten. She could not see her reflection in the murky waters.
There was an old German legend she'd heard one of the
electress's tiring women recount, of a fine lady who had lost

her shadow. Kat didn't remember how or why—it had something to do with love and marriage. Kat had nothing to do with either. She was alone, unwanted and unloved.

The wind brushed her cheek. Kat didn't bother to look up. The afternoon light was fading quickly as a new storm moved in. The rain began to turn to snow, obscuring the opposite side of the river. Kat felt like lifting a fist to rail at the unseasonable storm, at Susan Howard, at Elizabeth, even at God.

"You're not as big a fool as you look," said Stefan Dvorak from directly behind her. "Or so I would hope."

Kat's shoulders sagged. She didn't attempt to look up. "Go away," she said in an irritable voice.

He stooped beside her on one knee. "You weren't actually going to try drowning yourself, were you?" His tone was light, yet Kat detected a somber undercurrent.

"Don't be ridiculous," she replied in annoyance. "Where did you come from? I thought you'd run off to Prague with your pious priest."

"We leave today. Father John was asked by old friends to perform a marriage ceremony at Heppenheim." Stefan put a hand on her back. "Good God, you're chilled to the bone. Get up, it's snowing hard."

"Leave me alone," countered Kat, but her tone was now more sulky than bellicose.

"Get up, I told you." Stefan's patience was ebbing as he hauled Kat to her feet. "God's blood, you look a fright! Did you roll down the hill to the river?"

Standing, Kat realized that her legs were very wobbly indeed. "I rolled into Susan Howard," she replied testily. "For once she doesn't look so wonderful, either. Her tongue is forked. She insulted us both. Strumpet!"

"Zounds." Stefan brushed the rain from his eyes as he examined Kat's appearance. She was soaked, dirty, and as unkempt as any creature he had ever seen in his life. But

Stefan Dvorak had never wanted a woman as much as he wanted Kat de Vere.

"Damn all," he breathed, sweeping her up in his arms. She intended to protest, but was too weary. Or so she told herself, feeling the warmth of his flesh and the strength of his body. Snowflakes fell on her face, washing away the terrible sense of doom. He moved swiftly along the river-bank, not up toward the castle, but to the little dock where the boys had been throwing stones. They were gone now, apparently chased home by the oncoming storm.

Between the pier and the city wall stood the stone toll-house with its rounded red dome. It was empty on this late March afternoon, no doubt due to the lack of river traffic. An unlit brazier, a rickety table, a homely chair and a locked chest were the only furnishings. Dvorak set Kat down on the chair and immediately set about lighting a fire in the brazier.

"You'll be very fortunate if you don't catch a deathly ague out of this misadventure," he said in a severe voice.

"I was safer outside than I would have been with Susan Howard," Kat responded. "I'm going to have to leave Heidelberg, foul weather or not."

Dvorak was busying himself with flint and coals. "Why?"

"The electress has asked me to go. I'm like to cause a scandal." Suddenly, Kat felt very sorry for herself. She gave Stefan the bleakest of looks. "King James thinks my presence at Frederick's court is harmful. Is that not far-fetched?"

Dvorak regarded Kat thoughtfully. "I wish it were true. It might solve all our problems."

"You truly wish to prevent the elector from being your king?"

"I do." He moved restlessly around the small room. "Frederick is a decent lad, but he's not a leader. And he drinks too much. I only wish to God I knew of a better candidate. The field is barren." He gave Kat a wry look. "But such matters don't trouble you, do they?"

"I care about Bess. But politics—no." She shook her head. "I care about people. To me, Bess is not a queen, she's my friend. And Freddy is her spouse. I want no harm to come to them, but their aspirations don't interest me in the slightest." She lifted her shoulders under the sodden gown. "It seems to me that life is very simple."

But Dvorak shook his head. "Oh, no, little Kat, it's very complicated. You aren't looking beyond your nose." To prove his point, he ran his finger from the curve of her brow to her upper lip. "Even with your own dilemma, you rant and rave about individuals. But have you thought that your troubles are caused not by people, but politics?"

Kat pulled back and stared at Stefan. "Whatever are you talking about?"

"People *are* politics," he said evenly. "You've studied history. You know it's not just dry facts and dates and places, but love and hate and envy and ambition. So it is with the events that move us every day. Someone murdered Thomas Overbury and that same someone is trying to blame you in order to escape getting caught. Why? I give you two reasons, which may in fact be one—you are a likely suspect, having had reason to want Sir Thomas dead. And the king—or his favorite, Villiers—covets Windrush. The two could be connected, or perhaps one is the result of the other. But the point is, who had the most to gain by poisoning Overbury? I don't think you have to look too far—even in Heidelberg—to find the answer."

Kat's brow furrowed as she studied Stefan's chiseled features. "You don't mean . . ." She paused and swallowed hard. ". . . Susan Howard?"

"Not Susan herself, but possibly one of the other Howards. Frances is now married to Robin Carr. She got her annulment, she won the man she loves, she overcame every obstacle. Catholic or not, all the Howards are riding high. Their influence dominates, which bodes ill for Frederick and Elizabeth. And now Susan is given a post in attendance on the electress. Is she a tool of her family, or is she merely an acquiescent maid of honor?'' He took a step forward and lowered his voice. "Or did she come to create a rift between you and Elizabeth?''

Kat gaped at Stefan. He had spoken in a matter-of-fact voice, as if Susan Howard was of no personal concern to him. "But...she is your..." Kat fumbled at the words. "...Or was your...bed partner.''

Dvorak had turned back to the brazier. Satisfied that the coals had caught, he looked at Kat. "What? Oh, indeed she...was.'' He frowned slightly. Stefan Dvorak was not a man to let others influence his thoughts or deeds. Yet he was about to discard the inventively amorous Susan Howard because she might be Kat's enemy. "Here,'' he said gruffly, handing Kat his cloak. "I'll turn my back and you can get out of those wet clothes.''

"The fire will dry me out,'' Kat countered.

"With that puny blaze, it would take a month.'' He shoved the black cloak with its scarlet lining at Kat. "It will reach your ankles. You couldn't be more modestly attired.''

Kat relented, but didn't budge, waiting for Stefan to turn around. "Do you require accessories as well?'' Dvorak plucked a filmy white scarf from his sleeve.

Kat's eyes widened, but her expression was disapproving. "I'm not a child. Don't try to ingratiate yourself with those cheap conjuring tricks. The Frankfurt Fair has a dozen wizards more clever than you.''

The scarf floated in Stefan's hand. "The dons at Oxford didn't appreciate me, either. I was almost sent down for flushing a pair of squirrels from under the lectern during a particularly soporific discourse on the Roman satirists."

"How juvenile," murmured Kat with a scornful air.

"No, it was actually Juvenal," replied Stefan, his dark eyes twinkling.

Kat had to bite her cheeks to keep from laughing. The man was impossible, his moods unpredictable. "I used to read Juvenal with my father," she said with a placating note. "His works were quite scathing."

"Much more entertaining than the lectures," Dvorak agreed. The amusement had fled from his gaze. He stood with his thumbs hooked in his belt, the white scarf dangling from the crook of his arm. Kat thought he looked oddly ill at ease.

Kat's lips formed into a prim line. "I must change, if you insist. But you're watching me. Stop that."

Stefan drummed his fingers on the baldric sash that held the *schiavona* in place. "I can't." The sharp, strong jaw softened; the piercing black eyes glinted. Kat winced, yet the sensation was not unpleasant. She was about to ask him why he could not look away, when Stefan took three steps toward the chair where she was seated and planted himself so close that his boots touched her bedraggled hem.

He was looming over her, with Kat's eyes fixed on the lacings of his doublet just above the waist. Stefan put a hand in her tangled hair, tilting her head up. "I can't turn away from you," he said simply. "I want to look at you. I want to look at all of you."

Though his words were utterly forthright, the strange note of longing in his voice sent a shiver down Kat's spine, one that had nothing to do with her chilled condition. Uncertainly, she raised one hand, placing it against his chest. He leaned down, winding the scarf around her neck. How odd, he thought, being accustomed to taking and leaving women at his will and their whim, that he should find this prickly little English wench so difficult to resist. The taste he had taken of her had only whetted his appetite. But he would not force Kat, for that was not his way. Stefan Dvorak would rob no human being of free will.

"Do you find me repugnant?" he asked, with his cheek pressed against hers and his lips almost touching her ear.

"Oh, no!" Kat's response came out on a sigh.

"Good." He grinned, though Kat could not see him. Her eyes were closed and her hands fluttered over his doublet. "I will be gentle, if that is your will." He slipped down next to the chair and spoke very softly. His arms wrapped around her; his kisses rained at her temple, her eye, her nose and at last her mouth. Kat clutched more tightly at him, unaware that she was digging her nails through the fabric of the shirt he wore under his doublet. Stefan's kiss hardened, then he forced her lips apart to probe at will with his tongue.

Kat writhed in his embrace, her senses overwhelmed by the intimate contact. She should have protested, fought him off, fled the little tollhouse and summoned protection. Her brain registered each practical, virtuous response, but her body rebelled. These passionate kisses, those roving hands, the feel of that taut, muscular body against hers—all were what she had yearned for ever since Stefan Dvorak had skewered her with those Romany eyes in front of the Abbey on the day of Prince Henry's funeral. She knew that now, admitted it openly to herself, even as he slid the torn bodice over her shoulders and used his cloak to make a pallet for them on the floor.

The fire in the brazier crackled and the snow drifted past the small arched window. It was almost dark outside, and a church bell tolled in the distance. The room was in shadow, gold-and-crimson flames bathing their figures in an opulent light. He kissed her breasts, then slipped off both overskirt and petticoats. Kat trembled, as apprehensive at revealing her own nakedness as at seeing his. But when the final garment had been tossed aside, she smiled at the wonder of him, and he bowed his head at the temple of her beauty.

"You are so fair," he murmured, kneeling over her, with his hands at her hips.

"I'm a bit marred at present," she replied, allowing her fingers to stray to his muscular thigh. The contact made her catch her breath. "Oh, Stefan, why does touching you make me dizzy?"

He put his hand over hers, drawing it between his legs. "Gypsy magic," he answered, his smile crooked and his voice a trifle ragged. "No," he corrected himself, closing his eyes as he led her fingers in an exploration of his manhood. "Nature. This is the way between men and women."

But Kat gave a weak shake of her head. "Not all men and women." She gasped, growing breathless at the feel of him. "Certain men and women. Us."

Stefan moved back, bending to kiss the flat of her stomach. His hands strayed to her breasts, plying them expertly. Kat sighed with pleasure, entranced by the havoc he was wreaking with her senses. He was mouthing her hardened nipples, sending little spurts of flame through every nerve in her body. She grasped at his bare back, at the wide shoulders, the narrow waist, the muscles of his upper arms. Kat felt as if she were learning every inch of him, even as he savored her own most intimate secrets. If there should be shame in such mutual exploration, Kat felt none of it, only a total abandonment to shared desire.

At last his tongue parted the tender flesh between her thighs, making Kat's spine arch and her head fall back. The longing that had simmered for months, perhaps even years, began to overtake her like a rampant fever. There must be a remedy, she thought hazily; somehow the fire must be put out before it consumed her....

Cradling her shoulders, Stefan stretched out over Kat. His black eyes scorched her face. She could have sworn that his agony was as intense as her own. Had they violated some precept of nature? Was there no recourse for sinners who had stripped each other's bodies bare and exposed their very souls?

Succor came to Kat in a flurry of passion and pain, so sharp, yet so sweet that she cried out in astonishment. The sound of the rushing river echoed in her ears, the fresh wind from the mountains seemed to sweep over her, the peace of the pristine forest settled in to soothe her soul. Kat gave one final shudder and fell back in Stefan's embrace. Her longing was assuaged, a miracle wrought not by Gypsy magic, but by the mingling of two oddly matched creatures who had dared to become one.

By reason, Stefan's weight should have crushed Kat. Yet she bore the burden of him gladly, rejoicing in the sensation of his manhood still within her. Tiny beads of perspiration glistened on his skin. Kat turned just enough so that she could see his closed eyes and the short, thick fringe of dark lashes. He looked amazingly young and vulnerable. Tenderly, she stroked the back of his neck.

"Little Kat," he murmured, then shook himself and carefully withdrew from her. Slowly, he moved away, resting on one elbow. His fingers traced a path from her throat through the valley of her breasts to the burnished triangle between her thighs. "What shall I do with you?" he said in a musing voice.

Kat, still overcome by the wonder of their mating, gave him an odd little smile. "Do? You already did."

He uttered a truncated laugh. "I did indeed. I would do it again. I will." He leaned over to kiss her nose. Despite his response, he hadn't answered the question. At least not for himself. Over the years, women had been a passing pleasure, had meant a giving and taking that left each with the most pleasant of memories. But nothing more. A penniless half-Rom couldn't afford to love, let alone live, except on the move. And this willful English wench with her shimmering green eyes and bold tongue conjured up visions of well-stocked larders and carefully tended gardens and cradles rocking by the firelight. Those were *Gajo* images, intended only for the affluent, for those who belonged to a stable society and a happy home. Stefan gazed at Kat, trying to keep his unsettled thoughts to himself.

But Kat was too sated, too happy to read his mind. Stefan knew as much, and for the moment, he was glad.

"You will go with me to Prague," Stefan said much later when they were seated at an inn near the river. Noisy students drank and laughed near a huge vat of beer, while weary travelers dried out in front of the open fireplace.

The fork in Kat's hand stopped near her mouth. "To Prague? But that's impossible! I must go home!"

"It's a trap." He speared a roasted potato. "Do you think Sir Edward Coke has forgotten how you duped him? He will arrest you the minute you set foot in England."

"But I told you, my mother is ill and my father is distraught!" Kat put the fork down, the tempting veal uneaten.

"You also told me that that letter did not sound like either of your parents," he noted dryly. "Hasn't it occurred to you that that's because your father didn't write it?"

Kat's astonishment turned to skepticism. "I know my father's handwriting. I'd recognize..." She stopped, visualizing the page. "Yes, it *was* a bit different. More cramped. But I thought it was because of his distress." Disconcerted, she moved the fork around on the surface of the worn table, carved with centuries-old initials and epigrams. "But who forged that letter? And what of the one from King James to Elizabeth?"

Across the room, a scuffle had broken out between students from rival colleges at Heidelberg University. Fists flew and swords were drawn. Kat watched with apprehension, but Dvorak wore a resigned expression. "They'll settle down," he said, obviously used to such fracases among undergraduates, "or get thrown out."

Sure enough, in less than two minutes the altercation ceased. The former combatants rubbed at their knuckles and sheathed their weapons, then poured more beer and began to sing. Kat sighed with relief.

"The letter from James is probably genuine," said Stefan, as if the outburst had never happened. "But someone is goading him, probably the Howards. Northampton, the most influential of the family, is old, but he's wily. He's got James's ear these days. As for the letter allegedly from your sire, who knows? But remember that Susan Howard brought it to Heidelberg."

"It's stupid," exclaimed Kat. "I would have found out that my father never wrote such a letter. I don't understand any of this."

Dvorak regarded her with a wry expression. "You might not have found out if you'd been arrested immediately upon your arrival. The letter may have been a trick to make you return to England."

"But Susan said I shouldn't go," protested Kat. "She suggested I seek refuge in the Low Countries."

"Naturally," said Stefan with a half smile. "Susan knows you wouldn't take her advice. Indeed, you'd be inclined to do the opposite, merely because it came from her." He looked at Kat over the rim of his beer stein. "Well?"

Kat made a face. "It seems that you're not the only one who can read my mind. Am I so transparent?"

"No." He shook his head. "But you're open and honest. You make no secret of your feelings. Thank God." He reached across the table and put his hand on hers. "You are made for loving, little Kat."

Suddenly shy, Kat stared down at her uneaten food. "Oh, I never thought…that is, I had sworn not to…" She clutched at his fingers and gazed into his dark eyes. "Stefan, I'm not a rabbit!"

He squeezed her fingers and grinned. "I know that. I said as much. But you must eat your supper. This storm is blowing itself out. We'll leave as soon as it stops."

Kat squirmed in the chair, but didn't try to free her hand. "But…how can I travel with you? We're not married!"

Amused as well as dismayed by her naiveté, Dvorak chuckled. "We have a chaperon, remember? A holy priest. What more could you want in terms of decorum?"

Kat remained dubious. She wanted to go with Stefan Dvorak. To Prague, to Budapest, to Istanbul—the destination didn't matter. But she still felt duty bound to return home. "I'm torn. Whether or not my father wrote that letter, I know my parents are upset. I feel as if I'm running away from my obligations."

Letting go of her hand, Dvorak picked up Kat's fork and stabbed a piece of veal. "In my life, I've learned it's sometimes prudent to run away." Briefly, he glanced around the common room. He believed what he said, but the words conjured up images of his parents, of Albrecht Wallenstein, of militant anti-Protestants. Brecht had run away. He'd admitted it. Dvorak hadn't quite forgiven him. But perhaps it was time. "Here," he said abruptly, holding the forkful of veal near Kat's lips. "Eat."

Reluctantly, Kat obeyed. She was in disgrace with the king of England, her family home stood in peril and her parents must be suffering on her account. She had been turned out of Heidelberg by her dearest friend, to roam Europe as an exile. She was going to Prague with Stefan

Dvorak. The city sounded faraway and very foreign. There would be trouble, perhaps even war. But Stefan was feeding her braised veal and roasted potatoes and boiled cabbage. Kat couldn't believe that she actually felt happy.

Chapter Thirteen

In spite of herself, Kat was awed by the Bohemian countryside. After they crossed the frontier, they rode among snow-topped spruce and fir trees clinging to rugged mountains. In a few days, Stefan told her, the *fohn,* a hot, dry, early-spring wind would blow through the forest, creating torrents of water coursing down the cliffsides. Following the Eger River, they put the wild country, with its lair of lynx and cry of eagle, behind them. The land grew tame, and Kat saw fertile fields, with green shoots of grain peeking out of the ground. In the orchards, plum and cherry trees were in bud. Spring's first flowers grew along the roadside, under the hedgerows, on window ledges and beside tumbling streams. Kat found there was a lushness about rural Bohemia, a rugged land tempered by time and the hard labor of its people.

Yet there was also a sense of foreboding. The busy workers who tended the crops looked up from their tasks with wary eyes, afraid of what news—or commands—any band of travelers might bring. Currents of unease and mistrust seemed to ripple out of the rich earth as Kat noticed an increasing scarceness of ablebodied young men.

Outside of Prague, their little caravan passed among rocky crags, where the lower hillsides had been turned into vineyards. The journey had taken almost a week, and they had been joined by another half-dozen travelers along the way from Eberbach to Rakovnik.

Throughout the trip, Stefan had behaved as decorously as he had promised. Ironically, Kat had not been pleased. She yearned for his embrace, for his kisses, for that sweet surrender that was so new, so overpowering, so all-consuming. But Father Comenius's presence, as well as that of the others who joined them, forced Kat and Dvorak to keep their distance.

Father John was hardly the stern, solemn clergyman that Kat had pictured. Rather, he was a pleasant-visaged young man in his middle twenties, with a long brown beard, gentle brown eyes and a delightful smile. His manner was forthright, his conversation down-to-earth. Kat began to understand why Stefan was so taken with the young priest and his ideas of religious freedom.

"You English like to boast of your tolerance," Father John remarked as they neared Prague on the final day of their journey. "But in fact you persecute anyone who holds what you consider extremist views, such as Catholics and Puritans. That, my lady, is not true freedom."

Though the words were critical, Father John's manner, as ever, was genial. Had anybody else offered such a criticism, Kat would have argued forcibly. Instead, she merely smiled at Comenius and allowed that King James had often been provoked by certain sects, but perhaps there had been occasions where he wasn't as broadminded as he liked to pretend. At her side, Stefan Dvorak smiled to himself. It appeared to him that John Comenius was using his characteristic charm to make another convert.

But just up ahead, the rest of the little party had slowed its pace to exclaim over a handsome edifice they'd glimpsed through the trees. Kat and the priest also took notice, stopping to admire the long avenue of approach, the copper roof and what appeared to be various wings.

"That's the Hvezda Palace, actually a hunting lodge," Stefan explained. "It's built in the shape of a six-pointed star, with trees planted around it in the same configuration. It's quite beautiful, as are the gardens." He paused as a small band of riders approached from the other direction. Except for their leader, they were soldiers, attired in the emperor's uniform. "Damn," breathed Stefan, "'tis Cardinal Zittau."

Kat peered at the crimson-clad figure, his silken robes trailing grandly in the breeze. He was a heavyset man with ruddy coloring and a bristling mustache. Stefan saluted the churchman while the others watched in varying states of unease.

"By the mass," exclaimed the cardinal in a hearty voice that could carry into the far reaches of the greatest cathedral, "Stefan Dvorak! I have not seen you since I was a poor priest in Falkenau!"

"And how surprised you are to see me now, your eminence," Dvorak responded dryly. "Or are you just passing through en route to Vienna to call on the Emperor Ferdinand?"

Zittau was beaming at Stefan, with an occasional, benign glance at the others. "You might say I'm on a hunting expedition." He gestured with a beefy, beringed hand at the Hvezda Palace. "The sport here is excellent, as I'm sure you know."

With a flick of the reins, Stefan made as if to ride off. "The best of luck to you, your eminence. It's been a pleasure."

"Hold, Baron." Even as the cardinal spoke, the half-dozen horsemen behind him had maneuvered their horses to block the road. "Not all game is four-footed." He nodded in Father John's direction. "I've a mind to bag a priest."

Stefan uttered a short laugh. "You've priests a-plenty." He gave the cardinal a baffled look. "Who do you think is in this company? We are a varied group—a brewer, a corn merchant, a glassblower, a master of horticulture. We have no clergy among us."

The cardinal's small, gray eyes narrowed as they flicked from Dvorak to Comenius and back again. "Now Baron, would you tell a lie to a man of God? Is this not John Comenius of Moravia, or is my memory faulty?"

Stefan gazed at Father John, who was looking suitably confused. In his plain brown travel garb, he could have plied any trade. "He's our horticulturist, one Vaclav Palacky. Here," he continued, leaning across the saddle toward Comenius, "see what beautiful blooms he grows." With a flourish, Stefan produced a bouquet of red roses that matched the cardinal's robes to perfection.

The distraction was sufficient to catch the soldiers off guard. Comenius put spurs to his horse and raced off down the tree-lined road toward the elegant hunting lodge. Cursing, the emperor's men regrouped and started to follow the young priest. But Dvorak and his big gelding blocked their way.

"Stay, good fellows," Stefan commanded in that reasonable yet authoritative tone. "Master Palacky has a terrible fear of any weapon more lethal than a pair of garden shears. You frightened him away."

Cardinal Zittau's face had turned almost as crimson as his robes. His affable demeanor had changed to wrath, and he was shaking a fat fist. "Damn your heretical hide, Baron! I'll see you hang for your insolence!"

Kat and the other travelers watched with anxious eyes. But Stefan was unmoved by the threat. "No, you won't, your eminence. You're not as narrow-minded as you pretend."

"Don't underestimate me," fumed the cardinal, trying to get his temper under control. "I serve the pope and the emperor." He heaved his bulk around in the saddle, pointing to Kat. "Who is this? Your glassblower?"

The barest flicker of apprehension passed over Stefan's face. "A lawyer's daughter, visiting relatives in Prague. She's mute."

"Take her!" the cardinal barked at the soldiers. Frantically, Kat tried to wheel her horse around, but she was too late. Stefan, drawing his *schiavona,* charged at the men, but three of them drove him back. Kat tugged desperately on the reins, then felt them being jerked out of her hands. Surrounded by the other three soldiers, she was soon a prisoner.

"Now," said the cardinal to Dvorak, his voice again calm, "we shall keep this mute lawyer's daughter safely until you do one of two things, Baron." He paused, a bit out of breath from the sudden exertion. "You will send me Father Comenius, or you will agree to help me mediate between the rebels and the emperor's advisors. I'm a man of peace, not war. I'm quite willing to be reasonable." With a nod, he ordered the soldiers to lead Kat away.

Stefan, still gripping the *schiavona,* was tempted to test the cardinal's word. But if Zittau was fair, he was also tough. Stefan could not take chances with Kat's safety. Helpless, he watched her slim figure grow smaller as the cardinal's party headed back toward Prague.

Kat was not in the mood to appreciate the wonders of Bohemia's capital. The city's faintly exotic buildings, the silver ribbon of river, the great churches with their spires and domes, all were lost on her as she was led to a handsome palace in the northwest corner of Hradcany Square.

"Andreas Teyfl had this palace built a few years ago," the cardinal explained in his most convivial manner. "At present, two of the imperial councillors are living here. I will leave you in their care."

They were in a courtyard surrounded by the palace's four wings. Kat studied the Renaissance design, but gave Zittau a frosty look. Following her cue from Stefan, she had not spoken since the cardinal had led her away. Zittau had addressed her in German; Kat had picked up a smattering of the language during her stay in Heidelberg, but she was far from fluent. It occurred to her that she might as well be mute, since she didn't know a word of the Bohemian tongue.

"Vilem Slavata and Jaroslav Martinitz are both Jesuits," the cardinal was explaining, while several retainers emerged to assist with the horses. "They're fine men and will see to your comfort." He glanced up as another man, dressed in a green doublet slashed with gold, moved briskly across the courtyard. "Ah!" exclaimed Zittau, "'tis Slavata's nephew, Brecht Wallenstein."

Kat watched as the two men exchanged greetings. Wallenstein's name was not unfamiliar to her, but she wasn't sure where she'd heard it. He and the cardinal were now speaking in Bohemian, and Kat was left to guess what they were saying. She could tell from their gaze that part of the conversation pertained to her. Wallenstein, whose physical appearance was undistinguished except for his carefully tended beard and mustache, seemed to grow disturbed. The cardinal appeared to be reassuring him. Kat dismounted and waited impatiently. Perhaps she should announce her real identity and insist upon being released at once.

But before she could make up her mind about her course of action, the cardinal and the soldiers were taking their leave. Zittau bowed formally to Kat, adding a word of caution, "Don't consider anything rash, my child. This place is well guarded." In a swirl of crimson silk, he rode out of the courtyard.

Wallenstein approached Kat and also bowed, a stiff, uncomfortable gesture. His first words were unintelligible; then he switched to French. "His eminence doesn't believe Baron Ostrov," he said bluntly. "If you are not actually mute, please tell me who you are. This is not a game, it's very serious."

Kat studied his long, sallow face. With some misgivings, she decided on candor. "I'm Lady Katherine de Vere, an English maid of honor to the Electress Palatine. Her highness will not be pleased to learn I've been kidnapped."

"Her highness's sensibilities are not our concern," Wallenstein replied as haughtily as Kat. "My uncle and I will do our best to see that your stay here is a pleasant one."

"Pleasant!" cried Kat. "I'm a prisoner! What right do you have to hold me at all? I know nothing of your ridiculous politics! I'm English!"

Wallenstein frowned. "You are also a...friend of Baron Ostrov," he said, looking faintly embarrassed. "We are relying on his affection for you to gain our political ends."

Kat felt the color rising in her cheeks. Gossip had no nationality; it seemed to run amok all over Europe, just as it did at the English court. "This is absurd," Kat declared, turning her back on Wallenstein to cover her own embarrassment. Angrily, she stalked toward the small fountain that stood in the middle of the courtyard.

"I'm sorry," Wallenstein said stiltedly. "Stefan should not have tried to hoodwink his eminence. Had Father John complied, you would not be here now."

Kat swerved around and glared at Wallenstein. "But I am. And you'll be sorry for it."

A shadow crossed his sallow face. "I told you, I already am." The ironic look he gave Kat told her that he spoke the truth. But she wasn't sure what he meant.

* * *

Truculent and fearless, Count Heinrich Matthias Thurn would not give in. Dvorak had argued with the rebel leader far into the night, in a small, shabby room above an inn near Emmaus Abbey in Prague's Lesser Quarter. Comenius, insisted Thurn, could not be put to risk for anyone's sake, least of all for a foreign wench whose influence was virtually nonexistent.

"Sacrifice Father John for an English chit?" Over his tankard of pilsner, Thurn's broad face turned scornful. "What's gotten into you, Stefan? Don't tell me this Katherine has stolen your heart!" The mere idea strained Thurn's credulity. He let out a guffaw, spewing beer on the rickety tabletop.

"She's the Electress Palatine's closest friend," Stefan replied without emotion. "You favor the elector as the next king of Bohemia. Do you want to offend his consort?"

But Thurn remained adamant. "Comenius is the spiritual leader of Bohemia. God's teeth, Stefan, you know that better than anybody!" He scowled across the table and took another swig of beer. "Damme, that English schooling you got has softened your brain!"

Thoughtfully, Stefan studied the belligerent expression on Thurn's weatherbeaten face. Count Thurn was single-minded, practical, brave. There wasn't an ounce of subtlety in his body. But he was also a man of limited intellectual capacity. Stefan passed a hand over his forehead. Frederick of the Palatinate was a moody, hard-drinking, twenty-two-year-old man-child. Count Thurn had no vision for Bohemia. John Comenius was on the run, a fugitive from the emperor and the pope. Stefan sighed. The situation seemed so hopeless. And to make matters worse, he had lost Kat. Inwardly, he cursed himself. A few months ago, he could have ridden away from any woman he'd bedded and not looked back. But it was different with Kat.

As much as he hated to admit it, the little English lass had a hold on him. For a brief instant, he caught a glimpse of the future and was unsettled.

Dvorak poured more beer and talked of other things.

Albrecht Wallenstein had ordered a plump capon for supper. Its crisp, golden skin looked delectable on the silver platter. He smiled in appreciation, then gazed at Kat. "My uncle sends his regrets this evening. I trust you do not object to dining alone with me."

Kat fanned herself with her hand, for the April evening had grown quite warm. "He's a busy man, I gather," she replied, evading his direct question. In the two weeks that she had been held prisoner, her treatment had been just short of lavish. Uncle Villi and his fellow Jesuit, Father Martinitz, had been unexpectedly charming company. As for Wallenstein, Kat had found him more austere than the two older men, but reasonably gracious.

"Uncle Villi has been an advisor to Ferdinand, the new emperor, for several years," Wallenstein said complacently. "Indeed, he and Father Jaroslav are the real rulers of Bohemia at present, since Ferdinand stays in Vienna." He looked up from carving the capon. "That's not to criticize. The emperor must remain in the seat of his realm, after all."

"Yes, yes," agreed Kat a trifle impatiently. For the past fortnight she had heard nothing but the wonders of the Holy Roman Empire and the pope. It was almost enough to make her long for King James—to watch him spit and speak at the same time. "And you? Didn't I hear you were going back to Italy to fight for your emperor?" She tried to sound interested, but knew her effort was half-hearted.

"I leave tomorrow." Wallenstein's brow creased as he passed Kat her plate. "For once, I wish I weren't going off to war."

"Really," remarked Kat, wondering if the food she would have been given in the Tower of London would have been half so savory as her meals in Prague. "Why is that?"

Wallenstein put down his fork and looked vaguely disconcerted. "I'm a widower, you know."

"Oh?" Kat chewed on the fowl, and discovered it tasted as good as it looked. "I'm sorry for your loss."

"It's been awhile," replied Wallenstein, shifting about in his chair. "My wife was somewhat older than I." He cleared his throat, passed the buttered carrots to Kat and fidgeted with his napery. "How long have you known Stefan?"

Kat forced herself to look blank. "Who?"

Wallenstein, however, was a very shrewd man. "Did you meet him in England?"

"Yes," Kat answered with a note of what she hoped was indifference. "My family home is close to Oxford."

An enigmatic expression crossed Wallenstein's face. For a moment he said nothing, sitting motionless while the candlelight cast amber shadows over the handsomely appointed dining room. "Do you love him?"

The abruptness of the question caught Kat off guard. "What?" Her voice had risen an octave. She choked on a bite of bread, then coughed into her napkin. "Really, sir, what sort of impertinent question is that?"

Wallenstein saw the flush creep over her cheeks, and poured the wine with too free a hand. Some of it sloshed onto the gleaming mahogany. He made a face, then looked at Kat. "Pray excuse me, my lady. You're right. I'm impertinent." Carefully, he composed his features. "And what think you of Bohemia thus far?"

Kat gathered her scattered wits and tried to answer. But even as she recalled the wild, rugged beauty of the mountains and the verdant, fertile fields of the lowlands, her mind was elsewhere. She had to get away from this place, and she must do it soon. Comfortable or not, the palace was still a prison. Out there, somewhere in Prague, Stefan Dvorak walked and talked and ate and drank. Kat could endure the separation no longer. She vowed to be free before the sun set again.

The Gypsy tinkers arrived at midday. Kat saw them come into the courtyard shortly after Wallenstein rode off for the Italian front. The two Jesuits were absent, tending to business at nearby Hradcany Palace. Their servants eyed the Gypsies warily, but let them go about their business. Kat, who was free to move about inside the palace, asked what the visitors did. Mending pots and sharpening knives, was the general answer. Casually, Kat went into the courtyard and inspected the small wagon the Roms had brought with them. Their dark eyes and bronzed faces reminded her of the Gypsies she'd encountered near Windrush. She smiled at them, passed a few words in German, and started back for the south wing of the palace.

But when the tinkering was done, Kat was gone from her prison.

Stefan Dvorak knew he would be too late. The council chamber at the Hradcany was no doubt already rocking with the fury of men pushed to the breaking point. The emperor's advisors had rejected and reviled Count Thurn and his Bohemians for the last time. In Stefan's estimation, Thurn was a fool, though well-intentioned. He had led thirty men in full armor to the castle, set on the assassination of the old emperor's Jesuit advisors. Stefan had tried to talk Thurn out of the rash plan, but the outraged count refused to listen. Indeed, he had been furious with Dvorak for not joining the bloodthirsty band. But Stefan, who despised the herd mentality, resisted.

Wrapping his fingers around the compact grip of his *schiavona,* he shielded his eyes from the bright sun as he looked up at the sprawling stone walls and soaring towers that constituted the Hradcany. He could not stop Thurn's band by himself, and in some dark corner of his mind he wasn't sure he wanted to. The Emperor Ferdinand had broken promise after promise to his Protestant majority. Yet Thurn's plan to murder two hapless priests in a show of patriotic and religious fervor struck Stefan as reckless. Dangerous, too, for if it came to vengeance, the Holy Roman Emperor was not without resources.

Near the wing known as the Louis Palace a crowd was gathering, a motley mixture of Catholic nobility, Protestant merchants, German craftsmen and peasants in from the fields. Stefan froze as a hand tugged at his short serge cape.

"Stefan!" The husky voice stopped him in his tracks. Swerving, he saw a compact little person attired in vivid colors and wearing a bright green veil. With a sly glint in her dark eyes, she reached behind her ear and produced a robin's egg.

"Thirza." Stefan grinned, pulling the little gypsy to his side. "You taught me that trick when I was a lad." He palmed the egg, opened his empty hand, and then plucked it from Thirza's sleeve. "You see? I've not forgotten. But you should not be abroad. There is great trouble at the Hradcany."

Thirza wrinkled her nose and spat. "There is always great trouble. We Gypsies live with trouble. We live off of it." She tossed her head, the golden hoops swinging at her ears. Even though Stefan had leaned down, Thirza had to stand on tiptoe to watch his face. She was of an indeterminate age, her small, squat body brown as berry juice, her black hair flecked with white. "You are alone, as ever. Why do you not find a rich wife among the *Gaje?* You should have come back from England with a bride.''

Stefan met her gaze, but his face had taken on a guarded aspect. ''Who would want a wanderer like me, Thirza? Today I am in Prague, tomorrow Istanbul. Wives prefer husbands to stay home.''

''Then marry a Rom.'' She wagged a finger at him in a scolding manner as the crowd's cries grew louder. ''You need a woman. You should not grow old alone.'' Scowling at Dvorak's refusal to be baited, Thirza gestured behind her. ''Like that one.''

Stefan turned. Among the sea of curious faces, he saw an oval face, green-eyed and wary. Azure and gold veils covered the chestnut hair; double loops of silver dangled from her ears. He grinned; Kat fought to keep her expression impassive.

''Well?'' said Thirza, glancing quickly from one to the other. ''What think you of our newcomer? She has just joined the *kumpania.*''

Before Stefan could answer, shouts rose from the palace. Thirza was hopping up and down. ''Lift me, so I can see. Are they really going to murder those Jesuits?''

The crowd was pressing in around them as Dvorak hoisted Thirza onto his shoulder. Kat turned away, appalled at such violence. She couldn't imagine such a dreadful scene being enacted in London. Stefan should be at her side, comforting her, not helping Thirza enjoy the horrid spectacle. Had the mob not been surging forward, Kat would have fled.

''Remember what happened to the Catholic oppressors two hundred years ago?'' he reminded Thirza. ''Thurn has no imagination.'' His tone was as easy as ever, yet his face was suddenly drawn. Stefan recognized one of Thurn's victims: Vilem Slavata. Brecht's uncle. The generous man who had seen to the schooling of two orphaned boys. He winced inwardly.

"Eeeiyah!" cried Thirza, all but bouncing in Stefan's grip while the enormous gold hoops dangled from ear to shoulder. "You're right, they're going to throw those priests into the empty moat! Hear the screams!"

One black-clad figure was straddling the sill, fingers clutching at the embrasure. Kat peeked through her fingers, unable to fend off her curiosity. "Jesus! Mary!" the priest cried as hostile hands pushed him over the edge and into fifty feet of space. The crowd gasped, then let out another collective shriek as the second man hurtled through space, arms flailing, legs kicking. The priests landed one on top of the other as gunshots spewed from the tower, grazing one of the victim's arms.

The cruel death that the dry moat should have dealt to the unfortunate priests was averted not by the arms of angels, but by the presence of a large, reeking dung heap. The descent of a third man, flapping through the air like a crippled bird, was virtually anticlimactic. The onlookers, whose gasps had changed to a mixture of jeers, cheers and prayerful exclamations, were now arguing among themselves about rescuing the priests or finishing the job that Count Thurn's men had bungled. Except for a slight wound on Father Martinitz's arm from the musket ball, it was clear that the two Jesuits and their secretary had suffered more damage to their pride than to their bodies. Kat felt limp. Her colorful Gypsy garb clung to her skin. She sought an opening in the crowd, but was hemmed in on every side. Stefan's voice carried to her just as a troop of imperial guards cleared a path to the moat.

The majority of the crowd grew antagonistic. Hoots of derision competed with the shuddering ring of the Sigismund Bell in St. Vitus's Cathedral. Stefan, who had set Thirza back on the ground, was about to offer Slavata his assistance when he was stopped by a group of apprentices, sulking in their frustration and sniffing for fresh prey.

"Ah!" their stocky ringleader exclaimed, wielding a club. "A Rom dwarf! She must be a witch who conjured up a spell to save those poxy priests! Let's cut off her ears!"

Horrified, Kat pushed two gawking students aside and confronted the apprentices. "Begone!" she cried in German, pulling Thirza close. "What do you know of Roms, except for vile myths?"

The apprentices gaped at Kat, confused by the contrast of fair skin and Gypsy clothing. "They feast on human flesh," declared one of the young men, pugnacious and homely. "They steal babies from the crib." He lunged, as if to grab at Kat's breast. "They stole you, I'd wager. You're no Rom!"

"And you're an idiot," Kat shot back, fighting down fear as Thirza clung to her skirts. Scornfully, she spat on the ground, just as she'd seen Kore do to show his disapproval of *Gajo* ways.

This time, the apprentice squeezed Kat's breast, making her wince. "Viper!" she cried, reeling backward. The crowd seemed to be closing in, with not a friendly face in view. Panicking, Kat whirled, still clutching Thirza. Less than a foot away, Stefan Dvorak stood, shielding them with his body while he whipped the *schiavona* from its scabbard. His black eyes glittered at the apprentices.

"Are you willing to sacrifice your lives for a bit of sport?" He sliced the air with the three-foot blade, the cat's-head pommel catching the sun.

Though two of the half-dozen apprentices cowered as Stefan brandished the menacing weapon, the ringleader was drunk enough to be undaunted. Swinging his club, he gestured at his followers, three of whom had now unsheathed poniards. "Take them all! He looks like a Rom, too!"

Stefan swung the *schiavona*, aiming to wound rather than kill. One of the youths went down, clutching his wrist. But a lanky blonde with a broken nose dived behind Dvorak and swept Thirza off her feet. She kicked and clawed, but was no match for the sinewy youth, who held his weapon just under her earlobe. Kat screamed in pain as a rock grazed her shoulder. The lanky youth screeched out a warning to Stefan, "Desist, Romany devil, or I'll slice this side first, baubles and all!"

Dodging the ringleader's club, Dvorak lunged and cursed. The outbreak of violence was only one skirmish of many beneath the walls of the Hradcany. Fists, firewood, knives, even pieces of furniture were being wielded by various members of the crowd as Catholic grappled with Protestant, and the emperor's adherents struggled with Bohemian nationalists. As ever, Prague was a hotbed of religious and political chaos, the crossroads of Europe, a cauldron of dissent. A pair of Gypsy women and their rough-edged defender weren't worth notice.

Yet even as Stefan fended off his attackers with the formidable *schiavona*, a pistol shot rang out, followed by a stern voice ordering the mayhem to cease. Thirza's would-be abductor dumped her unceremoniously onto the litter-strewn cobbles. The other apprentices, in various states of disarray, faltered and turned to see who dared interfere with their nasty pleasures. A man wearing the garb of an imperial officer stood with his feet planted apart and the smoking pistol raised on high. Kat slipped through an opening in the crowd and fled.

"Ah! 'Tis Wallenstein!" breathed one of the youths, clumsily sheathing his poniard. His fallen fellows recovered themselves and stumbled off through the crowd. Only the ringleader remained, now leaning on his club and regarding Wallenstein with barely veiled insolence. "Since when does a colonel in the imperial army give protection to heretics and Roms?'' he demanded with a sneer.

Wallenstein's brown eyes flicked from Dvorak's wry expression to the figure of Thirza, still sprawled on the cobbles like a broken rainbow. "I see no heretic here. As for the little lady, she is firstly a woman, only secondly a Rom.'' He gestured fretfully with the gun as Stefan carefully lifted Thirza to her feet. "Lose yourself, young knave. I would arrest you and your minions for mayhem, but the emperor will need you for cannon fodder in the weeks to come. I trust your courage matches your bravado.''

The stocky apprentice shouldered his club. "There was another, comelier wench,'' he began, but caught the dark warning in Stefan's glance, reconsidered, and walked away at a leisurely pace.

As the crowd milled around them, Stefan kept Thirza at his hip and eyed Wallenstein thoughtfully. "I thought you were at Gradisca, Brecht,'' he said. His former companion seemed ill at ease. Perhaps his edginess had been triggered by the outbreak of violence. But Stefan knew that Brecht was not an easy man to unnerve. He shrugged off his reaction. "Your homecoming has proved spectacular.''

"I returned within the hour. What other wench?'' Wallenstein demanded, his long, sallow face severe.

Stefan gazed around him. He could not see Kat, and was relieved as well as puzzled. But when he turned back to Wallenstein, his expression was blank. "What wench? There were dozens of them, though not all comely.''

Wallenstein studied Dvorak briefly, then lifted one narrow shoulder. Noting that several people had recognized him and were exchanging comments with their companions, Wallenstein turned on his heel and headed eastward, skirting the ramparts of the Hradcany. "Take your little friend home. Is it a caravan, or a hovel outside the city?''

"It's Golden Lane," Thirza answered, her breath finally restored. "Not all Roms wander, Colonel Wallenstein."

He shot her a faintly amused glance over his shoulder. "I know that, don't I, Stefan?"

Stefan's jaw muscles tightened. "You know more about Roms than most *Gaje* do, Brecht."

Wallenstein flushed and said no more. He was a taciturn man by nature, and had already talked much more than was his custom. As they entered St. George's Lane, where peddlers pushed carts and farmers drove wagons out of the Hradcany, pigeons circled the Black Tower. The Sigismund Bell still boomed out across the Moldau, to the three towns that made up the City of Prague. Despite the clear blue sky and the sparkling waters of the river, a specter of disaster seemed to rise up over the White Mountain's outcropping of rock that stood guard at the edge of the capital.

They paused as a clutch of peasants in long homespun coats scrambled onto a haycart, agog with news. From the direction of the provost's lodging, Stefan heard drumbeats, then he saw a company of imperial soldiers marching in formation across the square. Wallenstein, however, shook his head.

"We are in for ugly days. Nothing will be done until the emperor gives his orders." He looked at Stefan. "Will you ride with me to Vienna to deliver the news?"

"No," Stefan answered flatly, steering Thirza into Golden Lane. "I prefer to stay in Prague and see what Thurn does next."

Thirza grinned up at Stefan, heedless of a missing front tooth. "You'd try to talk sense into that one? Don't waste your time, Thurn's a brainless fighting cock. See what havoc he has caused today. The Hussites will beat the drum made out of old General Zizka's skin and all Bohemia will be put to the sword!''

''She's right,'' said Wallenstein as they crossed into Golden Lane, with its tiny multicolored houses and stout chimneys that looked like tombstones.

Stefan shrugged. ''I know. I already tried to argue with Thurn. But Thurn is not the only man in Europe who can decide Bohemia's fate.''

''Stefan...'' Wallenstein began on a weary note, but knew it was as useless to dispute with Dvorak as it was with Thurn, if for vastly different reasons.

Thirza paused at the green door, then rapped three times in quick succession. Scurrying noises could be heard from within, then the door swung open, revealing a small, cluttered room that smelled of frying meat, incense and candle wax. Half-clad children tumbled on the floor with a menagerie of cats, dogs and a monkey. At a table covered with a bright shawl, Kore sat drinking from a bottle of pinard. Stefan had seen him only twice since their encounter in England. He was the nominal head of the household, though the family relationships had never been quite clear. In a corner of the room, Grandfather Yojo reclined on a battered eiderdown mattress, eyeing Wallenstein with suspicion. The house grew suddenly silent as Thirza shooed the children and animals outside, except for the monkey, which had leaped onto a wrought-iron chandelier that hung from the low ceiling.

''What's this?'' demanded Kore, banging the wine bottle down on the table. ''Is this not Wallenstein?'' He glared at Stefan. ''Are you mad?''

Stefan was umoved by the reproach. ''Are you stupid?'' He took the bottle from Kore, reached for a pair of mismatched tumblers and poured out the cheap young wine for himself and Wallenstein. ''Brecht may be a *Gajo,* he may serve the emperor, but I know him. Today he saved Thirza's life.''

Kore glanced at Thirza for confirmation. "So." He pulled the black-and-green kerchief from his curly hair and regarded both Dvorak and Wallenstein with shrewd dark eyes. "Then you must share our hospitality, Colonel. Go ahead, drink the fruit of our poor vineyards." He grinned at Dvorak as Thirza stirred a big iron pot that hung over a fitful fire. "You know many people, Stefan Dvorak, even Jews and Turks. How do you come to make this one's acquaintance?"

"From Falkenau. He spent part of his youth there, too." Dvorak's expression was unrevealing; Wallenstein's eyes had become evasive.

"He brings danger." Grandfather Yojo spoke with a rasp. "Drink up, then begone."

Stefan was about to refute the old man's words when Wallenstein set his tumbler down on the table and uttered a truncated laugh. "He's right, Stefan." He paused, his gaze wavering. "I must talk to you. Alone. Tonight, off the square by St. Salvator's Church?"

Stefan eyed the other man curiously. "Why? We've said all there is to say."

But Wallenstein persisted. "It's very important. Please." The brown eyes begged Dvorak to accede. "I must leave for Vienna at dawn."

With a short sigh, Stefan gave in. "As you will. Nine?"

Relief washed over Wallenstein's face. "Good. You'll not regret this favor." He bowed to Thirza and Yojo, then offered his hand to Kore, who gave a single shake of his head. Wallenstein lifted his narrow shoulders as the corners of his mouth turned down in his beard. "So be it. What is it the Gypsies say? 'There are lies more believable than truth.'" He turned to embrace Dvorak. "Our lives have turned out like that, Stefan. The stars have not been kind."

"Is it only the stars?" Stefan mused with an ironic gaze for the entire room. "We are not helpless puppets, Brecht."

Wallenstein's brown eyes grew sorrowful. But he said nothing, and a moment later he was gone.

Stefan's gaze rested briefly on each Rom in turn. "Well?" he inquired. "Where is she?" Before they could answer, he reached for the shawl that covered the table and flicked it up. Kat huddled on the floor, anxious and uncomfortable. Stefan grinned at her. "You're fleet of foot, little Kat. How did you get here in the first place?" He extended his hand as she scrambled out from under the table.

"I've been hiding here for days," she grumbled. "Your Rom friends rescued me from the Jesuits." Shaking her tangled hair and brushing at her borrowed skirts, Kat couldn't help but glare at Stefan. "You certainly didn't seem inclined to come to my aid. Indeed, you seemed overfriendly with Wallenstein just now. It's a wonder you don't hand me back."

Incredulously, Stefan stared at Kat. "Wallenstein! You met him? Where were you?"

Tersely, Kat explained, then shot Stefan an arch look while the Gypsies watched in amusement. "Where did you think I was, the moon? Did you ever try to find me?"

Dvorak was not accustomed to being put on the defensive by anyone, let alone a woman. "Of course I did!" he retorted a bit too heatedly. "But I was gone for over a week, finding a safe place for Comenius. When I returned, I heard vague rumors. Then the cardinal sent a message, again demanding Father John. I didn't answer it." He had composed himself and his voice sounded more normal. "I couldn't," he went on with a helpless gesture. "These past few days I was biding my time. I've learned how to wait, you see."

Kat gave a toss of her head. "Well, I haven't. I decided
to rescue myself." She smiled at the Gypsies, with special
warmth for Thirza. "And sure enough, these good people
gave me the chance. I've a mind to make my home with
them and take up fortune-telling."

Stefan had reached for the bottle of pinard. "Hold, little Kat—what is this you say about Brecht? I sensed something was amiss with him just now. Does he knew you
escaped?" For the first time, he studied her Gypsy garb,
gold skirts with azure petticoats and a laced bodice in black.
Her breasts strained at the homespun fabric, and a trio of
multicolored ribbons nipped her slim waist. It was no
wonder the loutish apprentice had made such a rude advance outside of the Hradcany. The effect was delightful,
but Stefan knew this wasn't quite the moment to say so.

"Brecht Wallenstein may be an excellent soldier, but he's
almost as dim as you are when it comes to women," Kat
sniffed. "He's been gone for weeks. I didn't know he was
back until I saw him outside of the Hradcany."

Trying not to let Kat's costume distract him, Stefan
sipped at his cup of wine. "So he doesn't know. Hmm…"
The black eyes gleamed as a slow smile spread across his
features. "This may prove quite useful."

"How so?" Kat asked, still testy.

But Dvorak intended to keep his own counsel. He shook
his head and gave Kat an off-center smile. "Will you stay
inside the house until I decide when you should go out?"

The request did not improve Kat's disposition. She had
envisioned quite a different sort of reunion, with Stefan
sweeping her off her feet and whispering tender words of
joy into her ear. "I've been mewed up here forever as it is,"
she replied crossly. "I wouldn't have gone out today except that Thirza said there was great danger in the city and
I didn't think she should venture out alone. Does it really
matter that much whether I'm seen or not?"

"It might." Stefan saw the anger sparking in her green eyes and considered making an effort to placate her. But he had very little time. Surely Kat would understand that the crisis in Prague must take precedence over personal feelings. If nothing else, her kidnapping should have taught her a lesson—that Bohemians took their politics very seriously.

"Well, I don't see what difference it makes," Kat declared, stamping her foot. "If Wallenstein is leaving Prague again, nobody else will recognize me. His uncle and that other priest are recovering from concussion, are they not? By heaven," Kat went on, gathering steam, "I've never heard anything so silly in all my life as people throwing each other out of windows! Don't you Bohemians own real weapons?"

Having had his hopes for Kat's enlightenment dashed, Dvorak sighed and put his hands on her shoulders. "Don't be foolish. Slavata and Martinitz have their underlings. I must insist that you remain inside this house until it's safe for you to leave."

Kat felt the pressure of his hands and wished he'd take her in his arms instead of looming over her with such a stern expression on his face. "Do you want me to squeeze berry juice all over my face and pretend I'm a Gypsy, too?" she asked with sarcasm.

Stefan glanced at Thirza. "That's an excellent idea. But I still want you to stay inside until after tonight." He let go of Kat, saw the mulish look on her face and leaned down to brush her nose with his lips. "Behave, little Kat. Please."

Kat watched him go, and wondered why Thirza was trying so hard not to laugh.

Chapter Fourteen

St. Salvator's Church was very old, unlike a second house of worship by the same name that had recently been built by Protestants in the brief days of tolerance under the Emperor Matthias. In Knights of the Cross Square, just off the Charles Bridge, Stefan Dvorak waited for Albrecht Wallenstein. It was the same place where Stefan had encountered him in the past. The square was virtually deserted, though not as peaceful as it had been on previous occasions. A warning tocsin sounded in the distance and shouts could be heard from the student quarter. On this mild May night of 1619, Prague was a restless city.

Wallenstein approached on foot, muffled in a dark cloak, crossing the bridge with quick, quiet steps. He wasted no time on pleasantries. "Where is she?"

Stefan was leaning against an ancient building where the weathered insignia of the Military Order of the Knights of the Cross still displayed its faded red star after almost four hundred years. "Who?" he inquired in his casual manner.

Wallenstein's narrow face was flushed. "You know who." His voice shook with anger. "Your English lady-love. She escaped. I didn't find out until this afternoon."

"Escaped!" Stefan evinced surprise. "What a clever kitten! How did she manage that?"

Wallenstein scrutinized Dvorak's face in the darkness. He couldn't be sure if the other man was lying. "With Rom help. Do you swear you know nothing about it?"

Stefan shrugged. "I haven't been in Prague, either. You must know that." He moved away from the old stones and stretched. "Damn it all, Brecht, the English are a queer race. They're very touchy about their independence. As much, in fact, as we Bohemians are. I suppose she didn't like being held a prisoner." Abruptly, he wheeled around, jabbing a finger at Wallenstein. "But I hold you responsible. You're Zittau's dupe, he abducted her, and if anything has happened to her, you'll pay. I might forgive you once, but not twice." He grabbed Wallenstein by the cloak and jerked him forward. "Never again. Do you hear?"

Repressing an urge to struggle, Wallenstein's eyes narrowed. "I want her back as much as you do, Stefan," he said, his words a trifle garbled by the stranglehold Stefan had on the fabric around his throat. "I'm in love with her."

"God Almighty!" Dvorak released Wallenstein so suddenly that he stumbled on the cobbles. "Brecht, you're a jackass!"

The two men eyed each other, with the tocsin still resounding and musket fire belching from somewhere close by. For a brief moment they were boys again, back at Falkenau, fighting over the miller's comely daughter. But Stefan was the first to regain his aplomb and bring himself back into the present.

"All right," he said. "You've managed to lose Kat de Vere. The price is not too high for such carelessness." He watched Wallenstein's brown eyes closely. "You must step aside, and let the Bohemian people choose their own king."

Wallenstein's long face fell. "No!" He made a threatening gesture, thought better of it and uttered a derisive laugh. "An English girl for the crown of Bohemia? Stefan, you're mad!"

Dvorak's initial reaction was to flare up at the accusation. But he saw the scorn in Wallenstein's eyes, and took a backward step. For all their differences, the two men had much in common. And Brecht had always been the elder, a source of wisdom, even brotherly comfort. Yet Stefan wasn't quite ready to back down. "You heard me," he said in terse tones. "Lady Katherine has disappeared. She was your responsibility. Do you think the King of England will be pleased to find out how disrespectfully his subjects are treated by the emperor and his minions?"

"I can't do what I can't do. The lass ran off on her own." Wallenstein was unmoved. "If King James knows Lady Katherine, then he's aware of her high spirits and independent mind." He paused and spread his hands. "You cannot ask me to do something so important for such a petty reason."

It occurred to Stefan that the English king knew far too much about Kat de Vere. But at least her sullied reputation had not followed her to Prague. Yet. Albrecht Wallenstein might think twice about falling in love with a girl who had been accused of poisoning her fiancé. Feeling uncharacteristically somber, Stefan tried to assume an attitude as obstinate as Wallenstein's.

"I've given you a choice," he said. "You must make up your mind."

Wallenstein made a slashing motion with his hand. "That's no choice at all!" He gathered the cloak more closely around his slender body and lowered his voice. "You're not acting like yourself, Stefan. What's gotten into you?"

For one brief instant, Stefan's intense gaze wavered. Then he squared his shoulders and stared hard at Wallenstein. "I don't know what you're talking about," he growled. Wheeling around on his heel, Stefan strode rapidly across the darkened square.

Moments later, approaching the steep steps that led up to the Hradcany, Stefan stopped. The night was still noisy, with shouts and alarms and an occasional burst of gunpowder. In the shadow of the Black Tower, he surveyed the city and pondered Wallenstein's words. Brecht was right. Stefan had indeed known what the other man was talking about. Kat de Vere, innocent, unwitting, beguiling, had set his world on its ear. Not since the death of his parents almost twenty years earlier had he felt such turmoil.

Screams erupted from somewhere in St. George's Lane. Unsheathing his *schiavona*, Stefan ran toward the gates that led to the Hradcany. They were locked; the night watch was nowhere in sight. The screams grew more shrill, countered by rough masculine voices. He shouted, hoping someone would let him into the castle precincts, or at least let him go to the aid of the victim.

But no one came, and a moment later there was an ominous silence. He cursed and sheathed his sword. No doubt there would be many such cries for help in Prague before Bohemia's troubles were over. He went back down the ancient steps, past the walled moat where the three Catholic adherents had been thrown onto the dung heap earlier in the day. There, all was quiet. But Stefan knew that the burst of violence had only signaled the beginning. As he headed for the provost's lodging and the main entrance into the Hradcany, he made up his mind: having pledged himself to his people's cause, Stefan could not go back on his word. The lure of Kat's arms was strong. But for now, he would have to put her aside. She muddled his thinking, made him lose face among his Rom friends, had even caused Brecht to doubt him.

The lamplights behind the gates at the Hradcany's west entrance cast long, thin shadows across Stefan's path. Like the bars of a prison, he thought to himself. Abruptly, he turned away. He would not go back to the Hradcany and

Golden Lane. He would not return to Kat de Vere until
Bohemia was at peace and her people knew freedom.

Frederick of the Palatinate had been elected King of Bohemia. In Prague, the people anxiously awaited the arrival
of their new monarch and his pretty English consort. Kat
was among them, garbed in Gypsy clothing, with her
chestnut hair cascading down her back, and her hands
roughened by months of hard work.

"Much too young and small-timbered to undertake such
a task," Stefan Dvorak had quoted an English courtier as
saying of Frederick. In his one and only letter to Kat, dated
in early June from Laun, he had also expressed the opinion that given the field, Frederick appeared to be the only
logical Protestant choice. "With reluctance, I am giving my
support to the elector, and hoping for the best. Perhaps responsibility will temper him."

As for Kat, he wrote that her care would be well provided by his Rom friends, but that in the event of danger
flight would be advisable. "The Gypsies know where to
hide—they are accustomed to persecution. Meanwhile, be
of good cheer. I will carry your face in my heart."

Only the last sentence had prevented Kat from ripping
the letter to shreds. Yet, five months later, she was still hurt
and angry. Dvorak had gone off without a word, a kiss, a
fond farewell. For several weeks, Kat had thought she hated
him, but she knew that was not true. Often, especially alone
in her narrow bed, nestled against the goose-down *sherande*
pillows, she would wish her love away. But it clung, more
than a shadow, a part of her so deep that even the greatest
sense of rage could not excise it.

In the months that had passed since Stefan left Prague,
Kat had become absorbed in the routine of the Gypsy
household. Along with Thirza, she cooked and cleaned and
occasionally went out into the fields at the edge of town to

pick berries or harvest fruit. The hard work wearied Kat at first, but soon she became used to it, and acknowledged that it helped pass the time. Little by little she picked up the Rom language, finding the words strangely soft on her *Gajo* tongue.

Kat had written only once to her parents, assuring them of her safety but fearful of pinpointing her whereabouts. Kore had found someone—he had never said who—to carry the letter out of the city. Kat could not be sure that it had ever reached England, and worried that even if it had, her parents would still be distressed.

But once Elizabeth was installed as Queen of Bohemia, there might be a ray of hope. The accusations against Kat no longer threatened Elizabeth and her husband. As the consort to a reigning monarch, Elizabeth would have more influence, even with her father.

Thus, Kat was even more anxious to greet the new queen than the others in the crowd that had gathered outside the Strahow Gate to the Hradcany. Trying to get a better view in the crush of shouting citizens, Kat stood on tiptoe and craned her neck. She saw Frederick first, looking almost handsome in brown and silver on a spirited charger. Then came Elizabeth, resplendent in a chariot decorated with gold and silver. Tears sprang into Kat's eyes as she watched her old friend smile and wave in the most gracious and regal of manners. Visions of scrambling up the ivy outside of Windrush, of surreptitiously trying on Lady Beatrice's finery, of racing their horses across Buckleberry Common flashed through Kat's mind's eye. But this Elizabeth, with her footmen in maroon velvet livery, was a far cry from the frolicsome girl of ten years past. Elizabeth Stuart looked every inch a queen.

"Is she fair? Is she kind?" Thirza bobbed at Kat's side, her short stature precluding any view of the royal proceedings. Kore had come with them, but had gotten lost in the crowd.

"She is all those things and more," asserted Kat, raising her voice over the throng. Elizabeth glanced in their direction; Kat waved frantically. But in her Gypsy garb, with her hair worn loose, Kat realized she looked quite different from the maid of honor that Elizabeth knew so well.

At the gate, a large cluster of people surged forward and hoisted a tattered banner. Kat noted that they looked like peasants. Scythes were raised as a lone voice called out to Frederick above the crowd. *"Vivat Fredericus Rex!"* Frederick smiled and Elizabeth giggled. A hush fell over the vast throng.

"This is no joke," Thirza muttered. "Those peasants are fierce Hussite fighters, whose forebears fought for General Zizka."

The awkward moment had passed. So had the new king and queen, under the archway and into the precincts of the Hradcany. Many in the crowd began to follow their new rulers, but others, satisfied that they had savored the historic moment, drifted away. Kat and Thirza remained where they were, on the lookout for Kore.

"I must seek an audience with her majesty," Kat said, more to herself than to the Gypsy.

"Half of Prague will seek an audience with the queen," said Thirza, her dark gaze still on the Hussite peasants who lingered just outside the gate. "I hope your friend and her man are strong. Their task is not for weaklings."

"Elizabeth is a very determined sort of person," Kat said just as Kore approached. "She will do everything in her power to be a good consort."

Thirza waved to Kore to acknowledge his arrival. "So you say," she said with a shrug that set her bangles ringing. "That being the case, I wish she were a man."

* * *

Three days later, one of Kore's confederates took a note from Kat to the new queen. But no immediate reply was forthcoming. Frederick's coronation was scheduled for the next day. Kat tried to be patient. Unlike Stefan Dvorak, she had not yet learned to wait. But life was beginning to teach her the lesson of patience.

"Your friend," Thirza said over a pot of boiling vegetables, "will be much occupied. She herself will be crowned in another three days' time, you know."

Kat did. With a sigh of resignation, she lifted little Pulika out of the bathtub. At three years of age, he was all chubby brown skin and cherubic smiles. Kat, who had never spent much time with small children, was finding the mischievous quartet of Rom youngsters an enlightenment.

"Elizabeth will send for me," Kat asserted, pulling a shirt over Pulika's tousled curls. "It's just a matter of time."

Thirza added a dash of salt to the pot. "Why do you want to see your friend so much? Do you want to go to court and live like a fine lady again?" The little Gypsy didn't wait for Kat to answer. "That only brought you trouble, as far as I can see. Why not marry a good man and have babies?" She gestured at Pulika with a wooden spoon. "Like this one, eh?"

"I'm English," Kat began to explain, not for the first time. "I have responsibilities. I have parents and a home in England. I can't just run off and—"

She stopped abruptly as the door opened. The sounds and smells of Golden Lane trickled into the little house along with the November fog. Kat, who had picked up Pulika and was about to fetch his favorite ball, turned with mild curiosity.

In the doorway, with a heavy cloak flung over his shoulder, stood Stefan Dvorak. Kat's heart leaped as she cried his name, then froze as she saw Father Comenius directly behind him.

"I have brought Father John back," Dvorak announced. "With Frederick as king, our renegade priest is safe in Prague."

Kore, who had been in one of the little house's other two rooms, pushed aside a striped curtain and beamed at the newcomers. "Is it possible? Are we to enjoy freedom after all these years?" He moved swiftly to embrace Stefan, then shook hands with Comenius. "Praise our ancestors! This is a happy day!"

From the corner where he had been dozing by the fire, Grandfather Yojo pulled himself to a sitting position on his eiderdown mattress. "Savor it," he murmured in his rough old voice. "Such joy never lasts."

"Now, now, old one," Kore began, but Father John put up a hand.

"He's right, my friends," the priest said in his pleasant voice. "This world is sadly flawed. We pass through it only to make ready for the next."

Kat was watching neither the Roms nor the clergyman, but only Stefan. So far, he had not yet met her gaze. Rather, he had gone to the table and was holding up an amber-colored bottle of brandy. "Here, let us drink *pliashka,* the old way." At last he turned to Kat and touched her hair. "May I?" he said in that deep, casual voice she had kept in her heart during all the long months of separation. Carefully, he removed the bright blue ribbon that bound her hair and wrapped it around the bottle. Seemingly from nowhere, Thirza produced a string of gold coins, which Dvorak also placed around the brandy.

"*Devlesa avilan,*" cried Kore, when his glass had been filled. "It is God who brought you!"

They all drank. Kat made a face as the burning liquor touched her tongue. Father John, sipping slowly, smiled at the others. "Perhaps you'll join me Sunday for services in whichever church I'm allowed to preach."

Thirza gave the priest a wily look. "Churches aren't for the likes of us. Do you know what the Roms did with their church?" She didn't wait for Comenius to respond. "We bartered away our beautiful stone chapel to the *Gaje* for a church made of bacon. Then we ate it." She chuckled, the golden hoops dancing in her ears. Noting that Kat looked more dismayed than amused, Thirza wagged a finger. "Never mind, Father John knows what we're like and loves us all the same." Squatting next to Kat on the floor, she arranged her bright veils around her shoulders and looked at Dvorak. "Now tell me, *churdo,* are you here to stay?"

Kat was puzzled. *"Churdo?"*

Thirza nodded. "Stefan. A *churdo* is half Rom, half *Gajo.*" She pointed to the festooned brandy bottle. *"Pliashka* is served only for betrothals and weddings. Are you going to marry this little English girl or not?"

Stefan's bronzed skin turned even darker. "Thirza, you ask too many questions. The brandy may also be drunk for other celebrations." He did not look at either Thirza or Kat when he spoke, but into his crude tin cup. "I'm only passing through."

"To where?" rasped Grandfather Yojo, emboldened by age and the brandy.

There was a pause. Kat watched Stefan keenly, hoping for some explanation. "Nurnberg," he said at last. "I will accompany the elector, to urge the Lutherans and the Calvinists to unite behind Frederick and help him keep his new throne."

"Bosh!" exclaimed Thirza. "He sits upon it, so it's his. Who is to gainsay the chosen king of Bohemia?"

"The emperor, for one," Stefan began, clearly entrenching himself in a political dissertation. But before he could continue, Kat jumped to her feet, all but fell over

Father Comenius and flew out the door. She was halfway
to St. George's Lane when Dvorak caught up with her.

"Kat!" he shouted, as she tried to make her way around
a load of lumber that was being drawn by cows. "What's
wrong? Have my friends treated you ill?"

Kat was trapped between the lumber and a quaint house
with a sign on the door depicting a swan. "No! They're
wonderful! It's you I hate!" With a snarl, she pushed past
the slow-footed beasts and started to run back in the direction of the Rom cottage. But Stefan was too quick for her;
he caught her billowing skirts, bringing her to a standstill.

"What is this mutiny?" he demanded, pulling her close.
The driver of the cart kept moving forward, but his gaze
strayed to the quarreling couple. So did that of a goodwife
carrying a basket of fresh bread on her head. Even an aged
yellow dog got up from its place by the door of a cheerful
red house and began to nose about in the cobbles near Stefan's leather boots.

"You left me!" Kat declared, trying to keep her voice
low. "You abandoned me in a strange city with strange
people and strange ways! And now you're going away
again!" She thrust her pugnacious face up at him. "Why
shouldn't I hate you?"

Stefan's grip tightened on Kat's arms. "You didn't hate
me in Heidelberg." His expression was unfathomable, but
his voice was just a trifle thick. The brandy, perhaps, Kat
thought, and wished he weren't so close. With a glance over
his shoulder to make sure no one could see precisely what
he intended to do, he let go of one of Kat's arms and idly
brushed at the thin homespun fabric that covered her
breast. "You seemed to like me. And my touch."

Inwardly, Kat shivered at the contact, light and seemingly undemanding. A stranger might have brushed against
her in a crowd. But the effect was not the same. Jerkily, she
turned away, trying to deny her feelings. "You don't like

me. If you did, you wouldn't leave." The petulant note in
her voice annoyed her. She wanted to revile him, to reject
him, to send him away as hurt and humiliated as she felt.
But his hand had now strayed to her waist, purposefully yet
casually caressing her flesh.

With the arrival of a stalwart young king and a beautiful queen, Prague's mood had changed. Dissension was on
the wane, at least during these festive coronation days. The
sight of young lovers in a sun-dappled lane brought smiles,
not frowns, to the faces of passersby. But Kat could not
permit herself the luxury of becoming a public spectacle. If
she and Stefan had been observed in such an unseemly, if
delicious, display of affection outside of Whitehall, her
embarrassment would follow her to the grave. With one
swift, strong movement she pulled free and regarded Dvorak sternly.

"Strangers are watching," she admonished him. "Take
me back to Golden Lane."

"Nonsense," responded Dvorak, allowing her to step out
of his embrace but not his reach. "That little house is
crammed with people. Come," he said, lightly taking her
arm, "let's walk."

Kat did not resist. They moved down the hill, toward the
river and the stone bridge that linked the Lesser Quarter
and the Old Town. A bronze crucifix adorned the span,
with the Savior flanked by the Blessed Virgin and St. John.
Kat eyed the sculpture with mixed emotions.

"'Tis handsome, I suppose, but smacks of popery. Why
does the Protestant majority tolerate it?"

Stefan steered Kat past the bridge with its twin towers,
obviously built for defense. "Tradition. We Bohemians
aren't as inclined as you English to destroy beauty for the
sake of doctrinal quibbling."

Kat ignored the criticism. To her right she saw a high
wall, and beyond, clusters of chimneys and steep dark tiled

roofs. A strange wail floated on the air, as did the cries of children and stale smells of food. "What's that?" she asked, pointing to the huddled mass of buildings.

Stefan glanced over his shoulder and his jaw tightened. "The Jewish Quarter—Joseph's Town, it's called." His stride grew brisker, as if he were anxious to get away. "Unfortunately, we are as guilty as any other nation of harassing the Jews. You English are no better. It's sad."

Kat was craning her neck, hoping for a glimpse through one of the windows that looked out over the high wall. "I've never seen a Jew. What are they like?"

"Like people. Like us." He turned a corner, putting Joseph's Town behind them. "We shut our Jews away, forcing them to live in cramped, filthy conditions. Do you know what a Golem is?"

Kat wrinkled her nose at the strange word. "A what?"

"A Golem. Several years ago, before I was born, it was said that a rabbi created a creature called a Golem." Stefan gave Kat a wry smile as they moved along a broad, busy avenue. "Such stories about Jews are not uncommon."

Kat shivered. "That's frightening. I don't like that place. Where are we going?"

Above them, the November sun flirted with the clouds, lending little warmth but a pale golden light. Stefan pointed to a hill crowned with trees. "The view from there is breathtaking. I will lay Prague at your feet." He gave her his engaging grin.

Kat tried to remember how angry she'd been with him only minutes earlier. But his embrace had cooled her temper even as it warmed her heart. Amid outcroppings of white rock they climbed the hills, passing an occasional wood gatherer who had branches piled high on head and shoulders. As they reached the crest, Kat saw a brightly painted wagon among the trees. A man in a crimson vest and dark blue breeks waved to Stefan.

"Kalia!" He saluted the Gypsy, who exhibited a broad, gap-toothed smile.

"You are early," said Kalia, whose expression changed to puzzlement as Kat came closer to him. "Who is this, Stefan? Not one of Nano Yojo's tribe, I'd wager."

"Not exactly," Dvorak answered, with his hand at Kat's elbow. "But she lives with Yojo and the others. For now."

"Ah!" The explanation seemed sufficient for the Gypsy. He made a little bow to Kat as a dozen wary men, women and children emerged from the woods like deer flushed out by huntsmen. "Shall we begin our *patshiva* now instead of after dark?"

Stefan shook his head. "Such a celebration must have firelight. Another time, perhaps. I have brought Katerina here to show her the city. Your camp commands the finest view in Prague."

Kalia spread his berry brown hands. "That's why we make it here. And it is safe. We can see who approaches." He glanced at the others, who sniggered behind their hands. With another bow, Kalia gestured toward the wagon. "Come see our traveling home, Mistress Katerina. It is called a *vurdon* in our tongue, for living on the *vurma*." Noting Kat's blank expression, he wagged a finger. "That means the trail. Our home, you see. You wish to be like a Rom?" He waved a hand at Kat's Gypsy garb.

"For now," Kat replied with a questioning glance at Stefan.

He was helping her up the narrow steps of the *vurdon*. "Kalia is the kapo, or chief of the Gypsies in this vicinity. His tribe, unlike Grandfather Yojo's, seldom stays in one place very long. They are true nomads."

Kat absorbed the information with half an ear, for she and Stefan had entered the wagon and her eyes were dazzled by the colorful clutter that provided the Gypsies with the necessities of life. Burnished copper pots, gleaming pewter vessels, sparkling cut glass, shiny tin mugs, glittering gold bowls danced against a background of brilliant fabrics, from purple velvet to scarlet satin. Kat felt as if she'd walked into a star-studded rainbow.

"Where," she gasped, "do they get all these things?"

Dvorak eyed her with amusement. "You think they stole them?" He didn't wait for her to answer. "Some, yes. But most of these the Roms make themselves." He picked up a finely wrought silver goblet, etched with a forest scene. "Their craftsmanship is generally excellent. It's one reason they're so hated by the *Gaje*. Gypsy workmanship offers too much competition, thus they are outlawed from most city guilds."

Kat fingered the goblet and shook her head in wonderment. "It's lovely. It's all lovely," she added with a sigh, taking in the brilliant, crowded interior of the *vurdon*. "But how do they all sleep in such a small place?"

Stefan grinned. "Gypsy magic," he said, reaching down to pull out what Kat had thought to be a drawer but what was actually a taffeta-covered trundle bed. He pointed to three more drawerlike panels rising up to the wagon's arched ceiling. "Four beds to a side. They could easily sleep two-dozen people."

"Oh! It's...quaint," said Kat, for want of a better word. She could scarcely imagine being crammed into such a small space with so many others. Sharing a tiny room with Thirza and two of the older children in Golden Lane had already strained her sense of privacy. "I suppose you get used to it."

Stefan shrugged. "It's their way of life." He replaced the silver goblet and rested both arms lightly on Kat's shoulders. "But it is neither cramped nor crowded now, little Kat." The black eyes scoured her upturned face.

"It's also the middle of the day," Kat noted, suddenly feeling both uneasy and expectant. "Where's Kalia? And the others?"

Stefan leaned down to push open the shutters of a small window. "Gone. See for yourself."

Kat looked out. Stefan was right—the only sign of life in the little clearing was the fitful smoke from the fire that had cooked the Gypsies' noon-day meal. Her face wore a bemused expression.

"How," she asked dryly, "did you manage that?"

"They come, they go," he replied in his easy manner. "That is the way of the Rom. You know that by now."

"Too well." Her green eyes held a hint of reproof. Stefan Dvorak was taking her submission for granted, but the reproach was for herself as well as for him. She had followed him willingly, and now he was pulling her close, his hands caressing her back. He and Kalia had mentioned a celebration. Could it mean that Stefan was going to ask for her hand? Kat shivered, not with the cold, frightened feeling of the enforced squalor outside of Joseph's Town, but with anticipation.

"Those Roms know," she breathed in feeble protest. "What will they think?"

His mouth brushed hers. "That we must be alone." He kissed her nose. "That your beauty stirs me to desire." He ran his hands from her waist to her thighs. "That you want me as much as I want you." He kissed her temple. "That we are making love." With a deft motion, he bunched up the bright skirts and petticoats, cupping her buttocks. "Am I right?"

Kat pressed against him, knowing she should deny what was so palpably true. Instead, she nipped at his chin with her teeth, then linked her hands behind his head, pulling his face even closer. "The Roms know everything," she breathed, allowing him to lower her onto the sky blue taffeta bed. "Like you, they seem to read my mind."

"I am one of them, after all," he murmured against her throat. He had promised himself he'd keep away from Kat until Bohemia was truly free. But she was so near, so enchanting, so ripe for love. Protestant Frederick had been crowned. Dvorak asked himself if he was being lulled into complacency. It was possible—but with Kat in his arms, delusion didn't matter.

His fingers were at the laces of her bodice, slowly yet adroitly undoing the yellow ribbons. Kat tugged at his white lawn shirt, making little circles on his bare broad chest. Stefan freed her breasts and grinned with pleasure. "How fair you are! How long it has been since the snows of Heidelberg!"

"Too long!" exclaimed Kat on a sigh. "How could you leave me thus?"

"A worthy question," he replied, tracing the valley between her breasts, then suckling at the taut, rosy nipples. Kat moaned with delight, feeling that now-familiar, ever-wondrous fire build within the well of her being.

"Oh, Stefan!" she cried, wrapping her legs around him, "why do you make my head spin?"

A low chuckle rumbled in his throat. "It is the way of men and women. We are meant to mate in joy and part in sorrow." His mouth caught hers, all restraint abandoned. Together, they freed themselves of their remaining garments, savoring each other's flesh, each discovering anew the wonder of the other. Kat reveled in the sinew and muscle of Stefan's hard strength; he delighted in the soft, guileless voluptuousness of her body.

It was Kat, burning for completion, who urged Stefan to drive them to the pinnacle of ecstasy. Captivated by her eagerness, he delayed his conquest only long enough to drive her desire to unexplored heights. Kat emitted a strange, keening noise from her throat, then felt the full power of Dvorak somewhere deep in her soul and cried out with triumph. In some shadowy corner of her mind, Kat knew that the long months of anxiety had not been in vain.

Kat dozed, nestled in the crook of Stefan's arm. Twilight settled in over the *vurdon,* and at last he got up to light a pair of candles on what appeared to be a small shrine. Yet, Kat noted sleepily, there were no religious pictures or icons, not even a cross. Instead, she saw a jumble of personal effects—a jeweled comb, a slim stiletto, a homely tankard.

"What are those things?" she asked, propping herself up on one elbow and realizing that without the warmth of Stefan next to her, the autumn air had grown quite cool.

Stefan was pulling on his breeks. "They belong to the Gypsies' ancestors. For all that the Roms give lip service to Christianity, they still worship their forebears." His expression was almost plaintive. "It's difficult for the *Gaje* to understand. They consider such ideas heresy."

A year ago, Kat might have held the same opinion. But she had spent too much time with Thirza and the others to condemn the Roms for their unorthodox ways. "Revering one's ancestors sounds harmless enough," she said, reaching for her petticoats. A sudden thought struck her; and her eyes narrowed at Stefan. "Do you follow those Gypsy ways?"

He shrugged into his lawn shirt. "No. But formal religion has no hold on me. I believe in the *Gajo* God, in Jesus Christ. But only people like Father Comenius make sense when they speak about the soul. Stripped of all its mummery, Christianity is nothing more than kindness. To me, the true heretics are those who forget that actions are more important than trappings."

Kat was interested in Stefan's opinions only as they applied to their future. For a moment she was silent, trying to maneuver the conversation around to his intentions. But he was smiling at the sight of her nakedness, disconcerting her and making havoc of her thought processes.

"Fie, Stefan, look the other way!" she commanded, holding the petticoats up to her neck. Subtlety never having been her strong suit, Kat gave up. "Well?" she demanded, struggling back into her clothes despite his reluctance to turn away. "What is to become of us now?"

"To become of us?" He seemed genuinely mystified. "I go to Nurnberg. You return to Golden Lane. What else?"

"Stefan!" She was covered, if in a haphazard manner. "I'm not a Rom! I can't spend the rest of my life dipping candles and mending pots! Nor," she added with a dignity that did not mesh with her disheveled appearance, "can I let you make love to me at your whim. Think what you like about Christianity, but its teachings tell me our lovemaking is a sin."

He sat down beside her and took her hand. "It would be a sin for us *not* to make love," he said reasonably. "A waste. But little Kat," he went on, looking deep into her troubled eyes, "I can't offer you marriage. I have no future. My world is upside down. You wouldn't want to be tied to a rootless, impoverished half-Gypsy nobleman. It would go against your English grain."

Both words and manner were so rational that Kat was momentarily speechless. Then her emotions caught up with her. "Rot! You're inventing excuses!" She yanked her hand away and stood up in a swirl of green and yellow and blue. "Could it be that you're afraid to marry a woman who has been accused of poisoning her fiancé?"

Stefan was abashed. "Do you think I believe such calumny?" He took a step toward Kat but she backed away.

"Then you're a philanderer, plain and simple! Don't talk to me of being rootless and my English grain! If your intentions aren't honorable, leave me be! You're toying not only with my body, but with my heart! Is *that* a kindness?"

Dvorak looked faintly startled. "Kat..." he began, sounding disturbed. With his usual grace somewhat impaired, he, too, got to his feet. "You don't understand. I've devoted my life to my people, to Bohemia. The emperor will do everything in his power to dethrone Frederick and your friend Bess. Until peace and freedom are assured for all Bohemians, I can't think of myself. Or even of you."

His obvious sincerity didn't move Kat a jot. "As if you or any other single person could make a difference!" She tossed her head, the chestnut tresses sailing around her shoulders. "You could wait your lifetime for peace! And for freedom or independence or whatever fine phrases you extol with such eloquence! But what will that do for you as a man? Don't you want sons? A home, a life of your own? What good is your precious freedom if there's nothing left for *you?*"

It was not a new thought for Stefan, at least not since he'd met Katherine de Vere. Even seven years earlier, he had felt a tinge of doubt about his footloose ways. But this was not the time to admit it, not when Frederick and Elizabeth had just mounted the throne of Bohemia and it might—just might—be possible to achieve the dream he'd cherished all his life.

Impulsively, he took Kat in his arms. Stefan felt her stiffen and try to pull back, but he held her fast. "Would you wait a year? Or two?"

The soft fabric of his shirt was pressing against Kat's cheek. Darkness surrounded the *vurdon,* with the pair of candles giving off a wavering amber glow. Kat could hear voices outside and musical instruments whose notes she didn't recognize.

"Wait for what?" she mumbled into his chest.

"For me." Stefan's lips were in her hair. "For us. To be together."

Kat pulled back just enough so that she could look up into his face, sharply etched yet cast in shadow. The music drifting in from outside had an exotic, almost mystical sound. "Do you love me?" she asked, and was aware that her voice was wistful, even pleading.

His hesitation made her tremble. Then Stefan's grip tightened. "I do. By God, I do."

He realized that until she had asked the question, he had not known the answer.

Chapter Fifteen

Kat did not attend Elizabeth's coronation. Nor was there any summons to court issued from her old friend in the month of November. Kat's only comfort was that none of the English courtiers, except for Albert Morton, had witnessed Elizabeth's crowning in St. Vitus's Cathedral. King James refused to acknowledge his daughter as anything but the Electress Palatine. His rigid attitude did not bode well for any English aid to the Bohemian national cause.

Thirza did her best to comfort Kat. "Your friend has made a good impression so far, but she must be very busy. And there is the babe, due any moment. You will hear, I am sure of it."

Kat was not so sanguine. Nor did she think Thirza's reports were entirely accurate. Rumors about Bess buzzed through Prague. Her attire was immodest, displaying too much of her white bosom. She allowed her personal attendants to be overly familiar. And worst of all, when a group of goodwives had brought tiny loaves of bread baked in the shape of flowers to commemorate St. Elizabeth of Hungary's feast day, the new queen had not been properly impressed. Kat fretted over Bess, but not as much as she worried about Stefan Dvorak, who had gone from Nurnberg on a progress of Moravia with Frederick. Unrest was rampant, and Spanish troops were said to be on the move.

Winter was setting in over Prague, and Kat despaired of ever seeing England again.

But in December, Albert Morton arrived in Golden Lane, his homely, honest face astonished by Kat's appearance. "If I had passed you in the street, I would not have known you," he insisted.

"That is the point," Kat assured him, rummaging in a chest for her traveling cloak. "This city is not a safe place for me. But at court, I shall have the king and queen's protection."

Albert was looking mystified, but Kat didn't choose to enlighten him at present. Now that Elizabeth had finally sent for her, she was eager to be gone from Golden Lane. But as she gathered her meager belongings, she saw Grandfather Yojo's wrinkled face and Pulika's huge dark eyes and Thirza's shoulders hunched over a pot in which she was cooking a chicken.

"I'll be back," Kat blurted in an uncertain voice. "I don't intend to disappear. Again."

Thirza looked up from the cast-iron pot. "You will not. You are *Gaje.* You will forget us Roms." She shrugged her little shoulders in a gesture not unlike Stefan's. "It is your way. You will be a fine lady again and someday you will go home to England."

To Kat's astonishment, Thirza's eyes were filled with tears. In four quick steps, Kat was at the other woman's side, leaning down to hug her. "Thirza! I could never forget you! Or any of the Roms who helped me! I will be back, I promise."

But Thirza sniffed, either from disdain or emotion, and shook her head. "No promises. They can be so easily broken. Then hearts break, too." She drew away and forced a smile. "For you, the *vurma* leads to England. Follow it. And follow your heart."

* * *

The previous week, Elizabeth had given birth to another son, named Rupert in honor of Frederick's ancestor. To Kat, the new mother looked wan, almost spiritless. The recriminations Kat had hoarded up to hurl at her friend now died on her lips.

"What's wrong, Bess? Are you ill?" Kat asked when they were finally left alone in the royal chambers. Unlike fusty but comfortable Whitehall and elegant, handsome Heidelberg, the Hradcany's palace showed outright neglect. Kat was dismayed by the dull leather upholstery and the faded, dusty tapestries.

Bess moved restlessly in the big canopied bed. "I'm well enough, all things considered. But Freddy is gone all the time and this place is so ugly. The people aren't friendly and all my attendants—especially the Germans—are homesick. I wish we'd never come to Prague." Fretfully, she tugged at the patched comforter. "It's gruesome, too. You wouldn't believe the tales of foul deeds. These Bohemians are a bloodthirsty lot. I'd give the world to be back in London—or Heidelberg."

"But you're a queen now, Bess," Kat pointed out, smoothing the skirts of her borrowed gown. Fleetingly, she wondered if she'd ever again have clothes of her own. "I heard your coronation was a wonderful spectacle."

"It was long and dull," Bess replied, frowning. "It would have been more of both, had I not been eight months gone with child." She sat up, brightening a bit. "Is it true you've been living with Gypsies? Were you really kidnapped? Tell me about your adventures, Kat. They sound very exciting."

Having lived through months of drudgery in the cramped quarters of the house in Golden Lane, Kat failed to see the romance of her predicament. But to please Elizabeth, she did her best to sketch a lively string of anecdotes. By the time she finished, Bess was laughing, some of the bloom restored to her cheeks.

"Oh, tell me again about the Gypsy wagon! To think you actually went inside! Why ever for?" inquired Elizabeth, pouring them each a glass of excellent beer.

"Why?" Kat turned vague. "Well, to see it, of course. The Roms make beautiful things. There were candlesticks and goblets and glassware and..." In her mind's eyes, the picture of the *vurdon* grew dim. All she could remember was Stefan Dvorak, lavishing caresses on her naked body and exploring every inch of her flesh.

"Jewels?" coaxed Elizabeth. Then she caught the dreamlike expression on Kat's face. "Oh, by heaven, I should have guessed! Kat," she went on earnestly, leaning forward, "you're quite smitten with that Gypsy baron, aren't you? Why don't you marry him?"

For Elizabeth, who had been lucky enough to make a political match that was also a personal success, matters of the heart were quite simple. Kat, however, was not as fortunate. Strange, she thought, that a royal princess should fare better in love than a mere noblewoman. She envied Elizabeth—her husband, her babes, even her worries. For now, Kat would gladly change places with her old friend.

"Someday, maybe I will," Kat answered evasively.

In mid-March, Frederick returned from his progress. Stefan Dvorak was not with him, having gone on to England to join Christopher Dohna in begging King James for military aid. Kat's heart sank. It was hard enough to be apart from Stefan, but to know that he was treading the cobbles of London, breathing the damp air off the Thames, speaking with familiar faces—that was enough to sink Kat into the deepest gloom.

Yet she dared not succumb to despair, if only for Elizabeth's sake. The Queen of Bohemia had rallied physically from her last delivery, but she still suffered from bouts of melancholy. At the end of March, Bess's spirits briefly soared for the christening of little Rupert. But Prince Anhalt's decision to engage the imperial troops at the earliest possible moment sent a shiver of disquiet throughout the Hradcany. Elizabeth attempted to divert herself by becoming better acquainted with her new capital.

"Mayhap I've been too harsh in my judgments about this place," Elizabeth confided to Kat as they strolled outside the handsome Belvedere Palace built by Ferdinand I for his wife, Anna Jagellowna. "The tennis courts are excellent, the riding school is very fine and St. Vaclav's vineyard is almost a rival to those of the Palatinate. I mustn't let all those ghastly tales of torture and death that surround the Hradcany dismay me. After all, the Tower of London has some hideous stories of its own."

"True," agreed Kat, thinking of Thomas Overbury for the first time in months. Indeed, she had not given much thought to her own dilemma with regard to Thomas until she had encountered Susan Howard walking with Prince Anhalt in the Gardens of Paradise outside the Hradcany. The two women had acknowledged each other—barely.

"Now that our young Freddy has been nominated to succeed my darling husband, I feel things will become more settled," Elizabeth said, going off on another tack. They had stopped to admire a colonnade with a frieze of graceful foliage interspersed with elegant medallions. Kat allowed herself to be impressed. "Father Comenius is trying to convince Protestants of every persuasion to rally behind Freddy. We're concerned about how any plans we make seem to reach the emperor's ears so quickly, but I'm convinced my royal sire will finally relent and send soldiers to protect us."

Kat took a short breath. "Does that mean you've heard from . . . England?"

Elizabeth eyed Kat with amusement. "From Christopher? Or Stefan?" She threw back her head and laughed, more merry than she had been in months. "Oh, Kat, you are without guile! Yes, a message came this morning. They will return before the summer is out. Are you pleased?"

Kat was blushing. "Of course I am," she replied a bit crossly. "Stefan has written only two letters. But he visited my parents." Kat had been elated to learn of his trip to Windrush, and to hear that Lord and Lady de Vere were in good health, if apprehensive spirits. He had not alluded to the Overbury affair, and Kat wondered if he feared that his correspondence might be intercepted.

With a lightened step, Elizabeth led the way back to the carriage where her other attendants were gossiping and eating sweetmeats under the bright July sunshine. They all looked up as Albert Morton rode into view on a sprightly gray mare.

"Albert!" Elizabeth hailed him as Bess Apsley was suddenly overcome by a fit of the giggles. "Are you going to take us to see the mixed bathing in the Moldau?"

For once, Albert didn't respond with his usual good-natured grin. Dismounting from his horse, he bowed jerkily and steered Elizabeth, as well as Kat, out of hearing range.

"Your highness," he began, out of breath. "Forgive my intrusion, but..."

His sudden hesitation brought fear to Elizabeth's face. "What is it? Not Freddy!" She looked as if she were about to shake the hapless Albert.

"No, no," he reassured his mistress, "naught such as that. But the Emperor Ferdinand has issued a decree stating that unless King Frederick renounces the crown of Bohemia, he will fall under the ban of the empire."

Elizabeth's fair brow furrowed. Kat thought she was about to burst into an angry tirade, but instead, she merely snapped her fingers. "Pah! Who gives a fig for the emperor and his silly bans? What does my lord have to say about this impertinence?"

Albert answered readily enough. "That as elector and as king, it is up to him to judge the emperor, not the other way round."

Elizabeth gave a swish of her silken skirts. "And so it will be. What nonsense!" She started again for the carriage, but caught Albert's still unhappy face. "Well? What else? Are the imperial troops at our gates?"

"No," replied Albert, fumbling with his cap. "Not yet," he added under his breath. "But the people are distressed. They heard about the crucifix being removed from the Charles Bridge last night."

Elizabeth looked blank. "What crucifix?"

Kat remembered the sculpture very well. "The one with Our Savior and the Blessed Virgin and St. John, in bronze. You've seen it, I'm sure."

"Oh." Elizabeth gave a little lift to her shoulders. "I suppose I have." She turned back to Albert. "What about it? It's gone, you say?"

"Yes, your highness, taken away under cover of darkness. The people, Catholic and Protestant alike, consider its removal a sacrilege." Albert wore a miserable expression. "It's said that you ordered their icon destroyed. You would not cross the bridge because you believed the statues were blasphemous."

The color drained from Elizabeth's face. "That's a lie!" she cried, grabbing Kat's wrist for support. "I would never do such a thing!"

"I know," soothed Albert, now sweating profusely. "I know, and so does your court. But the people don't know it, your highness. They are up in arms."

Elizabeth's chin quivered; her grip tightened on Kat's hand. "Damn them! Damn this foul country!" She used

her free hand to make a fist, and shook it at the broad blue
sky. "Damn Bohemia! I wish we'd never come!"

The late summer days seemed to mock the mood of the
Bohemian courtiers. The citizens of Prague no longer went
about their daily tasks with an air of hope. Rather, they
seemed to withdraw into themselves, suspicious and apprehensive. To Kat's amazement, Frederick had assented to
the removal of the revered bronze crucifix. His chaplain,
Dr. Abraham Schultz, had been busy since his arrival in
Prague, ordering the destruction of all artwork that
smacked of popery. To Frederick, the grouping on the
Charles Bridge was no more than a superstitious effigy. To
the Christian people of Prague, the statues were a symbol
of their faith, no matter what form of worship they practiced. It was easier to blame the pleasure-loving English
consort than the hooked-nose old German clergyman.

The first casualty in the controversy was Albert Morton, who resigned his post and left for England. The part-
ing was doubly bitter, since he took Bess Apsley with him
as his intended bride.

"My English circle shrinks by the month," Elizabeth la-
mented on an August afternoon in the orchard below the
Black Tower.

"A pity you can't send Susan Howard back," remarked
Kat, watching two speckled fawns drink from a brook that
danced among the pear and plum trees. The royal children
were nearby, playing with their dogs and monkeys.

Elizabeth nodded. "She has seduced Anhalt. I mistrust
her intentions."

A fanfare resounded above them, causing both young
women to look up toward the palace. Kat knew that
Bethlem Gabor, the Prince of Transylvania and one of
Frederick's staunchest adherents, was due to arrive any day.
But she hoped it was Stefan Dvorak instead of the Hun-

garian princeling. Christopher Dohna had ridden in the previous week, bringing news that King James had indeed sent troops. However, their number was not only disappointing, they were under orders to guard Heidelberg, not Prague. Elizabeth had wept tears of frustration. Kat had paced her chamber with anxiety, not for the sake of any city or country, but for her lover. Dohna, however, insisted that Dvorak had been set to sail just a few days after his own departure.

Kat wasted no time hurrying up St. George's Lane, past the basilica, across the square and into the royal palace. No guard of honor stood on hand; whoever had arrived was no Transylvanian prince. Out of breath, Kat scanned the vast entry hall. In front of a huge fireplace stood Frederick with a clutch of other men. Kat peered across the marble floor, trying in vain to find Stefan Dvorak.

"The swarthy pig isn't here," said a voice behind Kat. "Her highness's new secretary, Francis Nethersole, has just arrived. Perhaps your poxy lover's ship was sunk by pirates."

She whirled, coming face-to-face with a smirking Susan Howard. "He will come any day," declared Kat, trying to keep her voice steady.

Susan tucked a stray tendril of golden hair behind one perfect ear. She wore diamonds at her throat and, despite the hot weather, carried a sable muff. "Maybe he's come back already and someone has thrown him into Daliborka Tower. The cells are all underground, you know, and prisoners are lowered by ropes through trapdoors. They have only the rats for company." Delicately, she licked her lips.

Kat fought down an urge to pummel Susan with her fists. The gems that glittered on the Howard woman's white breast seemed to dazzle Kat's eyes. She tore her gaze away, glancing over her shoulder at the stranger who was gesticulating at Frederick's side. Nethersole, she supposed

vaguely, noting that the elector seemed sunk in gloom.
These were not happy days in the Hradcany. Kat started to
turn for the wide staircase when Prince Anhalt sauntered
in, beaming at Susan.

"My lady," he began, executing his most courtly bow,
"you grow more beautiful by the hour!"

Susan simpered, then languorously waved her muff at
Anhalt. "La, highness, you flatter me! I thought you were
with your troops in the field, singeing the emperor's tail
feathers. Pray tell me all about your manly military adventures."

Kat could stand no more of their fatuous badinage. She
all but ran across the marble floor and galloped up the
stairs like a gawky colt. Sanctuary was her tiny bedchamber, its single tall window overlooking the rampart gardens. Flinging open the door, she virtually fell into the
room. A shriek erupted from her lips.

Stefan Dvorak was lying on the bed, fast asleep.

"Where have you been?" he asked, stifling a yawn and
groping for his boots. "I got here this morning."

With shaky hands, Kat was pouring them each a goblet
of wine. "I was with Bess and the children, out by the
Stag's Moat. Susan said you hadn't come with Nethersole."

"I hadn't." Stefan accepted the goblet, took a sip and set
it down. "I sailed with him, but rode ahead. He was inclined to linger, this being his first trip abroad." With a
grin, he put an arm around Kat and pulled her to him.
"You look as if a Golem had been chasing you. Where did
you get that awful dress?"

Ruefully, Kat glanced down at the cream-and-green satin
that hung like a large load of laundry from her slender
frame. "It belonged to Bess Apsley. She's trying not to eat

so much now that she's betrothed, so she left most of her wardrobe in Prague.''

Stefan felt for Kat's backside, then kissed her mouth. "I can scarcely find you in all this fabric. Why don't you cut it up and make two gowns? Or a counterpane."

Kat laughed, and kissed him in return. As ever, his presence made her troubles melt away. "Oh, Stefan, I missed you so! What news of England and my parents?"

Kat felt him tense and draw back. "They are well. Truly. Of the rest, we'll speak later.'' He leaned down and caught her lips in a long, hard kiss. Kat leaned back in the crook of his arm, relishing his strength. Running her fingers through his crisp black hair, she felt his tongue touch hers in lazy exploration. Kat's senses quickened, and the heat of desire made her brain grow fuzzy. There were so many questions, so much she needed to know, so many problems to be resolved . . . yet for now, she required no more than the reassurance of his arms.

But the world was not about to give them peace. An urgent knock at the door forced them to break apart. Kat hastily rearranged the curls at her temples and asked after the caller.

It was Christopher Dohna, his fair skin faintly pink with embarrassment, seeking Stefan Dvorak. "His highness must see you at once,'' he began, looking beyond Kat to the window where Stefan now lounged against the embrasure. "Lady Susan thought you might be . . . here.'' He made a vague gesture that took in Kat's small chamber.

Stefan grinned. "Lady Susan is well informed.'' He moved easily toward the door. "Remarkably so,'' he added as an afterthought. To Kat's surprise—and pleasure—he paused to kiss her cheek. "I'll be back. Soon.''

After he and Dohna had left, Kat touched her cheek and smiled. For all the difficulties in keeping Frederick and Elizabeth on the throne, almost a year had passed since the elector had agreed to be named King of Bohemia. Surely he was entrenched by now, with Prince Anhalt's soldiers guarding the frontier and King James's men in the Palatinate. Kat hummed to herself and set about finding a more suitable gown.

She had just slipped into gimped green silk over ecru brocade when she received word that Elizabeth needed her services. Kat hurried to the royal chambers to find her old friend practically hysterical.

"Kat!" shrieked Bess, whirling away from a large chest that was being packed by two attendants, "we are done for! Spinola is marching through the Lower Palatinate, headed for Bohemia!"

It took Kat a moment to comprehend the scene. In the corner, young Frederick Henry was stuffing toys into another chest. He was dressed in riding clothes and his eyes were wet with tears. Elizabeth ruefully regarded her eldest son and tried to compose herself. "There, there, my darling," she said, rushing away from Kat to the little prince, "this will be a wonderful journey! You will adore your Dutch cousins! There will be ice skating and sailboats and all manner of amusements! Such a treat!"

As Elizabeth helped her son pack, Kat turned to Trina von Solms, Dohna's wife. "What is happening? I don't understand."

Trina, who was expecting her first child in the New Year, sniffled into a handkerchief. "It is as her highness said. The Dowager Electress sent word that imperial troops are marching toward the frontier. The crown prince is being sent away for the sake of his safety." Trina's plump shoulders shook as she blew her nose. "I wish to God her highness and the other babes would go, too!"

A glance at an ivory case told Kat that more than the prince's toys were headed for The Hague; Elizabeth was dispatching some of her jewels as well. Kat's expression was grim as she joined in preparing young Frederick Henry for his journey. He left, in the company of his nineteen-year-old cousin, Prince Louis, within the hour. There were more tears and a sense of panic as his unadorned black carriage rolled out of the Hradcany. Elizabeth collapsed in the arms of her husband.

Kat searched for Stefan but could not find him. Late that night, Christopher Dohna informed her that Dvorak had ridden out after the young prince's coach, to form a rear-guard escort and, upon his return, to determine the exact strength of the imperial forces. Desolate, Kat lay awake, alone in her bed under the sliver of a late-summer moon. She had been a fool to think their troubles were over. On the contrary, it appeared they had only begun.

Chapter Sixteen

It was mid-September before Elizabeth learned that her firstborn had reached his destination safely. The journey had not been without incident, however, despite the zealous secrecy that had attended Frederick Henry's departure. A few miles across the Silesian frontier, according to a hastily written letter from Stefan Dvorak, a band of imperial soldiers had tried to divert the prince's coach. Dvorak gave no further details, but obviously he and his compatriots had managed to get the young heir to safety.

"Praise God," Elizabeth murmured, sinking onto a divan and accepting a glass of red wine from Trina von Solms. Like her lady-in-waiting, the Queen of Bohemia was pregnant. She was also suffering an attack of nerves. "Now what to do?" she asked fretfully. "My darling has left for war. He wants me to flee Prague. How could I do such a thing while he faces death in the field?"

"If the battle is joined, he'll face it whether you are in Prague or Putney," replied Kat dryly. With so many of the English attendants gone, and the German women in a state of constant upset, it had fallen on Kat to keep up the royal circle's spirits. The task was daunting, especially since her anxiety over Stefan mounted by the day. "Here," Kat urged, picking up Jock-o and putting him on Elizabeth's

ap, "you've been neglecting the little fellow. Sing him a
ong, or teach him how to dance."

With a trembling hand, Elizabeth petted the monkey
while cradling Prince Rupert in her other arm. "Oh, Kat,
what would I do without you? You cheer me so!"

Across the room, Susan Howard sniggered.

At last the rains came to Prague. The Moldau swelled,
nd tiny rivulets poured down the cobbles that led away
rom the Hradcany. On a dreary morning in early Octo-
er, Kat thought she heard a thunderstorm brewing in the
west. But Francis Nethersole dolefully informed her it was
unfire.

"There have been skirmishes these past few days, but no
decisive battles," he informed Kat in his dour manner. For
a man schooled in diplomacy, Nethersole was utterly lack-
ng in tact. He was, however, capable and loyal, but his
pessimistic outlook on life was a far cry from that of the
good-natured Albert Morton.

Kat was unnerved by Nethersole's report. "How close are
he imperial soldiers?" she asked, keeping her voice low so
hat Elizabeth and her attendants couldn't hear.

Nethersole reflected. "Thirty, forty miles, with the Duke
of Bavaria at their head. To the west, Spinola's forces have
overrun most of the cities along the Rhine. Frederick won't
et on in his letters to Elizabeth, but the state of his army is
deplorable. And Count Thurn refuses to serve under Count
Hohenlohe's command. If I were Frederick, I'd make that
Bohemian a general—Dvorak, that's his name. A very dark
fellow, but he wears authority well."

"He's not a soldier," Kat snapped, and was dismayed at
her tone. She saw Nethersole's startled expression and
tempered her words. "That is, he's unversed in military
arts. Jock-o would do as well."

Her remark might have been construed as showing a lac
of confidence in Stefan Dvorak, but Kat felt little remorse
She could not bear the idea of her lover leading an arm
into the field. It was bad enough to have him in dange
while he scouted the enemy positions. Kat watched the rai
pour down and prayed that one way or another, the Bohe
mian question would soon be resolved.

In mid-October, Frederick returned to Prague for a brie
stay. He met with the English ambassadors, whose visi
cheered Elizabeth greatly. But the only news they reporte
from King James was that he hoped war could be avoidec
even at this late date.

Frederick, however, brought Kat more welcome news—
Stefan Dvorak was in excellent spirits and had sent her
short letter. Kat held it against her breast and hurried o1
to the privacy of her chamber. She glowed as she read th
salutation and felt tears sting her eyes.

My love,
The enemy advances each day. I urge you to convince
Elizabeth to withdraw from Prague before it is too
late. The king has begged her to leave the city, but fears
that her characteristic vacillation will prevent her from
acting decisively. Pray use your influence to convince
her she and the rest of the court are not safe, even
within the walls of the Hradcany.

Four days ago, I determined the quarters of the
Duke of Bavaria, conveying his position to the king,
who immediately set out in the rain to surprise the enemy. But when Frederick and his men reached the
camp, the duke had departed. From this incident, I
must conclude that there are traitors among us.

Kat frowned at the page, then read the last paragraph.

Do not distress yourself over my welfare. I move about the countryside with ease, and have not been hampered in my expeditions. Rather, be of concern for your own safety, and entreat your dear friend to make haste from Prague so that one day soon we may enjoy a happy reunion.

Having hoped for a more romantic missive, but grateful to receive one at all, Kat folded the letter very small and tucked it inside her sleeve. She knew it was useless to talk to Elizabeth while Frederick was with her. Indeed, it would be up to him to convince his wife that there was no virtue in remaining in the capital. Kat saw her own puzzled reflection in the mirror that hung over her little dressing table. How could it be that only a year ago Frederick and Elizabeth had entered Prague in such triumph? Even in the summer, which was not long past, there had still been hope. But the imperial armies had made havoc of optimism, laying to waste lands from the Rhine Valley to the Bohemian Forest.

By the end of October, Frederick was back with his army at Rakovitz. The days and nights with her husband had steadied Elizabeth's nerve. "My darling's soldiers have taken over the Star Park," Elizabeth said in a mood of euphoria as she ventured outside the Louis Palace on a day warmed by a fitful sun. "I should like to visit them and make a speech of encouragement, as Queen Elizabeth did at Tilbury before our English navy sailed to meet the Armada."

Kat marveled at Elizabeth's confidence, and tried not to look dismayed. "At least you should consider going somewhere else for your confinement," she suggested as they strolled by the equestrian statue of St. George outside of the old provost's lodging. "The Hague, mayhap, with Prince Frederick Henry."

Trina von Solms and a trio of German attendants were at their heels. "Kat is right," Trina chimed in, huffing a bit to keep up. "Once the babe is born, flight will not prove so easy, your majesty."

Elizabeth gave her lady-in-waiting a scornful look. But before she could further reprimand her for such timorousness, a large crowd began to pour in from the direction of Hradcany Square. The women paused, noting that many of the newcomers were peasants, ill-clad and haggard-looking.

"What's this?" whispered Elizabeth.

At least a hundred men, women and children were milling about outside the main entrance to St. Vitus's Cathedral. More were straggling in, some hauling farm animals, others towing carts and wagons.

"Refugees, I'd guess," said Kat, not much liking their sullen expressions. "Bess, let's go back to the palace."

Elizabeth was undaunted. "What for? These are my subjects. I shall address them." She looked around, apparently considering the best vantage point from which to deliver her greetings.

In the distance, cannons rumbled. Curses erupted from the crowd. Elizabeth started to climb up a short flight of steps that led to the pedestal of the equestrian sculpture. A woman screamed her name.

"Elizabeth! Heretic whore! She's brought us misery and war!"

More curses cut across the courtyard. At least forty people surged forward, waving their fists and, in some cases, crude weapons. Elizabeth teetered uncertainly on the top step, while Trina von Solms wrung her hands.

Kat pushed the other attendants aside. "Bess! Come down!" she commanded, gesturing urgently.

But the Queen of Bohemia was already hemmed in.
Though she stood above her irate subjects, Elizabeth might
as well have been their prisoner. Trina von Solms and the
other German attendants had dissolved into quivering
masses of helplessness. Fleetingly, Kat considered ordering them to start pushing the mob back by force, but she
knew such an effort would be futile. Instead, she broke
away from the angry refugees and fought her way toward
the Golden Gate entrance to the church. The side chapels
appeared empty. Kat raced into the nave and uttered a sigh
of relief when she saw Father Comenius at the high altar.

He evinced only mild surprise as Kat hurried up the steps
to meet him. As succinctly as possible she outlined Elizabeth's dilemma. Moments later, Comenius was in the
courtyard, his pleasant voice carrying above the crowd with
amazing force. Kat saw Elizabeth, with now at least a dozen
refugees clutching at her hem, reel slightly, then square her
shoulders and take a deep breath.

The mob grew silent, drawn to the clergyman who looked
so humble but exuded such uncompromising authority. "A
crowned queen, sanctified in this very cathedral...the
greatest gift of God, motherhood most holy...blameless
in the face of those who persecute and wage war..."

Comenius's impromptu homily wrought its minor miracle. The mob drew back, respectfully allowing Elizabeth to
descend the steps from the statue's pedestal. Kat went to
meet her, taking her arm and steering her back through the
crowd toward the Louis Palace. The queen's other attendants straggled behind, still shaken and murmuring over
the dire fate so narrowly averted.

And still the cannons rumbled in the distance.

The trunks were packed; the wagons were loaded. But
Elizabeth would not accompany her favorite belongings. "I
am the queen," she announced, recovered from her fright

outside the cathedral. "If Freddy stays, I stay." Only a wistful expression in her eyes indicated that she might be sorry to see her possessions depart without her.

But within the week, Frederick was back in Prague, gleeful with the news that the Count of Bucuoy had been wounded. "He is one of the emperor's best generals, along with Spinola. It requires two men to take his place, a Walloon named Johann Tilly, and that Bohemian buffoon Wallenstein." Frederick laughed at his own little joke and hugged his wife.

Kat did not share his majesty's mirth. She knew nothing of Tilly, but her personal knowledge of Wallenstein had indicated that he was no buffoon. Certainly Stefan Dvorak took Brecht seriously.

On that cool November night, Frederick and Elizabeth supped with their courtiers. An air of relaxation seemed to wash over the Louis Palace. As ever, Francis Nethersole was not so sanguine.

"The enemy is but eight miles from Prague," he murmured to Kat over a course of roast partridge in plum sauce. "Can Anhalt and Hohenlohe stop their march?"

"His majesty says his forces number twenty-five thousand strong," Kat replied, trying to sound hopeful, but in fact feeling as glum as Nethersole looked. "Surely this Tilly and Wallenstein cannot break through their ranks."

Nethersole did not answer.

Sunday morning fog sprawled over Prague, drifting through the narrow streets and nestling among the tiled rooftops. Kat, attired in wine red satin with a perky hat adorned with ostrich feathers, attended services with the royal party in the cathedral's St. Wenceslas Chapel. Father Comenius did not preach that morning, having succumbed to an ague.

The English envoys were present at dinner, feasting on boar, cod and capon. Elizabeth was dazzling in purple brocade and white satin. As the cod, floating in white wine and herbs, was brought to the table, the Queen of Bohemia announced that she and the English ambassadors would visit the troops at the Star Park that afternoon.

"The fog will lift, and I will make my little speech," she said with a smile. Obviously, thought Kat, her friend's confidence had not been shaken by the ugly encounter of the previous week. Kat mentally saluted Elizabeth for her courage.

"I shall be there to welcome you," said Frederick, rising from the long table. "I intend to ride ahead, so that all will be ready for your gracious eloquence." He kissed his wife's hand and exited the banquet hall.

Great platters of dried fruit and several cheeses had just been delivered by liveried servants when Kat looked up to see Stefan Dvorak enter the hall. She could not suppress a gasp of astonishment. His clothes were dirty and torn; there was a fresh cut on his forehead and a bloodied bandage on his left forearm. Kat leaped to her feet, but Stefan had gone directly to the queen.

"I bring unfortunate news, your majesty," he said, his deep voice echoing in the suddenly silent room. "There has been a major engagement at White Mountain. Our cannon is lost. The royal army has fled in disorder." He clamped his mouth shut, his face etched in disapproval as well as defeat.

Elizabeth uttered a little cry and pressed a hand to her breast. Others at table also made noises of protest and disbelief. Stefan was now standing erect, though it was not clear whether he was awaiting orders or about to give them. Then he raised his right arm.

"The king is safe, having headed out to White Mountain after the battle was over. He will return shortly. Meanwhile, we must all prepare for immediate flight."

A flurry of activity greeted Dvorak's pronouncement. Chairs scraped, wine goblets were overturned, cutlery clattered on the stone floor. Kat, who had been sitting about ten feet away from Elizabeth pushed past Francis Nethersole, Christopher Dohna and two footmen to reach Dvorak.

"Stefan!" she cried, just as he was about to turn away. "What happened to you? Were you wounded?"

His face was as grim as Kat had ever seen it. "My body is merely scratched," he said, the black eyes glittering with emotion. "It is my pride that has been dealt a mortal blow."

"Oh, Stefan..." Kat began, anxious to dismiss his distress as a casualty of the masculine soul. But she plumbed the depths of those dark eyes and took a backward step. "Oh." She took a deep breath. "Were you hurt in battle?"

"No." He gave Kat a bitter look. "My injuries occurred when our Bohemian soldiers fled the field. I was lucky not to be trampled by those cowards." Dvorak clutched the pommel of his *schiavona* as if he wanted to use the weapon on his own people.

"I heard they were ill provisioned," Kat said in a small voice, but realized her words made no impression. She still didn't understand men, still couldn't fathom Stefan's feelings for his country. But in this moment of crisis, she knew she had to try. "What can I do?" she asked almost helplessly.

He started to make a gesture of dismissal, then glanced at Elizabeth who was looking pale and tight-lipped as she fended off questions from the English envoys. "Take care of the queen," he said tersely, turning on his heel. As Kat's heart turned heavily in her breast, Stefan reached out with his good arm. "Then, God willing, some day I will be able to take care of you."

He wheeled out of the banquet hall, in search of his king. *And,* Kat thought, *his pride.*

She moved to Elizabeth's side, interrupting the barrage from the English ambassadors. Taking the queen firmly by the hand, Kat looked into her friend's stunned blue eyes. "Come on, Bess. We're going home. At last."

King Frederick had not yet left the Hradcany when Stefan Dvorak arrived with the terrible news. Despite Dvorak's advice to the contrary, the badly shaken sovereign had insisted on joining his army. Dvorak still hoped to stop Frederick. If his majesty was taken prisoner, the war, along with the battle, would be over. He caught up with the king's party at the Strahow Gate.

"Sire!" Stefan called, trying to make himself heard above the panicky crowd of Prague citizenry who had been rousted from their churches and wakened from their Sunday naps. "Sire!" he called again, this time eliciting a backward glance from Frederick. Stefan dismounted from his black gelding and hurried to the king, making a cursory bow. "I have given your lady wife the grievous news. I fear she will not leave Prague until you go with her."

Frederick's olive skin flushed. "I should have been in the field," he muttered. "I failed my men." The king held a leather-bound flask in one hand, the reins of his horse in the other. He hardly seemed aware of Dvorak's presence.

But shouts from Strahow Gate caught his attention. Cristopher Dohna was at the gate, exchanging rapid-fire conversation with the guardsmen. "Highness!" he shouted. "It's Anhalt and the others! They demand admittance!"

Frederick looked momentarily blank. "Anhalt? What others?"

Dvorak joined Dohna. A moment later, he called back to Frederick, "The army, sire. Or what is left of it. They seek sanctuary." He set his jaw and refrained from spitting on the ground.

"Oh, God!" Frederick reeled in the saddle. Anguish suffused his face, so youthful and carefree until this very day. With effort, he composed himself. "Open the gates!" the king commanded.

Dvorak and Dohna stepped aside as a horde of terrified soldiers charged into the Hradcany. Some were bloodstained, many were bandaged, most were ragged and dirty. The distraught residents of Prague stared at the remnants of the army that had been dispatched to defend their city. Some hooted with derision; other wept. Frederick drained his flask.

In the chaos that followed, Stefan managed to help steer the king back to the Louis Palace. Prince Anhalt, his dashing cavalry uniform torn in three places, was the color of slate and virtually speechless. With his head hanging, he kept close to Count Hohenlohe, an equally dispirited figure. Frederick dismounted at the entrance to the palace and turned to Stefan.

"I blame only myself," he murmured. "Why did I return to the Hradcany?"

Stefan was in no mood to be tactful, though his tone was not unkind. "Because you love your wife more than you love Bohemia."

Despite the liquor he had just imbibed, Frederick's gaze was level. "Is that so wrong?" The question was almost a whisper. Dvorak started to phrase a reply, but Frederick shook his head, "King or not, a man has to consider. Which would cost him more dearly—losing his woman or losing a country?" A tight little smile crossed his haggard

face. "I made my choice. And, by God, I'm not sorry."
Frederick placed his hand on Dvorak's shoulder. "Do you
understand what I'm saying?"

Stefan Dvorak gazed into his monarch's eye and drew a
sharp breath. "Yes," he said, a curious note in his voice.
"I think I do. Now."

Elizabeth was ready to leave the Hradcany. Having seen
her husband return safely, she was finally willing to take
flight. In a flurry of packing, the queen and her attendants
gathered everything they could carry from the royal quarters. Kat and Christopher Dohna supervised the frenzied
activities, and were among the last to leave.

"I think we have commandeered every coach and carriage in the Hradcany," Dohna told Kat as they gave the
state apartments a final inspection. "Let's hope there is
room for us, too."

Kat knew she had to go, but, like Elizabeth, was unwilling to depart without the man she loved. "We seem to have
everything that's necessary," Kat said, noting a small bundle that had been left lying on Elizabeth's canopied bed.
"What's that?"

Dohna glanced at the counterpane, then shrugged.
"Nothing of import, I should think. Shall we go?"

Kat put on her cloak. From out in the courtyard, she
could hear shouts, cries, even screams. There were rumors
that the dreaded Imperial Cossacks were about to invade
the city. Kat gave the bundle a last look, then started. The
bundle moved.

"Sweet Jesu," breathed Kat. "Is it one of Bess's pets?"
She raced to the bed and undid the satin-edged blanket.
Little Prince Rupert gazed up at her with innocent brown
eyes. Kat picked the baby up and stared at Dohna. "How
like Elizabeth to remember all of her menagerie and forget
her son! I don't know whether to laugh or cry!"

Dohna was as dismayed as Kat. "Let me take the babe. Come, we'll put him in the coach with her highness. We must not delay another moment."

But Kat was still reluctant to leave without Stefan. "Maybe Bess left another of her offspring somewhere," she said, making an excuse to linger. "You go. I'll scan the other rooms."

Dohna wasn't keen on leaving Kat. "The other children are old enough to be noticed," he said, but he saw the set look on Kat's face and guessed the reason. His decision was forced by the cries of Prince Rupert, who apparently had decided he was hungry. "I'll go, mistress, but I advise you not to tarry. This is not a safe place."

Kat knew as much. For the next ten minutes, she moved from room to room, occasionally glancing through the windows to see the string of vehicles wending their way out of the courtyard toward Hradcany Square and the Charles Bridge. By now, the royal party had been joined by ordinary citizens, hauling their belongings on every conceivable conveyance. Some were fleeing on foot, taking only what they could pack on their backs. The sight of so many people suffering from so much fear overwhelmed Kat with sadness. For the first time she felt a kinship with the Bohemians, as fellow human beings who had become history's victims.

But she could not find Stefan Dvorak. Its apartments stripped, its corridors empty, the Louis Palace echoed with her footsteps. Desolation held Kat in its grip. She decided to make one last turn of the council chambers, thinking that perhaps Stefan had agreed to meet there with Anhalt or Count Hohenlohe or even the disgruntled Thurn.

To her surprise, there were candles lit in the chancellery. Evening was setting in, cool and crisp. Kat saw a strip of light under the door and pushed it open carefully. Seated at the head of the long table, holding a goblet of white wine and wearing a rose satin gown, was Susan Howard. It was hard to tell which woman was more astonished at the sight of the other. They both spoke at once, with the same words. "You haven't left."

If Susan had been anyone else, Kat would have laughed at the exchange. Instead, she stiffened, her hand still on the latch. "Why are you here?" she demanded.

"I ask the same question," Susan said, adopting her customary languid air and setting down her wineglass. "Aren't you afraid of the cossacks?"

"Aren't you?" Kat countered. Then her hand fell away from the door. "No, of course not," she said in a curious tone. "Why should you be? You're waiting for them."

With studied nonchalance, Susan patted her artfully coiffed curls. "Whatever do you mean?"

Kat took four quick steps to the council table, lightly resting her hands on its gleaming oak surface. "You are the emperor's spy. You Howards are all Catholic, you would serve Rome before King James. That fool Anhalt was your dupe. You seduced him, you wrung information from him, you betrayed Frederick and Elizabeth! However did you wrest your appointment in the first place?"

Susan emitted her tinkling laugh. "That was easy. I told that parsimonious King James I didn't want wages, only the privilege of serving his illustrious daughter. He couldn't wait to send me to Heidelberg instead of some dutiful daughter who needed the stipend for her dowry." Susan turned suddenly sober. "I think you'd better go now, Kat de Vere. Your speculations are amusing, but unprovable. And your time in Prague is up."

The apprehension that Kat had felt for Stefan she now felt for herself. Flicking her tongue over dry lips, she glanced at the door. All she had to do was leave the council chamber, go down the stairs and out into the courtyard. Carriages would still be waiting. But Susan was so smug, so sure of herself, so steeped in the Howard power. Kat had one last thing to say.

"I know you forged that letter from my parents." She ignored Susan's wide-eyed denial. "Did King James really ask Bess to send me away because of the Overbury scandal?"

"Naturally." Susan had gotten to her feet, arranging the folds of rose satin. "He always believed you were guilty." Her lavender eyes narrowed at Kat. "You can't go home, you know."

Kat pounded a fist on the table. "Oh, yes I can! And will. All the Howards in the hemisphere can't stop me. Wait until James finds out that you're a papist spy!"

For just a brief moment, Susan's lovely face hardened, making her almost ugly. Then she relaxed and lifted one shoulder. "Such nonsense! You won't be able to return to England, I told you that. In fact," she went on, gliding toward the long windows, "you won't even get out of here if you don't leave now. Look," she said, throwing the casement open and letting in a rush of cold air, "the coaches have all left without you."

Hurrying to the window, Kat looked down—not into the courtyard, but into the moat. In her agitation, she had forgotten that she was on the south side of the palace; the courtyard was to the north. She could see nothing below but darkness.

Kat swung round. "What are you talking about? They're all on the other side, heading for Hradcany Square and the river."

"Oh, really?" Susan's expression didn't change. Without warning, she lunged for Kat, thrusting her through the window embrasure. Stunned, Kat tried to dig in her heels, but slipped, falling against the casement. Taller and seemingly stronger, Susan grasped Kat's shoulders, pushing her closer to the edge. Kat scrambled for purchase, trying to strike at Susan with her fists. Hampered by the folds of her cloak, she found the blows glanced off. Kat's balance grew precarious.

With her ribs pressed against the sill, she frantically fought to keep her feet on the floor. But Susan now had hold of Kat's legs, pulling them painfully up behind her. The ties of her cloak were straining at her throat, threatening to strangle her. With one last, desperate motion, Kat kicked with all her might. By chance, her feet connected with Susan's stomach, knocking the wind out of her.

Kat slumped to the floor, yanking at her cloak while Susan gasped for breath and clutched at her midsection. The lavender eyes were wild; the golden curls were a-tangle, like little snakes. Kat tried to rise, but her knees were weak. Susan staggered to her own knees, then stood up. With hatred in her eyes and teeth bared, she flew toward Kat, grabbing at the heavy fabric that covered her shoulders. Susan stumbled; the cloak fell free. Propelled by her own momentum, Susan Howard hurtled through the window.

Kat screamed, then looked down. She could see nothing in the darkness. But after living in the Louis Palace for almost a year, she knew that the dung heap was gone and that the heavy autumn rains had filled the castle moat.

Chapter Seventeen

Kat ran all the way from the council chambers, down the spiral staircase and out into the courtyard. Whether Susan Howard had lied about the carriages having left the Hradcany, Kat would never know. However, the last vehicle was lumbering away when she got outside. She considered chasing after it, but the effort of escaping the palace had cost her dearly. Exhausted and unnerved, she began to walk slowly, stiffly, toward St. George's Lane.

No one paid any heed to the bedraggled figure who moved among them like a sleepwalker. The citizens of Prague had seen too many strange sights already that day. People were still streaming through the Hradcany, riding top-heavy carts and driving wagons crammed with furniture, food, clothing, even an occasional bird cage. Kat turned near the Black Tower and headed for Golden Lane.

The little house with its green door looked even smaller than Kat remembered it. She started to knock, then realized that the shutters were closed. Stepping back, she looked up at the chimney; no spiral of smoke drifted on the autumn wind. The Gypsies were gone. No wonder, thought Kat unhappily. Their fate would be too cruel at the hands of the imperial army. Kat said a quick prayer for their safekeeping, then trudged back down Golden Lane.

She was turning at the Daliborka Tower, famous in gruesome legends, when she saw the soldiers marching in brisk formation. These were no ragged stragglers, flying from defeat, but men of victory. Kat glanced around the cobbled street. A handful of citizens were still struggling to load their belongings. They would not be much interested in a foreigner, left behind by the royal party. Indeed, they might even turn on her, blaming the king and queen for their troubles. Kat sought a hiding place, but found none. The soldiers were heading straight for her. She shivered, as much from fright as from the cold, for her cloak had gone with Susan Howard. Kat closed her eyes, hearing the relentless tread of the victors' boots on the ancient cobbles. If these were the hated cossacks, she could only wish that she had suffered the same fate as Susan....

"Mistress de Vere!" The voice was amazingly familiar, yet Kat could not place it. Warily, she opened her eyes. In the light from a pair of torches, she recognized Albrecht Wallenstein, somehow looming larger in his military garb.

The troop halted at Wallenstein's signal. "What are you doing here, my lady?" he inquired, almost as if they had met by chance in the marketplace at Hradcany Square. "Why have you not gone with the others?"

Kat could not tell him the truth. She pushed a strand of hair out of her eyes and sighed wearily. "They left without me. I was...ah...I forget." Too exhausted to lie, Kat avoided Wallenstein's shrewd gaze.

"Then you must come with me," he said. "It isn't safe for you to be alone in the city tonight."

Kat had no choice. Yet she still had to find Stefan. Or would he try to find her? No, he would assume she had gone with Bess and Freddy. Maybe that's where he was, even now—in their caravan. "Where are the king and queen?" Kat asked, evading Wallenstein's invitation.

"I'm not sure," replied Wallenstein, aware that his well-drilled soldiers were growing restive. "We just arrived in Prague. I suspect they are still somewhere in the city, and will wait until morning to head for the frontier."

"You'll let them go?" Kat asked in surprise.

Wallenstein assumed his sternest expression. "I would not. But I haven't yet received orders from the emperor." He held out his hand. "Come, mistress, you're cold, you're tired, you should eat. I must find quarters for my men, but I'll have an escort take you to my uncle's house."

Kat hesitated, than gave in. "As you will. But I'm not going as a prisoner, as I did last time," she added in a stubborn voice.

"Of course not." Wallenstein smiled faintly. "You're my guest. And a welcome one," he added. Kat could have sworn that he flushed.

"Very well." She tried to exude as much dignity as she could muster while Wallenstein commanded four of his men to take her to Vilem Slavata's residence. But as she mounted a dappled mare and allowed one of the soldiers to put a fur-lined cape over her shoulders, Kat still felt like a prisoner.

"Some day," said Brecht Wallenstein, gesturing at the rooftops of the Lesser Quarter, "I intend to build a grand house here, with magnificent gardens in the Italian style. Like the Farnese Palace. Have you ever been there?"

"No," answered Kat, preoccupied with her own problems.

"I shall hire Italians," he continued, far more loquacious than usual in the afterglow of victory. "Many of these present dwellings will have to be torn down. The town gate that stands over there should also be razed, since it . . ."

Kat didn't care if Wallenstein used explosives to blow up the entire city. She had been staying "under his protecion," as he so tactfully put it, for three days. Prague had officially surrendered to the imperialists. Frederick and Elizabeth had spent their first night away from the Hradcany at a wealthy denizen's home on the Bruckenplatz. But there was still no word of Stefan Dvorak.

"...to share it with me," Wallenstein was saying, and Kat felt his hand on her arm.

"What?" She glanced down at her crimson sleeve, now begrimed and rumpled. In a household of men, there was no one to borrow clothes from except the servants.

Wallenstein lowered his eyes and gripped Kat's fingers. "I'm a widower. Childless." His sallow face was turning pink. "Ever since I met you...that is, I've been alone a long time.... If you would do me the honor..." His expression was miserable, a far cry from the victorious warrior of the previous Sabbath. "Will you marry me, Katherine de Vere?"

Kat retreated as far as she could, but her fingers were held fast by Wallenstein. "Is that the price for my freedom?" Her tone was as cold as the sharp November air.

Abashed, Wallenstein stared at her. "No. Oh, no! I would not coerce you!" He swallowed hard, then released her. "I thought...I felt... Oh, mistress, you are so fair! And clever, too! We would do so well, you and I!"

In her soiled gown, with her hair streaming down her back and her nerves stretched taut, Kat felt anything but fair. But she took pity on Wallenstein, and tried to soften her words.

"I once vowed never to marry. I'm well beyond the age to wed—a veritable spinster, at least in my native land. Forgive me, sir, but I can't accept your kind offer." She gave him her kindest smile. "I think it's best that you send me home."

"Home?" Wallenstein sounded as if he'd never heard of the word. "But I'm told you have no home."

"Who said that?" Kat demanded.

Wallenstein looked genuinely mystified. "I don't recall. But I did hear it. Somehow." He still seemed quite miserable. "You are in disgrace in England, that's what I was told. And," he continued, moving closer again, "I don't care what you've done. I know only one thing—I love you."

"And so do I." Stefan Dvorak, wearing his familiar white shirt, black breeks and tall leather boots, spoke from the doorway. "Come, Brecht," he said in his easy manner, "let us barter. Like the Roms."

Kat ran to him, noting that his arm was still bandaged but that the cut on his forehead had almost healed. "Stefan! Thank God! I thought you were dead!"

"Hardly that." He put his good arm around her. "Well, Brecht? What do you say?"

Wallenstein was fighting for composure. "What do you mean, barter? You and your Bohemians have lost everything. What could you possibly offer me?"

Stefan grinned and looked down at Kat. "Your would-be bride. Will you give her up for the King and Queen of Bohemia?"

His proposal shocked both Kat and Wallenstein. "Are you mad?" gasped Wallenstein.

Stefan, with his arm still around Kat, lounged against the doorframe. "Hear me out. I don't intend to turn them over to you. Far from it. But there are many in this city—maybe a majority—who still prefer Frederick to the emperor. I will speak plainly. While I, too, prefer him to Ferdinand, I never thought him adequate as a ruler. But as long as Frederick remains in Bohemia, he is a threat to your Catholic cause. If you let me take Kat away from here—peaceably—I will see that the king and queen are safely escorted across the frontier into Silesia."

Wallenstein rubbed at his chin, then went to the double doors that led to the balcony overlooking the Lesser Quarter. As he stood deep in thought, Kat gazed up at Stefan, who kissed the top of her head and motioned for her to keep silent. At last Wallenstein turned, a wry expression on his face.

"This is not an easy decision," he said ruefully. "But you're right, Stefan. I want Frederick out of Bohemia. As long as he stays, he will be a rallying point for dissidents." He paused, gazing at Kat. "This does not mean that I don't love you, mistress. But I must put the empire above my personal happiness." His shrewd eyes shifted to Dvorak. "You know me too well, Stefan. You knew what I would do for the empire, just as you would have done for Bohemia."

But Stefan shook his head. "Not anymore, Brecht." He glanced down at Kat and gave her shoulder a squeeze. "Not ever again." He gazed soberly at Wallenstein. "Farewell. We will not meet again. *Nais tuke,* brother." He raised his bandaged arm in salute, then led Kat out of the room, away from the residence of Vilem Slavata and to the city gates that would put Prague behind them forever.

It was snowing in the mountains that guarded the Silesian frontier. Elizabeth sat in her coach, dejectedly watching the thick flakes fly past the little window. "They call me the Winter Queen," she said to Kat. "I came with the snows, I leave with the snows. Oh, Kat," she exclaimed, fighting back tears, "what is to become of us?"

Kat stopped watching Stefan Dvorak struggle to free one of the other coaches from a snowdrift and leaned toward Elizabeth. "You will be all right, Bess. You have Freddy and your sweet children, and the new babe is due in just a few weeks. If you can't go back to the Palatinate, you could come home to England."

"My selfish royal father doesn't want us," Elizabeth replied bitterly, a hand on the mound of her belly. "He didn't give a fig about Bohemia, but he blames us for losing the German possessions. And all he ever sent to help was a token force! Damn his niggardly Scots hide!"

"He's not well," Kat argued, glancing out the window again to discover that Dvorak and his companions had given up on freeing the coach. "Once your brother is king, things will be different."

Elizabeth sighed and wiped at her eyes. "Mayhap." She pushed open the door and inquired after their progress. Christopher Dohna was of the opinion that all the coaches were stalled. They would have to wait until the storm passed.

"I can't wait!" Elizabeth said fretfully. "I must join Freddy in Breslau! What am I to do if the babe comes early? Have my delivery in a pile of snow?" She saw Trina von Solms standing next to her husband and shook her head. "And Trina, too. Her time is also nigh. First babies come when they will."

Stefan was tapping on the door of the coach. Kat opened it, delighted as ever to have him near. He poked his head inside, snowflakes sticking to his dark hair.

"Highness," he addressed Elizabeth, "I have a worthy steed ready to take you across the frontier. Will you ride with its owner, Captain Ralph?"

Elizabeth beamed. "I'd ride with the devil to get out of Bohemia! Oh, thank you, Stefan!" Awkwardly, she emerged from the coach, letting Dvorak hand her down. She was still smiling as she greeted Ralph Hopton, whose handsome steed docilely awaited her. "Wonderful!" enthused Elizabeth, as both Dvorak and Christopher Dohna helped her climb behind the freckled-faced young soldier. "I'd rather ride a horse than be bounced along in a coach any day!"

And then it dawned on Elizabeth that the time had come to part with Kat. So caught up in her own affairs had she been that she'd failed to inquire about her old friend's plans.

"You're really not coming with us?" Bess asked now, turning wistful.

"Not now," said Kat. "Stefan is going to escort Father Comenius to Moravia. We'll have him marry us there."

"Oh." Elizabeth forced a smile. "That's wonderful. And then?"

Kat glanced up at Stefan, who had an arm slung casually around her shoulders. "We're going home. To England."

Elizabeth's fair face puckered. "But . . . is it safe? Especially after . . . Susan?" She left the rest unspoken.

"Susan fell," Stefan said calmly. "It was an accident. As we all know, on that Sunday in Prague many strange things happened."

Elizabeth lowered her eyes. "Yes. Of course." The steed was becoming restless; so, Kat reckoned, was Captain Ralph. "But Kat," protested Elizabeth, "are you sure it's all right for you to go back to England?"

Kat held her head high. "I'm prepared to find out. With Stefan's help, nothing will daunt me. I refuse to spend the rest of my life in exile."

The former Queen of Bohemia and Electress Palatine looked straight ahead, into the oncoming snow. "I would not want that, either. I swear it would break my heart never to see England again."

Impulsively, Kat reached up and touched Elizabeth's gloved hand. "Oh, Bess, don't make vows you can't keep! I did that once, you know. Your heart is strong as a lion's! And an English lion at that! Now ride off and roar into the wind! Remember, you've got another cub to care for!"

Elizabeth grasped Kat's fingers and gave them a squeeze. She smiled, if somewhat tremulously. "You always make me feel better, Kat. What will I do without you?"

Kat smiled back, then stepped aside as Captain Ralph put spurs to his steed. In the curve of Stefan's arm, Kat watched Elizabeth disappear into the snows, the Winter Queen making her way across the frontier.

They would never meet again.

Chapter Eighteen

Katherine Dvorak, Baroness Ostrov, returned to England on the last day of the old year under cover of darkness. She was accompanied by Stefan Dvorak and John Comenius, landing in a small fishing vessel near Great Yarmouth on the Norfolk coast. Thomas Howard, Earl of Suffolk and Fanny Howard's father, had been incensed over his niece Susan's death in Prague. Since word had reached England that Thomas Overbury's purported murderer had also been in attendance on Elizabeth, the Howards had demanded that if Kat de Vere ever returned to England, she should be immediately detained for questioning. When she heard the news just before leaving Scheveningen, Holland, Kat had become irate. She was still fuming when they stopped for the night at a small inn outside of Norwich.

"How dare they! Susan was trying to kill *me!* Now they'll dredge up the Overbury scandal and I shall never know any peace!" Kat stormed about the tiny chamber as the wind howled through the rooftops.

Stefan closed the flap on the inn's little window. "You know that would have happened anyway. The matter of Susan's death only gives the Howards more fuel to pour on the fire of your alleged guilt. The important thing is to prove your innocence once and for all." He pulled off his boots and grinned at Kat. "I wonder what Thirza will say when she hears we are wed?"

Despite her distress, Kat smiled. "She will say she saw it in our palms. Whether she did or not, I think she always knew we were meant for each other." Kat stepped out of the skirts of her makeshift riding habit, pieced together from oddments gleaned from Elizabeth's baggage carts. "Oh, Stefan, you must tell me what your plans are now that we're back in England. You've kept me in suspense too long."

But Stefan was placing his shirt over the back of a chair and admiring the curve of Kat's breasts under her silky chemise. "Just another day or two," he replied, moving to take her in his arms. "We must go to the village of Stratton Strawless."

"Stratton Strawless?" Kat wrinkled her nose as she slipped her arms around Stefan's bare back. The name sounded vaguely familiar, but her attempt at recollection failed as she saw the desire in Stefan's dark eyes. She could hardly believe they were man and wife, married by Comenius in a tiny stone chapel at Jesenik, near the Silesian border. "Why? I've never been to such a place."

He brushed her nose with his. "As I said, I'll tell you later." Stefan's hands roamed under the chemise, sliding it from her shoulders. The room was small, with only a table, chair and bed. The flame of a single candle wavered in the draft from the only window. The weather outside was raw, with the wind blowing up the coast, bringing winter to England. But in Dvorak's arms, Kat felt warm. She arched her back and let him kiss the curve of her throat.

"To think you were not the marrying kind!" she said, a note of laughter in her voice.

"Oh?" He caressed her buttocks, felt the flat plane of her stomach, let his fingers trail upward to the valley between her breasts. "And you had vowed never to wed. So," he inquired, grinning as she glowed with pleasure at his touch, "how did we end up like this?"

Kat's green eyes flashed wickedly as she tugged at Stefan's breeks. "I didn't plan on love. *Real* love," she said, stripping him as naked as she was. "I didn't know the meaning of the word." Boldly, she touched his manhood, thrilling them both. "Nor did you, I'll wager."

Together, they tumbled onto the bed. The straw-filled mattress groaned; the rickety frame creaked. Stefan lay on his back, delighting in the wonders Kat worked with his body. "You're right. I knew only freedom. Which means nothing without love."

"We thought we were so clever," Kat mused, spreading herself on top of him, chin to chin. She sighed, looking deep into those black eyes. "We weren't, were we?"

Stefan shifted her hips so that she could capture him between her thighs. "Not by half," he murmured, relishing the feel of her soft, warm flesh.

"True." Kat sighed again, this time with pure pleasure, and hazily wondered what they were talking about. For now, with Stefan penetrating her very soul, there were no more words, no unasked questions, nothing but the two of them made one. Kat gave in to the fire of passion, her entire being caught up in the miracle of love. She saw him watching her, a scant inch away, and fleetingly mused on what he was thinking in this sublime moment of union.

As ever, he seemed to read her mind. Yet he said nothing, and for once she knew what he was thinking—that Kat was no longer budding. Like the rose, she had come into full bloom.

Comenius had ridden to Oxford. Kat wished she and Stefan could have gone with him. "I'm anxious to see my parents," she said as they headed through a chill rain. "Why wouldn't you let me write to them?"

Stefan glanced at her over his shoulder. "Don't they like surprises?" He didn't wait for her reply. "Besides, it's better for them if they don't know we're in England. Until our task is accomplished, we can't take chances."

Kat resigned herself to letting her husband take charge, yet it rankled. She wasn't accustomed to giving in to anyone, especially not without an explanation. "What if nobody except those odious Howards care about the Overbury affair?" she asked, trying to keep her mount from getting mired in the mud.

"They care," Stefan said tersely. "I was in England just a few months ago, remember?"

Raindrops were running down Kat's nose. "What was being said? Did they mention my name? Is Edward Coke still in charge of the investigation?"

It was midday and they were approaching a village. Stefan espied an inn and signaled for Kat to stop. "Coke and Francis Bacon are like terriers worrying bones. In this case, the bones are those of Thomas Overbury. They have never given up the thought of bringing his murderer to justice."

Kat's cloak was wet. So was her hair, and even her feet felt damp in their leather boots. She studied the weather-beaten sign outside the inn, a dirty swan wearing a faded crown. "Then why haven't they found him?" she asked.

Stefan didn't answer. He had dismounted and was reaching up to help Kat. "I will tell you this much," he said, leading her into the inn. "Robin Carr had letters written to Overbury. I found them a long time ago, hidden in a Bible."

"What happened to them?" Kat asked as they entered the common room, where several other wet and weary travelers were warming themselves by the fire.

Stefan drew Kat into an inglenook and pointed to his cloak. "They are stitched inside. I've carried them everywhere."

Kat was aghast. But she had to wait silently until the innkeeper inquired after their needs. When Stefan had ordered beef, bread and ale, and the man had left, she expressed her incredulity. "What do they say? And why would Carr have letters *to* rather than *from* poor Thomas?"

"My question exactly," said Stefan. "That's why I thought they must be important. So I took them. It occurred to me that Carr must have wanted those letters after Overbury died because he was afraid the words he'd written to his old mentor might implicate him somehow."

Kat's green eyes were wide. "Do they?"

"They might." Stefan paused as the innkeeper brought their ale in tall pewter tankards. "Early on, Carr was all fondness and dispensing good cheer. Then his tone changed. He grew menacing. Yet he made no serious threats."

Sipping at the ale, Kat reflected. "But Carr had fallen from favor. Without Overbury to guide him, I'm told he was helpless to exert influence on James."

"Robin Carr is a stupid man," he said. Noting that the group of travelers was moving away from the fireplace as a trio of newcomers entered, he nodded at Kat. "Go warm yourself, you're wet as a newborn kitten. This is no time to catch a chill." Abruptly, he tensed, then leaned across the narrow table and spoke so quietly that Kat could barely catch his words: "Those are king's men. I saw their insignia under their cloaks."

Kat started to turn around, but Stefan clamped his fingers around her wrist. "Don't move. At the count of three, we'll get up and make our leisurely way out the door." Letting go of her, he put some coins on the table, then stood up. Kat, trying to control a rising tide of anxiety, got to her feet, careful to keep her face hidden by her hood. A moment later, they were outside, untying their horses.

"Are they looking for us?" she asked breathlessly.

"I don't know," Stefan answered, swinging into the saddle. "Someone may have recognized us along the way. We can't afford to take risks."

Stefan urged his mount to move as swiftly as possible along the muddy road. They were rounding the first bend when they heard shouts in the distance. Kat glanced back over her shoulder. The king's men were at the road's edge, waving their fists and calling for their horses. Kat put her head down and kept up the pace, riding heedlessly into the driving rain.

Even when the rain turned to snow, they did not stop until they were in Stratton Strawless. Once there, Stefan had to ask for directions. Kat stayed hidden by the roadside, lest the king's men were in hot pursuit and stopped to ask questions, too.

It was after dark when they reached their destination at the edge of the village. As the snow grew thicker and the wind whipped at their clothes, they stopped at a small cottage. A light glowed behind a shuttered window. The snowy path to the front door was unblemished. They dismounted and Dvorak knocked three times.

Shivering from the cold, Kat waited at his side. She knew it was useless to ask why they had come to this homely little place. From inside, she heard the meowing of a cat, then quick footsteps, and finally the door was opened.

Kat's eyes were momentarily dazzled by the light inside the cottage. Then she made out the brightly clad figure outlined in the doorway. For one brief moment, she thought Stefan had brought her to meet with some Gypsy woman of his acquaintance. Then she blinked and looked more closely.

The age-old eyes of Mary Woods returned her gaze.

* * *

"It's an herb tea, most bracing," said Mary Woods, handing her guests small bowls of steaming liquid. "Many people don't care for this new beverage, but I suspect they'll get used to it when they understand its healthful properties."

Cautiously, Kat took a sip and found the brew pleasant enough, if too hot. They were seated in Mary Woods's small, cluttered parlor, where a fire crackled in the grate and the cat now slept on the hearth rug. Kat could not rein in her curiosity any longer. "Why," she asked, glancing first at Dvorak and then at Mistress Woods, "are we here?"

Mary Woods looked at Stefan as if for a cue. Seeing him incline his head, she smiled, that enigmatic expression Kat remembered. "Long ago, you helped me. You and Baron Ostrov saved me from being arrested for theft. I don't forget such good deeds." Her strange eyes regarded Kat over the rim of her tea bowl. "Now it seems you need my help."

"I need *somebody's* help," Kat admitted. "But how can you help me?"

Mary Woods leaned back in her chair and her face turned pensive. The parlor was quite warm, the aroma of exotic spices filled the air, the fire flickered hypnotically. As Mistress Woods's voice grew deeper, Kat felt as if she were floating back in time.

"The Earl of Essex accused me of stealing money and jewels from his wife," Mary Woods was saying in that mesmerizing voice. "But the countess had given me both, as payment for a love potion. I thought it was for her husband, but she gave it to Robin Carr. The potion worked its magic—it always does—so the countess then asked me for another. But this one had nothing to do with love, only with hate." Lazily, her eyes drifted from Kat to the dancing flames in the grate.

"Having made Robin fall in love with her, I assumed she wanted to rid herself of the earl. I refused to make such a deadly potion. She became angry, and said I was a thief. Essex overheard her and assumed the worst. But of course she could not tell him what she was really trying to do. Then the two of you intervened, and I fled London, never to return. The next thing I knew, Thomas Overbury—not the Earl of Essex—was dead. Poisoned. And Fanny Howard had her marriage annulled and wedded Robin Carr." Mistress Woods sighed. "A very simple crime. And just as simple to blame you, my lady. How very wicked."

Kat had snapped out of her somnolent state. "Fanny! But how desperate of her to kill poor Thomas! Did she really think he would have stopped her from marrying Robin?"

Stefan had stood up, his back to the fire. "He would have and he could have. He hated Fanny, not only because she was a powerful Howard whose influence he feared at court, but because his affection for Robin was—like that of King James's—unnatural. Fanny had taken Overbury's place in Robin Carr's bed. That is what is indicated in those letters Robin wrote to Overbury in the Tower."

Kat jumped to her feet and snatched up Dvorak's cloak. "Let me see them! This is incredible!"

But Stefan reached out and retrieved the cloak. "Not yet, little Kat. Keep them where they've stayed so long in safety."

Defiance snapped in Kat's eyes, but she relented, then turned to Mary Woods. "Your testimony would prove helpful to my cause, of course. But to exonerate me and convict Fanny, the court would surely require more evidence."

Mistress Woods nodded complacently. "They would. And they will have it." She looked up at Kat, her face wreathed in a benign smile. "You see, when I refused to brew that lethal potion for the countess, she insisted I tell her the name of someone who would. To escape her cruel clutches, I did what she asked." The ageless brow furrowed. "I sent her to Anne Turner, sister of the royal falconer, Eustace Norton. I know Anne, and she will talk. It is, among others, a great failing of Mistress Turner's."

They sipped more hot tea and ate tiny seed cakes, then prepared to leave for the inn in the village. Stefan tried to give Mary Woods a handsome purse, but she rejected the offer. "It is not necessary to pay me. I learned much of my lore from your Gypsy friends. That's how I came to be near Windrush the day I first met you, my lady," she said to Kat. "Kore . . . he is known to you both, I think?"

"That's right," agreed Stefan. "Someday, I hope, he and the others will come again to England."

They were at the door. The snow had stopped and the wind had died down. The cat, having finished its nap, wound in and out between their legs. Out on the road, a lantern bobbed in the darkness. Stefan hesitated, a hand on Kat's arm. A group of riders came to a halt.

"Damn," breathed Stefan.

"Who is it?" asked Kat in a whisper as a bulky figure in a long cape pushed his way toward them through the newly fallen snow.

"Edward Coke," he said, and to Kat's surprise, he grinned.

The others were trailing behind Coke, whose thundering voice shattered the peaceful winter landscape. "Lady Katherine de Vere! At last! In the name of the king, you are under arrest!"

Stefan Dvorak stepped forward, shielding Kat. "You are wrong, sir, on both counts. This is not Lady Katherine de Vere, but the Baroness Ostrov. And by whatever name she is known, my wife is not under arrest. Unless, of course, you expect to make a public fool of yourself."

Coke's florid face glared above the miniver trim of his cloak. "Such bravado! Hold your tongue, my lord, lest you be arrested as well for conspiracy!"

Gesturing for Kat and Mistress Woods to step back inside, Stefan indicated that Coke should also come into the cottage. The others squeezed in, too, forced to stand in the cluttered parlor.

"A moment, sir," said Stefan in his easy, confident manner. He had removed his cloak and was slitting open the lining with the tip of his *schiavona*. Carefully, he extracted a packet of letters. "If you will read these, I believe you will discover who really murdered Overbury. Then, being a fair-minded man, you will allow my wife and me to depart in peace." He moved to the hearth and picked up the cat, stroking its black fur.

Breathlessly, Kat watched while Coke perused the dozen missives penned by Robin Carr. His face darkened with every page. At last, he looked up, first at Dvorak, then at Kat. "I don't understand.... Was it Carr? Or Fanny?"

"Both, possibly," replied Dvorak. "You will learn that when you question Mistress Anne Turner. She works in league with a physician, one Simon Forman of Lambeth. And I suspect that if you talk to Sir Gervase Elwes, Lord Lieutenant of the Tower, you will find that he is not averse to bribery, especially where pretty women are concerned. My wife and her mother already know as much. The rest should now be easy to uncover."

Coke's eyes narrowed. He had not forgotten the humiliation of Kat's flight from under his nose at Whitehall. "It would be even easier to arrest Lady Katherine, if for nothing more than obstructing justice. She has led me a merry chase!"

The fear that had begun to ebb now rekin̄ ̄
green eyes widened as she saw the determined expr̄ ̄
Coke's bearded face. But Mistress Woods was rumm̄
in a gaily decorated reticule.

"Sir Edward," she said, holding a long, narrow piece of
paper in her hand, "I had hoped not to bother you—or
anyone—with this. But your obstinacy forces me to act."

Coke eyed both Mary Woods and her paper with distaste. "What are you talking about?" he rumbled.

But Mistress Woods was not disconcerted by Coke's
overbearing manner. The timeless face and age-old eyes
remained serene. "It's a list," she said simply. "Put together by Anne Turner and Dr. Forman as a hedge against
their clients betraying them. I must confess I took it to do
the same for me, should I ever have to give evidence against
them. But these are the names of prominent people at court
who have consulted Mistress Turner and the doctor for
various potions, usually aphrodisiacs for their paramours
or mistresses." She put the paper virtually under Edward
Coke's nose. "A glance should suffice, my lord."

Coke's florid flesh paled. He gasped, sputtered and
wheeled around, his heavy cloak undulating like a murky
ocean wave. "To horse!" he cried, and stomped out the
door.

The first name on the list was his wife's.

Kat was crying, not tears of joy or even of sorrow, but of
frustration. Stefan stood in the doorway of the solarium at
Windrush, a brace of pigeons thrown over his shoulder.
"Whatever is wrong, little Kat? Only this morning you told
me you had never been so happy."

"I am," sniffed Kat, blowing her nose into a linen
handkerchief. It was true; with the arrest of Fanny Howard and Robin Carr, her reputation was restored. Her par-

ᴴad been delighted with her marriage, and to allow the newlyweds ample privacy, Sir Edgar had agreed to go to France to help negotiate Prince Charles's marriage to King Louis's sister, Henrietta Maria. Lady Beatrice had been thrilled at the idea of a trip abroad, as long as they could avoid the war-ravaged parts of the Continent. And John Comenius was settled at Oxford, resigned to his life in exile. The only sour note was the future of Elizabeth and Frederick, who were homeless, rootless and unwelcome in most of the courts of Europe, including England. The latest letter Kat had received from her dear friend had been written in Westphalia in mid-March. Elizabeth had tried to put on a cheerful face, exulting over her last delivery, a son named Maurice. But Kat no longer envied poor Bess.

All the same, Kat was feeling somewhat sorry for herself. Tucking the handkerchief up her sleeve, she waved at a table piled high with beautiful satins, silky ribbons and dainty laces. "I've waited for years to have my own clothes," she complained. "Before she left for France, my mother and I contacted the best dressmakers in London. She even said she'd bring back the latest styles from Paris. And now..." Her voice trailed away as she looked wistfully at the lavish pile of fabrics.

Stefan had set the pigeons down on a narrow bench. "What is it then? James no longer covets Windrush now that he can set his sights on some of the Howard properties. Is it money? Your steward seems most competent, the land quite lush. And the farm animals are breeding well this year."

Kat burst into tears. "And so am I!"

Stunned, Stefan almost tripped over the bench. With a curse, he came to Kat's side and put his arms around her. "What do you say, little Kat?"

She looked up at him, at the dark, chiseled face with the intense black eyes, and her heart swelled with emotion.

"I'm going to have a baby! I just realized it this morning! Isn't it wonderful?" She sobbed all the harder, burying her face against his chest.

Stefan held her close. "Good God, it's joyous news!" He was silent for a few moments, rocking her gently. "But why are you crying?"

Kat turned her tear-stained face up to him. "Because I can't wear all those new clothes! I'll have to remake my old ones. And my mother's. Am I never to have my very own gowns?"

Stefan knew he shouldn't laugh, but he did anyway, a great, hearty roar of delight. "Oh, little Kat! You're irrational!"

She sniffed some more and pummeled his chest with her fists. "Of course I am! I'm supposed to be! I'm pregnant!"

Still laughing, he scooped her up and swung her in circles around the room. At last he stopped by the long, wide windows that looked out onto the sloping lawns with their border of bright spring flowers. "When, little Kat? When will our child be born?"

The tears had stopped. "Early autumn, I think. Late September."

"Hmm." He gazed down into her face, with those wide-set green eyes and that catlike air. He kissed her cheek. "That's not long to wait."

"For you," said Kat. "But you've always been better at waiting than I." She traced his profile with one finger. "Stefan," she asked seriously, "are you happy here?"

He looked surprised at the question. "Of course. Windrush is all you said it was. And with you and now the babe, it's even more. It's home." He kissed her lips, then nudged at the glass-paned door to open it with his knee. Still cradling Kat in his arms, he carried her out into the fragrant spring sunshine.

"I wonder what it was like here at Windrush when the first de Veres came?" he mused.

"Forest, I suppose. Maybe some farmland. My father would know." She snuggled closer, hearing his heart beat. "Why do you ask?"

He was looking beyond the green lawn, the circular drive, even the broad horizon. "It must be exciting to start with nothing. To build a home and make a farm and bring in the first harvest." Stefan rested his chin on the top of her head. "What do you think?"

"I suppose," she answered somewhat vaguely, then sensed more than casual interest in the question. "What do you mean? Do you want to buy our own property somewhere else in England?"

"No. For you, England *is* Windrush. But," he went on more slowly, "if ever the urge to roam comes over me again, I'd want to go somewhere I've never seen, someplace so new, the land so untamed, that everything we did made it ours alone."

Kat bolted out of his arms, all but falling onto the grass. "Where?" she demanded.

He gave a little shrug. "Where else? America."

Kat rolled her eyes. "America!"

Stefan brushed dirt off her sleeve. "Not now. Someday. Maybe."

Kat shook her head. "You're insane. America, indeed!"

He was grinning again, if crookedly. "Ridiculous, eh?"

"Certainly." She started back into the house. "Let's look."

He matched her step in two strides. "At what?"

Kat's smile slid up at him and her green eyes danced. "Maps. If I'm married to a Gypsy baron, at least I want to know where I'm going."

Stefan dropped to his knees and reached under Kat's hem. Her lips twitched with anticipation as she waited for his touch on her stockinged legs. Then he removed his hand and held out a globe. "I once said I'd put Prague at your feet. Today, I give you the world."

"Very clever," said Kat dryly. "Some day you must teach me those cheap tricks." Tantalizingly, she lifted her skirts. "I can perform much better magic, Baron Ostrov. I can give you posterity."

Stefan wrapped his arms around her thighs. "And love," he said. "Which I can give back."

"Yes," agreed Kat, as she slipped down onto the carpet beside him. "That's the best magic of all."

* * * * *

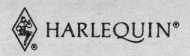

♦ HARLEQUIN®

THE TAGGARTS OF TEXAS!

Harlequin's Ruth Jean Dale brings you
THE TAGGARTS OF TEXAS!

Those Taggart men—strong, sexy and hard to resist...

You've met Jesse James Taggart in FIREWORKS!
Harlequin Romance #3205 (July 1992)

Now meet Trey Smith—he's THE RED-BLOODED YANKEE!
Harlequin Temptation #413 (October 1992)

Then there's Daniel Boone Taggart in SHOWDOWN!
Harlequin Romance #3242 (January 1993)

And finally the Taggarts who started it all—in LEGEND!
Harlequin Historical #168 (April 1993)

Read all the Taggart romances!
Meet all the Taggart men!

Available wherever Harlequin books are sold.

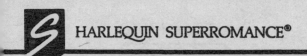

A PLACE IN HER HEART...

Tom Kennedy

Somewhere deep in the heart of every grown woman is the little girl she used to be....

In September, October and November 1992, the world of childhood and the world of love collide in six very special romance titles. Follow these six special heroines as they discover the sometimes heart-wrenching, always heartwarming joy of being a Big Sister.

Written by six of your favorite Superromance authors, these compelling and emotionally satisfying romantic stories will earn a place in your heart!

SEPTEMBER 1992

#514 NOTHING BUT TROUBLE—Sandra James
#515 ONE TO ONE—Marisa Carroll

OCTOBER 1992

#518 OUT ON A LIMB—Sally Bradford
#519 STAR SONG—Sandra Canfield

NOVEMBER 1992

#522 JUST BETWEEN US—Debbi Bedford
#523 MAKE-BELIEVE—Emma Merritt

AVAILABLE WHEREVER
HARLEQUIN SUPERROMANCE
BOOKS ARE SOLD

WELCOME TO

The quintessential small town, where everyone
knows everybody else!

Finally, books that capture the pleasure
of tuning in to your favorite TV show!

Join your friends at Tyler in the eighth book, BACHELOR'S PUZZLE by Ginger
Chambers, available in October.

*What do Tyler's librarian and a cosmopolitan architect have in common? What
does the coroner's office have to reveal?*

GREAT READING...GREAT SAVINGS...
AND A FABULOUS FREE GIFT!

Each book set in Tyler is a self-contained love story; together, the twelve novels
stitch the fabric of the community. You can't miss the Tyler books on the shelves
because the covers honor the old American tradition of quilting; each cover
depicts a patch of the large Tyler quilt!

And you can receive a FABULOUS GIFT, ABSOLUTELY FREE, by collecting
proofs-of-purchase found in each Tyler book, *and* use our Tyler coupons to save
on your next TYLER book purchase.
